A Time for Titans

Also by Viña Delmar

THE MARCABOTH WOMEN

THE LAUGHING STRANGER

BELOVED

THE BREEZE FROM CAMELOT

THE BIG FAMILY

THE ENCHANTED

GRANDMÈRE

THE BECKER SCANDAL

THE FREEWAYS

A
TIME
FOR
TITANS

. . . .

Viña Delmar

HARCOURT BRACE JOVANOVICH, INC.

NEW YORK

Printed in the United States of America

Library of Congress Cataloging in Publication Data
Delmar, Viña, date
A time for titans.
Includes bibliographical references.
I. Title.
PZ3.D3822Ti4   [PS3507.E494]   813'.5'2   73-18499
ISBN 0-15-190445-6

First edition

B C D E

CONTENTS

FOREWORD

Though interpreted where gaps in human knowledge provide leeway, occurrences recorded here have not been invented. What is there to invent? What has history failed to supply in the way of dynamic characters and sensational happenings? The startling news of two centuries ago has not yet been eclipsed. World leaders of that time are still quoted, still damned or revered, their opinions still influential in the affairs of their countries. For better or worse, their fiery words are owned by all, their deeds mysteriously lodged in the minds of men who never studied history.

Those were years of great changes, of unbelievable events. England, powerful England, had lost her American colonies. What now? How could backwoodsmen and provincial lawyers build a country? But wait! Here was something exciting. The backwoodsmen had not pushed themselves into high places, and the provincial lawyers, upon close observation, turned out to be intellectuals. Most amazing was that, though all men were created equal, it was an aristocrat who became president.

The next thunderbolt was the news from France. Revolution! And not at all a simply understood clashing of military men against dissidents who had secretly armed themselves. This was a nationwide bloodletting, and no one was given the privilege of remaining uninvolved. Neighbors murdered one another to demonstrate their loyalty either to the King or to the Cause. In turn they were murdered by other neighbors. France smelled of blood and death. No one was in more danger than the moderate, for both the royalists and the revolutionaries stalked him menacingly.

King Louis and Queen Marie Antoinette escaped from house imprisonment. They were captured. The King was executed, but that was not the end. There were the names that made men tremble—Marat, Danton, Robespierre. The world gasped as the horror of French madness was described in the newspapers. A woman assassinated Marat, and there were those who thought that might end the nightmare with a shuddering awakening. The execution of the Queen proved that hope to be illusory, and when Danton went to the guillotine there was only a sharp realization that France was now alone with Robespierre, the personification of the Terror. He trusted no one, and the blade of the guillotine dripped unceasingly, thirstily, until at last it was satiated by the blood of Robespierre himself.

A spurious respectability then settled upon France. Soberly, the Council of Elders and the Council of Five Hundred chose five men who would hold executive power. Paul Barras was the chief member of what was known as the Directory. He was notorious for his corruption and immorality, but these were venial sins to a nation that had heard the frightful screams of the condemned and had seen headless bodies stacked beside the scaffolds.

The Directory provided a brief season in which France regained its sanity, but Barras had made a terrible mistake. He had furnished his countrymen with a hero. He had singled out a Corsican officer who had been intended to do no more than add luster to the Directory's reputation. Barras's error was fatal. With the Terror safely behind, the people of France began to consider the Directory with less lenient eyes. They fretted about dishonesty in government and the threat of bankruptcy. What had become of the riches their hero had gained for them? Where were the honors he deserved? His passionate dedication to France exposed all five men of the Directory as worthless parasites who weakened the nation. Down with the Directory! Down with selfish leaders. Let us have Napoleon Bonaparte. It is the will of the people.

The Consulate was formed of three men. Bonaparte was First Consul. The other two were subject to removal, but no rule, no law, must ever rob France of a man who was a peerless general and a financial genius. With Bonaparte's gifts, France could govern the world.

Far away across the ocean there was a small island where French was spoken, where soldiers wore the uniforms of the French Army and sang the *"Marseillaise."* The flag of France floated over public buildings, but, curiously, the largest segment of the population had no love for France. They had cursed the kings, welcomed the Revolution, tolerated the Directory and now watched the Consulate uneasily. They were the blacks of the island, the ex-slaves, the majority. Their leader was Toussaint L'Ouverture, and his mind was a match for any in the world. Thomas Jefferson and Napoleon Bonaparte were no more than vaguely aware of his name, and perhaps neither ever realized that, but for the undying blaze of Toussaint's dreams, the history of the United States and France would have been vastly altered.

These, then, are the titans. First Consul Napoleon Bonaparte, President Thomas Jefferson and an ugly little black man whose tongue was tipped with flame. Napoleon Bonaparte? No one will ask, "Why is he a titan?" Thomas Jefferson? Look around you. The states of Louisiana, Missouri, Arkansas, Iowa, Minnesota, Wyoming, Kansas, Nebraska, Colorado, North Dakota, South Dakota, Montana and Oklahoma are testimony to his uncommon mind. They were carved from the greatest treasure in land ever bloodlessly acquired by any nation. Toussaint L'Ouverture? There will be those who have not heard of him and will demand to know what he accomplished. There are no answers in the back of a history book. One must judge for oneself.

One chronological rearrangement of importance has been made. In actual fact, the rescinding of permission for the United States to deposit produce and merchandise at the harbor of New Orleans occurred somewhat later than in this text. The privilege of using the harbor was not restored to the United States until three months before Louisiana became American. The original order denying the right of deposit has not been satisfactorily explained to this day.

No other major historical reality has been cut to the novelist's pattern, but much has been trimmed to avoid irrelevance, confusion and a multiplicity of detail.

A few apologies, though of minor consequence, seem worth making.

Mrs. James Madison's first name is deliberately misspelled. Throughout she is called Dolly, because one expects to see it so written. Her name was not a winsome shortening of Dorothy or of anything else. Her name was Dolley.

The families of the three important black leaders have not been mentioned. These men were all married and all had children. Because there was no intimate, comfortable home life for a Haitian patriot, the families could in no way add to or subtract from the story as it stands.

It may even be impudent to suppose that anyone could add to or subtract from a story that was born in the dazzling minds of Napoleon Bonaparte, Thomas Jefferson and Toussaint L'Ouverture.

ONE

The Duologues

. . . .

*G*ENERAL CHARLES VICTOR EMMANUEL LECLERC, under the striped silken awning of the flagship *Océana*, stared across the flashing blue water and shook his head disbelievingly. True, the island, despite its greenness, did not look inviting. It did not nestle softly against the sea in the way of sweet, misty isles that inspired gentle love songs. The peaks of the steep mountains seemed to rip, rather than melt, into the sky, and one could feel their bitter, brooding animosity.

Still, General Leclerc had not been prepared for what had happened. *They* had dared to shoot at French vessels. Blacks. Ex-slaves. They had opened fire on the ships of Napoleon Bonaparte. Two frigates and a cutter had approached the harbor entrance, and cannon had boomed. Though the outrage had occurred hours earlier, General Leclerc's fury had not subsided. Whoever had given the order for the hostile act would hang.

There had been no moment in which one could suppose the blacks had fired in error. The fleet Leclerc commanded was the largest that France had ever sent across the ocean. For months, in newspapers and pamphlets, the world had speculated upon its errand, and if blacks could not read they certainly could recognize French flags and insignia.

But blacks could read. And write. The letters in Leclerc's inner pocket said very plainly that there had not been the least doubt as to the identity of the ships. In fact, he knew now that the blacks would not have fired upon those of any other nation.

The commanders of the frigates had turned back at the demand of the cannon. Very sensible, of course, but nevertheless

3

humiliating. The cutter had been permitted to land. It was presently under armed guard, Leclerc had learned from the port captain, who had come out in a smart, well-kept launch, bearing a letter for the General.

> General Leclerc,
> Messengers have been dispatched to inform Governor-General Toussaint L'Ouverture of the arrival of the great French fleet. Until I have his order no warship can be admitted to the port.

Leclerc studied the handwriting and, for the second time, was disappointed to find it firm and rather stylish. The arrogant bastard who signed himself "Christophe" had not even bothered to mention his rank. Was the whole world expected to know that he was a general? Leclerc had had to send someone to question the port captain before he could address a proper reply. His first impulse had been to write, "Christophe, my good man," but that would have done no more than satisfy a childish urge to deflate Toussaint L'Ouverture's most important officer.

Instead he had written:

> Citizen General,
> It is with indignation that I learn of your refusal to receive the forces under my command on the pretext that you have no orders from Toussaint L'Ouverture. You now have orders from me which reduce all others to nothingness since I have the honor to speak for the First Consul, Napoleon Bonaparte. I must warn you that my forces are capable of overwhelming any rebels, and I will land fifteen thousand men. . . .

Leclerc had entrusted the letter to the Admiral's aide-de-camp, Lieutenant Lebrun, and had sent him back in the launch with the port captain. Along with Lebrun had gone many copies of Bonaparte's proclamation which had been printed on the ship's presses during the voyage. Among other things, the proclamation assured the blacks that, regardless of color or origin, they were all Frenchmen, free and equal in the sight of God and the Republic.

Leclerc could not be sure that Christophe had read Bonaparte's proclamation. However, he had read the letter. And he had answered it.

General Leclerc,

I repeat that I have sent messengers to Governor-General Toussaint L'Ouverture announcing your arrival and that of the fleet. Until his reply reaches me I can not permit you to land. If you make use of the force with which you threaten me, I shall offer all the resistance worthy of a general officer; and if the struggle should be favorable to you, you shall not enter the town of Le Cap until it is in ashes, and even then I will oppose you—

There had been a time when it had seemed plausible that bloodshed might be averted. Bonaparte had put forth the opinion that blacks were essentially lazy and incompetent, and that by now they would be weary of responsibility. It was likely that they would welcome back the French, who would repair all manner of things that had fallen to pieces during the long years. Yes, in Paris it had seemed that the blacks might come tamely to heel. But in this harbor Leclerc had heard the crack of gunfire and the roar of cannon. And he had read the letters from Christophe. There was no choice. He would have to subdue the blacks. They had fired on French ships, and were not repentant. It was still unbelievable. Blacks, ex-slaves had dared—

Was there any possibility that Toussaint L'Ouverture was truly unaware of the imposing fleet? How could he be? In all probability he had dictated the impudent letters and was trusting them to postpone any action until he had planned his tactics. There was just a slim hope that the black leader was totally unacquainted with the situation. If that were the case, a sensible accord could still come about. Suppose Toussaint turned out to be a realistic man who would immediately perceive the folly of opposing France. Then it would be only a matter of parades, speeches, reinstatement of French rule and the execution of that Goddamned Christophe.

There was no doubt that Toussaint L'Ouverture was a black with a thinking mind and extraordinary abilities. Right here in the harbor there was proof of that. Leclerc could see many merchant ships from the United States. Their men were now loading sugar and coffee, and the docks were piled with merchandise they had delivered. He had read in French reports of the prosperous trade Toussaint had instituted. Bonaparte must have read of it, too. What, then, had been the meaning of those empty words regarding the desolate condition into which the island must have plunged without French leadership? On the contrary, Toussaint's treasury had to be filled to overflowing with the profits of selling France's colonial resources.

Leclerc lowered his spyglass and pressed a handkerchief against his moist forehead. This was not the climate in which to wear a heavily padded coat with a stiff collar that touched one's ear lobes. But didn't the dignity of his position compel— He realized suddenly that here in the tropics the coat and the satin breeches might be ridiculous rather than impressive. Something must be done about officers' uniforms. Perhaps the fleet's tailor could devise acceptable garments in cotton.

Is the weight of my uniform all I have to think about? How long should I give Toussaint to learn of my arrival? Or should I assume that he already knows and is taking advantage of my tolerance? What if, on the generous premise that he is honestly without knowledge of my presence, I grant him more time?

Leclerc pondered the question. To what degree would the landings become more expensive if he threw his men against the blacks tomorrow instead of today? Or perhaps that was the wrong question. The right one might be, "Isn't waiting worth the gamble?" Toussaint, for some personal reason, could have placed himself beyond reach of Christophe's messengers. In that event it would be rash to land French soldiers, for it was apparent that Christophe, who would be in command on the island, was not a man with a preference for parley. Toussaint, an old campaigner, represented the one chance for a peaceable landing.

Leclerc felt a tingle of excitement at the thought that by way of temperate discussion the island might be returned to French rule. Without the loss of a single soldier he would be able— By God, that was worth a small delay. Moreover, it was in keeping with the spirit of Bonaparte's orders. Again and again Leclerc had been told that, in the beginning, Toussaint was to be treated with respect and consideration. That was the answer, then. In an effort to preserve French lives and to assure Toussaint that he was regarded as a leader and an equal, a day of grace would be extended.

For the first time Leclerc permitted his conscious mind to take note of the soft music playing unobtrusively in the background. It came from somewhere beyond the gilded iron latticework that formed the symbolic bulkheads of a private sitting room on deck reserved for Pauline and himself. She would be there, and certainly he owed her a visit. He had not seen her since the cannon had sounded. Perhaps she was in need of a heartening word.

He strolled forward and stood silently for a moment, looking at his wife. She was almost as beautiful as people said she was, almost as well formed. She was lying on a brocade-covered divan, wearing a Grecian gown and golden ornaments in her hair. Her attire was completely appropriate for shipboard, he conceded, since no precedent had been established for what was to be worn by a general's wife on a military expedition.

She glanced up at him with only languid interest. "Are those damned savages going to shoot at us again?"

"I hope you weren't frightened."

"You know I'm never frightened. I leave that to the crybabies we brought along to be my jolly companions. A couple of them fainted, and none of them will come out of their cabins." She moved restlessly on the divan. "I'm so sick of this ship that when the frigates were shot at I was delighted. It seemed that something was happening at last, but I suppose we'll just wait here until I die of boredom."

So it was not one of her sunnier days. Had she felt alarm, he

7

would have comforted her. Boredom was not a thing he understood. However, he seated himself close to her and made a few suggestions.

"Go find your brother Jérôme and have him invent a new game for you."

"After forty-five days of his company I detest my brother Jérôme. We're not talking to each other."

"Send for your child. Let him frolic here. You two will make a pretty picture."

"He has been so seasick on the voyage that he is not at all pretty. He brings me no pleasure."

"Why don't you learn to embroider?"

"I'm only twenty-one. I'll embroider when I'm forty."

"Tell Lieutenant Roncier to arrange another dance."

"I have told him and we will dance this evening. But what shall I do now? I want to go ashore. I'm tired of everybody and everything around here."

He overcame an impulse to shake her until the whining ceased. Strange that in moments when her voice was high-pitched and complaining he found it difficult to remember how adorable she could be. Just as strange that when she was pleasing him with happy nonsense he could never recall why, only an hour before, he had almost hated her.

What a pity he had not been permitted to leave her in Paris. Had that arrangement been made he would now be blessed with the delectable dream of returning to her. Or would he be disturbed by thoughts of how she was amusing herself?

"Victor, are we just going to sit in this harbor? How many tiresome hours do you expect me to endure before going mad?"

He kept his temper. "Don't you have any inner resources at all?" he asked quietly.

She puzzled over the question. "What are inner resources?"

"Strength, imagination, sympathy, patience. Those are valuable assets that make us tolerable to ourselves and to others."

"I don't need any of those things," she snapped. "I'm Napoleon Bonaparte's sister."

He turned from her abruptly, his eyes glowing with a new

intensity as they leveled upon the island. When he looked back at her he saw that her mood had changed. She was, at least for that moment, the sweet, teasing yellow-haired girl who, amazingly, had consented to marry him.

"Victor, I was just thinking—that island over there—what's its name again?"

"The Spanish say San Domingo. We gallicized it to Saint-Domingue. The blacks use an aboriginal name. They call it Haiti."

"Do they have a right to do that?"

He shrugged. "We've made no point of it. They use many barbaric words."

"I was thinking—could the island be named for me?"

"I shouldn't think so. We haven't discovered it."

"I'll just bet that if you'd ask Napoleon he'd say yes. Remember that when he said good-bye to us he told you that he liked to think of me sharing a little in the glory of your expedition. Oh, Victor, listen. Lieutenant Lenoir is singing that old Corsican song I taught him. I'm going to go thank him for entertaining us."

He watched her glide away in her golden slippers. Was she having an affair with Claude Lenoir? Why should she be? Leclerc, though not a popinjay, had a healthy awareness of his own good looks, and even Pauline could not consider him elderly. He was only thirty. Bonaparte at thirty-three was spoken of as a young man.

The thought of Bonaparte turned Leclerc's mind to other matters. A stab of pain pierced his eyes as he looked across the glittering water to the island. What was happening there? Were Christophe's messengers frantically seeking Toussaint L'Ouverture? Or had Toussaint himself ordered the firing of the cannon? If the monstrous act had been committed by Toussaint, then the subjugation of the blacks would be bloody. But no bloodier tomorrow than today.

He could hear Pauline's laughter, and it was disturbing. If she were in Paris now— But Napoleon had insisted that she accompany her husband. Was that because of the actor, Lafon, who was boasting in cafés and drawing rooms that he had conquered a Bonaparte? Leclerc had not believed the gossip, had not been convinced that Lafon had even been presented to Pauline. He remembered now how she had wept at being exiled, how she had pled with Napoleon to spare her the terror of cannibals and jungle serpents. Napoleon had remained firm and he, Leclerc, had sworn to her that the blacks of Saint-Domingue were not cannibals, and that she would enter a lively city where serpents were no more prevalent than in Paris. What a fool he had been. She had been weeping for the loss of Lafon. And why was she laughing now with Claude Lenoir?

Determinedly, he dismissed Pauline and her laughter. The decision to give Toussaint more time was right because, while offering the opportunity of preventing battle, it also demonstrated the forbearance of the French. Too, there was no risk involved. It wasn't as though the blacks could attack the fleet. There was nothing to lose except an insignificant amount of time. And one could think of that as an investment in good will.

Pauline was back, smiling, contented, a slight flush brightening her creamy skin. She placed herself once more on the divan and began to hum the song that Lieutenant Lenoir had sung. Leclerc looked away from her and tried to think of his first moves against the island if there were no conciliatory words from Toussaint by morning.

"Victor, that place over there where you sent Lieutenant Lebrun in the launch—is that the main city?"

"Yes, though Port-au-Prince is the capital. That's quite a distance south from here. I sent Lebrun to Le Cap. Informally, it's called Le Cap. It has been Cap-Français and Cap-de-la-République in the past. Now the blacks call it Cap-Haïtien."

Pauline's eyes blazed with interest. "That's exciting."

"Why?"

"Because if the place has had so many names, what would another change matter? Doesn't Cap-Pauline sound pretty? Is it a city in the way that we would think of such a thing?"

"Of course not. This isn't Europe. But I have heard that the architecture is surprisingly good and that there are restaurants, dance halls, a theater, many shops that sell all kinds of luxuries, and there are—"

She grinned and murmured, "Cap-Pauline."

There was a time when he would have promised her that small glory. Now he ignored the interruption and went on. "Also schools, churches, a prison, a hospital and two bookstores."

"Bookstores? You mean the blacks can read?"

"I am told that some speak and write two languages perfectly, in addition to their native patois." It occurred to him that Pauline had achieved no equal dexterity. Her French and even her Italian were only adequate. Perhaps, though, if standards existed for the Corsican jargon that exploded whenever the Bonapartes gathered, she was flawless in the language of her childhood. "Of course, many white families live on the island. It is they who support the bookstores." He considered what he had said, then added, "For all I know, the blacks may read a dozen books a day. We are in the habit of underestimating blacks. We ought not do that." He pressed his handkerchief against his face and the back of his neck, and sighed deeply.

Pauline's curiosity was roused now by a new thought. "Is that the kind of island Josephine came from?"

"She came from Martinique."

"I know that. I'm asking if Martinique is the same as the one we have in front of us here."

"Martinique is not so rich. It does not have the finest sugar and mahogany in the world, as this island does. But there are ways in which they resemble each other."

Her eyes gleamed mischievously. "Victor, what if Josephine has a black relative hiding somewhere?"

Leclerc's lips tightened to repress any comment; then, remembering her penchant for transforming surmises into solid facts, he said, "Josephine's people were without money but not without pride or pedigree. She's as white as anyone alive."

"I hope that's not true. Wouldn't it be wonderful if I found a reason that makes her unsuitable to be Napoleon's wife? Not that there aren't reasons, but I mean one that we could make public without the people laughing at Napoleon."

"Pauline, there is not and never could be anything about Josephine that is the business of our citizens. Napoleon is a superlative administrator and military leader who performs for France the services that keep the country strong and free. If he were a king, his wife and his descendants would quite rightly be of concern to the public. But your brother is not a king. France is through with kings."

"Is it really? Forever? Well, perhaps Napoleon will find something else to be. I'm sure he would hate your calling him an administrator. I won't tell him you did that."

"Thank you. You have saved my career." He rose from the small space he had occupied at the foot of the divan. "Now, if you will excuse me, I will go to my office and think about Toussaint L'Ouverture, another administrator and military leader."

"Someone told me that Napoleon refers to him as the gilded African. Does he splash some kind of gold paint on his face to draw attention?"

"I would doubt he'd find that necessary. People who have cannons rarely go unnoticed."

"Why did Napoleon let him get cannons? If he didn't have any, we could take the island from him more easily."

Leclerc had started away from her, but he stopped and spoke chillingly. "What is that you just said? Take the island from him! It's ours! It belongs to France!"

"Then let's go ashore," she taunted.

"When I give the command, we will go. Until then you will please remember that we are not stealing the island. It's a French colony."

"The blacks don't seem to know that."

"They know it but they've been outside our control. The British Navy was blockading the Atlantic. We couldn't get here."

"My brother has been First Consul for two years. Do you mean to say—"

"Toussaint has had things his own way for five years. We're here to put an end to that. The island is French property. Don't go around talking as though it isn't. Do you understand?"

She looked at him coldly. "Stop shouting at me."

"Well, do you understand the difference between reclaiming one's own possessions and seizing that which is somebody else's?"

"Of course. Don't talk to me as though I were a fool. I'm a Bonaparte."

"So are Joseph and Lucien and Louis and Jérôme and Elisa and Caroline," he said. "Of you all only Lucien's thinking would remind anyone of Napoleon's." He was silent for a moment, simmering with vexation. "How the blacks would love to hear that Bonaparte's sister speaks of taking the island from Toussaint. We can't take it from him. It's ours."

"Then why is he on it and we're out here in the harbor?"

Leclerc was exasperated enough to walk away from her question, but she would only carry it elsewhere and receive misinformation. "There was terrible trouble on the island some years ago. Though he now seems to call himself governor-general, Toussaint was appointed commander in chief by a commissioner of the Directory. The Directory controlled France before your brother was chosen to do so."

Pauline tossed her head in annoyance. "You don't have to tell me about the Directory. I knew those men. You didn't."

"Be that as it may, I won't let you go ashore saying silly things that will be accepted as coming from me." He saw that she was about to leave the divan, but, as he had expected, his next words held her there. "Napoleon cannot afford your ignorance."

She waited, her eyes lowered, her hands tightly clasped in her lap.

"About eighteen months ago," Leclerc continued, "your brother, wishing to establish some sort of tie with Toussaint, confirmed the man's position as commander in chief so it would be evident to all concerned that France still ruled the island. We had to have someone in charge, and Toussaint had been approved, at one time, by a French representative. Now that we have signed the preliminaries to a treaty with Britain, we are able to cross the ocean and appraise Toussaint for ourselves."

"He appraised us first," Pauline said. "Then he shot at our ships."

"Good God! Will you stop making irresponsible statements? We do not yet know that it was he who gave the order." Leclerc turned his back to her and stood again staring at the harsh outline of the mountain peaks.

Behind him Pauline spoke. "If I were you, I'd storm onto that island and kill everybody who has a drop of black blood."

Over his shoulder he said, "It's very reassuring that you are equipped to give advice on how France must deal with Haiti."

She did not answer. Her silence was a relief. He had made a blunder that she might have challenged. Carelessly, he had used for the island the name the blacks had given it.

. . . .

The tall black officer in the white uniform dismissed his servants and poured the coffee himself. His guest, a small, aging man in a wrinkled dust-colored jacket and shabby trousers, took note of the professional grace with which the coffee was poured. His eyes sparked briefly with amusement. Ah, what a fine headwaiter this glorious soldier must have been. A bitter thought cooled the spark and left the eyes sad and brooding. The officers of the accursed French fleet had been wearing dancing pumps and learning the cotillion while this superior man had been a slave. But that was a foolish, sentimental regret. One grew wise, then forgot the wisdom so laboriously acquired. He reminded himself now that because they had never been slaves the young white gentlemen had not taken any particular happiness from the gift of special privilege. Contrariwise, this tall black man, because he had never been a young white gentleman, appreciated life's better moments. Simple mathematics. Things evened out.

"Sit with me and share the coffee," he ordered.

"Thank you, General." The man in the white uniform filled a cup for himself and sat down at his own table, where the cloth was of lace from France and the china delicate and exquisitely designed.

The two men listened in silence for a time to the drums com-

14

municating between hills and valleys, the wild beating, the staccato questions, the sharp replies.

Toussaint twisted his mouth, his lined face, with its markedly undershot jaw, suggesting some uncatalogued animal that might be dangerous. "I should think that, after two days, they could cease mentioning Bonaparte's proclamation," he said.

"Sir, it is still being passed from hand to hand," the younger man told him. "We cannot risk having the ignorant place their trust in the words of Bonaparte. The drums must warn of the lies and of the emptiness of his promises."

"That aide-de-camp, Lebrun, must have brought many copies of the proclamation with him."

"Yes, and he surreptitiously dropped them from the carriage as he was being courteously escorted to Government House. Every day I learn another reason for despising white men."

Toussaint sipped his coffee and remarked that Lebrun had been but serving his cause as was expected of every soldier. "You would have done the same in his place, Christophe."

"And I would have been burned to death over a slow fire instead of being returned to my ship after an excellent dinner and a good night's rest."

But Toussaint was again listening to the drums. "Are you following? Have you noticed that your messages to Leclerc have been thoroughly understood? It has been guessed that you are not searching for me, that I have spent these days with you creating a battle plan. Our drummers are extremely perceptive."

With a gesture Christophe belittled the perception of the drummers. "Even the French have guessed that, sir." He stirred uneasily on his chair. "You have not referred to the principal order a second time. I must be certain that it stands. Do you still intend that Cap-Haïtien be burned?"

"Why not? Shall we present the city to Leclerc with all buildings and services intact? You know the order stands. It is one which you yourself would have given had I truly been out of touch with you."

"Yes, General, I would have given the order." Christophe lowered his eyes, not wishing to show the pain in them.

Toussaint understood. Better than anyone he knew that it had been the efforts, the energy, of Christophe that had caused the tiny tropical Paris down there on the harbor to know a second growth. Christophe had let no one rest until the city, in its own flamboyant style, had blossomed anew after bloody darkness.

I am being sentimental again, Toussaint thought. He has established a charming little city that pays its way, and because of that both he and I are regarding him as an admirable citizen. Mother of Christ, none of us are that.

He sat thinking, no longer interpreting the messages of the drums though they boomed on, telling all that was known, all that was hoped and supposed. He thought of the past, the rebellion of the slaves, the slaughter of the plantation owners.

Does Christophe remember, too? And is there something that he can find among his memories that permits him to sleep at night? Perhaps he is pleased to recall that he buried nobody alive, or soothed by the thought that he never slit a throat while children were watching. Toussaint sighed. The plantation owners and their overseers had invited the butchery. They had not learned the simplest of all lessons: Never place a man in a position where he has nothing worthwhile to lose.

And he thought of Dessalines, who had taken such pleasure in observing the behavior of his tortured captives that even today it was not easy to control him.

I could have him executed, Toussaint thought, but in so doing I would rob myself of a fearless soldier. Unfortunate, illiterate Dessalines. He had suffered the unspeakable indignity of having been slave to another black man. Perhaps I shall have the strength one day to inquire as to the disposition Dessalines made of his former master.

Toussaint gazed out the wide windows at the French warships on the far edge of the harbor, and he was seized by sudden laughter that had no sound and no merriment. To be the greatest and most respected man on the island was a lonely fate. To whom could he say that it was only by chance that laughter had come instead of sobs? Who would perceive the drama, the farce that lay in the sending of the stiff little notes back and forth between well-bred, perfectly trained French officers and hard black men who, with their own fingers, had torn out oppressors' eyes and fed them to the fish?

Toussaint reached for a small jewellike bit of pastry. How would he sleep tonight? What would he remember of the struggle that was on the verge of repeating itself? But, of course, that night he would not attempt to sleep. There was too much to do. It was good to have a reasonable excuse for not going to bed. Never had he found a recollection of the past that had helped him to drift into pleasant dreams. Certainly he was not calmed by remembering that he had protected and saved Bréda and his entire family. Many slaves had done as much. Stupid, ape-brained, they had placed their own lives in peril for men who had done no more than refrain from beating them. To have murdered Bréda and his wife and children would, at least, have proved that there was consistency and justice in the philosophy of the rebellion. As it was, anyone might ask, "If one master was to be saved, why not all masters?"

I delivered Bréda from a terrible death, Toussaint thought, because he had taught me to read and write, because he had instructed me in the methods of healing sick horses. And so highly did I value what he had done for me that I forgave him for being a slaveowner. And that is the rotten core that lies within all men and poisons the universe. If one condones evil merely because it has not dealt harshly with oneself, then one subscribes to the theory that nothing of importance exists beyond one's own well-being.

He became aware once more of Christophe. The man must have a hundred things to say, but it was not Christophe's right to break the silence of the Governor-General.

"And when the torches have been put to the city, Christophe, when the smoke and flames are rising and destruction assured, our armies will disappear into the mountains. From there we will give them a fight such as they never have imagined."

Christophe smiled thinly and poured more coffee.

Toussaint studied him carefully, noting the steadiness of his hand, and musing upon the remarkable capacity Christophe possessed for accepting all things as they were. Another man might have questioned, perhaps protested, even refused, but Christophe had never supposed his life to be more precious than Haiti's. Still, he should have the satisfaction of knowing that his generosity and courage were appreciated. To remain silent forever on the subject of the French frigates was carrying stoicism a whit too far.

"Christophe, have you ever thought that your faith in me may be deeper than any human deserves? If we are, by any chance, both captured by the French, do you expect me to reveal that it was I who ordered the cannon fire? Do you trust me to confess that the letters to Leclerc which you wrote and signed were at my direction?"

Christophe said, "If you did such a dramatic and useless thing as that, sir, I would think only that I had misjudged your strength and your love for Haiti. It could be only at Haiti's expense that you could gain for yourself the luxury of telling the truth. I have lived for quite a time now with the understanding that we lie for you, kill for you and finally die for you because that is what Haiti demands of us. If to save me or your soul you disclosed everything to Leclerc, I would feel betrayed."

Toussaint gazed with admiration at the man in the trim white uniform. "You will not be betrayed, Christophe. If we are captured, the false testimony I promise to give against you will result in your being hanged."

"It's one way of dying for Haiti," Christophe said.

"Yes," Toussaint agreed. "But I shall feel then as I feel now —that somehow I never succeeded in saying that no man was ever more valued than you."

"I have taken the liberty, sir, of supposing that I had your approval."

It was enough for both of them.

Toussaint said, "Fine pastrymaker you have, Christophe. Would you be so kind as to send my compliments to him, along with the information that you and I have been reduced to only one éclair apiece?"

Christophe rang the silver table bell, and the four servants who had been dismissed reappeared. Toussaint looked away from them. Their peach-colored livery with heavy lace dripping from the cuffs was always a source of annoyance to him. Christophe was originally from an English island. He knew that servants properly wore simple garb. Toussaint's distress rested on the fact that Christophe had learned well what delighted the hearts of Haitians. He had given his army officers uniforms of yellow, pink or purple, according to their choice. The gold braid with which they decked themselves, if carefully rolled, might make a ball of a size to equal the sun. Toussaint did not resent Christophe's understanding his soldiers. He only sorrowed that there was this about the soldiers to understand. Dear Jesus, was there still raw courage inside such gaudily appareled creatures? Or did a man, by what he wore, signal what he had become? How the French would laugh at those ridiculous black figures in carnival clothes, with jeweled decorations and gold chains dangling from their uniforms. How the French would laugh. How the French would— But, of course, Christophe had encouraged Haitians to indulge their love of frippery and dazzle. Why? Because he had known that the French would laugh. Toussaint rubbed his protruding jaw thoughtfully. He saw another dimension he could add to this infantile passion for mummery. But that would wait for a time when it was needed.

The fresh supply of pastries arrived, and the servants were waved away. More coffee was poured.

"Christophe, were you surprised when you first caught sight of the French fleet approaching?"

Christophe tapped upon a door of the wine cabinet, and a shallow drawer slid toward him. He handed over some newspaper clippings and a few pages torn from magazines.

Toussaint noted the names of the periodicals from England and the United States. "I have read these," he said.

"I know that, sir, or I would have delivered them to you."

"Wait. This one I have not seen. The *Gentleman's Magazine*. Does that mean only the upper classes are permitted to buy it?" He glanced at the date of the issue and then fixed his eyes on the article and read a portion of it aloud, in a rapid mumble. " 'The

Consular Government is making preparations for sending a military force of twenty thousand men to the island of San Domingo for the purpose of reducing Toussaint L'Ouverture to a due degree of subordination to the mother country—' " He shrugged. "They all say about the same thing."

"Except this one points out that Jamaica may also be subjugated rather swiftly once we have been dealt with."

"The French are busy making peace with Britain."

"But if, while in the neighborhood, Bonaparte cannot resist the impulse to press his attentions upon Jamaica—"

"He is not interested in Jamaica," Toussaint said flatly.

Christophe rose from the table to draw a drapery against the hot violence of the late-afternoon sun. He experimented with the velvet pull cord until he was certain that Toussaint's eyes were shielded from the glare. Then he stood viewing the French fleet that from his green hilltop looked so tiny, so remote.

"They still regard us as slaves in revolt," he said.

"Are we something else, Christophe?"

"Yes. The past is not the present. We are excellent officials of a fine, rich island. Bonaparte hates us more for that than had we lived in drunkenness and let the jungle cover the towns, more than had we foolishly eaten all the animals instead of breeding them, more than had we taken the sweet dreams of the ti-délice plant and let the buildings rot away while we lay in filthy stupor with our women."

"But Bonaparte is no fool. As First Consul, he recognizes the necessity of trading with everybody. I will be glad to talk business with him as I do with the United States. When anger has been replaced with a realistic viewpoint, he will want us to continue producing at the high level we have achieved."

"Oh, indeed, sir, he will want us to continue producing. In fact, he will insist upon it, but we will produce as we did in other years—as slaves." Christophe stalked from one window to another, first staring gloomily out toward the forests of mahogany, then limiting his vision to his own property, with its kitchens, stables and working quarters, its distillery and storehouses. Ah, how beautiful were the lush green lawns and the sparkling fountains that one could see from any window.

"Since their revolution, Christophe, the French might almost be in the position of having to prove to the world that they favor equality."

"For all but black men. There are no whites anywhere who would call us equals. Have you read what the American President, Thomas Jefferson, is reported to have said of us?"

"I do not trouble myself to recall any particular statement of his, Christophe. He is the product of a slaveholding state. You must tell me what he said."

"I am not sure I quote him exactly, but in essence he said, 'Black men can be led, and they can sometimes lead. The one thing they cannot do is co-operate.'"

"That is his hope, Christophe. Haiti has given him and his fellow Southerners something indigestible to chew upon. They ask themselves what if the slaves of the United States followed the example we set."

"Doesn't Jefferson know there is no chance of that?"

"Fear dulls the capabilities of the best thinkers. When a Southerner hears the stories out of our past he forgets that his country is too large for messages to be exchanged between any significant number of slaves. The vast distances also preclude any secret gatherings that could result in massive uprising."

"Most important," Christophe added, "they have no Toussaint L'Ouverture."

"Hush. Listen to the drums. There is news." After a moment's attention he said, "Well, no, not exactly news."

It was certainly not news that the whites on the island were blissful at the arrival of the fleet and the prospect of French rule. The return of slavery and increased profits must follow. Not news either that mulattoes and other mixed bloods believed the precepts of the Revolution would endow them with all the rights and honors enjoyed by their white relatives.

"The black man," Toussaint said, "knows the truth. People get what they fight for, but they must fight hard and with intelligence."

Christophe was thinking of another matter. "Though Jefferson does not like us, he trades with us. There are many of his merchant ships in the harbor. Would you permit Americans who are on the island to be placed aboard them and taken to safety?"

Toussaint meditated. "It is what we must do," he conceded. "But I don't want our time or our men wasted on the project. You must inform the American chargé d'affaires that the lives of his countrymen rest with American sailors who are now drinking and whoring in Le Cap. It is his responsibility to see that Jefferson's vessels remove every citizen of the United States from the island."

"He will be told, sir."

Toussaint worried a hangnail, and a small drop of blood appeared on his finger. "I don't want Americans killed. I can't see a way that that would further our cause. The maddening thing is that white men take pleasure in outwitting us. Where there is room on their ships the Americans will hide French nationals and carry them to the United States. How can we stop that?"

Christophe said, "We cannot stop it without posting troops at the harbor to question every passenger going aboard. Our hope must be that the American ships have so great an insufficiency of space that there can be no pity for French citizens."

The drop of blood was a small red island now, on the Alençon lace tablecloth. "Perhaps we can do something more effective than simply hope for overcrowded conditions. What would you think of choosing some unimportant Frenchman and having him publicly flogged to death? It could be said that he had tried to board an American ship." Toussaint reflected, his long jaw jutting to its outward limits. "Restraining the French from flight is quite justified. If we must sacrifice our beautiful city, there is no reason to permit French citizens—who made money from it— to escape without sharing our hardships."

The sky was violet now, and a fresh breeze carrying the fragrance of the sea entered the large room, bringing a strange illusion of contentment. The two men sat in silence listening to the drums, breathing the sweet air and stilling momentarily the feverish questions in their minds.

"I must go," Toussaint said. "You seek out Dessalines and tell him to take his troops to Saint-Marc. Forget the French citizens. What does it matter if a few escape? Admittedly, it was I who invited them back to contribute to our peace and prosperity after we rebuilt." He rose and stood contemplating the glimmer of lights in the harbor.

Christophe asked, "Did you know that Leclerc brought his wife with him?"

"Yes. She is Bonaparte's sister. She will want a residence worthy of her. Perhaps yours will do."

In the darkness Toussaint could feel the stinging rage of the man beside him.

Christophe said, "If she chooses to live here, her tenancy will not be prolonged. The house has secret entrances, and some night I will point out one of them to Dessalines."

Toussaint shook his head. "Do not teach Bonaparte or Leclerc to weep as black men have wept. When you do that, you teach them to fight as black men fight."

Christophe would have answered, but the drums broke into a sudden hysterical imitation of Haitian laughter. Toussaint laughed, too, and Christophe joined him. It had been learned that, earlier in the day, General Leclerc had sent boat parties ashore to a fishing village in search of men who, in exchange for gold pieces, would pilot them around the coast and into the harbor. The booming laughter of the drums was caused by the fact that Leclerc's men had found no fisherman who seemed to know anything at all about the coast of the island.

Toussaint demanded gleefully, "What was it Thomas Jefferson said about blacks being unable to co-operate?"

The drums stopped abruptly and there was a strange, thick silence, then a renewal of laughter. General Leclerc had boarded a frigate and had made an attempt to lead, under cover of darkness, a few armed sloops and corvettes toward a surprise landing. The vessels now lay without motion in a windless calm.

Toussaint raised his head as though trying to smell the meaning of a new sudden quiet. Again the drums had ceased, this time in the middle of their laughter.

Christophe said, "General, I never thought to make this request of you. I make it now. Will you do me the kindness of leaving my house?"

The drums clattered a curt signal for attention. There was another silence followed by a message that had no laughter. The men listened. Then Christophe asked, "Who is General Two?"

"Rochambeau. I know him well. He was here in the old days."

"And he has now cannonaded his way ashore at Fort Liberté, and possessed himself of the forts at L'Anse and Labouque. General, will you please leave this house?"

No further word passed between them. They embraced, and the small man in the wrinkled clothes was gone.

Christophe lighted a candle and held it high so that he could see the fine paintings on the wall, the lofty ceiling adorned with cherubs and holy saints. Affectionately, he fondled, with his large, dark hands, a tapestry woven for him by the black nuns of Port-au-Prince. He stooped and touched the deep silky pile of the carpet; then, calling all his servants to him, he handed each a burning candle. He sent for his guards and told them it was time for their torches to brighten the sky. He tossed his own flaming candle at the satin draperies and, without a backward glance, strode to the stables, where he chose one horse and freed the others.

Then he rode down to Cap-Haïtien, gave the order and waited, tense and hard-eyed, until he saw the city ablaze.

After that he galloped away to fight the forces of Napoleon Bonaparte.

. . . .

Secretary of State James Madison thought that the greatest sacrifice a man made in accepting the presidency was to move out of a comfortable home and into the unfinished structure known to many as the Palace. Madison made a point of calling the building the President's Mansion. Absurd to think of this place, with its leaking roof and ugly, untended grounds, as a palace. There were not even adequate stabling facilities, and no storehouses at all for coal, wood and other necessities.

As he walked through the first-floor corridor toward the flight of rough wooden steps leading to the President's office, he noted that nothing had been accomplished since his last visit. All rooms along his route remained unplastered. One would think that laborers might willingly toil without sleep, if requested, until every inch of the President's official residence had been brought to a state of perfection. Unbelievable that money would be a consideration when weighed against the honor of working on the most important home in the country.

Madison, with great care, placed his feet on the temporary steps and made his descent. He entered a spacious room that, in order to dispatch the business of the nation, had been made usable for John Adams. The most interesting features of the office were Jefferson's personal possessions. In the center was a long table with drawers on each side. Madison knew that in some of the drawers were small garden implements with which the President groomed the flowers and plants he kept in window boxes. Against the walls were maps and charts and tall bookcases crammed with volumes on every subject known to man. A large globe of the world was spinning on its cherry-wood axis as though it had, within the minute, been given a mighty whirl.

The President, unaware of his caller, stood with his back turned, his hands occupied unlatching the door to a large gilded cage. A mockingbird hopped forth and proceeded from the President's shoulder to his desk.

"Well, well, now," the President said, softly. "You just stay there and enjoy— Oh, good afternoon, Madison."

"Good afternoon, Mr. President."

"Sit down. I trust you have no dislike for my recently arrived house guest."

Madison chose a Windsor chair on the visitor's side of the desk. "Not at all, and I see that he does not object to me."

In a stately march across several books and letters, the bird had come to peek inquisitively into Madison's hat.

"If he becomes a bother to you, please ask me to return him to the cage. I should not like any human to charge the atmosphere with unfriendly feeling. Such a thing could hamper the bird's domestication. I am hoping to make of him a pet as acceptable as any dog might be."

Poor Jefferson, a widower with two married daughters who visited him infrequently. They had their lives to live. Jefferson had the presidency and a mockingbird. But it is not so hard on him as it would be on others, Madison thought.

He glanced again at the bookcases, where he knew he would find the French Encyclopedia in the original, the history of Tacitus, with Latin text on one side and a translation into Spanish on the other. With a mind like Jefferson's there really could not be the ordinary suffering of mortal men. There could not be, for instance, loneliness. Jefferson's interest in the mockingbird was purely scientific. Could mockingbirds give and receive affection? That was a question Jefferson might want answered. But the man who had written the Declaration of Independence certainly was not bedeviled by trivial or commonplace emotions.

"How are you feeling, Madison? And how is your good lady?"

"We are both in the best of health, thank you."

"I am delighted to hear that. Would you be so kind as to make inquiries as to when the lovely Dolly might again serve as my hostess?"

"Why, I can answer that now, Mr. President. She will be happy to be present at your table on any date you mention."

Jefferson shook his head. "I don't think I would like it quite that way. She must understand, and so must you, that she is not being summoned. She is being asked on what day it would please her to do me a great honor. In my opinion, this distinguished task of heading the state in no way entitles me to become the peevish master of the social world. Anyone has a right to refuse an invitation from me, and on any grounds. God save me, Madison, from using my position to impede my friends from doing something they would rather do."

"And what might that be, Mr. President?" Madison was thinking of the needle-witted conversation one heard at Jefferson's table, of the wine cellar he maintained, and of the talents of his French chef. It was strange, Madison mused, that those of indifferent breeding did not recognize Jefferson as a man of elegance. They judged him by his old brown coat, his corduroy trousers and heelless house slippers. "He is not a gentleman," some whispered, and the Madisons were amused. No one qualified to judge a gentleman ever spoke such words of Jefferson.

Tall in stature, spare in flesh, grave, sedate, the President had a charm that only political enemies could resist. He was capable of horrifying people who spoke of tradition. "To what tradition do you refer?" he would ask. "This country has no grandmother. There were no Americans before us."

It was his earnest desire to put an end to all aping of royal courts. Here at the Palace the door was opened by the butler— or any other servant who happened to be unoccupied—and if the visitor had a familiar face he was permitted to find his own way to the President. Anyone could call on Mr. Jefferson. Ladies who enjoyed comparing their silks and jewels with those of others were embittered by the President's ban on formal entertaining. The customs of George Washington and John Adams were not for Thomas Jefferson. Dinners planned for four or six good companions were agreeable, and, of course, an occasional stately display for some diplomat who was not too pompous or empty-headed. But huge crowds of dancing, chattering people were destructive to sanity, the President said.

Sir Augustus Foster, of the British legation, was infuriated when informed that Mr. Jefferson regarded no nation to be bound by the social decrees of another, and that every representative of a foreign country was equal to every other representative of a foreign country. The power or riches of no nation would be permitted to place one man above another at the President's table.

"Mr. Jefferson knows too well what he is about," Sir Augustus fumed. "As minister to France, he has lived in good society in Paris and knows how to set a value on the decencies and proprieties of life."

"Indeed he does know," Madison had commented. "He knows very well how much value there is in pretension."

Jefferson bent forward and stroked the mockingbird as it

goggled at the shiny surface of the glass inkwell. "It will not hurt you, friend," he whispered. Then, turning his attention back to Madison, "I thought to give a dinner party for Yrujo and his pretty little wife."

Madison smiled. "Did you know he thinks she looks quite Andalusian?"

"Yes, I did. I knew that. But her father is Governor of Pennsylvania, not Andalusia. I had intended to wine and dine Sally and Yrujo on their wedding anniversary but I forgot. Since I have missed the date I aimed for, do tell Mrs. Madison that it is completely at her convenience when we will entertain the representative of Charles the Fourth of Spain and his lady."

Madison thought it was a stroke of luck that the President had missed the actual date of the anniversary. Though there was certainly justice in the argument that Jefferson should have a citizen's right to celebrate the anniversaries of his friends while ignoring those of his acquaintances, much jealousy would have been aroused.

"Odd," Madison said. "Very odd that I was thinking of the Marquis de Casa Yrujo this morning."

The President studied the feathers of the mockingbird. "Were you? Why was that, Madison?"

"Because he is a friend of yours. Because you have invited him to Monticello many times. Over a glass of fine Spanish sherry you and he must have talked of serious matters that concern Americans and Spaniards. For that reason I wondered if it would be in order for me to consult him on a worry of mine. Or, with your friendship so firmly established, would you prefer to approach the Marquis personally?"

The President rose from his desk and, with gentle hands, replaced the mockingbird in its cage. He sat down again and fixed his gaze on Madison. "I have already passed a word with him. He is investigating."

"Then you are familiar with the situation?"

Jefferson laughed unexpectedly. "Assuming that each of us has the same situation in mind. Of course, if an underling of the Spanish diplomatic corps has insulted an overling of the British diplomatic corps, then I know nothing about it and will thank you not to inform me."

Madison said, "I am sure you know of what I am speaking, but let me review what has been presented to me as fact. Perhaps you will then be kind enough to correct my thinking if I have been misinformed. The Spanish Intendant at New Orleans, someone named Morales, has denied us—quite suddenly, after all these years—he has denied us the right to deposit our merchandise for shipment. Since the produce of Kentucky and Tennessee depends on an outlet to the sea, we cannot reach our markets without the port of New Orleans. Cotton season is approaching, and a severe wound will be inflicted on agricultural and commercial interests if the port remains closed to us."

"You have not been misinformed, Madison. However, Yrujo swears that no such order could have possibly emanated from Madrid. He tells me that he has written Morales a most unpleasant letter."

"I want him to do more than that," Madison said resolutely. "I want him to send a swift packet boat immediately to New Orleans to demand the same use of the port that we have had in the past. I want him to communicate with Madrid at once. I have already written to Charles Pinckney at the Spanish court, telling him that we must not lose a moment in expressing our outrage."

The President lowered his head thoughtfully. "Madison, I'm going to leave this problem in your hands, where it properly belongs. I wish most dreadfully that I had not mentioned it to Yrujo." He looked into Madison's troubled eyes. "I wouldn't have you think that I tried to usurp your authority."

"That was not my thought, Mr. President, and had it been, I believe I can claim that I would have felt no resentment. I live contentedly with the knowledge that you excel us all in dealing with whatever difficulty arises. If there is a weakness in the present situation, it lies with the Marquis who did not take all measures available to him." Madison fell silent. When he spoke again it was to ask, "May I tell him that hard-working Americans who are trying to build secure lives for themselves and their families are seething with fury, and that they know no way of overcoming obstacles other than shouldering muskets?"

Jefferson said, "May I tell you that will sound like bluster?"

"It would not be said in that spirit. It is not intended to threaten but to explain how the hot tempers and direct action of Americans could create a crisis that the United States would give much to avoid."

Jefferson shook his head. "You must take my word, there is no way on earth that Yrujo could be convinced that men without orders from their commander in chief would shoulder muskets and march on New Orleans. Nothing has prepared him to understand the temperament of Americans."

"Not our history, Mr. President?"

"No. Yrujo believes that Washington—looking as he does in the Gilbert Stuart paintings—stood on a high hill and controlled every thought and every action of every fighting man. Oh, intellectually, he doesn't really believe that, but it will give you a fair idea of his comprehension of us."

Madison considered a moment. "I shall not address any remarks to the Marquis that might cause friction. I see I have been mistaken about him. His affable manner leads one to suppose that a sincere and candid conversation would be quite easy to conduct with him."

The President leaned back in his chair and half closed his eyes. "I trust you are not readying yourself to oppose the dinner of which I spoke."

"Dissent between the Secretary of State and the representative of King Charles the Fourth must not be allowed to destroy harmony between Madison and Yrujo."

"Splendid, Madison. Would you care for a glass of wine?"

"I would enjoy that, thank you."

The President poured, and the two men settled themselves on a worn and faded sofa.

"What do you think, Madison, about the French fleet? The talk is that it is almost as stupendous as Bonaparte's vanity."

"I would suppose that it has by now reached its destination in the Caribbean. The unfortunate blacks, who were living rather well, as I understand it, have probably been returned to cutting sugar cane. There should be some reports in another few weeks on their fate." Madison paused, then added, "I daresay Yrujo still hears from what was the Spanish portion of the island."

"No. The diplomatic link has been severed. Everyone there is now French regardless of language and tradition. However, the black man who decided he was governor-general—what is his name?"

"Toussaint," Madison said promptly.

"Yes. Toussaint. He has somehow managed to exercise authority over the people who are officially French, and those who were once officially Spanish."

The Secretary of State said "Oh" very innocently.

"Yrujo, under the circumstances, may not care to be questioned about the island."

Madison's eyes were engaged in a study of the threadbare carpet. Why was it that Jefferson never objected to the condition of furnishings or clothes? If they were but clean, he considered them presentable. The sofa, now—it had been Washington's, though Washington had never lived in this house. Had Jefferson purposely arranged to have in his office something that had been used by the first President? And had the carpet belonged to Adams? It looked rather like a New Englander's choice, Madison thought.

He turned his eyes back to Jefferson. "I do believe that the arrival of that massive armada in the West Indies is going to disturb the British greatly. I cannot imagine why Bonaparte is not behaving in a more circumspect manner when peace is all but secured between the two countries."

The President tipped the decanter and refilled the glasses. "Bonaparte's motives have not always been clear to everyone," he said.

Madison shook his head in wonderment. "Isn't it amazing how the name Yrujo simply can't remain out of our conversation today? I just remembered he spends more time in Philadelphia than in Washington, doesn't he?"

"Sally is a Philadelphian," the President said. "Her family

and friends are there." He studied the calm, intelligent face of his secretary of State. "Is there some connection between Bonaparte's fleet and Yrujo's mother-in-law, Madison?"

Madison favored the whimsical query with a small smile. "I was just thinking that Philadelphia has recently acquired a singularly huge population of French. They have arrived by hundreds, some say by thousands. If you really desire opinions on Bonaparte's fleet, Yrujo could easily bring them to you. He is acquainted with Moreau de St. Méry, as is every highly educated person familiar with Philadelphia. The gentleman is the owner of a bookshop on Front Street near Walnut. All new arrivals from France seem to flock to his shop for warmth and conversation. Yrujo could ask him if his French friends believe the great fleet menaces a peace treaty between the two strong countries."

"Moreau de St. Méry." Jefferson repeated the name with languid interest. "I once ordered books from him. He shipped me several. Yes." Jefferson reached across to a desk drawer, and Madison guessed that he was about to produce the invoice. Instead he brought forth a tiny pair of pruning scissors, with which he began to clip at the frayed edges of a sofa cushion. "I do not think I will ask Yrujo to run an errand for me. And I do not think the average French citizen knows whether or not Bonaparte values peace with England very highly."

The Secretary of State watched the small scissors flashing in the sunlight. "Oh, do you suppose these are average French citizens?" he asked. "The bookseller is such an intellectual that I had thought he might associate only with superior people. Besides, never before have I heard of immigrants who, upon arrival, immediately feel the need of a bookshop."

The President said, "I imagine, Madison, that Yrujo knows this shop and its proprietor well, as you have suggested. The world has been hearing of Bonaparte's armada for quite a while. Yrujo has said not one word to me concerning it. If he had gleaned some particular bit of knowledge in a bookshop, I think he might have mentioned it."

"Of course, of course," Madison agreed. Clip. Clip. He wished the President hadn't chosen this moment to improve the appearance of Washington's sofa. Clip. Clip. But this was the moment the President had chosen, so— "Mr. President, could there be any reason why Yrujo would not mention the bookshop in Philadelphia?"

Jefferson dropped the pruning scissors and went to sit at his desk. The look in his eyes drew the Secretary of State away from the comfortable old sofa and back to the stiff Windsor chair.

"Madison," the President said sternly, "you and I have been dancing about trying to discover which of us has learned the latest steps. When I am alone I will think more on that subject and decide whether you thought it unseemly to be in possession of facts unknown to me, or if I was reluctant to spread before you the conclusions I have reached."

The Secretary of State waited.

"No sensible man," the President said, "could believe that Bonaparte has sent warships and his best generals to subjugate ex-slaves. He will do that, of course, but only as one kills a rabbit on the way to a stag hunt."

"That is the truth, Mr. President."

"His fleet is not principally in pursuit of the blacks or even of a lost island. Such specified goals may furnish plausible answers to the world's questions, but I am not satisfied. That island, once properly in hand, will be an invincible French garrison, a supply line, a splendid storehouse and a position to fall back upon if one is needed. We are a young country, newly born into the midst of great and greedy powers. We are weak. Now, if ever, is the time for a conqueror to attack us. James, Napoleon Bonaparte intends to do just that."

Madison's face was expressionless, his tone matter-of-fact. "Yes, Mr. President, I know. When the assault on San Domingo has been concluded he will come through New Orleans to strike at us. And he will not have to fight Spain to do it because there is some kind of devil's pact between him and Spain. My God, would a relatively unimportant man in New Orleans decide on his own authority to close the port to us?" He got to his feet and walked back and forth on the threadbare carpet. Suddenly he stopped walking and looked squarely at Jefferson. "Accepting the premise that there is a madman who will try to get into the nursery and strangle the most precious infant alive, what ought we be doing?"

The President said, "Your metaphor is very apt. I could continue it by saying that we have not sufficient bars for the windows or locks for the doors. But I will speak more plainly. We haven't, and never could have had, the naval force to challenge Bonaparte or the land force to defeat him. His generals will bring their men almost intact from the skirmishing in San Domingo, and it must be remembered that Bonaparte, if he wishes, can send reinforcements at any time."

"Yes, and the French arrivals in Philadelphia understand how to use our freedom. They travel everywhere to appraise and report our strength—and weakness. When the time is right they will cause disturbances and uncertainties in Philadelphia or perform any other service Bonaparte may ask of them. Mr. President, what ought we be doing?"

Jefferson made a small rearrangement of some articles on his desk. When he raised his glance, the Secretary of State saw that his eyes burned with the fire of that inventive mind.

"Madison, we could just possibly mount a fair defense against Bonaparte's fleet at one particular harbor, but, clearly, we cannot plant our defenders on the soil of a foreign country. New Orleans answers that description. It is the soil of a foreign country. Now, by what means could we change that situation? Under what circumstances would it be possible for us to give Americans the opportunity to fight for this land of ours?"

In a very quiet voice Madison asked, "What are you thinking, Mr. President?"

"Sit down. I want to talk to you about the one thing in God's world we may be able to do. I want to talk to you about buying New Orleans."

Madison sat down. He said, "As I remarked earlier, isn't it amazing how the name of Yrujo simply can't remain out of our conversation today."

T W O

Landscape of the Past

. . . .

*W*HEN PAULINE was seven years old she saw her brother Napolione for the first time. He had come home to Ajaccio, on the island of Corsica, after his long years at the school of Brienne and the military academy at Paris. The idea of seeing his brother Giuseppe might have interested him some-what, but the small children could not be expected to capture the attention of a serious-minded seventeen-year-old lieutenant. He had not even thought of Girolamo or Maria-Paola or Maria-Annunziata, who had been born since his departure. Now, as he received the embraces of his family, he noted that the little ones were untidy and ill-mannered. Also, he did not care for their names. It had already occurred to him that Girolamo could be called Jérôme. Maria-Annunziata, Maria-Anna and Maria-Whatever could decide what to call themselves. It didn't matter very much about girls. Sometime before the visit was ended he must suggest to Giuseppe that one did not go far in life with such a name, and certainly Luigi and Luciano sounded outlandish. His own name, he thought, had a dignified solidity to it once one had removed the final *e* and tampered slightly with the spelling. And something should be done about the spelling of Buonaparte. The French thought it odd, and since the opinion of the French was really all that mattered—

Well, not really all that mattered. The strong woman, his mother Letizia, was still in command. Her eyes, as she looked at him, were filled with the love he remembered, but she had been no more impressed by his uniform than a general would have been.

"What was that madness of yours, Napolione, criticizing the head officers of the military academy and telling them how they could improve their methods of instruction?"

"It was not madness, Mama."

"It was madness." To welcome him she had put on her best black dress, the one she had worn to her husband's funeral a few months earlier. The dress was now sprinkled with flour. Letizia was not a woman to reach instinctively for an apron.

Two neighbors had been paid a bottle of wine each to cook dinner on this first day of Napolione's visit, but Letizia had pushed them aside and had taken possession of her kitchen. The women were shouting angry words at her. The baby, Girolamo, cried, while the little girls argued shrilly over which of them should carry him about. Luciano and Luigi wrestled and shrieked on the newly scrubbed wooden floor. Giuseppe hammered at a sagging shelf that had just dropped all the herb pots and spice jars into the washtub below. Letizia's forceful voice scorned all rival sounds. It rang out clear and firm.

"They could have expelled you. What a heartbreak that would have been after all your poor father had done to get you a free cadetship. Can't you imagine the effort it was for him to see all those officials and get all those letters proving that we are two hundred years in Corsica? Not every family is of Corsican aristocracy, but *we* are—and of Italian aristocracy before that, I have no doubt. Your father had such pride that he would not die until he knew that you were an educated man. And you repay him by insulting the officers!"

The young lieutenant, who had grown unaccustomed to the bedlam of a Corsican kitchen, walked away. His head ached, he was dismayed by the undisciplined conduct of his brothers and sisters, and bothered by his mother's claim to aristocracy. From a distance he had seen aristocrats in Paris. Could he explain to her the difference between those glittering personages and the noisy, screeching Buonapartes? Would she understand that the family of an unsuccessful Corsican lawyer was of no consequence outside Corsica?

Here in the dim dining room, shuttered against the heat of the day, there was a chance to sort out the confusions that beset him. He loved his mother, and she was a widow. That added up to a simple tally. He must do everything possible to bring her happiness and prosperity. He felt that he had the gifts which would lead him to an outstanding military career, but might his advancement be hampered by this family of his? Would fellow officers joke among themselves of the Corsican "aristocrats" with the bizarre names? If so, then he would remain forever a nobody and unable to be of much help to his mother. She would live and die in the old house, always poorly dressed, always without comfort and security. So then, facing it all unemotionally, the sensible course would be to walk alone, to forget these Corsicans except for writing dutiful letters to his mother enclosing unfailingly whatever money he could afford. Despite love or longing, it must be his policy forever to be silent on the subject of family, and to let no gentleman of France ever meet these people who belonged only to the world of Ajaccio.

The seventeen-year-old lieutenant, having reached a conclusion that seemed a perfect guide for the future, turned his attention to the furnishings of the dining room. He remembered well the old, dark table and chairs, the rough walls, the candle-holders that needed scouring. He had just noticed an ugly wad of rags that had been jammed into a rat hole when he became aware that he was not alone in the room. There was a Maria-Something standing very still, just staring at him.

He smiled, and she walked toward him. It was rather like watching a ray of sunlight move across the floor. Why, this tiny thing was beautiful, and she was going to scramble up on his lap. He changed his position to accommodate her, and she put her arms around his neck and kissed his cheek.

"You are my brother. I love you," she said.

He felt suddenly weak. Senseless laughter broke from him, though deep inside he felt the agony of guilt. What had he been thinking? That his mother and all her fatherless children could be dismissed with a few miserable francs from his army pay?

"You are my sister, and I shall love you always," he managed after a time.

"Will you stay here with us tonight?"

"Yes, little one."

"Will you stay here with us forever?"

"I can't. I am a soldier."

"Will you come back to see us?"

"I will come back to see you. Will you remember me? What is my name?"

"Napolione."

"Good. What is your name?"

"Maria-Paola." She wrinkled her pretty little face into a knot of discontent. "I hate my name."

"Then I will call you Pauline."

During the first years of the Revolution he came back frequently. Corsica was in turmoil. The island had been seized by antirevolutionists who fought to deliver it to England for safekeeping. Letizia taught her children to sing the *Marseillaise.* She harangued crowds in the market place and became an acknowledged leader of the French faction. When the red, white and blue cockade that she wore on her shawl was torn from her and her face slapped by an angry man, Napoleon sent word for her to leave Corsica.

Letizia was not in the habit of obeying orders. She delayed until it was almost too late. She and her youngest children fled to the hills of Ajaccio only an hour before Corsican neighbors set fire to her house believing she was still there. It was an exhausting march to the sea, but Letizia and the children finally boarded a merchant ship that outwitted the British patrols and made its way to Toulon. Toulon was burning, the local government in revolt against the forces of the Revolution. Letizia, followed by the weary children, journeyed on along the coast to Marseille. Near the old port at the foot of the Cannebière she found two rooms on the top floor of a dreary house and informed her daughters that if they wanted to eat they would have to work. Work at what? Well, knock on doors and inquire if there is not a need for a healthy young laundress.

In Toulon something was happening that Letizia could not

have imagined as she gazed at the flames. The people of Toulon had called upon the English and the Spanish to assist them in their splinter revolution against France. The English responded by capturing the Toulon arsenal and fortress. France swiftly promoted a youthful artilleryman to lieutenant-colonel, placed him in command of reinforcements and rushed him to Toulon. The arsenal and the fortress were returned to France, and Letizia's son, Napoleon Bonaparte, was awarded the rank of brigadier-general for his sparkling victory.

With the pay increase, the enclosures in Napoleon's letters became more substantial. Letizia, never a shy woman, sought out the commissioners of the Republic, newly arrived at Marseille to stabilize local government. She told them of the dangers and losses she and her family had suffered for their loyalty to the Revolution, and so persuasive was Letizia that she was granted a pension for her brave stand.

Prosperity had touched the Bonapartes. They now had three rooms, and the girls were no longer laundresses. The day would come when it would be said that they never had been laundresses, that the indomitable Letizia had known a more profitable way to put her daughters to work. Had the sisters of Napoleon been holy messengers from heaven such a story was bound to circulate. Nevertheless, even friendly neighbors and acquaintances in Marseille were to remark later that the Bonaparte girls had been extraordinarily uninhibited. Their mother, who indisputably had been a laundress, whose hands throughout her life remained red and coarse, had often admitted that she had no idea where her daughters were. In any case, the three young sisters gave up whatever it was they had been doing and applied themselves to the business of imitating their new sister-in-law. Joseph had taken his younger brother's advice. He had changed his name, joined the Army and married Julie Clary. Julie was not pretty, but her deceased father had been a successful silk merchant. There was a dowry that made Julie extremely attractive. For all Letizia's claims to aristocracy, Julie was the only refined person any Bonaparte had met on an informal basis. Assuredly she came from the most imposing home the Bonapartes had ever entered.

For a time Napoleon's headquarters were in Marseille, and he spent his free hours with the family. He brought many officers to meet his interesting mother, his vivacious sisters and amusing brothers. "No one has a family like mine," he would boast. He would look at Pauline as he spoke, as though in some mysterious way she had given him his family. There was no doubt that he had a particular affection for this sister. He took long walks with her. They whispered and laughed together and shared secrets that drove their brothers and sisters mad with jealousy. Letizia counseled patience. "They are Bonapartes, too. Soon they will not be speaking to each other."

Napoleon was moved to Nice as artillery commander. For a few worrisome weeks he was under arrest. He had been identified too closely with the Terror. The month of Thermidor, when Robespierre was sent to the guillotine, was a bad time for those who had known him. However, Citizen Barras, one of the Directory of Five, recognized a brilliant officer when he saw one. Popular opinion was easy to come by; brilliant officers were in short supply. Release Bonaparte!

So, on the whole, life was pleasant for Corsicans except that Pauline, at fourteen, ached to marry. At first it was only the idea of marriage that appealed to her. Joseph and Julie were such a romantic couple. It was adorable to see Julie crisply taking charge in the pretty house Joseph had bought with part of the dowry. Julie's mother had sent a strong young servant girl to do the cooking and cleaning. Julie had lovely frocks and a solid gold necklace, and she knew how to give dinner parties and manage a carriage horse.

"You fool," Letizia said to Pauline. "You are not ready for marriage."

"You were my age when you married."

"But I was ready for work and children and trouble."

"You treat me as though I were a child."

"That's because I know you well."

Pauline thought of marrying a soap merchant named Billon,

but Napoleon wrote to Joseph telling him that the match was not to be considered. Junot, a staff officer of Napoleon's, had dreamed of Pauline since meeting her. Upon hearing that her family had rejected Billon, he was delighted and surprised at this evidence that she was not judged too young for marriage but only too precious to be given to a soap merchant. He now asked for Pauline's hand, but Napoleon squelched him. "She has nothing. You have nothing. Total, nothing." Pauline was not disturbed at the loss of either suitor. Without argument she accepted the fact that Napoleon was the wisest, dearest brother in the world and that he would choose well for her. But then Pauline fell in love.

Among all the men in Marseille, Pauline's heart could scarcely have made a more unfortunate selection. Louis Stanislas Fréron, aged forty-two, a dandy in rose-colored breeches, lived with an actress whose two children he had fathered. The actress was pregnant again, but Pauline saw it all in rather simple terms.

"If she really loves you she will want you to be happy, so tell her you're going to marry me. If she is selfish about the matter, then you'll know she never loved you and therefore her feelings need not be respected."

That made sense to Louis Fréron, although, as founder of the inflammatory journal *L'Orateur du Peuple*, he was ordinarily esteemed for his clear thinking. He had been one of the two commissioners who had come to Marseille to settle grievances and punish evildoers. He had been responsible for Letizia's pension and had voted for the death of the King in the National Convention. Admirable decisions, Letizia Bonaparte conceded, but neither a good reason to approve his marriage to Pauline.

"I love him," Pauline wailed.

"You are addlepated. He is old and cross-eyed and has an awful nose. You will have ugly children."

"I will have no children unless they are his. Don't you understand what love is?"

"No. Who does?"

"My brother Napoleon. He understands everything. I will get his consent."

"Be sure to show it to me when you get it."

Napoleon did not reply to Pauline's letter as promptly as expected. There were difficulties. The commissioner who had originally been sent to Marseille with Fréron was Barras. Barras now sat in a position from which he could influence Napoleon's fate. How great was the friendship between Barras and Fréron? Would it be dangerous to let it be known that Fréron, the friend of Barras, was not, in Napoleon's view, an acceptable brother-in-law?

It was an unnerving situation. Napoleon did not want his lovely sister married to Fréron. Still, though Barras had been lenient at the time of his arrest, Napoleon had not been sent back to his command at Nice. He was performing routine assignments in Paris and greatly feared that he was in grave disfavor. To permit the marriage of Fréron and Pauline would not improve his situation any, but to oppose it might alienate Barras forever. Napoleon perspired, went sleepless and read Pauline's pleading letters over and over.

She was writing to Fréron, too. At least she was sending him letters. Who composed those tender, graceful outpourings so richly filled with lines from Italian poetry and references to more ancient, tragic lovers? "I love you as Petrarch loved Laura." Was Fréron amused by that? He was an educated man. Surely he knew his little inamorata would have been tongue-tied if asked, "Who was Petrarch?"

Pauline wept. Letizia scolded. Napoleon worried about his career, his sister's love affair and the future of each and every Bonaparte, even the ones to whom he was not speaking.

The people of Paris settled the matter. A conservative insurrection menaced the Directory of Five and set Barras to thinking. The diehards needed an unforgettable fright, but where did one find a French officer willing to deal sternly with French civilians? Well, that little fellow Bonaparte was not truly French. Besides, at the moment he was not contributing anything worthwhile in exchange for his upkeep. Let him take over the command of the Paris troops.

Napoleon took command. The counterrevolutionaries marching in massed crowds toward the Assembly building were astonished at what happened. They were availing themselves of the rights of citizens. They were appealing to have their church and their privacy restored. They wanted the calendar to date from the birth of Christ instead of from the birth of the Revolution. They wanted an end to government spying, with its attendant evils of buying information from children and neighbors. Suddenly more than a hundred of them were lying dead in the Paris street.

Barras said, "What I like about Bonaparte is that he does what must be done instead of waiting until it's too late to do it." In high good humor he invited Napoleon to dine with him.

The dinner was far from dull. Napoleon learned that he was to be reinstated as artillery commander at Nice. But there was more, much more, to the evening. Napoleon found a way to introduce Fréron's name into the conversation.

"You cannot think how often my mother speaks of you. She remembers with gratitude that it was you and Louis Fréron who recognized her as a patriot."

Barras's brow puckered at the mention of Fréron. "Fréron? Oh, yes, of course. Fréron. Poor fellow. He has come to nothing." Barras shrugged. "Somehow he lost his way. I had almost forgotten him."

A servant bent over Barras and spoke very quietly. Barras nodded. "Ask the lady to join us, and see that her carriage attendants are given refreshments." He turned to Napoleon. "A most charming friend has arrived. She is the widow of Vicomte de Beauharnais, and is herself of noble birth. Her husband was an enemy of the people and paid the extreme penalty in the dark days that are now behind us."

He rose to his feet, and Napoleon stood, too, waiting.

She came into the room, lithe and enchanting, her eyes flashing, the jeweled bracelets on her arms jingling faintly. Her gown was a soft white cloud that swirled widely about her ankles but clung closely to her bosom and thighs as though in love with her.

"My dear Josephine, a pity you were not able to dine with us, but surely I may offer brandy or a sweet."

Her dazzling smile encompassed both men, and the introduction to Napoleon brought a flush to her cheeks. "How I admire you," she breathed. "You have given Paris back to the people."

There was no innocence in Napoleon. The situation was as comprehensible as the maps of Italy and Austria. At a glance he grasped how the campaign had gone thus far. The Widow de Beauharnais was the mistress of Barras, a mistress anxious to be a wife. Barras had gently discouraged any ambitions she had concerning him but had promised to find for her a man whose star was ascending, a man who would listen willingly to the fine things Barras would say of her.

"This lady has two of the most entrancing children I have ever seen. Do pardon me if I briefly rob you of a share in the conversation. I must find out what they have been doing recently to please their mama."

Honest of Barras, Napoleon thought. The fact that there were children was not to be concealed until a man was helplessly in love. Well, the children had done no harm to Mama's figure or to her glamour. How amusing she was as she told of Hortense's thoroughly insane music teacher and of Eugène's desire to grow vegetables in the rose garden.

"I must meet these children," Napoleon said.

Barras smiled and touched his arm as one who gives friendly advice. "Do not delay, Citizen General. You will be leaving Paris soon."

Napoleon breathed deeply of the fragrance that Josephine had brought with her, looked closely into the face that was like none he had ever seen, listened to the soft voice and lazy laughter. She is an aristocrat, he thought. I need one. God, You have been generous. She is glorious beyond description, and because I am a realistic man I ask, If she had not a questionable past, what would she want of me?

All the anxieties that had plagued him had been banished here at Barras's dinner table. The thought of ordering Pauline never again to see Fréron was distressing. To hurt her even when he knew it was in her interest was not easy. But she would forgive him. A change of scene was what she needed. Soon, oh, very soon now he would give her a world she had never known, a world full of gallants competing for her love. At last he was in a position to put forward his plan for a campaign in northern Italy. It had been gestating in his mind for a year. At this moment he could have explained in detail how Lombardy could be taken from Italy, and Mantua wrested from the Austrians.

It was all as he had dreamed at Barras's table. The Austrians surrendered to Napoleon, and northern Italy was in his hands when his family came to Milan. He was living in the manner of minor royalty and was hard pressed to restrain himself from an undignified show of exultation as he led his mother to the luxurious suite of rooms he had chosen for her in the Serbelloni Palace.

"You have done very well," she said. "But I do not need quarters such as these. My tastes are simple."

He knew that she was saying something quite different, saying it obliquely in the Corsican way. She was saying that she did not like the woman with the jeweled bracelets who presided over the palace, the woman he had given her as a daughter-in-law.

"These are not elaborate quarters, Mama. They are only tasteful and comfortable. I hope you will like them better tomorrow."

He was disappointed that Pauline had not come. What did he care about Caroline and Louis and Jérôme? Pauline's letters had stopped completely, and he knew that he would have to plead and coax to bring her here.

He sent her a dozen letters and a dozen gifts, and at last she came. He had not given his mother the finest rooms. He had saved them for Pauline. She pretended to be unimpressed by the grandeur.

"You broke my heart," she said. "Do you expect me to live again simply because my rooms have pink velvet carpets and gold-framed mirrors?"

"The pain will grow less, little one."

"Did I interfere with your marrying that woman who thinks herself some sort of goddess?"

He smiled at her jealousy and whispered that in time she would learn to be as elegant as Josephine. He knew that would never happen, but Pauline had her own kind of beauty and style. It would not be difficult to marry her off once she stopped sulking. There was Victor Leclerc, for instance. Yes, Victor Leclerc. He was a brigadier-general and had distinguished himself in the fighting around Fort Faron at Toulon. He was of excellent family and there was money, Napoleon remembered, as well as good looks and youth. Perfect. Why look farther than Victor Leclerc?

After a week of theaters and gala dinner parties Pauline managed to put Louis Fréron from her mind. When Leclerc was presented to her she found him irresistible. She told her sister Caroline that life had had no meaning until the moment Leclerc had danced with her.

"Don't tell Mama that," Caroline said. "She'll hit you. You almost drove her crazy with all your tears and tantrums over that terrible Fréron. You mean they weren't real? You mean you didn't love him?"

"Love," Pauline said, "is a man Napoleon approves of."

Pauline and Leclerc were married at Montebello in the chapel of the huge castle where Napoleon and his family were spending the summer. Letizia, stunned by the power of God's will, took note of the date. It was exactly four years to the day since she and her children, homeless and moneyless, had been driven from Toulon by flames and fear. She looked about her in honest wonderment at those who had been invited to the chapel. "Only my closest friends," Napoleon had said. The lion of St. Mark and the key of St. Peter glittered on foreign epaulettes. Envoys from Vienna and Genoa had brought their wives to weep happily at the wedding of Napoleon's sister. Only the sight of Josephine curdled Letizia's joy. Josephine of the sweet smile, the gentle voice and the wit to have landed legally in Napoleon's bed. But there was always God's will, Letizia reflected, always God's will.

It was a year before she came to look again at Josephine. The occasion was the christening of Pauline's child. A grand review of troops was held in Milan, and artillery roared salvos in honor of Napoleon's nephew. The guests were again solemnly appraised by Letizia as she listened to the cannons and drumbeats and band music. Incredible. All of it. One would suppose a royal heir had been christened. But it was only a child of Victor Leclerc's. Hatefully, Letizia's eyes rested on Josephine. Give Napoleon a child, she thought, or I will curse you all my life. And Josephine's glance turned to her just then, and Letizia saw the sudden pallor that swept across her daughter-in-law's bright face.

Leclerc bought Pauline a house in the Rue de la Victoire and a country place near Soissons. Napoleon took his armies to Egypt. When he came back, he came alone. Nelson had destroyed the French fleet at the Nile. The soldiers of France were cut off from any discernible chance of reaching home. The people were unaware that their husbands and sons might never return. They knew only that Italy, which Napoleon had given to them, had now been taken away. Nothing had prospered without Napoleon. France was again on the brink of civil war and bankruptcy. Napoleon would repair all the damage that had been done in his absence. Bells rang in the villages through which he passed. Bonfires lighted his way to Paris.

There was so much the people didn't know. Napoleon had come back to them in a frigate that dared show no lights, that moved secretly, that feared the British. There had been four hundred French ships in his fleet when he had gloriously sailed forth to conquer Egypt and strike at India. The people did not know that he had stolen away from Egypt without letting the soldiers guess that Kléber was now their commander in chief. The announcement was made after Napoleon had gone. Mutiny had been avoided by the good sense of French soldiers who knew themselves able to fight anything but a *fait accompli.*

From time to time Napoleon acknowledged the shouts of the happy crowds as he sat in a carriage and was driven from Lyon to Paris. He thought of the immediate future. The stupid men of the government will say I have deserted, that I have left my men to rot in Egypt. God alone knows that I have come here to save them. Help for them can come only from France. If I am not in France no one will send it. My victories have propped up the government. What other general has sent bullion valued at millions to the national treasury? Who but I makes war a financial success, *and* an artistic harvest? I have filled the Louvre Palace with Italy's great paintings. Because of me Paris will have the bronze horses of Venice and the Venus de' Medicis of Florence. But I am hampered by idiots.

And in that mood he faced the Directory. "What has become of the France which I left in your hands?"

"What has become of our fleet?"

"I am not an admiral."

"What has been accomplished by your expedition?"

"I have beaten the Turks, and we are in command of Egypt."

"For how long?"

"Hear me. I have been in peril on a sea possessed by British ships. I endured that so I could stand here and tell you how to save France."

"You are the only one who knows how that can be done?"

"No. You are the only ones who do not know how that can be done."

"We are waiting to be told."

Napoleon bellowed at them. He bellowed, "Ask the people!"

By the following midnight, 18 Brumaire, Year VIII, on the Revolutionary calendar, he was First Consul. He moved into the Tuileries, the last palace of the Bourbon kings. He lay upon his new bed and had no feeling of having attained the zenith. There was too much to do.

Josephine, uncertain that he wished her to disrobe, spoke quietly, beseechingly, explaining why she had not been present upon his triumphant arrival.

"Learn this," he said to her. "I regard any explanation as no more than a complicated maze of lies. Now go to your room and leave me to my thoughts."

She left him alone, and he did not notice. He was thinking of the precarious French currency, and the men who would be needed in the establishment of a solid financial fortress that would be internationally respected. It would be known as the Bank of—no, no, that was a dream ahead of its time. It must be known simply as the Bank of France.

In the month of Floréal he swept into Italy over the Grand-Saint-Bernard Pass. It was known that other commanders had led their armies across the Alps—four other commanders in the space of two thousand years. Napoleon stopped the mighty Second Coalition that had been formed against France. At Marengo, on 11 Thermidor, he broke the victorious streak of the Austrian Army and discovered that recapturing was the greatest excitement in the game.

He came back to Paris with a new dream: the former French possessions in America. He brooded upon the loss of that vaguely defined area extending from the Gulf of Mexico to the Great Lakes. Lost. All of it. Forfeited after Wolfe defeated Montcalm at Quebec in 1759. If only I had been there, he thought, angrily. France was victimized because I had not been born. It galled him that Spain had acquired the wide territory of glorious promise that was known as Louisiana. He urgently needed that land. He needed all the land that had ever belonged to France. And more. There were ways to get it. Spain could be persuaded. He thrilled as he thought of expanding the borders of France into that new, rich world. He could do it. He knew how.

The first step would be small but pivotal. That damned little island where ex-slaves had dared to write their own constitution must be secured before anything else could be achieved. At least the island belonged to France. Nobody could argue that point. He pondered. If the blacks were reasonably docile, the island could be occupied at once and soldiers set to work building bases for future operations. If the blacks made trouble there would be a slight delay. It might be necessary to kill all the natives who had a talent for organization and leadership. But there was always the possibility that such chaos existed on the island that French troops would be received with welcoming cheers.

In any case the island was the key to all the rest. It would be the perfect supply line. Whatever was required to make it functional would be done. He thought about England. Everything would move more easily if there were peace with England, but peace was not the *sine qua non*. If it seemed wise at the time, he would give England the assurance that he had no designs on Jamaica. But that was as far as he would go. Let England wonder. Let the world wonder. Even now the newspapers were guessing as to the use he would make of the warships that were under construction at Brest and Marseille.

In his imagination he called his brother-in-law Leclerc to him. He carefully inspected and catechized Pauline's husband. Yes, Leclerc would be placed in command. He could be trusted. Why not? Everything that was a gain for France was a gain for Bonaparte, and whatever was a gain for Bonaparte improved the position of all family members.

Such ecstasy and vigor flowed through Napoleon that last year of the new warships' building that he enthralled Josephine with the tenderness and power of his love.

"I think of you every moment that we're apart," he whispered to her.

It wasn't so. Even when they were together he thought of conquest.

. . . .

On lavishly verdant Saint-Domingue a very long time had passed without people complaining too bitterly of the fate that was theirs. The white plantation owners lived in luxurious houses built on steep slopes and surrounded by palms and fountains. They grumbled occasionally because, being a colonial possession, Saint-Domingue was permitted to sell its sugar and coffee, its sisal and mahogany only to France. Thus their profit was limited while French importers grew fabulously wealthy.

Too, it was distressing that many mulattoes on the island were as proud and prosperous as any white, and as well educated. Of course, the mulattoes were not allowed to vote in the elections of the colonial Assembly, but it was maddening to see their fine horses, their jewels and their Parisian clothing. There was, however, one thing about mulattoes that pleased the whites tremendously: there were no harsher slave masters than rich mulattoes. Their extraordinary cruelty toward blacks was comforting to remember. It meant that never would the two castes unite to cause disturbance.

The white shopkeepers and artisans were necessarily city people. They lived in small and pretty houses that were pink or yellow or so covered with flowering vines that one could make no guess as to color. The city people kept a slave or two for housework and errands. Mulatto money was as valuable as the money of the white plantation owners, so shopkeepers greeted all customers courteously. But a customer was something quite different from a competitor. There should be laws against mulattoes living in cities. Oh, it was all right for them to own sugar land and cotton fields. They could come in to Port-au-Prince or Cap-Français to spend their money. But those not fortunate enough to own plantations had the brazenness to settle down in the city. They opened shops or became skilled craftsmen. That ought not to be allowed. It took bread out of the mouths of white children.

Here and there in Saint-Domingue were some free blacks. The excessive sentimentality of owners, grateful, perhaps, for the saving of a child's life, created most of these anomalies. Some blacks had, in special situations, bought their freedom, but the number was too small to bother counting. One could say, if one was not a quibbler, that all blacks were slaves. They lived on their masters' plantation lands and were given nothing beyond sufficient food to keep them in working condition. They or their parents or grandparents had been brought from Senegal and Ghana and the Congo. The ones who survived the voyage were strong-bodied and produced a great many sons and daughters. So many, in fact, that it was not considered extravagant to shoot a few of them in the testing of a new gun. There was also a game that a planter invented for the diversion of his friends. It consisted of burying nine blacks up to their necks and bowling with cannon balls against these surprising "pins." Slaves were too plentiful for a man of means to deny himself any pleasure.

In Saint-Domingue there were forty thousand whites, twenty-four thousand mulattoes and a half-million black people who were slaves.

When word arrived that revolution had gripped France and that the Bastille had fallen, a shiver of excitement pulsed through the island. Ah, the white plantation owners gloated, that would be the end of colonialism. They would be full partners with France and send their wares to any world market that offered the highest price. Ah, thought the mulattoes, no more having to rise to our feet in the presence of the least worthy of white men. Even the slaves in their compounds stirred, aware of a compelling something in the air that, though unnamed and unrelated to themselves, must have significance.

The whites, even if some retained a secret love of royalty, elected a new assembly. Saint-Domingue was no longer obliged to obey edicts from the appointee who had represented Louis Capet. The mulattoes, feeling that the new assembly served them no better than the old, sent one of their most admired sons to Paris. His name was Vincent Ogé, and his mission was to plead before the National Assembly for the concession of equal rights to the mulattoes of Saint-Domingue. He returned with an inspiring message from the new leaders of France. The privilege of voting and of taking part in every aspect of political life had been granted to all free men regardless of color.

The mulattoes celebrated. The white people of Saint-Domingue did not celebrate. They held meetings and informed members of the new assembly that the ruling class would tolerate only that portion of Revolutionary absurdity that seemed pleasant and harmless.

Vincent Ogé was warned that he was in danger and hid himself in the home of a friend. At an hour convenient to the Assembly and the plantation owners, both Vincent and his friend were dragged into the public square and all their bones were broken. After that they were tied down to lie in the dreadful blaze of the sun "as long as it would please God to preserve their lives." That was the way the court decree read.

Everyone without a good excuse had been forced to attend the spectacle. There were those in the crowd who watched with satisfaction. There were those who became ill and fainted. There were those who grew thoughtful. Among the third group was the coachman for the Bréda family. His name was Toussaint, and he was a small, ugly fellow with a protruding jaw. He had no hatred for the two suffering men even though they were mulattoes. Toussaint never thought much about hate or love or pity or fear. He thought only of who and what could be used to bring about the freedom of blacks.

He looked around at the people in the crowd. Friends of Bréda's stood on the other side of the invisible barrier that separated blacks from whites. Some were kind enough to fling an agreeable word to the little coachman. Toussaint bowed his head humbly in answer or saluted with the carriage whip. He knew well which form of reply was more pleasing to each gentleman of Bréda's social circle.

He spoke to a few of the slaves standing close to him and was amused to note that they, too, had made a careful study and knew what sort of rejoinder was preferable to him. Though he made no distinction between field hands and house servants, Toussaint did not speak to every slave he knew. To do so would remove the honor of special favor. He was keenly aware of the high regard in which he was held as a man of education. The value he placed upon his prestige was in no way related to vanity or childish conceit.

Standing not too far away was the headwaiter from the Auberge de la Couronne. He is a fine-looking fellow, Toussaint thought. Tall, neat, well washed and combed. Naturally, his owner can't run a profitable restaurant unless the help looks clean, but I like to think this man enjoys presenting an appearance that is just a trifle more polished than that of any customer.

Toussaint greeted the young man, who responded politely but without any show of surprise at having been noticed.

"You are well, Christophe?"

"Extremely well, thank you. And you, coachman Toussaint?"

The accent brought to mind that Christophe had come from another island. Which island? English, of course. But which? No matter. The screams of Vincent Ogé and his tortured companion trembled in the airless morning. The men no longer had the will to endure in silence. Their discipline had been shattered by their agonies. Death was near, but the crowd would be told to wait until the heads had been severed and placed on pikes for display.

Toussaint's eyes wandered to the white men across the unmarked barrier, and then to the mulattoes, who, because of their inferiority, were not allowed to stand with the whites and, because of their superiority, not allowed to stand with the blacks. Toussaint's own slave throng was predictably the largest gathering of all. He contemplated it with interest. Facial expressions, postures and signs of illness were all catalogued for future reference.

Suddenly his attention was completely captured by a huge black man, ragged and sullen-eyed. He is uglier than I, Toussaint thought, but younger, much younger. A field hand. My God, he is dirty.

Defying his long-standing rules of deportment, he walked over to where the big man stood in his torn and filthy clothes. The stench was almost overwhelming, but Toussaint, in his dignified livery, looked up into the face of the young giant.

"What's your name, boy?"

"Why you ask, you dressed-up old flea?"

Toussaint blinked at that and listened for laughter, but the friend of Ogé was shrieking in delirium and no one had heard the insult.

"What do you think of all this?"

The field hand shrugged, and the rotting material of the shirt he wore split above one of his tremendous shoulders. "You kill to make people do what you want. You kill with bad pain to show it not good to do what he do. Too late to make dead fellow do what you want, but maybe scare some other fellow to do what you want."

Toussaint wondered what animal had taught this animal to speak. The answer came to him. Of course. This man was the property of one of the few freed blacks who now farmed some scraggly piece of earth with the help of a slave of his own. That

56

would account for the sullen eyes and foul condition of the field hand, and for his speech, which was a mixture of garbled Africanisms and almost unrecognizable French. Only the slave of an uneducated black could speak so abominably.

"What is your master's name?"

"Me, I don't have a master." The anger was back, very black now and very cold.

"You are a free man then?"

"Not today. Maybe tomorrow." The giant spat accurately just to the side of Toussaint's polished boots. "His name is Des Salines."

Toussaint turned away from the ill-smelling young man and thought, No point in asking him how to spell it. I suppose he said Dessalines. Merciful God, with my brains and his anger what could we not do?

A numbing doubt flashed into his mind.

But, of course, we could do nothing, he told himself, without one other factor. We would need a third man, a man fashioned by the God of vengeance, with the intelligence to understand me and the patience to reach the mind of an ignorant field hand.

If the white plantation owners thought that everything had been settled by the swift action taken against Ogé, it was because of a deep-rooted conviction that they constituted the ruling class. They had drawn up the regulations. If the regulations were violated, then punishment followed. After that, it would be accepted anew that indeed the white plantation owners were in control. Only, this time there was a new spirit walking the land.

In the southern and western parts of Saint-Domingue the mulattoes held councils in their great houses. They organized and plotted and armed. The blacks picked up the rhythm of revolt, and no one noticed. The whites were watching the mulattoes. The mulattoes were watching the whites. Nobody thought about the blacks. Nobody understood the strange African words that were exchanged by slaves from different plantations as they passed each other on a dusty road. Nobody suspected that there were messages in the little songs that women sang and in the drumbeats that throbbed in the darkness. Nobody feared to speak his mind in the presence of valets or waitresses or butlers. The blacks were only uncomprehending animals or so faithful and loving that they were harmless.

There was a slave named Buckman, and he believed that no power on earth could withstand his voodoo gods. He called his followers to him, and there was a girl with the eyes of a devil who danced and chanted and cut the throat of a boar and passed the warm blood to be drunk by those ready for freedom. Toussaint, the good Roman Catholic, drank and cried out to pagan gods for strength. He could not afford to alienate any of these fools. He would have a use for the survivors after Buckman and his voodoo gods had given up the fight.

Though they did not know it, the mulattoes were appointed to sound the call to battle. The blacks waited, and finally the mulattoes struck. They were not primitives. They struck against the soldiers of the new assembly. They were fighting a political war. Buckman and his wild-eyed men, armed with hoes and axes, old swords and a few stolen guns, wanted personal revenge against all whites and all mulattoes.

The blacks burned two hundred sugar refineries and six hundred coffee plantations. The city of Le Cap went up in flames, and every white and mulatto within reach was murdered. It was a week of incredible brutality, but at last the drunken laughter of Buckman's black hordes was silent. They had quarreled among themselves and had begun to kill each other. The soldiers, occupied with the well-armed, disciplined mulattoes, turned their attention to the blacks just long enough to round up the last dazed and wounded remnants of Buckman's rebellion, to clear away the corpses and to make certain that Buckman's mutilated body was seen by all.

Toussaint had invested a night or two in rampage, running with the ignorant butchers he disdained. How would one prove on another day that these were one's well-loved brothers if one held oneself aloof? And, occasionally, across a mound of mangled bodies, one looked sharply and learned something. For instance, the fastidious headwaiter from the Auberge de la Couronne had had a score or two to settle. Apparently it was true that the red-haired plantation owner, when displeased with his dinner, often struck Christophe. True, that a beautiful blonde lady, failing to draw a longing glance from the headwaiter, had accused him of fondling her breast as he bent to serve the *potage*. Her charge against him could have meant his disfigurement or his death, but Christophe's owner had influence and had used it. Toussaint almost admired the skill with which— But of course Christophe, by his profession, would know a great deal about carving.

Toussaint had spent most of that terrible week thinking, observing and prostrating himself before the plaster saints in his church. He now came forward and pled forgiveness for the misguided blacks.

He was a free man. The Bréda family had been grateful for his protection. Too, the family had been more than a little awed by the power he exercised over towering, blood-smeared blacks who turned aside at his words or at the sight of curious symbols he placed upon the house and around the grounds. Toussaint had happily accepted his freedom but had requested that he be retained as coachman until he had properly acquainted himself with his new condition. The Brédas had embraced him and wept a little.

There was really nobody to listen to Toussaint's plea for the misguided blacks, no government with which to deal. The Assembly had disappeared. Some members were in hiding. Some had jumped on American ships and fled to the United States. One had gone mad when he had seen a group of blacks carrying dead white babies on the points of sharpened sticks. The soldiers and the National Guard were actively engaged with the mulatto insurrection and could not listen, but Toussaint knew that blacks were listening. Those who had shunned Buckman from the beginning respected the freed coachman's plea for his own people no matter what evil deeds had been committed. Buckman's men who had escaped arrest were lurking in the mountains. The word was brought or sent to them: Toussaint is a true friend of his brothers.

There was no confusion as to where Toussaint's sympathies

lay, but in every other matter there were deep and painful uncertainties. In the West Province mulattoes and whites were joined in combat against loose bands of runaway slaves and any islanders who favored the Revolutionary government of France. The strange confederation collapsed with much bloodshed when news came that the National Assembly in Paris had reversed its decision and would permit mulattoes to vote only if the idea was satisfactory to local white residents. The soldiers of France, depleted by native fevers, weary and hardly alive, now gave up the struggle. They weren't missed. Everyone on the island had become a leader or a partisan and thus had enemies enough to slaughter without the participation of French soldiers.

The news of what was happening in Saint-Domingue at last had reached the Paris desk of someone with authority. Ships arrived in the harbor of ravaged Le Cap bringing thousands of fresh young soldiers to relieve the exhausted veterans. And on the ships were three French commissioners, who had come to restore order to the complex, bloody little island.

Toussaint was a member of the deputation of slaves and ex-slaves that was granted an audience with the plainly uniformed men of Revolutionary France. He spoke eloquently but left little latitude for negotiation. He asked freedom for the blacks. In return for which he promised their loyalty in peace or war. The commissioners, giving no hint of their personal thinking, said only that his words had been noted and would be considered.

His words certainly had been noted, but not considered. Rumors had spread that the request of Toussaint had been granted, so more battles had to be fought. The white plantation owners who had survived the hell of Buckman's rebellion sent out their troops to demolish the new French garrison. The commissioners went home to France convinced that the shrewd thing to do about Saint-Domingue was to forget it until its factions had destroyed each other and the island could be repopulated by sensible families from the French countryside and new shipments of slaves from Africa.

This opinion was not accepted in Paris. The National Assembly chose a new trio of commissioners, and accompanying them was a bombastic ex-mayor of Lyon upon whom had fallen the honor and title of governor-general of Saint-Domingue. Also aboard the ships were an additional six thousand well-trained soldiers.

Upon arrival the commissioners found that mulattoes were now enlisting blacks to fight the whites. That was a great pity, because from Paris had come a splendid message for the mulattoes. They were positively going to be permitted to vote and to hold positions of importance in local government.

The latest men from Paris had brought a new attitude with them. They had what seemed very much like an interest in Saint-Domingue. They restored order at Port-au-Prince and moved on, intending to end the fighting in the South Province, where savagery between whites and mulattoes had reached an unspeakable level of inhuman behavior.

The ex-mayor of Lyon, who did not think the title governor-general an empty honor, now declared that, on the basis of their bestiality, the mulattoes were certainly not going to be permitted to vote. The commissioners, deciding that here was a blockhead who did not understand how to achieve peace, ordered him back to Paris.

It was not that simple. The Governor-General called out the National Guard and sailors from French ships anchored in the harbor, and now all Saint-Domingue watched, openmouthed, while the white overseas French fought each other. Someone found a few houses and shops that had not been burned in Le Cap. The city sent more flames skyward and relapsed into a sooty, smoldering mass of nothing. Port-au-Prince was next, the stories went.

Toussaint had been patient. He had his followers. He had his cause. Now was the moment to use one and further the other. He scorned the Governor-General and asked for an audience with the commissioners. They stared in weary wonderment at the little black coachman, bemused that they were wasting their time with him. He had brought a useless bit of information, they thought, for which he would ask a hundred francs or the punishment of some white man who had once beaten him.

"What is it?" one of them asked.

"It is this: You have troops in the west and troops in the south and not enough troops anywhere," Toussaint told them. "You are fighting your so-called governor-general and the sailors from your own ships. You are thoroughly disorganized. I have come to help."

That was good enough to earn a tired smile from the Frenchmen.

"I have three thousand men who will fight for you."

As though rehearsed, the three commissioners leaned forward and fixed their gazes sharply on Toussaint.

"Three thousand men for a beginning," he said. "More will come later." He paused and waved his coachman's whip idly at a buzzing fly. "Of course, there is a price."

The fat commissioner with the straight black hair was named Sonthonax. He seemed to be the most important of the three. He said, "We are not authorized to make military payments."

Toussaint smiled and killed the fly. "There are men who do not fight for money. There are men who fight for freedom, not in the abstract French meaning of that word, but in a very personal way. To them freedom is the promise that they cannot be murdered by whim or have their ears cut off for eating a banana without permission. Freedom is your order that their women and children cannot be sold and sent away from them."

The commissioners understood now but did not look at each other.

"Who could lead these men?" the fat commissioner asked.

"Naturally, their leader," Toussaint said. "I."

There was a silence. Then, "What do you know of leading men into battle?"

"In Europe? Nothing. In Saint-Domingue, all. I know every inch of the island. I know the courage and cowardice of every man who lives here. And I am not without practical intelligence."

"You could guarantee that your men would not run amuck and become murderous and destructive?"

"No. They have been raised as beasts. Is there an abused and hungry dog whose gentleness you would vouch for?"

Now the commissioners looked at each other, troubled and still.

"I can guarantee you this," Toussaint said. "If you give the dog enough to eat and an occasional word of kindness he can be taught very quickly which throat to rip open and which hand to lick."

The fat commissioner said, "France has declared war on England. We would like to return home with news that Saint-Domingue, at least, is at peace."

Toussaint asked, quietly, "Do you remember that I said there was a price?"

"To be paid in advance? How can we trust you?"

"To be paid afterward? How can we trust you?"

"Coachman, you ask foolish questions. If we accept your proposition you will have in your possession the weapons of war that we have handed you to fight the enemy. If we prove false, you can turn them upon us."

Toussaint shook his head. "Not good enough. You three who sit here now dealing with me will be at home in France, forgetful of any loose agreements you might have made on an anxious day in Saint-Domingue. You will not be here for us to punish for your perfidy. In frustration we will kill thousands of your innocent, pink-cheeked soldiers, but that will gain us nothing. We will still be slaves."

"Do you really have three thousand men?"

"At minimum."

"And there is a possibility of more?"

"A probability."

"They will take commands from you?"

"From no one else."

The commissioners noticed the sudden glitter in the coachman's eyes and became aware of the undeniable magnetism the little man exercised. Uncomfortably, they asked themselves why they were taking him seriously. Why did they believe he was not exaggerating? Or that he was not a madman who thought himself a leader?

"Go away, coachman. We will see you again in an hour."

When the French commissioners issued their proclamation freeing all slaves, the South Province immediately placed itself and all property under the protection of England. The Royal Navy, rather pleased, landed a detachment of troops. And since France had also declared war against Spain, it seemed fitting for the representative of the English government in Jamaica to treat with San Domingo, as the Spanish portion of the troublesome island was called. The English, it was decided, would take the South Province, while the Spanish troops from San Domingo invaded from the North.

"Where is your army?" the commissioners demanded of Toussaint.

"It will march any day now."

And when it marched, the Governor-General, who had been mayor of Lyon, did not wait to see how it would all turn out. He found an American merchant ship willing to carry him to the United States. He had had enough of honors.

The white plantation owners looked with terror upon the strong black bodies clothed in tatters. They saw fire in the eyes of men they had held in captivity, men who were now in control of cannon and muskets. They saw a face here and there that was familiar, and they remembered what had been done to the possessor of that face when he had worked slowly or had stolen an egg. They hurried to the harbor and made arrangements with sea captains and went home to pack hastily.

"I did not mean for the French to be driven from the island," Sonthonax said.

"They will come back," Toussaint promised. "I myself will invite them back one day. They will think of the beauty of the island and the profits of growing sugar and coffee. They will return and become rich again."

"Without slaves it can't be done."

"I will show them how to do it." Toussaint's glittering eyes appraised the commissioner. There was something else to say. How would it be taken? "Now we have kept our bargain, you and I. You have made the black man free, and I have delivered an army the sight of which frightened away your silly enemy, who was of your race and nation. My army, happy not to fight French sailors and the National Guard, will fight the English and Spanish for you. But there is still a thing I would ask of you. You and the other commissioners wished to return to France. Go now."

"Now?"

"Yes. We have done all we can do together. We have reached a peak in our relationship. From this moment on we can only misunderstand each other. We will destroy what our mutual faith has built. We will begin to criticize and disapprove and suggest until there are angry words and finally hatred. Go, please."

Before he had seen Saint-Domingue the commissioner had never dealt with blacks, but in his blood and bones he knew that he had no choice. He knew, too, that he must try to give every man in that dangerous black army a reason to remember that liberation had come by the grace of France.

"I will do as you say, Toussaint. May I have a word with your men before I sail?"

It was true that most of the men did not understand all that he said in his fine French. Their owners had spoken to them in the quaint dialect they had learned from each other, part African, part French, simplified and limited to a few hundred words. But everyone understood the gift and the warning of Sonthonax.

"You are free men. Remember that always. In the supply depot there is a gun for each man. Your leader will attend to the distribution. The gun he will give you is separate from the weapons that are issued to you for fighting the enemies of your country. Once in your hand, the gun will not be the property of France or of any other country or of any other man. It is your personal possession to keep throughout your life, given to you as a symbol of my trust, of France's trust. I warn you that the person who tries to take it from you will return you to slavery."

A roaring scream of exultation almost shook the island. Some blacks wept, others laughed and some stood marveling that a white Frenchman had given them guns and spoken so to them. En masse they marched to the harbor and watched the commissioners' ship sail away. When it was out of sight, Toussaint gave a command and led his men away to join the forces of Spain.

The Spanish ranked him as a general because he had brought five thousand men to them. He moved with flashing style through the island, taking whatever stood in his way. As he advanced, his army grew, though his recruits often had no idea for what country they fought. "We fight for Toussaint," they said. And he picked up the name L'Ouverture because he opened all things before him.

The deadly green jungle, the jagged mountain peaks and sinister valleys held no malevolence for Toussaint and the men who followed his orders. They moved as shadows and as avengers, and they were accustomed to the risks of life and reconciled to the inevitability of death. Frequently after a halt for sleep or forage Toussaint's sharp eyes would light upon a peculiarly miserable corpse. The body was never that of a black, and, because many soldiers did not know which uniform the enemy wore, it was sometimes English and at other times French or Spanish. The shocking thing was that a heart was always clenched in the rigid jaws. It was the heart of the dead man himself. Toussaint would see the great bloody hole that had been slashed to remove it. He would cross himself and say a quick prayer, for it was always a chilling sight.

The island was now almost entirely in the hands of the English and Spanish, except for a pocket of mulattoes still fighting determinedly in the South. Toussaint was learning much about Spanish thinking and how the high command planned battles and made decisions. And because the Spanish Army of San Domingo heard news of the outside world from dispatches sent to the British Navy, he was able to verify what he had suspected. Alone he would never take the island away from the Spanish and the English. The French had no new troops with which to replenish the Saint-Domingue garrison because the campaigns of Europe required every man of military age. So it was time he brought his ruthless, untiring soldiers back to the French while that army still had some hope, some confidence. This great black beast of a fighting force would be a stimulus. It would make the

French dream again of victory. Together he and France could make Spain and England wish they had not heard of Saint-Domingue. And afterward, after the collapse of the mutual enemy, the French would be weak, drained of all strength—

Toussaint reversed his course, and with the speed of a demon he led his ill-clad legions over the ground they had taken such a short time before. They took it now from Spanish troops and hoisted the tricolor in every town they passed and drove the Spanish out of the valley and back over the frontier. They crossed the forbidding mountains and came at last to Le Cap, where nothing stood but the crude wooden lath buildings of the French garrison that had been hastily nailed together after the fires.

The great columns of ragged black men were hailed as heroes when they appeared carrying French flags and singing the *"Marseillaise."* Throughout the homeward march blacks had been deserting the Spanish and English to follow Toussaint L'Ouverture, and here in the ruins of the city more blacks gave him their allegiance.

From a charred beam that lay upon the ground a tall young man rose and bowed respectfully to Toussaint. He was dressed with care and his hair gleamed cleanly. Toussaint recognized Christophe, the headwaiter of the Auberge de la Couronne.

"What have you been doing, Christophe?"

"Sitting on what was left of the restaurant."

"You do not care for soldiering?"

"Yes, and I had thought to join you but I was puzzled when you went to the Spaniards. I think I understand now. Will you have me?"

"I will gladly have you, Christophe. You begin as a sergeant. Get a book and find out what a sergeant's duties are." Toussaint sighed, remembering that he had not many men to whom he could issue such an order. He thought of the coarse, gorillalike face that represented the typical soldier of his army, and suddenly into his mind popped the memory of a man he had seen on the day that the mulatto Vincent Ogé had died of his desire to vote.

"I have a task for you to perform, Christophe. Find me somewhere on this island an ex-slave named Dessalines. Perhaps he is dead. If so, bring me the information on how he died."

It took Christophe only an hour. "He is with your troops, General. He has been one of your men since you passed through the village of La Guêpe a year ago."

Toussaint thought of the dead bodies with the slashed chests and the hearts jammed between blood-soaked teeth. "I should have guessed," he said. "Did you speak to him, Christophe? Could you understand him?"

"Why not, sir?"

"Because he is a barbarian."

Christophe nodded. "Other barbarians respect him."

"Of what did you speak?"

"Of the army and of you, sir. You are all in the world that he does not hate."

"See that he develops a high opinion of you, too, Christophe. That's an order."

Toussaint rallied the French troops, and together they went against the English. They made immediate gains, for they picked up an unexpected ally. The French plantation owners had turned on the English under whose protection they had placed themselves. The protectors were now sandwiched between the furious landowners and the mixed army of French and blacks.

In Europe, France made peace with Spain, so England lost Spanish support on the island. Worse still for England was the news that even neutrality could not be hoped for from San Domingo. The area had been ceded to France in a war settlement.

When that news reached Toussaint he did not delay. He hastened east and found the Spanish Army short of supplies, the soldiers who were native to San Domingo disgusted with the situation.

"But you are French now," Toussaint exhorted. "Join us and rejoice. The Spaniards will sail home and forget you, but as Frenchmen you will share our victories and prosperity. We are all one."

Toussaint left a battalion to watch the inhabitants, and he marched the soldiers away to become Frenchmen. The English, with one misfortune and another, found themselves suddenly opposed by four times the strength they had expected on that bright morning when they had come to aid the frightened plantation owners of the South. Brigadier-General Maitland was sent to command their island campaign because he knew so well how to handle the simple blacks. Within three weeks Maitland wrote to the commander of the simple blacks promising to leave all public works undamaged if British forces were permitted to depart without interference. Toussaint permitted the English to depart without interference.

What was there still to clear up? Oh, yes, the mulattoes led by that plucky little Rigaud and the courtly Pétion. They knew it was their last stand. They inspired uprisings wherever possible and fought their men well. Toussaint's army, which was now an indestructible machine, took the mulattoes seriously. With full power to choose his methods, Dessalines was sent to show Rigaud and Pétion the kind of war that was waged by a man who could not read French textbooks on honor and glory. The mulattoes were not cowards, but they had thought only of fighting soldiers. Dessalines was a wild, bloodthirsty animal. Rigaud fled to France, and there was a stillness on the island. Toussaint, unlike Alexander, had no time to cry. His domain was rubble. The cities had to be rebuilt, the wounded countryside brought back to health. The planning would occupy every hour for months. The reconstruction would take years.

And suddenly there was the fat commissioner, Sonthonax, with the black, straight hair.

"I have come to salute you, Toussaint."

"Very kind of you."

"I have brought you a gift."

"I am honored."

"Welcome me, friend. I am a Frenchman and this is France. I suppose I may visit."

"Of course. As you see, we have not yet recovered. There is no worthy place to entertain you."

"I have a friend with me. You are invited to dine aboard the ship with us."

Toussaint politely declined. "It so happens that I have arranged with a woman to cook for me tonight. She runs a tiny eating place in her home. I would be happy for you to dine there with me."

The fat commissioner smiled. "You do not think yourself safe on a ship of your own country?"

"Forgive me, but only in poetic terms can I think of France as my country."

The three men dined in the parlor of a tidy, handsome woman who had been Bréda's cook. At Toussaint's request Bréda himself had financed the small venture. Toussaint was presented to General Rochambeau.

"He is a hero, Toussaint. He has fought all the important battles of our day. For his services he has been honored by George Washington, Citizen Capet, and today by all of our glorious new France."

Toussaint thought, What have I done that you judge me an idiot? This man, indeed, had a look at the American Revolution. But it was a greater Rochambeau, his father, who was honored by Washington and Capet. I know this one is only another French officer, and I know he has been sent here to govern the island.

"It has been a perfect dinner," Sonthonax said. "Do tell the lady how much we enjoyed it. And now—" He leaned down and felt for the box he had placed between his chair and the wall. He handed it to Toussaint. "With respect, admiration and affection," he said.

Toussaint opened the black leather case and found a pair of pistols. "Beautiful," he said. "My deepest thanks."

"They were made at the national arsenal in Versailles. I wanted you to have them."

The benefactor who had given guns to black soldiers and had won their hearts saw no demeaning parallel in the gift he offered to Toussaint. Will he tell me, Toussaint wondered, that the man who tries to take them from me will send me back to slavery?

And at that moment Rochambeau reached over and lifted one of the pistols from its case.

"Replace it, sir," Toussaint said. "Perhaps you have heard

that black men harbor superstitions. Personally, I consider it unlucky to have my firearms touched by strangers."

"Yes. Put it back in its case." The commissioner's tone was somewhat irritable, and Toussaint saw that Rochambeau had been instructed to make himself likable and had failed the first test.

In the days that followed he failed many more. He stood at the side of the commissioner as the men of Toussaint's army marched in review and he remarked that he could see no harm in slavery when it developed such healthy specimens as these. He ignored the outstretched hand of a mulatto gentleman to whom Sonthonax had introduced him, and he suggested to one of the remaining white plantation owners that the trouble on the island no doubt had been exaggerated by hysterical women. He was a constant companion of the commissioner and was even present when Toussaint was asked to contribute some ideas for the restoration of the island. Ideas? In a hundred pages of well-considered directions Toussaint had drawn up a complete and itemized plan. He would not reveal it now. Instead he would sketch out a vague proposition or two.

"The plantation houses that have been abandoned should be claimed by the government. They can be rented out and—"

Rochambeau laughed. "Who's going to pay rent for them? I never saw such a poverty-stricken populace in my life."

"Under normal conditions we are at least as well off as other Caribbean islands," Toussaint said.

"Except by geographical accident, this isn't a Caribbean island at all," Rochambeau argued. "It's pure African in its thoughts, actions and inability to function. Let me tell you what must be done."

Toussaint looked at Sonthonax. "Your friend will explain the needs of the island to you," he said, and got up and walked away.

In the morning he managed to see the commissioner alone. "I cannot work with Rochambeau," he said. "And I will not work for him. Don't waste my time with lies or evasions. I know why he was brought here and I know that you think as little of him as I do. Is everything we worked for to come to naught because of an order given in Paris?"

The following day a ship took Rochambeau home to France.

"Thank you," Toussaint said. "And when are you going, my friend?"

The fat commissioner ran his hand through his hair. "Very soon. I have important work to do in Paris. However, you will admit, I suppose, that there are matters we must discuss."

Toussaint agreed. "For instance, your tired, homesick soldiers who are dying of fevers to which black men are immune. What are your poor boys doing here? The wars are over in this part of the world. My men could repel any challenge to the island and they live off the land. Think of the saving to France."

"That is not a decision I'm empowered to make."

"But it is a suggestion you could outline in one of your dispatches. Or, better still, when you've arrived home."

It did not occur to the commissioner that Toussaint was arrogant or officious. Here was a man who had pledged an army and peace. He had delivered both and had won the right to talk to any Frenchman on even terms. And the thought came to him that the soldiers of France, of whom Toussaint spoke, were no match for the laughing, singing black men who walked as though they owned the earth.

"I appoint you commander in chief of the Army, Toussaint, and accept your recommendations regarding its structuring and staffing."

And so the French soldiers went home, but the fat commissioner with the straight, black hair married a mulatto girl and talked no more of his important work in Paris. Toussaint needed to be rid of him. Through narrowed eyes, staring out at the flashing blue water, Toussaint admitted to himself that it was regrettable. He is the one man I have ever seen to whom I could be a friend and who could be a friend to me. But I was born without time for friends. I was born for this island, and while one white man is here in a commanding position he can be replaced by another white man in a commanding position. I am not going to transform their scorched and ugly Saint-Domingue

72

into my beautiful Haiti so that they can take it from me. He must not be hurt, but he must go.

Somehow the word flew from soldier to soldier that the good man who had freed them was very ill and needed the services of his French physician. The story ran that he felt obligated to remain with the heroes who had made peace even though, in his strange white way, he needed the cool air of his native country and the administrations of the one doctor who knew how to cure him. Someone thought—and again no one knew just who—that if the Army itself asked him to go home—

They came by the unsmiling thousands, their bodies glistening in the sunlight, their eyes solemn with concern for their benefactor. They marched up and down the grassy slope on which the commissioner and his mulatto wife had their home. They surrounded the house and clogged the roadway, and they called out, "Go home. Go home. Go home." It all seemed very ominous.

The fat commissioner and his wife sailed away. The French ships in the harbor sailed away, too, and there was only one more threat. It was made by a man who called himself a nephew of Toussaint's because he had worked on the Bréda plantation. He was now in command of the North Province, and it was this Moyse Bréda who circulated the report that Toussaint intended to reinstate slavery. Armed groups were suddenly gathering in small towns of the northern section. Fires had started. Whites were being massacred. The entire district of Le Limbé was in revolt. Port-Margot had been seized by the rebels.

With fixed bayonets Toussaint's forces advanced. When Moyse Bréda realized that he had jumped too soon, he grasped a sword and slaughtered a dozen of his own adherents, then mounted a horse and, avoiding capture, rode to Toussaint claiming credit for having killed the leaders of the revolt. Toussaint promptly had Moyse arrested, then rode out himself to slay with his own hand every official who had sworn loyalty to Moyse.

When Toussaint returned from the North Province he found that the court-martial had returned a verdict of insufficient evidence against Moyse and had acquitted him. Toussaint convened his own court, with himself presiding. Moyse was convicted, and directly afterward he was shot.

Now at last it was all over. Toussaint proclaimed a constitution for the island and declared himself governor-general. With a personal guard of honor numbering two thousand men he rode into the tortured city of Le Cap. He attended high mass and took communion in the gutted, desecrated shell that had been the cathedral. Church bells pealed, and there were trumpets and drums and a new beginning.

In his address to his people Toussaint did not trouble their minds with the thousands of details over which he had agonized. What did they know of tariffs or judicial systems or public educational facilities? He went directly to matters they could understand, sacred promises for which he vowed to die rather than see them broken or altered.

All abandoned plantation lands were the property of Haiti. The land could be rented along with the house if, indeed, a house still stood. The tenant must agree to divide one-quarter of his gross revenues among his workers and to furnish them with acceptable lodgings, and care if they became ill. Tenants who abused workers would forfeit a year's harvest. No one would be permitted to strike another except in a fair fight. Field hands would be in ample supply since the army was discharging twenty-five per cent of its more recent recruits. Number of work hours per day would be decided between employer and employee. A worker would leave his assigned task at the risk of becoming an outcast from Haiti's bright future. Idlers would have their stake in the plantation's earnings reduced. Inefficient tenants would lose leases and face immediate eviction.

Army officers, in return for their valiant contributions to freedom, would be permitted to select a house and a plantation property commensurate with the rank they had held. All rules applying to treatment of workers and division of profits were as binding upon the officers as upon civilian tenants. But Haiti would bestow a gift upon her heroes. For a period of two years, while they were learning to operate their plantations, they would be exempt from rent and taxes. After that if the officer showed no ability to produce successfully for himself or for Haiti, the lease, as in the case of any other unsatisfactory tenant, would be canceled. On the other hand, an army officer who demonstrated talent as a planter and administrator would stand, after the period of his two rent-free and tax-free years, on equal footing with the civilian and be allowed to rent as much ground or as fine a house as he could pay for.

"This is the way we must begin," Toussaint told his people. "To survive we must work. There must be rules. Freedom is a fragile thing that perishes when not fed on earnest effort. The army will rebuild the cities and the countryside. I will cause trade to flourish with the United States and other countries. Do not tell me we should ignore the United States because it tolerates slavery. We must solve our problems in a realistic way. Let us trade with the devil if he makes us strong and keeps us free."

Within two years sugar production increased fivefold. The harbor was full of merchant ships buying and selling. The cities were rising again. The island resounded with the clang of hammers and the buzz of saws. Fresh paint almost overcame the fragrance of flowers. A building called Government House leaped from a drawing board to a hillside. No one on the island had ever seen its like. It was wrapped in beauty, with windows flashing in the sun and tall doors with carved and gilded lions' heads upon them.

Toussaint made constant inspections of the growing economy. At times he rode a hundred miles in a single day to surprise a tenant here, a moneylender there. He had drunk the warm blood of a boar, and he had lied and murdered for Haiti. Had there been another way? The island was at peace. It was rich and happy. Carefully he had loaded the dice, and a winning combination had turned up. Whites in the administration. Blacks in the army. A scattering of mulattoes in both. And himself as governor-general.

It was some time since France had been heard from. Oh, there was news of France. Ships brought mail and publications of all kinds. The Revolution had blown across France and was gone, but the innocent souls who thrilled at being called citizen did not yet know. They had replaced Capet with Bonaparte and believed there was a difference. What a master stroke it had been to design a calendar so artfully that Frenchmen thought they lived in a new and better time. Toussaint wrinkled his forehead, trying to remember the names France had given to the months of her great adventure. Germinal, Floréal, Prairial, Messidor, Thermidor—there were others, but in the end there had been only November 9, which the poor sheep called 18 Brumaire, Year VIII. That was the day Bonaparte had revealed that he, too, knew what Toussaint had always known. There were no Rights of Man. There was only the right of an individual man who had the mind, the determination and the courage to govern.

France had killed her king so a Corsican and his family could live in the palaces. And what had changed for the average Frenchman? Why, his sons had the honor of dying in Italy, Austria or Egypt—or perhaps even on a hot and hostile island.

Toussaint raised his eyes to the sparkling windows of Government House. He knew it was only a matter of time.

. . . .

All the people in the United States thought they knew Thomas Jefferson. That was not because he was an artless man. It was because of his deep understanding, his exquisite courtesy and the vastness of his knowledge. Everyone who held conversation with him came away feeling quite ready to describe the inner Jefferson.

Scientists were convinced that he spent every free hour studying science. Farmers were pleased that obviously he cared more about agriculture than anything else. Doctors were certain that he read only medical books. Musicians were regretful that he had not made a career of music, for it was apparent to them that he was happiest while playing his violin. Philosophers were of the opinion that his clear and penetrating political statements resulted from long hours of constant meditation on questions that had disturbed Anaximenes, Anaximander and Thales. Inventors guessed that there must be a hidden workshop somewhere, so quick was he to notice the flaw or to suggest an improvement in a snowplow, a jewelry clasp or a device for snaring lobsters. Poets shyly asked if they might read some of his verses, for certainly his remarks on poetry through the ages revealed a lifelong absorption in the muse. Botanists quoted him as an expert source of information and felt that upon retirement he would occupy himself writing a book on plant biology. Architects studied the technical drawings he had made for Monticello and saw at once that their profession could easily have been his. Jefferson's daughters believed he was mainly interested in babies and cooking recipes.

Thomas Jefferson had been a lawyer, a leader in the colonial House of Burgesses, a member of the Continental Congress, Governor of Virginia, Minister to France, Secretary of State and Vice President.

On the day of his inauguration he discovered that there is no preparation for the presidency.

Like a mysterious envelope, the new term waited to be unsealed. There would be perils of which the former President had never heard, situations to awaken unimagined enmities, and questions that never before had arisen. No departing president could say, "This is how to do it, friend. Here are the rules."

Jefferson remembered that as Secretary of State he had given President Washington the information, opinions and loyalty to which Washington was properly entitled. But there was that about the high office that militated against a president's knowing the all and the everything of a Cabinet member's thinking. To a president one did not say, "Now wait. You've got it wrong" or "Let's talk a little more about this because you weren't listening to what I said." Sometimes Jefferson had sat gnawing his lip as President Washington turned to speak to Alexander Hamilton or Henry Knox. Jefferson had been annoyed, but President Jefferson was willing to admit that there were times when the Secretary of the Treasury or the Secretary of War had more urgent business than did the Secretary of State.

Jefferson wondered if Washington had been aware that the presidency forced a man into an unreal world where everything was maddeningly magnified. Friends turned into worshipers.

Gadflies became destructive enemies. The most casual kindness created a sensation and was mentioned by partisan newspapers to illustrate the President's greatness of character. Conversely, a small blunder was blown into a national scandal by detractors.

In the relative privacy of Cabinet status Jefferson and Hamilton had been able to dislike each other without the eyes of the world focusing upon them. President Washington had tried and failed to draw his two brilliant advisers together. Jefferson had thought it a friendly act on the President's part. He knew now that the nerves of a president, his mind filled with worries and plans not yet ready to be shared, could not endure sarcasm or even polite wrangling between Cabinet members.

Jefferson had resigned from the Cabinet because of Hamilton. He had found the Treasury Secretary's views not only unpalatable but unconstitutional. Officially, the handling of the Treasury was not Jefferson's affair, but as a citizen who would have to live within the economic structure fashioned by Hamilton he was outraged. Even so, for the man personally he had felt nothing but a mild dislike and had supposed that that feeling was cordially returned. Upon becoming president, he was startled to see the naked hatred in Hamilton's eyes, amazed at the venomous reception given to his inaugural address by newspapers whose owners were friends of Hamilton's.

Only an insensitive man could have ignored the black-bordered *Columbian Centinel* with its horrid message:

YESTERDAY EXPIRED
Deeply regretted by MILLIONS of grateful Americans
And by all GOOD MEN
The GOVERNMENT of the United States

Jefferson tilted his head and read the message again. So, in part, this was the presidency, was it?

When he had considered the possibility that it would be he instead of Aaron Burr in the big, unfinished house, Jefferson had known which man he would select for Secretary of State. He could not picture anyone but his old friend James Madison at his side. For Secretary of the Treasury, Jefferson daringly chose

78

Albert Gallatin. Gallatin, forty years old, of a patrician Swiss family, was a highly respected financier. He had come to America, married a lady of a prominent New York family and purchased an estate in Pennsylvania. He had interested himself in the politics of his new country, and Pennsylvania had elected him to the Senate. The senators had angered Pennsylvania by depriving Gallatin of his Senate seat on grounds that he had come too recently to the United States. The current joke was that the United States had come quite recently itself. Jefferson had approved of all he had ever heard of Gallatin and had his name first on a very short list of possible secretaries of the Treasury.

The newspapers of Hamilton's friends greeted the appointment with a vicious flow of lies. "What shall we say of Albert Gallatin?" one editorial writer asked. "Shall we say that to save his life he was compelled to flee his country, on account of the enormity of his crimes? Shall we say that the vagabond, having landed on our shores, ragged and lousy, took his course at Harvard University and offered himself as an instructor of the Italian language, and when, by the charity of the benevolent students, his necessities were answered and his pockets filled with money, he took to his heels, and fled into Virginia where he opened a school for instructing in the principles of infidelity, and of despising all laws both sacred and divine? We say it and truth confirms our word. Such is the President, and such his partisans."

"We now have a country governed by blockheads and knaves," said the President of Yale.

At a banquet Jefferson's enemies drank a toast to him. "May he receive from his fellow citizens the reward of his merit—a halter."

Alexander von Humboldt, scientist, explorer and guest of Jefferson's, picked up a newspaper from the President's desk and was appalled by what he read.

"Why are these libels allowed? Why is not this journal suppressed or its editor imprisoned?"

Jefferson smiled into the anxious eyes of his friend. "Put that paper in your pocket, Baron, and should you hear the reality of

our liberty, the freedom of our press, questioned show this paper
—and say loudly where you found it."

Strange, Jefferson thought, that he and Alexander Hamilton
should share a secret. What Hamilton did not tell his newspaper
friends, and what Jefferson had perceived at once, was that
Hamilton was directing all his energies toward the very outcome
Baron von Humboldt thought proper. What a triumph for Hamilton if he could provoke the President into robbing the people of
a guarantee of the First Amendment. How joyously Hamilton
would cry "Tyrant!" What a brave show he would make of
defending the editors who had been his pawns.

For the War Department Jefferson took General Henry Dearborn, of that district of Massachusetts which was called Maine.
Dearborn was a doctor who had given up his practice on the day
the first shot was fired at Lexington. He had mustered sixty volunteers and marched them to Cambridge, and afterward had
lived through Valley Forge with Washington. His two years in
Congress had not been marked by any show of brilliance, but
Jefferson thought him a man blessed with common sense and
loyalty.

A wealthy maritime lawyer of Baltimore, son of a shipowner,
seemed suitable for the position of Secretary of the Navy. His
name was Robert Smith, and he was handsome and socially
accomplished. Actually, no one was quite certain what purpose a
Secretary of the Navy served. President Washington had not had
one, and President Adams had not consulted his very often. The
men Jefferson had preferred to Smith had been of the opinion
that the position had no intrinsic importance since the Secretary
of War was not likely to regard the Navy as a department
separate from his own. "To get a Secretary of the Navy," Jefferson had said wryly, "I probably shall have to advertise in the
newspapers."

Levi Lincoln, a distinguished member of the Massachusetts
bar, was appointed Attorney General. The Postmaster General
had not been of Cabinet rank in the past, but Jefferson appointed
Gideon Granger, of Connecticut, and placed him on equal footing with the others. Aaron Burr, of New York, was Vice Presi-

dent. Burr and Jefferson had tied in the popular voting, so the matter had been settled in the House of Representatives. Burr, upon receiving the second-greatest number of votes, automatically won second position in the government, though he and the President agreed on nothing at all. It was the way things were done, and no one found much fault with the system.

At the first gathering of the new Cabinet, Jefferson was still living in his perfectly satisfactory parlor and bedroom suite at Conrad's. He had invited a young captain named Meriwether Lewis to be his private secretary but did not yet know whether or not Captain Lewis would accept. Meanwhile there was not even a messenger to run Jefferson's errands or a clerk to write his letters. It appealed to his sense of the ridiculous that there he sat in his unpretentious parlor without a staff or even a single assistant while splendid parades in his honor were taking place in Philadelphia, Baltimore, Norfolk and elsewhere.

Fortunately he did not have to serve the drinks and the light repast himself. Conrad's was not able to provide an office force, but their waiters were unexcelled. Jefferson wished he could take a few of them to the house in which he would be living within a week or two. The thought of that house bothered him. Not because it was unfinished. Monticello, after almost a decade, was also still far from completion, but he called it home, entertained quite lavishly there and thought of its construction as a never-ending diversion. He remembered with amusement that Edward Thornton, the British chargé, had said that Monticello was in a state of commencement and decay, that only Virginians inhabited an unfinished house until it fell of old age about their ears. But the President's Mansion had no charm, no intimacy. Could he explain to the people of the country that Conrad's was just what he wanted? No. That would be taken as an insult. The president's house, the mansion, was their gift to him. They longed to see him living there. Jefferson knew that Americans suffered from chronic ambivalence. On the one hand, still yearning for the trappings of royalty, they would forever deeply desire that their leader live in kingly fashion. On the other hand, they would vote against him as soon as he appeared to be enjoying their generosity.

Jefferson brought himself back to the moment and the occasion. Sitting partly in shadow, his strong face and piercing eyes turned toward the men of the Cabinet, he spoke quietly.

"Let us have harmony at all times, gentlemen. You know I do not mean that I expect no disagreement. Disagreement is the substance of which national policy is formed, the essential root from which grows the well-considered decision. It is, however, my belief that a man of good will can oppose or approve an idea on the basis of its worth rather than by the degree of congeniality he feels toward its author. Beyond these rooms we have our friends and admirers. Let us keep them. Let us even add to their numbers. Out there also stand our defamers, waiting to hear that among us there exists disrespect or aversion. We are a very small group with terrible powers, and we must restrain ourselves from the slightest, most innocent criticism of each other. What we say, even with tolerance, will be shockingly reshaped by those who wish us to fail, by those who, at any cost, hope to provoke dissension and disaster. If it is unnecessary to warn you of this I ask your pardon. I ask you, too, to believe that I have not spoken so because I view myself or my Cabinet as sacred and above other men. It is only that we represent to the people of this young republic the strength and the rectitude that will carry them and this country ever onward. Let the people never suffer a doubt or disappointment that you and I could have spared them."

Bearing in mind that he would not have tendered his resignation to President Washington had he been able to avoid constant association with Hamilton, Jefferson outlined the manner in which business would be conducted.

General conferences would take place only infrequently. What circumstances could make necessary the simultaneous advice of the Secretary of War and the Postmaster General? Private meetings with individual Cabinet members were far more meaningful and could be requested at any hour of the day or night either by the President or a secretary whose department was enmeshed in some particularly thorny issue. Ordinarily in the course of a week he expected to receive in his office each Cabinet member for the exchange of ideas and opinions, even if nothing of great moment was on the horizon.

Letters addressed to the President would be read and sent on, with marginal notes, to the appropriate department. Letters to a member of the Cabinet were to be treated similarly and placed on the President's desk. In this way Jefferson would be familiar with all that was occurring, and no one would have to present a lengthy preparatory statement before discussion could begin.

Jefferson looked encouragingly at each man and waited for questions. He saw that none would be asked at this time. The Cabinet members were cautious, cogitative, unwilling to expose a train of thought at this unique meeting. And so he shook their hands and let them go. He let them go from his mind as well. He had thought much about them. What more was there to think until he had worked with them?

He lay down upon his bed, but his daughters would not let him doze. They troubled him for what they were and what they were not. Would they come to visit soon? Would they sense that his first weeks in the mansion would be lonely? He thought of Martha. Strong, healthy Martha with the five stalwart children. He thought of Maria, who was delicate and beautiful. She had produced one delicate and beautiful son. Memories of Paris passed through his thoughts. What a pleasant time it had been. Martha at his side and in his home. Except for her keen intelligence, she had been like other girls, delighted with theaters, parties and new friends. The elegant dressmakers and milliners of Paris had cost him too much money, but he had happily carried the packages. Maria, aged twelve, had come from Virginia at the close of the school year. The girls had seen the first frantic days of the French Revolution and had been thrilled. He had believed that all the hours of his life would be brightened by these lively companions and the men they would eventually marry.

It had been a blow to discover that such expectations had been illusory. The girls had come to regard luxurious surroundings, laughter, fine clothes and even comfort itself as well-loved toys that had no place in the lives of grown women. Each lived on a remote plantation. Each thought it was an extravagance to use slaves as house servants instead of as field hands, so both girls were burdened with heavy domestic duties. Jefferson loved his daughters dearly, and he was depressed by the gloominess of the lives they had embraced, alarmed at the willingness with which they had surrendered intellectual pursuits. He thought about his sons-in-law and in all fairness could not blame them.

He wished he had not sent the letter to Maria concerning her withdrawal from the life that existed beyond her plantation. He had not meant to meddle. But did a parent ever give advice that was not considered meddling? Ironic that for most of his adult years he had been paid well to give advice. Now he had given it lovingly to Maria and was haunted by the fear that he had angered her.

"I think I discover in you a tendency to withdraw from society more than is prudent," he had written. "I am convinced our own happiness requires that we should continue to mix with the world, and to keep pace with it as it goes, and that every person who retires from free communication with it is severely punished afterwards by the state of mind into which he gets, and which can only be prevented by feeding on sociable principles. . . ."

There had been more. Too much more. Why had he not the grace of restraint where his daughters were concerned? His diplomacy had been praised in many countries. Why could he not deal with Maria and Martha as though they were France and England? Why did love for one's children transform one into an annoying old man who fussed and fretted?

Jefferson sighed. "Get up, old man," he said to himself. "You are President of the United States."

He got up and began to dress. James and Dolly Madison were to be his guests that evening. Should it be Gadsby's Tavern, in Alexandria, and canvasback duck? Or would Dolly prefer beefsteak and oysters at the Anchor? McLaughlin's, in Georgetown, had an excellent wine list, but Aaron Burr frequented the place. He would have enough of Aaron Burr without— Was he avoiding the sight of Burr because Theodosia, that gorgeous girl with the hungry mind, would certainly be at her father's side? Was he envious of the Vice President's good fortune in having a daughter who, though married, still felt herself part of her father's life?

Jefferson disliked pettiness in others and loathed it in himself. He resolved to take his guests to McLaughlin's. Surely Dolly would entertain him royally with fearsome tales of her encounters with carpenters and plasterers. The Madisons were redoing a house on F Street between Thirteenth and Fourteenth. Dolly had loved the house on sight because of its cupola. She had not dreamed how much time and effort interior remodeling would take. She detested hotels and complained bitterly about the delay. Jefferson, looking in the mirror as he combed his hair, ordered himself to stop hoping. His daughters were not coming to alleviate the cold solitude of that mansion on Pennsylvania Avenue. Tonight he would ask the Madisons to move in and remain until the house with the cupola was ready to receive them.

I must learn to live in that unfriendly place, he thought. I must learn what the people want of me. If they do not tell me what they want then I must guess.

In Washington there were no churches. The Treasury building or the hall of the House of Representatives was used for religious services. There were few sermons preached. A chaplain or a visiting minister was rarely available. The Marine band played hymns. People prayed. Whether there was a clergyman or not, the families of the capital city, remembering with longing the little white churches of their home towns, felt better for having gone. The President never failed to appear. Good weather or bad he came riding on Wildair, his favorite horse. And so certain was his arrival that everyone waited outside watching for him. His admirers took great pleasure from his presence. He had been accused of atheism, yet every Sunday here he was, giving positive denial to the charge. True, when asked by the National Church Committee to make a simple declaration of faith, he had declined, saying that such a declaration would imply that it was necessary for a citizen to be a Christian. Freedom of worship, he said, was only as tenable as the freedom not to worship. Sensible people told each other that, of course, the President was a religious man. Why else would he ride out on a rainy Sunday morning?

Why would he ride out on horseback any morning? The fault-finders asked and answered the question themselves. Why? Because of vanity. This fifty-eight-year-old Virginian was conscious of the magnificent equestrian image he presented. The spirit of America. The strong, incorruptible leader on horseback. Something for men to approve, for women to romanticize and for children to remember throughout their lives. There's the President on his horse!

There was no doubt that Jefferson rode well. He would have thought himself a dunce had he not acquired a mastery of horsemanship and a certain masculine grace. He had ridden all his life and assumed that any man of similar background rode as well as he.

The fact was that dignity demanded that he be driven to church in a proper carriage. He would have preferred that means of transportation, but it was not at his command. The departing President Adams had informed him that there were two carriages and seven horses furnished by the United States for his use. Unfortunately this was not exactly the case. Adams had purchased the carriages and horses without consent of the government, taking the money from the allotment intended for furnishing the mansion. On the day that Adams retired from the presidency, Congress ordered the carriages and horses sold and the proceeds returned to the furniture account.

Jefferson knew what would be said if he remained away from religious services explaining that he had no carriage. He was having one built in Philadelphia and had instructed his son-in-law John to find him a half-dozen perfect carriage horses.

The President's salary was twenty-five thousand dollars. Jefferson had thought the amount would prove sufficient even for the Palace. Abigail Adams said that thirty servants were an absolute necessity. Dolly Madison said yes, thirty servants for

Mrs. Adams, but for Mr. Jefferson, who was not a frugal New Englander with a liking for boiled dinners and heavy pies—

"But, Mrs. Madison, one chef, regardless of his ability, still represents only one servant."

"Not so, Mr. President. You know very well that a suitable French chef requires four or five assistants."

Neither mentioned how politically tactless it would be to transport a dozen servants from Monticello. Southerners may call them servants, but New Englanders knew them to be slaves and would say so.

Rather quickly Thomas Jefferson saw that he could not live on twenty-five thousand dollars a year. Sensitive to how enormous that sum of money appeared to the average American, he confessed to no one that his personal funds would have to augment his salary. But he had not been elected to waste time on housekeeping accounts. What was not paid for by the nation would be paid for by the President. That was all there was to that. Without comment he gave Meriwether Lewis a list of items that were to be treated as personal expenditures, and dismissed the matter from his mind.

Lewis had his office and living quarters in what had been called the East Room. Seeing no use at all for an unplastered audience chamber, Abigail Adams had had clothes hung there on rainy days. Now the room was still unfinished, but a thin, rather shaky wall had been installed to provide two rooms for the President's secretary.

Jefferson, as he spoke to the young man, noticed the sad eyes, the listlessness, of one who has lost all joy in living. It had nothing to do with his inelegant quarters. Jefferson had heard the gossip. The secretary had been spending his free hours with Aaron Burr's daughter, Theodosia Burr Alston, and had fallen in love with her. The President had little pity for Lewis. What a fool's game it was to dine, dance and go galloping over the countryside with a young and beautiful married woman. Hadn't Lewis expected to fall in love and suffer? And how ill-mannered it had been of him to bare his heart to Theodosia. If true, her response, which was being repeated all over Washington, thanks to Lewis's trust in friends, was quite worth repeating.

"You are a romantic idiot," Theodosia was reported to have said. "If I were a weak and silly girl I would blush and relinquish the happy times we are having together. I refuse to do that. We would both lose. I invite you to be my good friend, Captain. It's an invitation that includes all but the special privileges reserved for my husband."

Jefferson, thinking of his own diffident daughters, did not wonder at the pride Burr took in his poised and outspoken Theodosia. Lewis was lucky to be offered the friendship of such as she.

"I am not feeling very well, sir," Lewis said.

"Neither am I," Jefferson replied. One of those dizzying headaches had swooped down on him again, but there was no time to think about that. There were national immediacies to be considered. Taxes, Barbary pirates, Army, Navy, the Naturalization Act, unnecessary appointments created in the past for political purposes.

"If this administration does not reduce taxes," Gallatin had said, "they never will be reduced."

And far into the night, every night, Gallatin worked. Jefferson urged him to spare himself, but the Secretary of the Treasury was indefatigable. He had other respected qualities, an incisive intellect and a genuine gift for making an authoritative statement without a trace of arrogance. The people must be relieved of internal taxes. For what reason was there a tax on an article made, sold and used within the United States?

Every project of Gallatin's was viewed by Alexander Hamilton as a studied insult to the manner in which he had managed the Treasury. "The removal of internal taxes," said Hamilton, "might be injurious to the energies and especially to the morality and industry of the Nation." He went on to suggest that if the taxes were not needed they should still be collected. Great rulers had never permitted the common man to grow accustomed to retaining a large share of his earnings. Tax reductions were granted by "only the indolent and temporizing rulers who love to loll in the lap of epicurean ease, and seem to imagine that to govern well is to amuse the wondering multitude with sagacious aphorisms and oracular sayings."

Hamilton did not care for the new administration's attitude toward the Barbary pirates, either. Tripoli had declared war on the United States because Algiers was being paid a higher price than Tripoli for not plundering America's commercial vessels. Blackmail had been enriching the pirates throughout the terms of Washington and Adams. Jefferson had thought it humiliating and had never approved. But in considering the situation now from his new position he saw that the limitations of the American Navy, coupled with the vast expense of spanking even a small power, made war with the Barbary States a foolhardy enterprise. He contented himself with sending a few frigates to blockade Tripoli. Smith, the Secretary of the Navy, was disappointed that it wasn't to be a splendid, flashy naval triumph, with world attention concentrated on his department. Jefferson soothed him. Smith meant no harm and was motivated by no more dangerous an emotion than that which could be found in most men.

It was different with Hamilton. He meant harm. "What will the world think of the fold which has such a shepherd?" he asked in disgust.

Jefferson felt that the fold was content and that he was not a dishonorable shepherd, but it pained him to be shown again this evidence of Hamilton's animosity. He knows as well as I, Jefferson thought, that to fight that brutish little amalgamation would take forever and would be costly beyond belief in men and money. Yet to discredit me he would, if he could, inflame the people into demanding war. He would consider the ruination of the country a fair price to pay for my undoing.

In the spirit of reducing governmental squandering of the people's money, Jefferson disbanded all foreign legations except in Great Britain, France and Spain. The collectors of internal taxes had disappeared with the tax itself. So it was now time to consider the War Department and the Navy. The Navy first. Since there was no possible way that the young United States could enter into competition with major sea powers, there was no logic in spending huge sums for a navy that would still be relatively insignificant and easily defeated by any of the great fleets. Moreover, the United States, in Jefferson's opinion, should be concerned with defense only. If the country should be menaced, he would have to prove his favorite point, which was that diplomacy was the weapon of civilization. Yes, he would have to prove it because there was neither money nor time for the United States to match the strength of any aggressive European navy.

"For defense against invasion their number is as nothing," he told Congress on the subject of the Army. And still it was frightfully expensive. It was a waste of manpower and of funds. It would discourage no enemy, and since it would be foolish to dream of equaling a foreign army bent on the destruction of the United States, there was only one way to proceed. He asked Congress to draw up rules and regulations concerning the militia. It was difficult to imagine why it ever would be called on to fight, but the same was true of the standing Army. What was not the same was that the men of the militia maintained themselves until called to arms.

The amendment of the Naturalization Act stirred furies. Fear and hatred of foreigners was a threat to a nation that must grow or perish. The original law had stated that citizenship could not be granted until after fourteen years of residence. Jefferson thought this unreasonable and harmful to a nation that counted little more than five million souls.

By now, Hamilton had founded his own newspaper. It was called the New York *Evening Post*, and it existed only so Hamilton could harry the administration while hiding in the anonymity of a sincere editorialist. The protection this device gave him was particularly desirable in the case of the Naturalization Act. Hamilton was not a native American. He had been born in the British West Indies, and for that reason the cloak his newspaper furnished was essential.

"The influx of foreigners is corrupting the national spirit," the New York *Evening Post* cried. "It is the Irish and Germans who elected Thomas Jefferson. Did honest native sons want him? No, but their voices were stifled by the rude shouts of those from foreign shores. The foreigner is a curse. Who rules France? A foreigner. Ask the French if they want a man of Italian ancestry guiding their future. Who rules the councils of our ill-fated and unhappy country? A foreigner. A man from Switzerland who speaks our language and handles our money with equal lack of ability."

Words of former President John Adams written in a private letter to a friend were printed with or without permission. "A group of foreign liars encouraged by a few ambitious native gentlemen have discomfited the education, the talents, the virtues and the property of the country."

To all of this Jefferson replied with a question, an eloquent question that could not be ignored by men who had fought for freedom. "Shall oppressed humanity find no asylum on this globe?"

Adams's legacy to the new administration was a bottomless pit of annoyances. What were commonly known as his "midnight appointments" were creating a storm. Jefferson was not an executive to accept quietly wrongs done by a predecessor in hope that his own sins would be overlooked by a successor. Adams had made innumerable appointments after it was already known that the political opposition had won the presidency. Jefferson rejected nineteen appointees, and when it was agreed that Adams had acted improperly his friends and Hamilton's still thought of something to say. "Everyone who speaks of pinching pennies is sure of an affectionate reception from the people."

An affectionate reception indeed. Hamilton himself was beginning to wonder how public confidence in his enemy could be shaken. It would take a miracle or, at least, some momentous event not yet within range of vision. The *Post* lay back and took idle potshots at the President. "It is well known in official circles that Thomas Jefferson will resign. He is mortally ill. Though the nature of his complaint has not been disclosed, physicians have agreed the case is incurable."

Hamilton was only sniping and he knew it. While waiting for a crisis that could be manipulated to the disadvantage of the President, Hamilton and his associates met and talked and plotted. Of them all, Hamilton was the most realistic. The others fed on each other's dreams. They talked to no one except those who hated the party of Jefferson, and they came away convinced that Jefferson was losing stature in the country. Hamilton knew better. In less than a year New England and New York had come to respect the man who had repealed internal taxes and had purged government offices of parasites. The West and the South had always been Jefferson's, but now the whole country was impressed by the millions that had been paid toward the reduction of the national debt, and proud that the United States had been recognized by the bankers of London and Amsterdam. The press was free, the public encouraged to speak its mind, and the foreigner welcomed as a full partner after only five years of residence. Hamilton knew it would take a very unexpected development to give him an even chance at containing Jefferson's rising tide of popularity. A very unexpected development.

While the visit of Tom Paine certainly could not be regarded as the great event that would rob Jefferson of the country's affection, it could be used to some advantage. Tom Paine was a man with a violent, twisted mind, and there was no one left on earth who admired him. Like a mad dog, he had turned on friends and had sought to destroy everyone who had done him a kindness. Yet there had been a time when Paine had been, in George Washington's view, worth an army in the field. He had written *Common Sense* and *The Crisis*, and these pamphlets had so marvelously bolstered the morale of weary soldiers that Washington had ordered the pamphlets tacked on trees about his camp so that all might read the inspiring words.

Paine had gone abroad in 1781 and had involved himself in all manner of difficulties in England. He had fled across the Channel and had become so enamored of the French Revolution that he had renounced his American citizenship and had sworn his oath to France. Because he was a born enemy of himself he managed to alienate his new compatriots and was condemned to the guillotine. By this time George Washington had read and heard what Paine had been saying of him in recent years and had no desire to plead mercy for the man. Gouverneur Morris, Minister to France, had loathed Paine but, for the sake of old mutual loyalties, had fed him for a time. When Paine had been thrown into prison, Morris left him to French justice and forgot him.

James Monroe, who followed Morris as United States minister, petitioned to have Paine freed. He was successful and soon regretted that he had not followed Morris's course. Paine remained in France for some time, writing nothing of value and sinking into drunkenness and slovenliness. Now Paine wanted to return to the United States. He wrote to President Jefferson and made the request. Jefferson could not forget that there had been a bleak time when Paine had done more for American freedom than any other individual, and he had responded graciously to the letter. Characteristically, Paine claimed that he had never thought of the United States until a surprising invitation had come from the new President.

The newspapers made the most of Tom Paine's return. The *Courant* inveighed, "The President has publicly, in the light of day, cordially, nay, affectionately invited the most infamous and depraved character of this or any age to take refuge in our country."

The *Columbian Centinel* addressed an open letter to Jefferson: "Is it because Paine has libeled George Washington, insulted our Government and blasphemed his God that he was considered peculiarly worthy of this pointed mark of your friendship?"

The *New England Palladium* asked, "Why insult the sense and virtue of the country by exhibiting an attachment for a man so offensive to decency, so smitten with the leprosy of scorn, the natural enemy of every righteous person?"

It saddened Jefferson that no newspaper thought it worthwhile to remind readers that during a long, terrible winter Paine's pamphlets had kept the breath of life in the American Revolution. Even ordinarily helpful editors did not protest the public degradation of Paine, but kept a hard silence.

"It seems you have imported a fine, new topic for the journalists, Mr. President."

Jefferson smiled at Madison. "Yes. I shall have to quote Paine's most famous observation: 'These are the times that try men's souls.' "

"Did you know Paine is pretending that you opened correspondence with him by sending a completely unexpected invitation?"

"Yes, James, I knew that. Am I supposed to shame myself and expose that unfortunate drunkard to further abuse by shouting 'I did not' at the newspapers?"

"No, but let me suggest that you plan on a very small dinner party for him. Dolly has found that there are ladies who will develop headaches, colic and sprained ankles if they are invited."

Jefferson looked into the distance, and with unusual bite he said, "And some of those ladies were dancing with British officers in New York while our Army suffered at Valley Forge."

"Nevertheless, Mr. President, it has to be admitted that Paine is not even physically clean, and the strange thoughts of his brilliant mind frighten many people."

"I have sent a valet to him at his hotel, James. His clothes are spotless and so is he. In sodden state, Paine is carried each day and dumped into a hot bath. As for his mind, it is not so brilliant any more. He has destroyed it and he speaks little. Would you like your Dolly spared the ordeal of sitting at table with him?"

Madison laughed. "Unless you issue an executive order, neither you nor I could keep her home. She is not the finicky sort. I, on the other hand, would enjoy missing Paine's company, but you know I will not."

"Is it safe to invite other Cabinet members and their wives?"

"You can be sure we will all stand by you, Mr. President."

The Gallatins did better than just stand by Jefferson. The following week they gave a dinner party of their own for Tom

Paine, and so prominent was the New York family of Mrs. Gallatin that no Washington lady of fashion dared refuse an invitation.

Hamilton's friends had some small malicious fun hinting that the President was assisting Paine in writing a book defaming Jesus, and that the two "splendid authors" got drunk together every night. The scurrilous remarks paid a pleasing dividend. When Jefferson next went to the grave of George Washington, the newspapers reprinted some of Paine's abusive attacks against the first President: " 'Treacherous in private friendship and a hypocrite in public life. Has Washington abandoned good principles, or did he ever have any?' This quotation, dear readers, is from the repulsive pen of the repulsive man who has recently been so charmingly received by Thomas Jefferson. How dare Jefferson stand at the grave of President George Washington after lavishly entertaining a sot who has no respect for God or man? Are Jefferson and Paine kindred spirits? What irony that our great Washington befriended them both."

Dolly Madison wept at what was written of Jefferson.

"You must learn to interpret the true meaning of all this, my dear Mrs. Madison." The President turned to her husband. "James, have you not explained that this but signifies the helplessness of our enemies? The country is so contented that those who wish to create disharmony are forced to manufacture lies and to state, as though it were news, that Tom Paine is a disreputable fellow."

"But, Mr. President, they're telling the people that you approve of him," Mrs. Madison complained.

"Do you really think anyone believes them, Mrs. Madison? Do you really think so?"

In August, Jefferson mounted Wildair and galloped along the red dirt roads to Monticello. His daughters and their children would meet him there. He carried with him materials for inoculating his entire family and his slaves against smallpox. Dr. Benjamin Waterhouse, of Boston, a medical pioneer, was a man in whom Jefferson deeply believed. The doctor had taught him to administer the inoculations, and the President now regarded the extinction of smallpox one of his missions in life.

He rode with contentment. Deep within him was a feeling of satisfaction at what had been accomplished in Washington. But the immediate future caused his heart to swell with happiness. His daughters and their families.

Behind him he left the captious newspapers complaining that the people had been deserted, the nation abandoned. The President had taken himself to Monticello, while the Secretary of State had gone to another corner of Virginia. The rest of the Cabinet was heaven knew where. To be sure, Gallatin, the Secretary of the Treasury, was still in Washington, but of what use was he in an emergency?

No matter that Adams had spent long and frequent holidays in Massachusetts. The papers were concerned only with the shocking news that Jefferson had gone to Virginia. The *National Intelligencer*, a friendly periodical, pointed out that the President had not had a day to himself since ascending to his high office, and, besides, he was going to be only a hundred miles away. It would take less than a week to send him a message and have the answer returned.

Jefferson was not thinking of the newspapers. He had left all that behind him. He was gazing in awe at the beauty of his blue Virginia sky. There was not, in any direction, the slightest sign of a cloud.

THREE

Soldiers and Statesmen

. . . .

$\mathcal{I}$N THE FIRST FORTNIGHT the coastal towns are to be taken." That was order number one from Napoleon Bonaparte to his brother-in-law General Leclerc. Leclerc read the orders that followed carefully but pigeonholed them in appropriate compartments of his mind. So far, there was no point in concentrating on anything beyond order number one. He was a methodical officer, and he had under his command the veterans of Campo Formio and Arcola, Napoleon's finest soldiers. Order number one would be carried out as directed.

Leclerc went ashore with a detachment of five thousand men, and when they had searched every inch of the ruins of Cap-Français and were certain that no ambush or trap was waiting he permitted his wife to disembark. It was not what he wanted. There was no reason why she could not remain on the flagship with her ladies and servants and personal hand-picked guard. No reason at all except that she refused to stay there.

"I'm tired of the ship. If you don't make arrangements for me to land properly, then I'll jump into the water and—"

"There are sharks," he said. "A great many of them."

"I swear to you I'm going to see the island or die trying."

He placed his arm around her. "Dear one, you are not going to be deprived of any pleasures. The island is interesting and I want you to see all of it, but have patience. Within a few weeks—"

"I want to go now."

There had been two thousand buildings in the city of Cap-Français. The fire had left fifty-nine. Pauline wept when she saw the remains of what had been the theater.

"We could have had such lovely evenings there. Oh, I hate these people for burning up all the shops and everything. Jérôme, couldn't Victor order his soldiers to rebuild the theater?"

"How do I know what he could do? He never speaks to me."

"Oh, it's so sad that we don't have the theater."

Pauline stood weeping charmingly, her ladies surrounding her, their lacy bonnets and silk gowns forming a piquant tableau in the devastated square. Civilians from the fleet who were attached to the Army and Navy as clerks and office assistants had evidently been given permission to come ashore. Pauline noted that most of them managed to post themselves in positions that afforded an unobstructed view of the wife of General Leclerc, the sister of Napoleon Bonaparte. She put her handkerchief away and smiled and turned from left to right, chatting brightly with her ladies. She even glanced toward the sky because the line from her chin to her bosom was said to be the most beautiful in the world. There was one man who did not look at her, so she looked at him. It was a full minute before she realized that the shabby, aging man was Louis Fréron, the founder of *L'Orateur du Peuple*, the firebrand who had voted for Louis Capet's death, commissioner to Marseille, her first and long-forgotten love. She could not control her laughter. Her ladies, happy that she no longer wept, laughed with her. It was an enchanting scene. Louis Fréron slunk out of the square.

Now there was another diversion. A group of well-dressed people was arriving. Pauline saw their spirited horses and smart carriages and was delighted. A captain, performing the double duty of cementing friendship with prosperous whites while still keeping them at a distance from the General's wife, went forward to greet them. The gentlemen bowed. Their wives curtsied to Pauline. There was a spokesman. He was a big, square-faced man who had a speech impediment that made Jérôme giggle.

"Madame Leclerc, the sight of you, and the knowledge that your brave husband is not far away, fills us with joy. We feel safe for the first time in many years. Always we have known that your noble brother, the First Consul, would deliver us from the humiliation of being governed by the children of ignorant Africans. We had patience. We waited and prayed. Now you are here. Madame, we extend to you a welcome and a promise. The welcome is loving and sincere. The promise is that if you will remain among us you will forever receive our loyalty and adoration. Dear lady, you have made this the happiest day of our lives."

Pauline replied that she hadn't seen anything of the island yet but it looked sunny and nice. "This is my youngest brother," she said, waving toward Jérôme. "He is eighteen and he's an officer in our navy already." She thought perhaps Jérôme would say a few words because the people seemed to expect more and she couldn't think of anything to add. But Jérôme was still giggling.

A child dashed up with a bouquet, which Pauline accepted, then threw away hastily. Some kind of shiny green bug was crawling on it.

She knew she had failed to exhibit the grace that would have marked Josephine's first meeting with the Saint-Domingue aristocrats. She sought the eyes of the captain of her guard. Within them perhaps she'd find proof that she had underestimated her performance. The captain wasn't looking at her, and there was a sour expression on his face. Pauline was angered. She couldn't have been *that* much of a failure.

It would have surprised her to know that the captain was not thinking of her. He was preoccupied with something else. It had to do with the quality of the horses and carriages and the clothes that were worn by the people who felt "safe for the first time in many years," the people who were to be delivered "from the humiliation of being governed by the children of ignorant Africans." They seemed to have done very well, these rich planters. The captain found them sickening. They had probably bowed and curtsied to the black Governor-General and made pretty speeches to him, too. Devoted followers of the winning side, the captain concluded, and resolved never to trust anyone on the damned island, regardless of color.

He whispered to one of Pauline's ladies, "Ask Madame if we may return to the ship now."

"I don't think she'll say yes. She wants to drive around and look at everything."

"Impossible."

"She's talking to her brother about borrowing one of these splendid carriages and being driven up there." The lady indicated a high hilltop overlooking the city where a rather large house had once stood. One flame-touched wall remained. Part of the roof, black and upended, was just visible from where they stood. "I'm sure these people would feel honored to carry Madame's party wherever she wants to go."

The captain shook his head. "Only the city has been searched to assure her safety. I have orders that she is not to venture beyond it."

"Oh, dear. She'll be so cross."

The plump, oily-skinned Jérôme was approaching now. "Captain, look up there. Isn't it odd that a house on a hilltop so far above the city also got burned? My sister wants a better look at it. She wants to—"

"Very sorry, Lieutenant. We have not yet investigated who or what—"

"But all these people came from outside the city. It's obviously quite safe."

"Very sorry, Lieutenant."

The vapid face of Jérôme Bonaparte turned sulky. "Now, look here, my sister may want her house built up there. It seems a very desirable site, but she has to have a closer view before deciding, doesn't she?"

"Yes, Lieutenant. Before deciding, she has to have a closer view and that, no doubt, will be her privilege on another day. Right now I am going to escort her back to the flagship."

"You think that is what you are going to do. My sister's not in the Army. Neither am I."

"But I am. I was told by Colonel Thermes to exercise my best judgment, and he was told by General Leclerc to give me that order. Will you inform Madame that we are now ready to return to the ship?"

Pauline lodged a complaint against the captain. He had been insufferably rude to Jérôme, and completely indifferent as to whether or not she enjoyed her visit to the island. General Leclerc was not listening. Port-au-Prince had fallen. Le Cap was so completely in his hands that his wife had spent the afternoon there. The South Province had capitulated without a struggle. The mulattoes assigned by Toussaint to hold Port-au-Prince had surrendered it with cries of *"Vive la France!"* La Plume, another mulatto officer, had yielded the South Province. He, at least, had pretended to be heartbroken at his defeat. Defeat? Leclerc smiled. The mulattoes had not even made an effort to defend the province. That was a promising sign. It showed that Toussaint was no judge of men. He had placed his confidence in cowards and traitors.

This is not going to be the debacle I anticipated, Leclerc thought. His mind went back to the night before the fleet had sailed from Brest. He wished he hadn't drunk so much with his old friends from Pontoise. They were also army officers, so there was a chance they would not repeat what he had said. He had certainly strung together a lot of theatrical and dangerous words.

"If I succeed, no glory will redound to me. Every favorable action of mine will be viewed as having been dictated by my brother-in-law. If I fail, the responsibility will be mine alone. I shall be accused of not having known how to carry out the plans of the First Consul, which were expressly designed to break down all resistance, overcome all hazards and assure victory. I shall, of course, do my duty, but I have no illusions regarding the fate that awaits me. I have, moreover, neither the right nor the power to attempt to escape it. All of us now have merely to obey. We have found a master where we had hoped only for a protector."

Good God, how he had been carried away by the excitement of that farewell dinner, the close fellowship and the drinking. If only he had known then that mulattoes were wretched soldiers.

What a merry speech he could have made, larded with loving references to Napoleon, who had given him such a wonderful opportunity to serve France. Well, all he could do now was pray that everyone at the dinner had drunk more than he and remembered nothing.

Enough of worrying about that. He was on his way to becoming Napoleon's favorite relative and most honored officer. If mulattoes—who were only half black—shrank from battle, it was clear that men who were all black would become pitiable cravens at sight of the French Army. This business could be wrapped up in—

Leclerc knew himself rather well. He knew he had a foolish streak but that he was not a fool. Except when intoxicated, which was rarely, he allowed his good sense to speak to him while he listened. Now it was saying that mulatto soldiers were half white as well as half black. Had it been proven that the cowardice he had witnessed was attributable to their black blood? Had he never heard of a white man who had deserted under fire? There wasn't any reason to suppose that the black men of Toussaint's army were going to shout *"Vive la France!"* According to the information he had on them they were strong, brave fighters, and, as Leclerc knew, the most formidable enemy was the one who fought to hold on to what he regarded as his own. Ah, yes, that explained something about the mulattoes, too. Neither whites nor blacks had ever let them feel that this land was theirs. In many cases they had been allowed to grow rich, and under Toussaint's rule they had even held political office. Still, there was no question that Saint-Domingue had been white and that Haiti was black. When had it ever been mulatto? By what sentimental distortion of fact could a mulatto convince himself that he should die willingly for the island? On the other hand, the blacks would fight to the last man because they considered Haiti theirs. He must not deceive himself. This business was not going to be wrapped up as easily as the foolish streak within him had been about to promise.

But Port-au-Prince had fallen, hadn't it? Yes. The other main coastal towns had been taken, hadn't they? Yes. Then you have carried out order number one, haven't you? Yes. Very well. How does order number two read?

Order number two read: "The coastal towns are captured, and the enemy has retreated into the interior. With a converging movement, advance upon his stronghold and demolish his resistance."

General Leclerc felt suddenly depressed. The order was as simplistic as though a cadet had written it for his first composition on battle planning. He wished Napoleon were here so that there might be a little talk about order number two.

You see, dear brother-in-law, the enemy did not run in terror to his stronghold. We have not exactly beaten him in the coastal towns. The big black army marched away intact before we ever saw it. The coastal towns were given without dispute to us by your admirers. So far, we are not really conquerors in the true sense. You are right about one thing, respected brother-in-law. The enemy has retreated into the interior. I wish you had some notion of what the interior is like.

Leclerc pushed the desk chair back and walked out of his cabin. For the thousandth time he stood on deck staring at the high outline of the island. The mountains, secretive and frightening, stood like stalagmites on a card table, rising out of the sea without the mercy of plain or beach. Just up, up, up into unknown green disaster. He had been told that there were villages from which men were lowered by ropes so that they might cast their nets in the bountiful waters.

Is there an order, number two and a half perhaps, that tells me to starve them out? Brother-in-law, breadfruit, bananas, melons and a score of other healthful and delicious foods are everywhere. A man need only put out his hand to be fed abundantly. But you used the word "advance," and that I shall do. I chose to be a soldier. I shall advance.

If the damned drums would only stop for a little while, a man could think. The drums, the drums, the drums, the throbbing and the booming of the drums. Leclerc could not guess at the messages, but he knew now that there was a complete system of communication. There were swift runners, shifts of drummers and precise knowledge of the distances at which drummers must be posted for repetition of the original message so that no pair of ears was beyond hearing range.

In every part of the world one found a traitor. Rochambeau gave a silver-gilt snuffbox to a skinny, one-eyed black who cocked his head and listened to the drums. Christophe was in the valley, thirty miles from the sea. Dessalines was in the plains behind Saint-Marc. Toussaint? Oh, the drums never mention Toussaint.

"Why not?"

There was a cool smile from the one-eyed black. "Too smart to mention Toussaint. Everybody hear what drums are saying and everybody know there are people like me." He fell silent and cocked his head again. He laughed then and pounded his bare feet upon the dusty road in appreciation of a great joke. "Here's some news you will not like, but it is funny. Those mulattoes! They are dirty sharp. Them you can never trust. You know what they do to you? Before they give you Port-au-Prince they send six hundred whites to Dessalines. You don't know Dessalines? Ha, French officer, he love to see your people die slow."

Leclerc, upon hearing of the six hundred white hostages, declared that Dessalines and Saint-Marc must be the first objective.

Rochambeau disagreed. "General, don't be swayed by sympathy. You'll never get those people back. If they're not dead now, they'll be dead tomorrow. If not tomorrow, then they will die just before Dessalines surrenders. They're lost. Do what we've discussed. Get Christophe first. That won't be easy, either, but I think this: I think the capture of Christophe will demoralize Dessalines, whereas Christophe wouldn't be shaken by the loss of Dessalines."

From under a frowning brow Leclerc gazed steadily at Rochambeau. It was a mannerism of Napoleon's that he rather liked. "You speak of these black generals as though you knew them well."

"I think I met Christophe. I certainly was acquainted with

Toussaint. He's an ugly little black bastard who thinks he's a military genius."

"A failing of successful soldiers," Leclerc commented.

Rochambeau smiled. "The point I was making, General, is that Toussaint and Christophe are educated. Those two won't think themselves less capable simply because the stupid Dessalines gets defeated."

"How do you know Dessalines is stupid?"

"Oh, I have a lot of snuffboxes. I really do recommend that Christophe be taken first. If we are fortunate, it might cause Dessalines to surrender, thus relieving us of a painful duty."

General Leclerc marched two thousand men toward the interior, thirty miles back from the sea. Christophe's encampment was in the valley. As it turned out, the valley could be reached only after a heart-pounding climb and a descent so steep that it would have been judged infeasible except for the suspicion that Christophe's army had managed it.

The descent was delayed at the summit while scouts were dispatched to cover the ground in all directions, searching for another approach. Leclerc watched the scouts disappear in the thick mass of overgrown foliage. They had gone in pairs, prepared for anything, and God knew that anything was waiting for them. No terror known to man seemed impossible in that wild, menacing silence. It occurred to Leclerc that some of the scouts might never again find their way back to the summit. He looked at the soldiers within his view, his white-clad troops, their boots, so recently polished, now scraped and torn by the climb.

Fast enough they had learned that they had not brought sufficient water. Rochambeau had heard that there were wells. It was true. There were wells—but none in which there were no corpses. Fresh corpses. Animal and human. Christophe had paid the French the compliment of recognizing their valor. He knew they would come after him.

Leclerc experienced the sudden, stunning thought that God had never meant Frenchmen to stand where he now stood. On three sides he was surrounded by unholy, giant-sized plant growth that exuded the odor of rottenness even as it flourished. In the distance he saw smoke and the orange blaze of plantation houses discoloring the sky. His heart perversely hardened against people who had built their homes and hopes on this abominable island. They were avaricious fools. He suffered a small delusion that powder-soft ash was settling upon him, turning his hair white, his skin old and dry. He looked at the cliff beneath him and saw that there were tangles and loops of liana to which man could cling. There were even meager footholds to be glimpsed, and an occasional ledge. It was not impossible, but, dear Jesus, let there be another way.

He and Rochambeau had spoken of capturing Christophe. Leclerc thought now that such a nicety need not be observed. Considering the burning plantation houses and the corpses in the wells, it would be absurd to grant Christophe the military courtesy owed to a European general. Besides, to hold such a celebrated prisoner would be to invite plots to effect his escape. Leclerc played with the idea of hanging Christophe the moment he was seized. To leave him in the valley for the vultures' pleasure seemed completely in conformity with the barbarity of the landscape. Still, to hang Christophe would not be a good thing for the character of French soldiers. After the battle, when the blacks had surrendered and were disarmed, there would be a military court convened and Christophe would be shot and properly interred in the valley. Actually, Leclerc had doubt about taking any prisoners. Napoleon had slain thousands of them in Egypt. The covenant of respecting the rights of prisoners was largely a matter of geography anyway.

He thought about water. Obviously, the blacks had clean wells from which they drank. Guards must be detailed at the first possible moment to protect whatever water supply there was. He pushed aside thick, fleshy vines that fought him like the arms of a strangler. He raised his spyglass and looked down upon the valley.

What he saw startled him—bare-legged, shirtless black men sprawled on the ground chewing sugar cane. Some were asleep.

Others slouched against trees exchanging lazy conversation. There was a group engaged in a witless sort of game that put no greater strain upon a player than that he manage to throw a stone slightly farther than his competitors had thrown one. There was no drill field, not one tent, nobody preparing a meal or policing the grounds to insure cleanliness and order. Leclerc watched, fascinated and unbelieving. He took another position and leveled the spyglass again. The view swept a good part of the valley. Not a uniform in sight. Not a man on guard. It couldn't be, no, it couldn't be the army of Christophe. Christophe was a stern officer, and Toussaint a fanatic on military standards. Their soldiers who proved to be less than perfect were promptly detached from service and assigned to agricultural work. Or, at least, those were the stories one heard. Leclerc looked again, trying to detect something soldierly or disciplined in the posture of the black men. They were lounging about scratching their backs against tree trunks or lying spread out, not moving more than an inch when others tripped over them. A vulture circled above the valley. A man lifted his gun casually and shot at it. He missed, and on the summit Leclerc could hear the derisive hooting of other blacks. He watched and waited, but no officer came to demand an explanation of the shot or to reprimand the silly fellow.

This, then, was the great black army of Christophe? It was an insult to the veterans of Campo Formio and Arcola. Leclerc saw two things clearly now: the terrain was what made fighting on the island so fearsome, and the armies of Toussaint had been measured by a generous yardstick. He called his adjutant and handed him the spyglass.

After a moment of scanning the scene below, the adjutant asked, "Who are those men, sir?"

Leclerc laughed. "Would you care to guess? Would you believe that is Christophe's army? Aren't you terrified by it?"

Still laughing, he sat down on the campaign chair that had been brought for him. There were serious things to consider, and reluctantly he put his laughter aside. The ascent had been more rugged than expected. The men should be given time to rest before confronting even this enemy. If the scouts did not find an approach other than that almost perpendicular mass of rock on which he sat, then the valley could only be reached after a dangerous, bruising descent. More rest would be needed after that ordeal. There might even be injuries to treat. The sobering factor was the shortage of water. At which point would rest be more welcome? Now, at the end of that lung-bursting climb? Or when the effort to hang on to the side of the mountain had been successfully concluded?

He gave an order for more scouts to be sent, this time in search of wells that had not been contaminated. Then he closed his eyes and paid careful attention to the condition of his own physical being. Was his heart still pounding? He discovered that he no longer could hear or feel it at its work. He tested his breathing. It seemed normal. He questioned the degree of his weariness. It had been excessive, but an hour had passed and recuperation was almost complete. His soldiers were younger than he, so it was reasonable to suppose that, for the present, no prolonged idleness was indicated. It might be obligatory following the descent. He could not afford the luxury of wasting time. Time, thanks to those black devils, was now measured in water. So if there were no pure wells and no less difficult entrance to the valley, then after one more hour he would give the word.

He thought of his brother-in-law, who had taken an army over the Alps. He pictured himself saying, "We couldn't do it. You see, the mountains of Haiti—" Right there his brother-in-law would laugh at him. There wasn't any way to describe Haiti to a man who had not been awed by the Alps.

Leclerc called a half-dozen officers to him, and they held council. After eying the encampment of Christophe and his warriors, relief and amusement were openly expressed. But even a mob could do great damage. A descent slightly west was decided upon. It was unlikely at this distance that their approach would be discovered until they had gained the valley floor. To make quite certain of surprising Christophe they would descend from a position where a jutting body of rock would conceal them completely.

"We will wait until the scouts return," Leclerc said. "That is, we will wait a sensible length of time."

The scouts brought disappointing news. They had skirted widely around the valley seeking a hidden slope that would guarantee an easier access. There were no passes between the mountains, no paths leading gently downward. One pair of scouts had not returned. Leclerc waited for them, and in the interval the water seekers brought their report. No wells had been found except one in which a mule had been drowned.

Finally the order was given and the descent began. It was understood that the manner of advance would operate against any customary procedure. Once in the valley they would properly regroup, but for now there could be no thought of dignity. The order was to get down the mountainside.

Slipping, scrambling, clinging to liana vines, feeling for footholds, Leclerc and his men clawed their way downward. The General's hands were scraped and bleeding within the first few minutes. He heard a gasp beside him and saw a captain plunge almost a hundred feet before his fall was blocked by an unyielding tangle of giant ferns. Leclerc thought of the men with the weapon carts. He would ask of Napoleon some special honor for those men. The cannons had been left at the summit under guard. An officer would have to be mad to think they could be dragged into the valley.

Leclerc felt a terrible ache in his back and bones. His hands, slippery with blood, made his hold uncertain, made it doubly necessary to place his feet slowly, surely in the small natural hollows of the cliff. Above and below him silent men, their faces pale, their hands as lacerated as his, crept arduously downward. Sometimes one gained unexpected distance by the tearing away of a vine that refused to bear a man's weight. It was not a gain one desired. There were scraped faces and bleeding heads. Someone had broken a leg and lay on a narrow ledge waiting for God knew what.

Halfway down, Leclerc paused and breathed deeply. He tested

the depth of the hollow in which his foot rested. He tugged
with his wounded hands at a strange-looking bush and found
it crazily, but securely, rooted between rocks. Satisfied that it
would hold, he bent his body outward to survey the condition
of as many men as he could see. Like himself, they were doing
what must be done, descending into hell, clutching at anything
that seemed safely embedded. And as his eyes slowly followed
the men within his range of vision, he became aware of a movement in the distance on the far side of the valley.

He would have given a great deal for a ledge and his spyglass, but neither was available. He squinted and stared, and
finally, with a rage that made his heart thunder, he saw the
figures of three riders. Three men on horseback entering the
valley down a trail that seemed no more than a slight incline.
So there *was* another approach. He felt no rancor toward the
scouts who had not found it. Perhaps the two who had failed to
return had, indeed, set foot upon it. His rage was directed
against the fate that had thrown him and his men into this unnecessary agony. And the cruelty of that fate was well marked
by the coincidence of his sighting the second entrance at the
halfway point of their travail. It would be as painful to continue
as to go back to the summit and try for the secret path. He
muttered oaths but he wanted to shriek his anger and make
someone pay dearly for the anguish of this day. Yes, he would
hang Christophe.

His forehead was cold with sweat and his eyes hot with scalding tears of frustration. He let go of the bush and began again to
move toward the valley. "Come on, men," he cried hoarsely. It
was the first time in this terrible descent that he had implied that
anyone's effort could be increased.

He watched now, casting a glance from time to time, for more
movement, more horsemen. Also, it would be worthwhile to
impress upon his mind where the path ended in the valley. If
he were certain where it ended, it could be traced to where it
began. Never again would he believe that there was no way
except the hardest. God damn Rochambeau and his filthy
traitors. Why hadn't they told him about the other approach?

How could it have been harder to go after Dessalines, who was holding six hundred whites? Too bad that Rochambeau, who knew all about the splendid wells, was not in command of this expedition.

The location of the path that gave an approach to the valley was fixed in his mind now. There was a row of mangroves, a gap and another unbroken line of mangroves. He glanced again, and as he did he saw the three riders cantering away through that very gap. What had they brought? A message? He became aware then that the drums had been silent. Why? It could be only that there were no messages. No messages? While he and his men were descending the face of the mountain, accomplishing what he was now willing to wager never had been done before by an army? He looked at his hands. Blood had begun to stream from under the nails, and there was a gash on his left cheek that throbbed maddeningly.

But the miserable feat had been accomplished. Men were jumping to the ground, risking broken ankles rather than cling any longer to the mountainside. Leclerc hung on yet a while; then he, too, jumped. He found that he ached from head to toe and that his legs, back and arms had been slashed by needle-sharp rocks each time his uniform had been torn.

He ordered rest for the men, and he walked among them appraising injuries. Some had been luckier than he, others not quite as lucky. One man was writhing in pain from a shoulder that had been wrenched or broken. Everybody was bleeding, yet, strangely enough, spirits were high. There wasn't a man who did not know that he had done something remarkable, something that on a distant day he would narrate to his grandchildren. Not I, Leclerc thought. Of them all, only I will be silent, lest my grandchildren tell me that Grandmother's brother was Napoleon Bonaparte, who took his army across the Alps.

Water was handed out freely. There would be more after the errand was completed. The men needed to quench their thirst and daub at their bloody skin. They were a sorry-looking army unless experience had taught one to study a soldier's eyes and to listen for his voice. Leclerc saw excitement in the eyes and heard good cheer in the voices. No matter that the white uniforms were ripped and stained by blood. No matter that the thick juices that spurted from crushed vegetation were sticky on their hair and eyebrows. All they needed was a brief period for recuperation and the chance to talk a bit of the adventure they had shared.

The men who had handled the weapon carts were heroes and so acclaimed. They were congratulated, embraced and surrounded by admirers. Leclerc gravely offered his own words of praise, knowing that, though among his equals a soldier may scoff at a general, for all his life he would cherish that same general's acknowledgment of his achievement.

And after a time, when Leclerc's own aches had diminished, he knew the men were ready. From him down through the ranks the order flashed, and pridefully he watched the columns form, four abreast, perfect order.

"March!"

As though parading on a patriotic holiday in Paris, the soldiers moved forward, some trying to conceal a limp or a wince. Dear God, bless them, Leclerc thought as he took his place at the head of the line. On and on across the valley, over the loamy earth that sometimes sucked unaccountably at a torn boot as though hungry creatures lived beneath the ground. And at last Leclerc's men saw the soldiers of Christophe, and there was no question that Christophe's soldiers saw them.

Leclerc was prepared for a rabble of hapless, awkward blacks, but he had not guessed at the shameful display of disorganization that met his eyes. The blacks stood open-mouthed, staring. Some picked up muskets, then dropped them. Others ran, reversed direction and came to a full stop yelling with fright. In proper parade formation the French kept marching and watching the amazing show of childish dismay. Suddenly one of the black men among the milling, terrified hundreds seemed to have a constructive thought. "Run, Christophe!" he screamed. The others took up his cry. "Run, Christophe!" The valley echoed with the warning, and, as one man, the blacks sped toward a massive stand of manchineel trees that, as could now be seen, hid an African-style hut held together by mud-daubed twigs and roofed with palm branches. "Run, Christophe! Run, Christophe!"

As ordered, the French followed the blacks at quickstep. They were at their heels now, into the dark-green shadows, and they heard no more frantic pleas that Christophe run. There was a split second of silence, and then the hut seemed to explode. Frenchmen lay dead and dying. Every twig in the hut was a resting place for the nose of a musket. Those who tried to remove the wounded died looking surprised and reproachful. Leclerc rushed more men forward. Christophe was there. He must be taken. That was their mission. But nobody lived to reach the African hut. Nobody lived to come away from the treacherous beauty of the manchineel trees.

And suddenly Leclerc knew that Christophe was not there. From his painful position on the mountainside he had watched Christophe depart. Three horsemen had entered the valley. Three horsemen had left the valley. One of those who had come in had stayed, and his place had been taken by Christophe. Leclerc turned to his adjutant and spoke wearily.

"A purpose for remaining no longer exists. We are withdrawing. Pass the word."

He pointed to the gap in the mangroves, and the officers along the line, without understanding, also pointed to the gap in the mangroves. The troops saw with relief that the face of the mountain need not be scaled, unless, of course, the General had only guessed that the missing trees signaled a path to safety.

Leclerc knew they would not be permitted simply to walk away. "Turn and fight if necessary." That was the order he passed, and, with the first shot fired at them, the retreating French turned and fought. They were mowed down with their own cannons. In a stand that was no less than suicidal, a hundred men protected Leclerc and the bulk of the force as they made for the slope that led out of the valley.

Brother-in-law, I have advanced into the interior. I have met the enemy, and I am leaving him now—if I can.

The enemy was not scratching his back against a tree or

yelling in fright. He had become an efficient soldier who knew
how to handle the stolen French cannons. Leclerc backed up the
slope, firing his pistol when it was useful to do so. Some of his
men were weeping with frustration and anger, as he had wept on
the mountainside.

Amazingly, the slope led to a deserted road. Not an enemy in
sight. The officers were doubtful and issued orders for watchful-
ness and readiness. But the army marched, fatigued and dazed,
without encountering anyone. They skirted the entire valley, the
terrain steepening in a slow, easily managed rise. Suddenly,
with no notice, they were up against a wall of jungle-thick plant
life. Sore and mangled hands tore an opening. Men with knives
hacked away until their bloody fingers slipped from the handles.
Others then took the knives and continued the effort. When they
broke through, they found themselves only fifty yards from the
summit where they had started. Nobody had the heart for even
ironic laughter upon discovering that, had they explored the
area, they would have seen the opening through which the enemy
had dragged their cannons.

The guards they had left on the summit lay dead. Men crossed
themselves, but noted with relief that the canteens were still
strapped to the dead men's belts. It was disappointing that the
canteens had been emptied.

Volunteers buried the guards in shallow graves. They were
too tired, too thirsty to provide more than the skimpiest of resting places. It was enough that they had volunteered. Someone
of unusual energy or humanitarian principles scrambled down
the mountain as far as the ledge where the soldier with the
broken leg had been left. The leg would hurt no more. The
soldier's throat had been cut, and his canteen flung some distance
below. The man who had come to rescue him had, on this day,
learned a great deal about Haiti. He knew that the canteen
would be empty. He knew that someone would be watching and
laughing as he ripped himself again on the evil rocks in hope of
a little water. And he knew that he was not going to carry the
dead soldier to the summit or ask anyone to help him do so. In
Haiti it was the living who needed pity.

Leclerc sat on a rock and gave himself up to agony of body and mind. Presently he raised his spyglass and looked into the valley. He saw the French dead lying where they had fallen. From this height one might suppose that large white handkerchiefs had been knotted into grotesque forms and allowed to drift from a mountain peak. They would never be buried, he thought regretfully, but, then, neither would the blacks. He lowered the spyglass and stared blindly toward the place where there had been no drill field, no tents, and, as he had arrogantly believed, no one worthy of facing the veterans of Campo Formio and Arcola.

He got up and walked to the opening through which his cannons had been dragged. He examined the ground carefully. Spiky rocks and tough, rotting entanglements of liana as thick as large snakes. He thought about the men who had delivered those cannons to the valley. Was he facing gods or giants?

Why had he, or someone else, not seen the arrival of the cannons? There was still another approach to the valley, he concluded. The path of the three horsemen, the path by which he and his troops had returned to the summit, had not been the route of the cannons. And it came to him that the African thatch-roofed hut he had glimpsed was an illusion. It was not a hut at all but only a façade that hid a convenient notch through which the cannons had been pulled.

He scowled. It did not hang together. If the hut were a deception, if the notch existed, if the blacks had known of the French presence, why had the horsemen not arrived and departed from behind the façade? Why had they gratuitously pointed out an escape from the valley? Leclerc pondered the matter and, in the end, rejected obvious answers. They had not underestimated his vision. They had not committed an error. Obsessed by the gnawing dread that the enemy was more astute than he, it was easy to accept that they had sought to demoralize the French. They had timed their entrance down that gentle incline just as he and his bleeding men had been halfway to solid ground. Halfway. They had hoped to create in him a sense of self-pity and despair. They had not been without success, he thought. But

117

why were we not engaged and annihilated on that path to escape? Is there a design craftier than I can possibly guess?

A captain came to him and asked if the men might sleep for a time.

"Yes, let them be as comfortable as they can. The hill we climbed this morning must be descended if we are to get back to the ships. Thank God, it will not be as harsh as the other. Has any pure water been found?"

"No, General."

"Disturbing," Leclerc said. "But I do not think dangerous, provided we do not rest too long."

He returned to the rock and seated himself heavily. He thought about the black men who had made him laugh when first he saw them. Suddenly the throb of the drums began, and, though he could not read the message, he knew what was being told. He could sense the exultation in the booming beat, and when it was picked up in a faint reprise from the distance, he was able, for the first time, to distinguish a variance in style among the drummers. The second chattered like a grinning ape, and Leclerc thought that probably the French soldier was being ridiculed. Fair enough, he reflected, fair enough. But there will come a day when you, too, will learn that one must not laugh too soon. Boom-boom boom-boom boom-boom chatter chatter chatter chatter boom-boom boom-boom.

You bastard, do you have the count of how many men I lost? How many? Tell me.

The final count was five hundred and seventy-three. Of the men who had returned, only eight were in the infirmary. One would have an arm amputated. A complete and normal recovery was promised for the ambulatory, with their sprains, wrenches, friction burns, gashes and gunshot wounds.

Leclerc took to his bed for a day, sick in spirit as well as feverish and aching. Pauline had retched when he had staggered aboard the *Océana* and tried to embrace her. He had forgotten the caked blood on his cheek and the ghastly appearance of his hands.

His orderly bathed his wounds, helped him into a soft, clean bedshirt, and delivered Leclerc's message to the doctor. The General would receive him only after all others had been treated.

"I don't want to sound heroic," Leclerc said, "but I sent them into a trap. It was my fault. It's always the general's fault."

Pauline said, "That's nonsense. Napoleon thinks a general who blames himself disheartens the whole Army. I didn't know about the rocks. I thought you had caught some disease out there. Do they have leprosy on the island?"

"I'm sure they do," Leclerc sighed.

"I'll give you a kiss now," Pauline offered.

"Never mind."

The next day he wrote to Napoleon. It was difficult to strike the balance he sought. It had to be about midway between his dejection at what had happened and his hope that future encounters with the enemy would be more successful as a result of hard lessons now learned. He wished he had more time to elaborate, but a ship was sailing for home at noon. Napoleon had every right to expect regular reports. Leclerc's state of mind improved as it occurred to him that by the time Napoleon received the letter there well might have been a tremendous victory. The island conceivably could be in French hands within a month or so. What a letter he would write then!

He unlocked a drawer in the desk and took out his most secret papers. He had not even studied these yet. He would do so, he thought, directly after the island had been secured. He gazed with melancholy upon order number three: "Resistance from enemy army in interior has now crumbled. Fast-moving columns must swiftly hunt down and exterminate any troublesome individuals who have not surrendered."

Brother-in-law, there are not yet any troublesome individuals. There are only the black forces of Haiti, who do not appear to be crumbling. Yes, I know you said to advance with a converging movement. How could I? I did not then know that there was more than one approach to the valley. Brother-in-law, do not sneer. Remember that all men are fallible. For instance, you never did get to India, did you?

119

He was not ready for order number three, but to strengthen himself he read on to the brighter day beyond. In a somewhat chatty style Napoleon had written: "In the first period of your victory, dear Leclerc, you will not be exacting. You will treat in friendly fashion with Toussaint. You will promise him everything he asks in order that you may get possession of the principal points. Confirm all his favorite officers and leaders in their rank and position. Later you must trap them all, in one way or another, and send them to me. I want Toussaint on board a frigate and in France as soon as this can be done without the threat of awakening further hostilities."

Of course, brother-in-law, of course. I will send you Toussaint any day now. Forgive the delay. I don't know how I came to overlook sending him. I guess I've just grown idle and pleasure-seeking on this beautiful tropical island. By the way, it is raining today. Do you think that is of no moment? It rains a great deal at this season of the year in our carefree paradise. Do figures impress you? The heavens empty as much as one hundred twenty-two inches in a single season. I venture to say that you have not seen rain of this sort. If one is caught in the deluge, breathing becomes a frightening experience. There is the sensation of drowning, and I swear to you that a deep breath cannot be drawn without danger. Then there is the fear of being beaten down into the mud by the incredibly powerful bayonets of water. If one loses one's footing there is the chance of never regaining balance, and then indeed one is drowned or suffocated. Brother-in-law, they keep no count here of those who have been killed by rain.

Leclerc looked with curiosity at the sheaf of papers that dealt with moves to be made when Haiti was no more, when Saint-Domingue had been safely turned over to the commissioners Napoleon would dispatch from Paris. He hesitated and decided he had not yet earned the right to bask in the warm glow cast by Napoleon's flaming ambition. Well, perhaps just a peek.

He broke the seal of the first folded document and saw with disappointment something he had seen before. A copy of Napoleon's letter to Decrès, Minister of Marine. Oddly, Decrès had been asked to signify his approval of the copy as well as the original upon receipt, and to return both to the First Consul.

Napoleon had written: "My intention, Citizen Minister, is that we shall take possession of Louisiana from its most southern edge to the Great Lakes with the least possible delay. The expedition must be carried out in the greatest secrecy so that the intention appears at all times to be concerned only with the reoccupation of Saint-Domingue."

Leclerc wondered why it had seemed important to the First Consul to send across the Atlantic duplicates of every word, note, letter and document that pertained to the expedition. Of course, there must be instructions. But why records? Could it be that Napoleon was protecting Pauline's husband? In the event of the First Consul's death and the rise to power of Bonaparte enemies, would there be those who would claim that they knew nothing of the wild schemes of Napoleon and his brother-in-law? Very farseeing of Napoleon, and very kind. But there was no need to be overcome by emotion. If Pauline's well-being were not involved, one Leclerc more or less would not matter.

The next broken seal disclosed a letter addressed to "General in Command of Saint-Domingue Expedition." Ah, Napoleon thought of everything. If he, the First Consul, could meet with unexpected death, then why not Leclerc? Why place his name on the letter? Leclerc read the instructions. They had been discussed in Paris. They were all familiar to him: "Once you are in control do not allow any black to remain on the island if he has held a rank above captain. Disarm all blacks, no matter what side they are on, and reinstate the laws which acted so efficaciously for us in the past. Begin by issuing an ordinance against the sale and purchase of small properties. This will virtually put an end to any increase in black ownership. Explain that only large plantations are of sufficient productivity to bring prosperity to all inhabitants. This will result in blacks seeking employment on said large plantations instead of wasting their energy on small farms that are of no profit to France. At first, you must encourage (later demand) that all blacks return to the practice of using the family name of their employer. Emphasize

that this simplifies all municipal and legal matters. When blacks
have once again become accustomed to this regulation, you must
decree that no fanciful additions to names are permitted. Much
harm was done to childish minds by the fact that Toussaint
Bréda called himself Toussaint L'Ouverture. This black man
became a legend because the appellation suggested splendid
victories. Create a law forbidding marriage or cohabitation
between blacks who work on different plantations. This can be
interpreted as a plan for promoting morality and improving
health. A man will always have his own wife at his side. This can
be a very happy law and also will be beneficial in curbing the
spread of any discontent from one plantation to another. When
all is smoothly accomplished there is no reason why slavery
cannot be reinstalled. You will be able to judge at what point
this can be done with the least disruption. Blacks must be returned to agriculture under proper guidance as swiftly as can
be arranged. They are of no value unless they are performing
the tasks for which they are naturally suited."

Though Leclerc had known every word to be found on the
page, he read it all with deep interest. It was amazing how much
more practical the orders had sounded in Paris. By using logic
and a firm course of action one would simply proceed to do this
sensible thing, then the next sensible thing, and at last all blacks
would be slaves again without having guessed what the French
had in mind.

Brother-in-law, have you ever met a Haitian?

Leclerc considered again the sheaf of papers that outlined the
course to follow when the business of Saint-Domingue had been
completed. He knew little of those future plans, and in breaking
the two seals he had hoped to learn what initial steps were
expected of him as the second stage of the great adventure began.
He thought of breaking all seals and devouring at once every
bit of information at hand, but he was engulfed by a sudden
wave of weariness. While the present weighed so heavily upon
him, what need had he to know the future?

He placed the papers back in their drawer and locked it.

Having a desire to speak freely of the happenings in the valley, he sent for his second-in-command.

Rochambeau came to him almost immediately.

"I hope I did not take you away from important work."

"No. As a matter of fact, I was holding myself in readiness. I thought you might want to see me. I sorrow with you that the attempt to capture Christophe was not successful."

"It was a nightmare. There are some strange things to tell you. Please sit down."

He told Rochambeau everything, calling particular attention to the behavior of the blacks, their display of helplessness upon seeing the French, their open fear, their warning shouts to Christophe.

Rochambeau nodded knowingly. "They are an inferior people, General. They have no rules of conduct."

"You have missed the point. These inferior people put on a superb performance and slaughtered us."

"General, forgive me, but I don't think they put on any performance at all. It just seemed that they did. In absolute panic they were running to protect Christophe, and you followed. They were lucky. Without plan, by sheer accident they completed the oldest military trick in the world, the classic ambush."

"Yes, the classic ambush." Leclerc raised his hand to his poulticed cheek. "As a cadet I did an excellent paper on the subject."

"I am sure you did. Tell me, are you in great pain?"

"You mean physically? No. Please continue to give me your impressions of the events in the valley."

Rochambeau obeyed. "Of course, being blockheads, the blacks must have cut down a lot of their own men. They couldn't have avoided that, but, then, life doesn't mean anything to them."

"There was a small space of time before they fired," Leclerc said. "I have the feeling that those we followed had been trained to run behind the hut."

Rochambeau grinned and shook his head. "I know these people. They're not that clever."

"Did you ever fight against them?"

"No. As I told you, I came here to look around and decide whether or not I'd be governor-general. I had to be honest and say that I really loathed the place and couldn't endure living among blacks and half-blacks. They're filthy people, you know. Vicious, too, and—"

"Pardon the interruption. I'd like to mention a few other things. As you know, while we were descending into the valley, our cannons were stolen and our guards were killed. Don't you see that we were being watched? Doesn't it strike you that Christophe's soldiers knew we were coming?"

"General, a few blacks were wandering around. Stealing is second nature to them, and they don't care if they have to kill to do it."

Leclerc was determined to keep his temper. "So they just happened to run across our cannons, and, indulging the demands of their second nature, they hurriedly, and damned expertly, dragged the cannons directly to where they were needed."

"You keep flattering the black wretches. If they had run across a dozen silver teaspoons, they'd have stolen those and rushed them to Christophe. Yes, and they'd have killed the guards to get them."

Leclerc thought his story over once more. "Rochambeau, how do you think that crazy, yelling mob turned so suddenly into a steady line of respectable soldiers?"

"Fear, General. They're more frightened of Christophe than of us. When they ran into the manchineels he was there to tell them that at one more sign of cowardice he'd have their bellies slit open. So they quieted down and went to work."

There was no proof, but Leclerc knew that Christophe had not been there. Christophe had given instructions and ridden away. Toussaint, aware of impending battle and unwilling to risk losing his best general, had ordered him out of the valley. Christophe had done more than plan an ambush. He had rehearsed a play with very convincing actors. But there was no use going over all that again with Rochambeau. Rochambeau was a disappointment. He had no imagination, no insight. Leclerc was only half listening as his second-in-command continued.

"General, God knows where Christophe is now. Do you realize that some of these mountains are nine thousand feet high and that there are hundreds of secret valleys all over the island? You had bad luck, and now we can't hope to capture Christophe until we get a hint of where he is."

Leclerc nodded.

"So there's no choice, General. We have to go for Dessalines. I want to do that, please. Will you give me the honor?"

Leclerc blinked in surprise. Rochambeau was more than fifty years old and had been expected to contribute little more than advice. Leclerc studied him speculatively and noted that there was certainly the appearance of vigor in the man. It was a matter that must be considered carefully. How carefully? Was time limitless? When would he himself feel equal to the task of leading troops against Dessalines? Could Rochambeau do it?

He was embarrassed that Rochambeau had read his mind, that he had left his chair and was standing tall and straight, giving the commanding general an opportunity to judge the condition of his health and strength.

"The mountains—" Leclerc murmured.

"I know. I could not do what you did," Rochambeau admitted. "But Dessalines is not guarded by mountains. To be sure, he has an ideal position and it is elevated, but I intend to capture him. He has twelve hundred men. Because we are fighting on his terms I would like to put twenty-five hundred against him."

"I hope," Leclerc said, "that you can rescue the whites he kidnapped."

Rochambeau did not bother to hide his annoyance. "Please accept that they are dead. I cannot do miracles. I cannot make them live again, but I will bring you Dessalines."

Rochambeau picked his men with care. Though every day mulattoes of considerable experience and ability were deserting Toussaint's forces to join Leclerc's, Rochambeau would have none of them.

"They know the island," Leclerc remarked.

"And I know mulattoes. I like them less than I like blacks. Blacks, at least, are simple-minded and understandable."

"Rochambeau, that may not be true. Just in case my impressions of them were not entirely caused by fever and misfortune —" He let his words trail off. His cheek was not healing well. The doctor had drained it of pus, but it was still hot and sore. He felt silly sitting there like a sick old woman telling her grandson to be careful in battle.

Rochambeau, after much thought, asked for three thousand men, and they were willingly granted to him. Horses were provided for officers. Mule-drawn carts carried great barrels of water and food. It would not be a swift onslaught. Dessalines was at Crête à Pierrot. Ordinarily, it was not what Frenchmen would call a fort, but in other times it had been an acceptable redoubt where plantation owners of the region had deposited their wives and children when slaves began to act suspiciously. It was, as Rochambeau had been told, still quite serviceable, though it predated the great island-wide slave rebellion by almost a century.

The approach of the French could be no secret to Dessalines, since it would take several days to reach Crête à Pierrot. Little difference, Rochambeau thought. Dessalines could not dig himself in any more deeply. However, close vigilance must be kept. Sometimes, as had happened with Leclerc, these black animals blundered into small triumphs through pure luck.

He knew he had been seen by troops of the Haitian Army. Troops? Those fools who were either almost as naked as the day they were born or wearing gold-braided uniforms in all colors of the rainbow? He had ridden up to a small overhang of rock and watched them as they straggled by, singing and jabbering. They had no idea of how soldiers marched. All of them slouched along, choosing a pleasing pace and even occasionally dropping out to chase a lizard or pluck an avocado. One could laugh at them if one were in the mood. Rochambeau was not in the mood because the bastards had set fire to every plantation house for miles around. Arson was a mania with them. Well, someday they'd all burn in hell.

It was on the morning of the second day that the wind carried to Rochambeau and his men an odor of putrefaction that cut through the smoke from the blazing sugar mills. There was no soldier who did not recognize the horror toward which he marched. But still it came as a shock to see what had been done to the white men, women and children Dessalines had received from the mulattoes at Port-au-Prince. They had been hacked to death with sugar-cane knives some days earlier, and thrown into a ravine.

Rochambeau rode on, thinking, as other men before him had thought, that there was no reason by the standards of God or man that these blacks should be permitted to live. Forgetting conquest, profit and power, civilized nations ought to band together and send a force of whatever size necessary to kill every single inhabitant of the island.

But before killing them, Rochambeau told himself, they must be severely tortured.

His first view of Crête à Pierrot was through his spyglass. He saw its long moss-covered walls rising from an ancient moat. He had expected it to be surrounded by jungle, but Dessalines had evidently felled trees and burned low-growing bushes to insure a clear view of the approaches. Rochambeau could see a few black soldiers on the hillside below the fort. One of them was an officer wearing a pink uniform and a black tricorn on which a huge jewel sparkled beautifully. Rochambeau found this so ludicrous that he burst into laughter.

He thought about rushing the fort immediately. To take Dessalines would be no effortless achievement at any time. The French would have to march up that hill and keep marching. When they fell, replacements would have to be swiftly thrown into the line. There was no way to take Dessalines without losses. It was going to be bloody but rewarding. And once the fort was surrounded—

He temporized. It was late in the afternoon, and his men were tired. Also, to let darkness end the battle would be an advantage for Dessalines. During the night he could slip beyond grasp. Rochambeau postponed the battle until morning.

When the sun rose, red and hot, over the island, he outlined the objective once again to his officers. The objective was Dessalines. He was to be captured at any cost. Preferably alive. Dead would be only a second choice. The fort looked more substantial than it actually was. It could not withstand cannon fire. However, the cannons must be almost a last resort, because a living Dessalines could play an enormous role in finishing the conflict.

"I know these people," Rochambeau said. "He'll tell us anything and betray anybody if only we give him enough food, women and drink. And, of course, we'll do that—as long as we need him."

Rochambeau's men marched toward Crête à Pierrot with the pride and determination for which French soldiers were famed. Four abreast. A straight, precise column. Rochambeau rode in front. There were a hundred or so black men lying halfway up the hill. Having apparently just breakfasted, they lay in a litter of melon rinds and banana peels.

When they saw the French, the blacks leaped to their feet and did exactly what Rochambeau had told Leclerc was natural to them: they darted about like lunatics, screaming in terror, having lost all sense of direction and purpose.

Rochambeau pulled his horse to the side as his men started the upward march. The blacks ran toward the moat and stopped one by one at the edge, as though gathering the courage to jump. They stood with their backs turned, uttering mournful cries. Occasionally, they glanced over their shoulders with wild, rolling eyes to see if the French were still advancing.

The French were still advancing and holding their fire when, suddenly, to the amazement of the onlooking Rochambeau and his men, the blacks actually did jump into the moat. And at that moment, and at the level where the blacks had stood, muskets poured death from the fort. Replacements were ready, and, after a fatal attempt to pick up the injured, the advance proceeded.

128

Those who reached the moat found it empty of water and of blacks. With trees and brush, its floor had been raised so that a man could drop into it without damaging himself. But no Frenchman lasted long enough to test its safety.

Rochambeau ordered more men into the battle, and late in the day he had the cannons brought up. By the time they were in place the musketmen on the walls of the fort had disappeared and the fire from the gun embrasures had ceased. It was mid-afternoon, and the heat and the dead and the weariness and the groans of the dying were all one great confused and unendurable agony. An officer scowled up at the mountain that pushed its eerie black peak toward the sky behind Crête à Pierrot. He expressed the opinion that Dessalines and his men had made their way out of the fort.

"No. No, they haven't," Rochambeau said, and his tone was that of a man who must believe himself or die. "But something else has happened." His eyes flashed as he pointed balefully toward the fort. "The black bastards have run out of ammunition. Let's go get them."

"General, perhaps we ought to—"

"Don't tell me they're in the mountains. They couldn't have escaped without detection. Tell the men we're going into the fort. I'll lead them."

The French soldiers formed their perfect line once again. Rochambeau, on his horse, watched from halfway up the hill as they came toward him. They marched as though there were nothing in the world to fear.

"On, men. They're out of ammunition. We're going to take them, every last Goddamned black one of them."

The soldiers came to the moat, and, though it was an awkward maneuver, they scrambled through the dead branches and thorny bush. They regrouped properly and advanced. There were some who held their breath, for they had heard disturbing talk from the men who had been with Leclerc on that other, ill-starred expedition.

But Rochambeau had been right. The blacks were out of ammunition. That is to say, the blacks who remained at Crête à

Pierrot were out of ammunition. They were also out of guns, knives and almost out of life itself. At the sight of the cannons, Dessalines had left his wounded and made for the mountains. Rochambeau's soldiers found the underground passage that had been dug within the last few weeks.

There were perhaps a hundred and fifty wounded blacks within the walls of the fort. Not even the man with only a bleeding foot bothered to beg for his life. Hot, sullen glances turned to the French, then slid away. The blacks waited indifferently.

Rochambeau gave the order himself. The blacks were beaten to death with shovels, chairs, wooden boards—anything that Dessalines had not carried with him. They died silently, which was infuriating, and the French, resenting this display of stoicism, continued the violent attack long after there was a chance of drawing a plea for mercy from any black in the fort.

Nobody marched down the hill. No order had been given. Rochambeau's men reeled past their own dead and were allowed to collapse anywhere they wished, and to sleep if they desired. A few chattered incessantly. Others bit into mangoes and let the juice run down their chins and onto their uniforms. One man, glassy-eyed and trembling, laughed loudly as he chased a lizard.

Rochambeau permitted his horse to carry him where it would. He had not captured Dessalines. That was going to be difficult to explain, considering that two thousand Frenchmen lay dead at Crête à Pierrot.

. . . .

On a high mountain ledge, where the silver flame of stars was only just beyond reach, the woman who had been Bréda's cook readied a midnight meal. She had selected flat stones, arranged them to her satisfaction and with a candle had set fire to the bed of dried wood chips within. Now she sat back on her heels and from time to time stirred the *riz djon-djon* and the *zœuf au lait*. She had brought her own chickens to Mont Vautour, so she knew the eggs were fresh, but she had never before prepared *zœuf au lait* with goat's milk. It was a great worry to her that it might have an unpleasant flavor. Well, she consoled herself, there was always a melon or bananas dusted with sugar to serve in an emergency. She laughed suddenly, remembering how funny she must have looked riding a mule and clinging to a cage of chickens and her favorite kettles and mixing bowls. She covered her mouth to still the laughter and glanced apologetically toward the men. She had not disturbed them. They were unaware of her.

They sat with their backs against the trees talking, talking, talking. This time, embarrassed by the sound of her laughter, she had not prepared herself for the sight of Toussaint. Her surprised heart shook as it had shaken upon her arrival at Mont Vautour. How ancient he had become, how withered. Always he had been ugly, but the strength of his face, the glitter of his eyes had marked him as a special man among men. The strength had left him. His temples were sunken and his eyes dull. She turned away. Christophe was speaking, and his words had no power to divert her from her anxieties. She often had trouble understanding his accent, and, besides, she had never cared for the manner in which he carried himself. It was as though he thought his height and the breadth of his shoulders were owed to some particularly clever trick he had performed. The other one, that Dessalines, was not even a man. He was a huge, wild animal who smelled bad and was uglier than Toussaint had ever been. There was no friendliness in his face, no evidence that a mind existed behind the small, mean eyes. And, yet, she had every reason to believe that he felt affection for Toussaint.

Christophe had stopped speaking. The woman stirred the rice, dropped in the black mushrooms and fretted about the dessert, but she listened to Toussaint's voice.

"Yes, it is a thing that all leaders forget. A leader often assumes his high position because the masses are abused and in great want. Immediately, to the extent that circumstances permit, he corrects inequities, he fills empty stomachs and supplies acceptable shelter. Whether or not all this is altruistic is beside the point, the point being that when a leader has given the common people comfort, they grow so frightened of losing it that they endanger the nation. They whimper and grow soft once they have a cow and an acre of land. Their stupidity is monumental. One does not retain comfort—or liberty—by licking an enemy's boots."

Christophe said, "Everybody is a peasant farmer now. If his barn door is locked, he feels safe. I speak to hundreds who were good soldiers, and I literally beg them to return to me. Do you know what they say? They say, 'I have to think of my woman and children and the farm.' I try to convince them that they'll lose all those precious things if they do not join me. They smile and say that the French are not bothering them."

Dessalines roared his anger. "I tell you we stop burning big plantations and sugar mills. We burn small farms and tell men their wife and baby get treated like white people if they don't help fight French."

Toussaint spoke with annoyance. "Is that the way to enlist a good soldier, Dessalines? Or is it the way to guarantee you have men in your ranks who will kill you at the first opportunity?"

Christophe stood up and paced nervously. "Every last man of Leclerc's valley expedition could have been finished off, but there weren't enough troops to put out on the slope. The French could have been cut to pieces, but instead they returned to their ships. What I would have given for a few hundred men waiting there behind the mangroves."

"No doubt you were watching, Christophe, but you weren't there at that painful moment."

"No, neither were the Goddamned mulattoes who were supposed to confront the French on the slope. If we hadn't been depending on the mulattoes, we wouldn't have shown the French the way out of the valley. They'd all be rotting there now."

Dessalines turned and studied Toussaint thoughtfully. "Why you trust mulattoes? You tell me that, General? You tell me why, after all they do to us, you trust mulattoes?"

Toussaint answered as though he were very tired. "Christophe has just told you why. Black soldiers are scarce and getting scarcer. There was just a chance that this particular mulatto unit was trustworthy. If it had proven so, we'd have destroyed

Leclerc. If it proved false—which it did—the worst that could happen was what happened. The French got away with only medium-sized losses."

"But you trust the mulattoes, General, after they give up Port-au-Prince and the South Province and—"

"I didn't trust them completely, Dessalines. If I had, I would not have ordered Christophe to leave. I had to think that perhaps the mulattoes would join the French right on the battleground. In that situation, there wouldn't have been enough blacks to protect Christophe."

Dessalines puffed out his great scarred cheeks and emitted a long *oh* of surprise. "I see something. The mulattoes did plan to do that. They did plan to give fine present to French so French maybe will be good to them. Then they hear, or maybe see, that Christophe is not no more in the valley, so they turn around and go home. They spend the day maybe having good time. After that, they go join Leclerc. He got a lot of them now."

"I know," Toussaint said. "Mulattoes still love the French."

"Why, General? Why they love French? You, me, we all see in the Place d'Armes that day what French do to Vincent Ogé and other fellow. Why mulattoes love French?"

"Because they hate the part of themselves that is black. They keep believing that the farther away they move from you and me the whiter they become."

"Big fools," Dessalines said. "I got no time now, but in next war I kill all black women that got inside them white man's baby."

Christophe shot an amused glance at Dessalines and asked, "What will you do with a white woman who is carrying a black man's baby?"

"Those women I treat good. Poor things. You know, they been hurt bad, real bad. No white woman ever go to black man unless he say he kill her if not." Dessalines' great, loud laughter must have driven the bats from their caves.

Toussaint, disapproving, did not show a flicker of a smile. He managed to convey the impression that he had been absent while some small talk had passed between the others.

The woman served the *riz djon-djon* and secretly tasted the *zœuf au lait*. It was very good. Who would have believed a goat had such fine milk to give? Strange that even in the villages it was never offered to the children. Toussaint should make a law that goats were not to be butchered. He must tell the people that the milk was delicious. She looked at the men. They were eating with evident enjoyment, and she was pleased.

Dessalines finished running his thick, purple tongue over the sea shell in which the rice had been served. "What it mean to *outlaw?*" he asked. "I hear yesterday that Leclerc make printed papers that say he outlaw us."

Toussaint said, "Yes, but that goes with other things I intend to mention when we have something sweet to put in our stomachs. What I have to say will be bitter for us all."

Dessalines looked at him in surprise. "Bitter? What going to be bitter? My men fight good. They fight like sons of bitches against Rochambeau."

"But you had to run, didn't you, Dessalines?"

"Sure I run. Not enough good sons of bitches."

"Yes," Toussaint said mildly, "that's what we've been saying."

The woman brought the *zœuf au lait* in a hollowed-out gourd. Nobody expressed pleasure at the sight or taste of it, but there was not a spoonful left when the men returned to their conversation.

"Dessalines," Toussaint explained, "Leclerc has issued orders that all citizens are to hunt us down and turn us over to him. There is no punishment for killing us. I believe if there are not immediate results, he will offer a reward for our capture. We are outlawed. That means we are not considered soldiers, but, instead, criminals."

Dessalines spat contemptuously. "Who going to catch us?"

"Somebody will," Toussaint assured him. "Not tonight or tomorrow, but soon. I don't know a white or a mulatto who won't be interested when money is mentioned. For that matter, I would not trust the black peasant farmers to reject the idea of enriching themselves."

Dessalines looked at Christophe. Christophe nodded. Dessalines always knew himself to be wrong when there was no difference of opinion between the other two.

"So what we do?"

Toussaint drew a long breath. He laid his head back against the tree trunk and gazed up at the stars. After a time he spoke. "We don't have enough men to fight the French. When we lose fifty in battle we feel that loss. Bonaparte will keep sending reinforcements to Leclerc. We can't match their numbers, and don't forget that in every battle Leclerc and Rochambeau and all the other officers will become more familiar with our ways. Add to that the fact that presently every man on the island will be devising a scheme for our undoing. As matters stand, we are on a road which leads to defeat and death."

The other two men waited, their eyes fixed on him, their bodies taut and still. A nocturnal lizard slid by and broke the spell of silence. In a hoarse whisper Dessalines repeated his question.

"So what we do?"

"We surrender," Toussaint said.

Dessalines leaped to his feet. "Goddamn no!" he cried. "We beat the French before and the Spanish and the English and we can—"

Toussaint said, "Sit down."

Dessalines obeyed, but his small eyes flashed rebellion.

"Explain to him, Christophe."

In all their three-cornered conversations there came a moment when Toussaint saw himself bereft of the patience needed for a lengthy discourse. While Toussaint rested against the tree, Christophe carefully reviewed battles and situations of the past, answered the questions of Dessalines, repeated, rephrased and simplified until he had awakened a spark of comprehension.

"And perhaps the most important thing, friend, is that we had every black on the island fighting on our side. We have only a quarter of the men we had then. No use arguing against what is real and true."

Dessalines bit at his lower lip and gazed fiercely at Christophe. Then suddenly he lowered his head and began to sob noisily.

Christophe turned away. Toussaint seemed not to notice. Suddenly Dessalines uttered a profanity and shouted up at the mountain peak.

"If Dessalines surrender hundred times, it will be to betray them hundred times!"

Toussaint reached out and touched his shoulder. "Exactly," he said. "Exactly. You have summed up the entire plan of action by which we will now operate."

The eyes of Dessalines went to Christophe. "Tell me plain what the General say."

Christophe smiled tightly. "I am not yet certain."

Toussaint sat taller against the tree. His eyes glittered and he spoke rapidly. "They cannot win, you know. The French cannot win; but if we are not smart, we will be dead by the time they lose. To survive we must play some undignified little tricks, such as we taught our soldiers to play. Remember that a white man is always willing to believe that a black man is a coward and an idiot. We will let him have his myths, and we will live to see him defeated."

"If things so bad, how we defeat him?" Dessalines asked.

"We outlive him. Do you remember how sick the French soldiers were years ago? No, perhaps you don't. We paid little attention to them because we fought every day against someone. Now we try to spend only enough men to keep the French off balance. We do no more than prevent them from winning, so there is plenty of time for thought. For instance, I have been thinking that Leclerc's men will die in fever season. They will die by the thousands because Bonaparte will send them here by the thousands. He wants this island, but he can't get it unless he knows a way of making white men as safe from fever as we are."

"Then why not we sit and wait?"

"We can't wait. They'll come get us. We are outlaws. If we are taken like helpless beasts, that is the way they will treat us. If we surrender like sensible generals who have had second thoughts, then there is room for bargaining."

Christophe said, "I know that to be the truth." He reached into the pocket of his coat and drew out a letter. "I received this in a way which proves to me, Dessalines, that we can't sit and wait, that others know the mountains, too. The letter comes from a mulatto who was once a friend of mine. He is now a loyal officer of Leclerc's." Christophe glanced at Toussaint, asking for sympathetic understanding. "I don't think I'll speak his name."

Toussaint's eyelids flickered in reply. It was an injustice to mention an individual enemy in the presence of Dessalines unless the enemy deserved a slow and screaming death.

Christophe took the candle from its niche in a rock and brought it close to him. "To save time, may I read this aloud?" The question was an old convention used to accommodate the illiteracy of Dessalines.

"Yes, please do that," Toussaint said.

Christophe proceeded to read. " 'My dear friend, with mortal regret have I watched your refusal to submit to the French general whom the First Consul has sent to maintain the order which you so successfully established in the city of Le Cap and in the region of the North. You have sacrificed both happiness and fortune. General Leclerc is so persuaded that it was bad advice that caused you to resist that he is quite ready to pardon you if you care to bring under his authority the troops which you command. We can guarantee you a fortune and the peaceable enjoyment of it under the protection of France. Quit your vagabond existence and abandon a cause which can come to nothing—' He goes on from there in the same general direction." Christophe folded the letter and put it away.

"Did you answer?" Toussaint asked.

"No. Should I?"

"Of course. It gives us a place to begin. You must not raise his suspicions by falling too easily into his basket, but fall you must, Christophe. It's our only chance." Toussaint waited, looking at the solemn faces of his generals. "All of us would rather be on a battlefield. That we cannot do much longer. I don't like treachery, but it has its place. Like opium, treachery is degrading to the one who uses it. It should be scorned by the strong until pain becomes unendurable."

Dessalines turned to Christophe inquiringly, anxiously.

"No. Nobody is going to have any opium. The General is just philosophizing, and I've explained about that to you."

"Yes. It means he think too big for me."

Christophe nodded. "Too big for me, too, my friend."

"Not too big for either of you. It is a simple stratagem. Christophe will surrender first, because he has been invited to do so. Then, when you and I, Dessalines, observe how happy and well rewarded he is, we will do the same. Something that is in the letter Christophe received has concerned me since first I thought of surrender. There is the demand that Christophe bring his troops with him. Of course, that will be expected of you, too, and I will be responsible for delivering my staff and guards and the regiment of L'Ouverture Elite. The French will be extremely suspicious if every man surrenders along with us. They will be equally suspicious if too few surrender. We have to decide how many of each is just right. Now, here is the poser: Do we take the most intelligent, the best fighters to the French? Or do we leave them outside? Obviously, there must be men to continue the war. If not, then our surrender is a reality rather than a ruse."

Christophe answered quickly. "Only the best fighters and best thinkers are going to be able to mount any kind of action against the French."

"I didn't mean to leave our men totally without military guidance, Christophe. That is not the major problem. However, entwined in it is what I see as a dreadful question upon which all else depends."

Christophe was up and pacing again. He said, "Sir, at the finish of each battle there will be fewer blacks. We can't get reinforcements. Five thousand or even twenty thousand French can be replaced, but we can't replace a dozen blacks. It's a few months yet to the fever season that you're counting on so heavily. Leclerc could well wipe out every black soldier on the island before that and sail home in triumph."

"Sit down, Christophe."

Dessalines laughed like a school child who has heard the

teacher's pet reprimanded. He rocked back and forth in delight as Christophe returned to his place against the tree.

Toussaint regarded Christophe from under thick and drooping eyelids. "I will have comments on your statements. I had just mentioned that military guidance for our men was not the major problem. I would like to continue from that point, if I may. The almost insurmountable concern is the matter of secrecy. How will we tell our soldiers who go with us to the French that it is not a genuine surrender? How will we tell the brave men whom we expect still to fight against Leclerc that we have not betrayed them? It is not only a question of holding their respect and faith. It is much more. How do we trust so many people with the information that our surrender is insincere?"

Dessalines studied his boots and frowned deeply. At last he turned to Christophe. " 'Insincere' mean not so real?" At Christophe's nod he beamed. "Then I say the answer. No reason for telling men I take to French that we are 'insincere.' I tell them nothing except that now we are French soldiers. The ones I don't take to French I don't tell them nothing, too. I pick out twenty or thirty officers, and them I tell everything. And I tell them that if they talk too much I kill them. Good idea?" He looked from Toussaint to Christophe and back again to Toussaint.

"Actually, yes," Toussaint said, "with certain refinements added."

Christophe agreed that the plan Dessalines had offered would work well in the army of Dessalines. "But I shall have to tell all officers who surrender with me that we're acting out a deception. The men who are not taken over to the French will have as their commander Hercule Drouet. He's an intelligent young captain and very trustworthy."

Both Christophe and Dessalines waited then for Toussaint to say how he might handle the situation with L'Ouverture Elite, his guards and staff.

Toussaint uttered no further word on the subject. Instead, he shifted back to Christophe's earlier remarks. "Blacks are going to get killed, of course. When was it otherwise? Perhaps more

139

blacks will have to die than you think, Christophe. I will tell
you why. If only by the law of averages, the French must have
some victories. In the opposite case, they will begin to wonder
about Trojan horses. We must fight enthusiastically for the
French. If we are not willing to do that, then we might as well
let civilians capture us. The French will shoot us as traitors.
The civilians will hang us as outlaws. I don't want either fate.
Do you?"

There was a stillness on Mont Vautour, except for the distant
drumming. Tonight blacks had raided the environs of Le Cap
and had crept into Fort Liberté. They had set many fires, and
the French had suffered losses, but there had been losses for the
blacks as well. The blacks had expected to die and they had
died bravely. Died bravely, the drums repeated, as though this
were so cheerful a message that it must be heard by all.

"I guess I surrender," Dessalines said dispiritedly.

"When I give the order, not before," Toussaint snapped.
"There must be negotiations and assurances. I want you to ride
to the French as a respected general of the Haitian Army."

Dessalines grunted. "Respected general of Haitian Army
does not surrender."

"Oh yes he does, but always bearing in mind the words
thundered here on this mountain tonight. Don't ever forget what
you said about surrendering a hundred times and betraying them
a hundred times."

Dessalines brightened. "I remember that. It was good speech.
I mean it. I surrender a hundred times and I betray—"

Toussaint said, "There is one other thing, Christophe. This is
by no means as sure as the fever season, but I feel that it will
happen. We won't get our black peasants into the Army soon
enough to be of any help in our present plight, but we will get
them eventually. We will get them on the day that Bonaparte and
Leclerc make their first moves toward restoring slavery."

Christophe pulled a leaf from a flowering bush and tore at it
angrily. "I have told those dull-witted farmers that they'll be
slaves again, but they don't believe it. I believe it. The French
are the French. They're the most ferocious people in the world.

Have you read accounts of their behavior in the Revolution? I swear to you, General, nothing ever happened on this island more grisly than the things that occurred on the streets of Paris."

Toussaint shrugged. "I've known the French a long time. Their manners are exquisite and their literature sublime. These two great talents of theirs have enabled them to walk about disguised as human beings."

"But the mask has been thrown aside."

"No, Christophe. The French Revolution will become very romantic when interpreted by their novelists. You know, I find it fascinating that French cadets are taught to fight in gentlemanly fashion and to bring glory upon the banners of France. On the other hand, the English are told quite bluntly that the battlefield is not a drawing room. Why do you suppose that is?"

Christophe said, "Because it's not necessary to teach a Frenchman the art of cruelty. One trains him to be a soldier or a planter and sends him forth. As soon as he encounters helpless people, his own nature instructs him in the ways to deal with them. How do you think Haitians learned which methods inflict the greatest degree of agony?"

"Why, Christophe, I always thought it was the other way around. Didn't my people teach the French to be unspeakably savage?"

"You can't claim the honor. In Paris the citizens dragged the headless body of a princess through the streets. Then they dismembered it, and her heart was cooked and eaten in a tavern by, one supposes, a patriotic gourmet. Other groups of merrymakers sliced up the neighbors with whom they had political differences. Then they dipped their bread in the blood and ate it."

"Please, Christophe, I am a squeamish man."

Their laughter was dark and mirthless, and they sat then in a silence that was interrupted by snores from Dessalines.

"What a pity. We were on his favorite subject and he missed it all." Christophe stood up. "I shall answer the letter and think well of arrangements, then report further. Perhaps two nights hence." He yawned. "I am as tired as he is, but I do not sleep that easily."

"Where are you going from here?"

"Do you worry for me? Or is that a casual question?"

"I worry for you, so the question cannot be casual."

The candle flame was a bright reflection in Christophe's eyes when he spoke. "All this month from dawn to dark French soldiers, mulatto artisans and stupid blacks have been building a house for Madame Leclerc. It stands where my house stood. At night I go to look at it. I look until my eyes can no longer bear the sight. Then I go away and try to sleep."

Toussaint shook his head. "God help us, we are always asked to give everything we have and then to find something else to give."

"Yes, I know. It is the way of the world." Christophe poked his boot at the sprawled body of Dessalines. "Wake up, friend. It's time to let the General retire."

"I will see you then very soon, Christophe?"

Christophe was back the following night, this time without Dessalines. "General, the messengers have been active, the correspondence heavy." He handed Toussaint a sheet of paper. "This is what I wrote in answer to the letter. I copied it so you could see."

Toussaint reached for the candle and read: "I am ready to retract. But my doubts must be removed, my suspicions cleared up. There is no sacrifice that I will not make for the peace and happiness of my fellow citizens if I am but convinced that they will all be free. Produce the proofs necessary. You speak to me of fortune. I no longer have any. Honor is the only possession now left me."

"Exactly right," Toussaint approved. He was surprised to see that Christophe was extending to him another letter.

"This came to me an hour after I had sent my answer. I have been turned over to a more important correspondent. Would you have believed that Leclerc could be such an absolute ninny?"

Toussaint stared. "You mean Leclerc himself wrote to you?"

"Yes. Read what he said."

It was only a few lines of hurried scribble: "Think of the

essential service you could render the Republic of France by furnishing the means to secure the person of General Toussaint."

"Did you answer this one?"

"Immediately, and with great dignity. Here's that copy."

Toussaint scanned the few cold words Christophe had written: "Toussaint is my commander and my friend. Is friendship, Citizen General, compatible with such baseness?"

"Ah, how well you are handling this, Christophe. Such self-respect, such loftiness." Toussaint sat back against the tree. He clasped his hands behind his head and rested one small, booted foot upon the other. He was quiet, lost in thought. The woman who had been Bréda's cook moved, mouselike, just beyond range of the candlelight. Suddenly Toussaint spoke. "What shall we fear, Christophe? We are all so clever, so devious. Can you trust me? Can I trust you? Does it alarm you, does it alarm me that someone can find you at will and place a letter in your hand?"

Christophe gazed down the mountain into the blackness of the uneasy night. "General, I trust you because there is nothing else in life to trust. I am educated beyond voodoo, and too wicked for the church that was once mine. You are all there is in which I can place my faith. You and Haiti are one, and Haiti is all I live for. Haiti is all there is."

Toussaint did not reply. The woman poured coffee and disappeared around the sharp turn of the mountain.

Christophe said, "The messenger who brought the letters was a mulatto, and, indeed, he placed the first one in my hand. Leclerc's suggestion that I betray you was given by a white lieutenant to a black peasant woman, who passed it to her grandson, who climbed a mountain and found a black soldier, who brought it to the captain of my guard. Leclerc's second communication—"

"There was a second communication from Leclerc?"

"Yes, General. You would have had it immediately, but a matter of faith intervened." Christophe set down the heavy earthenware cup and handed Toussaint an envelope.

The letter began with an apology for having supposed that Christophe would deal deceitfully with his commander and friend. It went on to state that Leclerc, representing France and the First Consul, guaranteed freedom to all blacks, complete pardon to surrendering rebels and an appropriate rank in the French Army for Christophe.

"Well, Christophe, when do you plan on becoming a Frenchman?"

Christophe turned and looked directly into Toussaint's eyes. "You tell me, sir. Please give me the hour and the date. Already I am shivering with the cold of being removed from your command. Since the day that you made me a sergeant I have lived with the assurance that you would always tell me what to do. Sir, give me the day of my surrender. Give me my orders."

Toussaint rose to his feet. "General Christophe, at noon, on Wednesday, April fourteenth of this year, you and two thousand men of your army are ordered to place yourselves under the command of General Charles Victor Emmanuel Leclerc, in the city that is popularly known as Le Cap. It is my hope and my belief that you will always do your duty, and that those who shaped your illustrious military career will forever take pride in you."

Christophe saluted, performed a precise military right turn and marched into the dark night.

Toussaint made his way along the ledge to where the mountain curved abruptly. The woman who had been Bréda's cook was waiting in a cave, where candles burned and blankets carpeted the floor. She searched his face, and, because she was not a fool, she knew that sometimes a man needed a woman and that sometimes he did not. More important, she knew which time was which.

She said, "I want more coffee. I go make more."

She left the cave and gave Toussaint the solitude in which he could unashamedly lie upon the ground and weep. He did not ask himself if he wept for Haiti, for Christophe or because life was always hard and vengeful. He cried until at last sleep came, and in the morning he went out on the ledge to gaze with bitter eyes upon the new day.

Standing there, high in the mountains, with Haiti spread

before him, he could see the silver flash of a waterfall, the coastline, the blue sea and the brightly colored sin of flowers, fruit and trees that had not been created for the meek but for the powerful, not for the simple heart but for the cunning mind. He thought that God might well be all that the priests said of Him but certainly He lacked reason. Why was not this island the property of the only people who had ever loved it, the only people who had ever labored in its fields and forests?

God, we did our best. You leave us now with only evil ambitions. We deal in deception, though with Your help we could have dealt in honor. We pray for fever to remove our enemies, though always we died uncomplainingly in battle. And it was they, God, not we, who forced the fighting. Had they been kind, had they been fair, with what motive would we have become monsters? In the beginning, what did we desire beyond that which is given freely to a willing horse? God, You know how to make a world, but You don't know how to manage it. Have I discovered a truth? Can it be that You are without common sense and without feeling?

After a time he went to sit beneath a tree, and the woman brought his breakfast. She looked at him shrewdly and thought that it was a morning when he needed conversation. And she knew that his attention could not be held with talk of the tethered goat or by amusing recollections from the past.

"How will it go for Christophe?" she asked. "Tell me a little about that. Have they set a trap for him?"

"No," Toussaint said. "He will be welcomed as though he is their hero, not ours."

"Describe to me what will happen."

And Toussaint told her that there would be a French guard of honor for Christophe, and music and much cheering, but he did not guess to what lengths France would go to make clear that a forgiving heart was her national characteristic.

Christophe was astonished at the splendor of his reception. As he rode down out of the mountains with his two thousand men behind him, he became aware that a crowd had gathered in front of the city gates. Women. Mulatto women displaying their enticing smiles, tearing the flowers from their hair and flinging them to the ground to be walked upon by Christophe's men. Black women singing sweet songs to Christophe's army because it did not matter who owned Haiti now that Christophe would stop hounding their men to go fight the French. The women threw garlands over his horse's head as the gates were swung open, but he did not give the women a glance. His eyes were fixed upon lines of French soldiers in parade uniform who stood at attention to receive him and his warriors. In the harbor every ship of the French fleet fired a salute as he entered the city that he had burned only two months earlier. It had been cleared of rubble, but the rebuilding had not yet started. Taverns operated beneath awnings, booths had been set up by industrious merchants, and under large umbrellas luxury merchandise was on display. In the scorched arcades, honey-colored girls struck poses and flashed their eyes at Christophe's soldiers. Everywhere there were decorations and flowers. Unorganized groups of dancers and jugglers blossomed colorfully in hastily created costumes, and on a platform a mighty chorus, when signaled, burst into the rousing *"Marseillaise."*

General Rochambeau, on a frisky horse, rode toward Christophe. He spoke warm, friendly words and presented other officers. A French lieutenant-colonel exchanged a greeting with Christophe saying that he had been assigned the happy task of conducting the two thousand new French soldiers to their barracks.

Rochambeau, his staff and an honor guard now led Christophe and four of his officers out of the city and toward the hills. Christophe turned and saluted the noisy civilians who screamed his name in rapture. You are a bunch of bastards, he thought as he smiled at them, pig swill, scum. Rotten mulattoes and cowardly blacks, too comfortable to fight for Toussaint, the man who got you your freedom. In case you don't remember slavery, you crawling lice, the French will refresh your memory. If you had rallied as I asked, I would not now be on my way to clasp the hand of General Leclerc and to bow respectfully to the sister of Bonaparte. To my beautiful hilltop, for which I worked and fought, you have made me go, carrying pleasant words with which I will endear myself to the garbage of France and Corsica.

They were there awaiting him on the terrace. The golden-haired people. The General and his lady. Christophe was embraced by Leclerc and sweetly received by Madame. He was presented to the soft and pretty women who made up Madame's little court. He met the officers who had been selected because they had charm and good singing voices and looked like poets. The more important plantation owners had been invited to the reception. Christophe drank with them and toasted Bonaparte and the Leclercs and the new understanding that was building between France and the beautiful island of Saint-Domingue.

Christophe wondered that a bolt of lightning did not strike the flower-decked galleries, where hatred and hypocrisy ran masked. I, too, had galleries, he thought, right here, and I stood upon them looking with love at the city I had built. My house, my city I destroyed because you were not good enough to touch them. Now here I stand saying how splendid it is to feel the warmth of your friendship. And you, plantation owners, what are you doing here? Don't you remember the slave rebellion? Don't you remember that blacks are animals? Stop smiling at me. Have the guts to tell Leclerc that you don't drink with savages.

Later there was entertainment in the drawing room. One of Madame's ladies struck plaintive chords on a harp while a lieutenant sang tenderly of his home in Normandy. General Leclerc maneuvered Christophe into an elegantly furnished room that was his office.

Part of my dining salon was here, Christophe thought. Where you are sitting, Leclerc, there was a satinwood chest in which the table silver was kept.

Leclerc was smiling. "Sorry I had to subject you to all the stuffy formalities, but, of course, people wanted to meet you."

"It was not unpleasant. I have had a delightful day, thanks to you, General."

Leclerc reached for a bottle of brandy and poured generously.

"Let us drink together and have a few private words before my wife decides there should be dancing or supper or God knows what. I will have a fine, long letter to write to the First Consul tonight, and I would like to anticipate a few of his questions. Forgive me, perhaps you have a few of your own you would like to ask before I begin."

"Only one," Christophe said. "What is my rank?"

Leclerc waved his hand in a gesture implying that Christophe was the one to be satisfied. "I had thought of you as a major-general in the French Army."

Christophe nodded. "Thank you. Now to your questions."

Leclerc looked at him earnestly. "Try to understand that I am speaking for the First Consul, who has a lively curiosity. He is interested in everybody and everything. Please believe that otherwise I would let time shape my judgments. But immediately the First Consul would ask: Why did you come over to us?"

"There are many reasons, General. I want peace and justice for the island, and I know that will be gained only through suppressing the rebellion. Too, I am not a man who can live his life as an outlaw. Such an existence would be repugnant to me. Your proclamation reducing me to the status of a criminal was very disturbing. To be honest with you, I could live a hundred years in the mountains and never be captured. But that is no life for a self-respecting military man. What I want, what I have always wanted, is to be an excellent army officer. I would like to give my talents to a major nation that can use me in different parts of the world and perhaps in many capacities. It is my hope to benefit the army I serve, and to improve my own position by enlarging the scope of my activities."

Leclerc considered the reply. "Then you'd have been as pleased to join the English."

"No. I am English by birth. I know the English well and have no love for them."

"Have you love for France?"

"Sir, you are a reasonable man and I am sure you will see the sense of my answer. I respect France above all other nations.

148

That must be enough for now. How could I love France when I was not born or reared there, and have not even seen it?"

"Properly said. Do you love Saint-Domingue?"

"I like it well, but it is not a place to which an ambitious officer gives his love. Let me lay my dreams on your desk, sir. I want as great an army career as God will let me have. After that I would enjoy retirement in a small, quiet town where intellectual standards are somewhat above those of Saint-Domingue. Would a French town accept a retired black officer?"

"With open arms, General Christophe. The Republic looks with favor upon all men who serve France well. Please drink again. This is a day to celebrate." Smilingly, he refilled Christophe's glass. "You will forgive my not keeping pace with you, I hope. I have had some slight indisposition in my cheek, and the doctor has instructed me to cultivate abstemiousness."

"Oh, I am sorry. Are there other questions?"

"Yes." Leclerc hesitated. Then, "Were you present at the skirmish in the valley?"

"I was present."

"Then you must solve a puzzle for my military mind. How was it that the slope was a safe escape for us, that none of your troops attacked as we withdrew?"

Christophe looked at him with disappointment. "So you did not understand. I had hoped that you would. Had we been English you would have recognized the tribute we paid to your incomparable bravery. Men who approached the valley down the face of the mountain and afterward fought so courageously deserved to have their gallant lives spared."

Leclerc studied the reply, his eyes narrowed. "It is not true, then, that a mulatto detachment deserted you?"

"A mulatto detachment?" Christophe stared at Leclerc. "I don't know what you mean. Toussaint does not have mulattoes in his army."

"I was told that on the slope we were to have been slashed to pieces by mulattoes, who, after determining where their best interests lay, refused to fight for Toussaint."

Christophe sipped his brandy and said, "Sir, perhaps the fact that you were told that story explains why Toussaint does not have mulattoes in his army. With few exceptions, they are unstable, imaginative people who have a greater grasp of dramatic values than of reality."

Leclerc was silent and thoughtful. Christophe let his eyes rove about the room. The window frames had not been correctly fitted. The delicate green finger of a fern stabbed experimentally through the space where the bottom of a pane did not meet the woodwork. The house, he had noted earlier, lacked the stamp of superior skills. Madame Leclerc, no doubt, had badgered her builders into proceeding too rapidly. The brandy bottle had been set beside Christophe's glass, and he had been urged to please himself. He poured lavishly and waited.

"General Christophe, why was the slope revealed to us as a means of escape?"

"It was not intentionally revealed to you. There was an urgent message from Toussaint. In that army, messengers are accompanied by two guards. They had been instructed to use another entrance into the valley but, at the time, that entrance was blocked by—what shall I say?—the unexpected delivery to us of some cannons. The message from Toussaint has no importance to you or to me today, but it was considered by the messenger so urgent that he used the slope to enter the valley."

"And to leave," Leclerc said.

"Yes. He had an answer to carry and could not permit the cannons to delay his departure."

"What sort of person is Toussaint?"

"He is what he appears to be. He is a good man, an excellent general and a splendid administrator. As a man, he has made and kept friends. As a general, he has produced victories. As an administrator, he wrote the Constitution, which worked very well."

"I have read the Constitution. It is a simple document for a simple set of circumstances."

"Oh, do you think so, General? I suppose I was rather overwhelmed by it because I would not have known how to create law courts or stabilize currency or levy property taxes or sponsor schools, or even where I wanted roads built. Toussaint knew how to do all those things, as, obviously, you would know. But I was greatly impressed."

"Apparently, you still are. You admire Toussaint greatly, don't you?"

"Of course I do. I think you and the First Consul, too, feel a certain respect for his abilities." Christophe paused to drink. "Sir, I think so highly of Toussaint that my hope is that he will offer his services to you. He is aging but his mind is still knife sharp, and I would wager he has ideas that would be of use to you."

Leclerc's expression was a mixture of amusement and irritation. "General Christophe, may I remind you that Toussaint is an outlaw? There is no question of his offering his services. He will be brought here by force before much time has passed."

"I was an outlaw also, General, and you have accepted me with great kindness and many honors."

"True, but you had not— Well, I'll mention that later. Is there any chance, do you think, of Toussaint's coming to us willingly?"

Christophe moved his hands in a gesture of uncertainty. "I tried to convince him that he belongs here, but older people are very reluctant to change their ways."

"Will he not have to make adjustments whether he will or no? I have sources of information from which I gather that Toussaint is rather short of manpower."

Christophe sat in silence, his face frozen in enigmatic blankness. Then, "I have just fought a battle with myself. I am, and always shall be, Toussaint's friend, but I am now a general in the French Army. Everything of military worth that is known to me must be your property also. So I am obligated to say that Toussaint has no dearth of men. I beg of you to remember this in any battle plan. The blacks, like other soldiers, are not invincible, but there is no scarcity of them."

"My informant was in a position to know the truth."

Christophe smiled. "Do you think I am not, sir?"

Leclerc laughed pleasantly. "What an easy man you are to

talk to, General Christophe. I already feel that we have fought side by side in other times, in other places."

"Yes, remarkable. I have that feeling about you."

They looked at each other with surprise and friendliness. Amazing, their eyes said, we were enemies and we are of different color, and, yet, already there is a bond of trust and affection between us.

"You know, dear Christophe, I was going to say before that it might be difficult for me to accept Toussaint. He usurped the position of governor-general."

"There was no one else who could have kept the island in order. Had he said he was merely a caretaker, who would have obeyed him?"

"He did not behave like a caretaker. Since I never have had a word of explanation or regret from him, I must conclude that he gave the order to fire upon French ships."

"General, there is no denying that a state of rebellion exists. However, it so happens that Toussaint had left the city and was not even aware of the presence of the French fleet."

Leclerc glanced toward the brandy bottle. The level of its contents had fallen considerably. "Your glass is empty, General."

"So it is. Thank you." Christophe poured again.

"But Toussaint returned and gave the order to burn Le Cap," Leclerc said, casually.

Christophe looked surprised. "Assuming that you save your correspondence, you have a letter signed by me declaring that I would make ashes of Le Cap if you came ashore. Toussaint was still absent when I wrote that. I thought the burning of the city was what he would want. As it turned out, I was quite wrong. He was furious with me."

"I have your word for that?"

"My word, a thousand times over."

Leclerc reserved judgment. "Tell me about Dessalines. Is it true that he is demented?"

"Demented? Certainly not. I will say that he has little interest in matters that do not concern fighting. Sometimes he doesn't bother to listen to what is being said around him. Were it not for his military abilities, which are extraordinary, he would be the typical, illiterate ex-slave. As it is, he is not typical of anything. He is a genius at warfare."

"He has a reputation for being exceedingly cruel."

Christophe said, "I think you'll find no one to dispute that charge. However, in the army from which I come there is more talk of his phenomenal flair for winning battles."

"Do his men like him?"

"Let us say they're proud of having a general who is feared."

Leclerc nodded. "That trait in soldiers is not confined to Saint-Domingue. Of course, Dessalines is an outlaw, too. However— Do you think the French Army would appeal to him? Is he ambitious?"

"Oh, indeed. He is ambitious to keep fighting until the day he dies."

"Astonishing," Leclerc said. "I think this is one of the most interesting conversations I have ever had in my life. As you can guess, Madame Leclerc will be vexed that I have kept you so long from our other guests."

They moved toward the drawing room, and Christophe saw wonderment upon Leclerc's face. Yes, Christophe thought, I can walk with a firm step and talk with a clear mind. What were you looking for? A drunken, babbling black? How you people believe in your myths. And how innocent you really are. White general, poor little man, I'll bet you even trust Corsicans.

Madame Leclerc smiled charmingly at Christophe. "I thought the General would never bring you back to us. I have something surprising to tell you. Would you believe it was only today I learned that you used to have a house on this site?"

"Really? Only today?"

"Yes. Madame Chevert told me. Isn't it strange that no one had mentioned it? She knows everything about the island. Her family has been here, except for occasional travels, since the beginning of the old century. She is very sympathetic about the loss of your house. Hers, too, caught fire."

"Carelessness, no doubt."

"I didn't ask her. I was fascinated by something else she said. She said you had solid gold place plates on your dinner table."

"I'm amazed that Madame Chevert said that."

"It isn't true?"

"Oh, yes, it's true. I'm amazed that she knew, because she never saw them."

Madame Leclerc pouted cutely. "I never did, either. I wish I had. I must say that Haitian generals evidently get paid a lot more money than French generals do."

"Oh, no, madame. The French are richly rewarded, but, you see, when I had gold place plates I was also a planter fortunate enough to reap the harvests of three great properties."

"But you must have earned much money before you could have such properties."

"I earned no money at all, madame. The army in which I served in those days was unique. It paid nobody anything, but it gave every man a chance to become an officer; then it gave every officer a chance to become a planter."

She frowned in perplexity. "I don't think I quite understand that."

"Few people do, madame."

"Then I shan't bother with it. I'm building another house, you know. On Tortuga. That will be our country place. This I regard as a city residence. And I would dearly love to have the theater in Le Cap restored. I am going to ask my brother to send some important actors as soon as there's a place for them to perform." She pointed to Jérôme, who stood eating pastry and talking to two pretty girls. "When I say 'my brother,' I don't mean that silly navy boy with the whipped cream all over his chin. I don't even speak to him. When I say 'my brother,' I mean the First Consul, my brother Napoleon."

"I had guessed that, madame."

"One day you will meet my brother."

"I cannot imagine that such an honor would ever be mine."

"I promise. I will take you right to him and present you."

"You are very kind."

She giggled and asked suddenly, "Did you ever wonder, General, what sort of impression you made on someone else?"

"Are you about to tell me? Shall I run, madame?"

"No, don't run. You'll like this." Upon her arm there hung a satin reticule beaded in pearls. She plunged her hand into it, and, laying aside her tiny gold mirror, her rouge pot, her ivory fan and a half-dozen unrecognizable articles, she came at last to a single sheet of stationery. "When I knew I would meet you I asked my husband to find out what you were like. I shan't tell you the name of the person who wrote this, but he knows you— or once knew you."

The handwriting was unfamiliar to Christophe, but perhaps the comments of someone summoned to Leclerc's office had been jotted down by a clerk: "General Christophe is perhaps thirty-six years old and of unimpeachable morals. He is handsome in physique, chilly in manner, urbane in conversation. There is much pride in his character. Although long accustomed to speak English, he speaks our language with ease and has distinguished manners."

"I do not find you chilly in manner," Madame Leclerc said when he looked up from reading.

"I'm glad of that, madame."

This time her smile was more than charming. It was absolutely bewitching. He was quite certain that she used this one preceding a request.

"General Christophe, do you suppose that you could order a number of your men to rebuild the theater?"

He smiled back at her. "Madame, I would be so happy to serve you and I know my men would be delighted. The trouble is that I've never been a French general before. I don't yet know what my orders are. My men and I may not remain very long in the neighborhood of Le Cap."

Nor did they. Within a week Christophe received his orders and two days later marched back into the mountains with his men. Six white officers had been assigned to his command. They were, as Christophe well knew, observers of his behavior. The order was: capture Dessalines.

Christophe did not know where Dessalines was and hoped he would not encounter him. Yet if his mission failed, why should Leclerc believe he had undertaken it in good faith? Dessalines would fight as hard against him as against Rochambeau, because Dessalines knew no other way to fight. The nagging worry was that one or more of the white officers might be killed or taken prisoner. Mother of God, suppose all six of them were slaughtered? What Frenchman would mark that down to coincidence? Christophe thought of Toussaint and the woman living in the cave on the high ledge of Mont Vautour. Unlikely that Dessalines was with them. Toussaint could not bear his company for long.

I should consider myself lucky that I was not ordered to bring in Toussaint. That I would not have, could not have, done. I could not seize Toussaint. Dessalines is different. He will treat me as a French general, and I will treat him as my captive if I am fortunate enough to survive a meeting with him. But why did it have to come to this? How long will Toussaint wait before sending Dessalines to surrender? How long will Toussaint wait before surrendering himself?

When they paused to rest, Christophe looked searchingly at the white officers. Their faces were impassive, and they evidenced no fraternal feeling for black officers. But who could blame them? They had been ordered to capture the most awesome soldier on the island, and even the men with whom they marched might be their enemies.

Christophe jeered at himself. It must be a beautiful day for you, eh, Christophe? Only on a beautiful day would you have nothing to do but feel sorry for Frenchmen.

He sat down on a fallen tree and spoke in friendly fashion to his officers, both black and white, who were grouped about. Some had removed their boots and were massaging their feet. Others had cut into juicy melons or had thrown themselves full length on the ground beneath a shade tree.

"I don't know where Dessalines is, but that is not to say that I am as bewildered as if I had never been acquainted with him or had never lived in the mountains. For instance, I know where he will not be. He will not be in a valley. He greatly mistrusts the constrictions of valleys. Anyone who thinks I may be wrong about that is free to question at random among the troops. It is well known that Dessalines is—yes, I will say he is afraid of valleys."

One of the Frenchmen cleared his throat and leaned toward Christophe.

"Yes?"

"How many men might he have with him?"

"He has eleven thousand under his command, but more than half have been detached and are fighting at Le Pouce under General Toiras. We may find Dessalines in hiding, with only his guard for personal protection. On the other hand, men who did not follow me into the French Army may have joined him. If so, and they are bivouacked together, we have a desperate situation."

A young captain with large pink ears asked, "Would it not be an impossible situation, General?"

"That depends on several factors. I don't like to think of any battle being impossible to win, especially when I know so well the fighting technique of the man I face."

"Will he be well armed, General?"

"Yes. The Haitians have been buying for many years from the British, the Americans and the Spanish. But, then, we are well armed, too. At La Croix the horse-drawn cannons will meet us, because it is in the vicinity of La Croix that I expect to make the first search. We will spend tomorrow morning questioning the farmers and other inhabitants of the district while scouts are taking a close look for signs that an encampment exists or has existed. If you are wondering why I have chosen La Croix, it is because there are some ruins close by. Dessalines once mentioned them to me. If I could remember of what we were speaking at the time, it would be helpful. At any rate, there are old walls, decaying structures and such. There is also the probability that Dessalines does not recall ever having spoken of this to me."

The French officers retained their impassive expressions, and after a time the march began again. At various points on the long, tilting path that led toward La Croix there was a pause while a dozen or so men from the ranks slipped silently into the trees to seek traces of Dessalines. Occasionally, black women carrying baskets of eggs upon their heads would approach. Always at sight of the soldiers they would turn, prepared for flight. Twice the troops encountered black farmers weighed down with bags of fruit to be sold beneath the awnings of Le Cap. The men, too, were startled by the soldiers.

With cold hatred in his heart Christophe watched as fear died and small, respectful smiles appeared on the faces of the villagers. You lousy, dirty worms, you've recognized the French uniforms, haven't you? You know you aren't going to be asked to do anything for your country, so all is well. Go sell your fruit and eggs. Soon you'll be getting your Goddamned skin whipped off you because you stole a banana.

Both men and women were questioned politely. There were no answers of value. The farm people were allowed to go their way. There was one man whose actions were beyond immediate understanding. With a sack of chicken feathers clutched in his arms he stood trembling and staring. Then he pointed to Christophe and asked in a voice that was out of control, "Is that General Christophe?"

A black lieutenant answered that it was, and ordered the man to come closer for questioning. But the man had flown. With the speed of a hurricane, he had run back in the direction from which he had come.

Christophe laughed. "He has confused me with Dessalines. They do, you know. His exploits have been widely proclaimed. Then my name is mentioned, and soon it is I, in the imagination of these isolated people, who become an ogre."

Now, what was the meaning of that unknown man's performance? It was a performance, of course. But for what purpose? Did Dessalines send him to find out if I was leading the hunting party? It's clear that an identification was wanted, so he is a man who has never seen me before. Dessalines would have sent a soldier who knows me by sight, and there would have been no need for such nonsense. With a bucket of milk in his hand and a few rags tied around his middle, any soldier could have passed for a farmer and then slipped back to Dessalines with the word that he had seen me. So he came from someone who has no soldier to send, someone who has to know if I am here. Who would that be? Something is going to happen. But what?

Christophe kept a watchful gaze on the road ahead and did not allow his hand to stray far from his pistol. He now began to question the villagers himself. They had seen no one, knew nothing of soldiers, had never heard of Dessalines. He let them go and resumed the march with his attention riveted on all around him.

When the troops came upon a sagging, arched gatehouse to the right of the road, Christophe called another period of rest. Beyond the gatehouse was a vast clearing that had once been carefully tended lawns and gardens. Now hibiscus, bougain-villaea and jasmine ran wild from the arch all the way up the incline to where the house had stood. Christophe remembered that house. It had belonged to a mulatto family with a reputation for murdering sickly slave children and all workers who met with accidents that reduced their usefulness. Toussaint had claimed the land for the Haitian government, but no one had cared to rent it.

Christophe walked under the arch and a considerable distance along what had been the private road. There was nothing to indicate that Dessalines or any other soldier had been there. The blackened columns of the house lay rotting in mounds of ashes. There were no hiding places. He beckoned for the officers to come, bringing the soldiers with them. There was room for everyone to spread out and rest beneath the cedar trees. The men passed on to the grounds and arranged themselves in friendly clusters. When every man was off the road, an improbable figure brought up the rear.

A woman in a snowy cap and apron, riding upon a mule, followed the last straggler under the arch. She looked about her, unabashed by the presence of so many men. Her eyes fell

159

on Christophe and she moved toward him, not bothering to lower her voice when she spoke. He saw that she was the woman who had been Bréda's cook.

"General, lady say to tell you she cannot meet you tonight."

A soldier laughed coarsely, then hurried to lose himself within his group. The French officers smiled. The black officers grinned broadly. Christophe let everyone see his embarrassment.

The woman waved an envelope at him. "Lady tell me she say to you everything in here. She say, 'Tell General I explain in letter why I can't meet him tonight.' "

Christophe looked like a man who wished the earth would swallow him. He tried to cover his face with his hand, then made an attempt at regaining his dignity. "Very well, woman. I have the letter. Now go."

She said, "I can't go so fast. I have to tell you something else. Lady feel very sad about not meeting you tonight. I don't think she tell you that in letter."

Christophe threw up his hands and glanced sheepishly at his officers. He plucked a camellia from its shrub and handed it to the woman. "Give this to the lady and tell her—" He broke into a boyish laugh and addressed the white officer at his elbow. "I guess there's no use trying to hide anything now." He turned back to the woman who had been Bréda's cook. "Tell her I love her."

The woman sighed sentimentally, induced the mule to reverse his position and rode away.

Christophe went through the regular routine of ordering guards. He saw that they were posted at the gatehouse and all side paths leading to the abandoned property. Then he picked up the letter, which he had tossed aside with his military cap.

"Since this is all the romance I'm going to get," he said to those within hearing, "I'd better enjoy it." He carried the letter to a moss-covered rock and sat down to read it. He knew the white officers were watching. He fixed a moon-struck expression upon his face and remembered to smile dreamily from time to time as he read. The lover separated from his lady was not an easy role to play because the first page that spread itself beneath his eyes was a copy of a letter from Napoleon Bonaparte to Toussaint:

I am pleased to recognize and proclaim the great services that you have rendered to the French people. If their flag floats over Saint-Domingue, it is to you and the worthy blacks that they owe this. In the circumstances in which you found yourself, surrounded by enemies while the mother country could neither help you nor send you provisions, you were justified in proposing a constitution that gave you extraordinary powers. But today, when circumstances are so happily altered, you will be the first to render homage to the sovereignty of the nation which counts you among its most illustrious citizens. What is there for you to desire? The freedom of the blacks? You know that in all countries where we have been, we have accorded it to those who did not have it. Respect? Honors? Fortune? After the services that you have rendered, and that you still will render, and with the special feelings that we have toward you, you need have no doubt about the respect, the fortune and the honors that await you.

Christophe widened his smile and beamed and smirked as he turned to the second page, a copy of a few lines dashed off by Leclerc to accompany the First Consul's letter:

Have no worries about your personal fortune; it will be safeguarded for you since it has been only too well earned by your own efforts. As for your rank, you may rely upon the promises of the First Consul, whose letter you have in your hands. From his solemn declaration contained in his attached proclamation and in the letter, you can see that you need have no further anxiety about the liberty of your fellow citizens.

There was also a note to Christophe from Toussaint:

This was delivered to me by way of a very twisted grapevine. I would have great fear that a man can know no privacy even on a mountaintop, but I had already made my decision. With the messenger went word of my surrender. Tomorrow I ride down into the city and become a Frenchman in good standing. Dessalines will be with me and he will also offer his heart and soul to France. L'Ouverture Elite will surrender en masse, also my guard. I will be an honored man indeed with that showing of loyalty. Dessalines will give three thousand men to Leclerc, but perhaps it would have been enough to have a tame Dessalines at one's disposal. While on the subject—he is not and has not been at the ruins behind La Croix. However, go there. Take your white officers to see the evidence that your intuition was good and your intentions noble. I am only guessing that you are headed there. Still, how could you approach La Croix without having the ruins in mind? Come visit me when you can. I shall be in retirement at my plantation. I have been asked to give advice to the French on crops and municipal matters. I do not think I have the strength to exert myself. I'm old and ill. I send my affection and prayers.

Christophe raised his eyes and caught a white captain gazing steadily at him. Again, he allowed embarrassment to show. He laughed self-consciously and placed the letters inside his shirt next to his heart. He sat thinking, his face set in an expression of lovelorn yearning.

They do things well, the French. That letter of Bonaparte's must have been written months ago so Leclerc would have it handy when the moment was right. I wonder how many of Bonaparte's letters Leclerc has stacked away awaiting the proper occasion. What effect will Toussaint's surrender have on other officers? Will Belair give up? Will Geffrard? Has Toussaint let them know we are playing a terrifying game? Or is he depending on their determination to fight the French savagely until the day they die?

He thought of the letter he had placed next to his heart. It belonged there. Toussaint had delivered his life to him to do with what he would. In his own handwriting, he had proved beyond possibility of doubt that he trusted completely the man who had been his favorite general.

There was no reason for haste now. No danger. Dessalines had become a Frenchman and would not attack. Within an hour there would be need to make camp for the night. What would he find that would suit the purpose better than the grounds of the old mulatto house? He passed the order that they would remain until dawn.

At dusk, new guards were posted and a few fires lighted. The French officers boiled coffee and ate bread that had been baked in the kitchens of the fleet. The blacks cooked rice, though most of them were satisfied with fruit. Christophe felt a strange contentment. The voices and activities of the men, the leap of the campfires, the sudden outburst of song produced a paradoxical feeling of peace known only to those who had dedicated their lives to war. The French officers could not understand the words that the black men sang, and their unfriendliness was somewhat conquered by their curiosity.

"*Zeb* is grass. *Touton* is uncle. *Ti moun* is a little child. *Ti* always means little. It is a very simple song. Oh, yes, *bourik* is a donkey. Now that you are really able to speak French, you sing with us."

And as black officers teasingly taught whites how French had sounded to slaves and how it had been spiced with Africanisms, Christophe took Toussaint's letter, along with Bonaparte's and Leclerc's, and gave them to the campfire. Then he let drowsiness overwhelm him, and he fell asleep thinking of La Croix, where Dessalines would not be.

Before sunrise he was on the upward path again, this time with only three French officers and two blacks. It was too early for the arrival of the cannons at the designated crossroads. "So," Christophe had said, "let us go very silently, just we six, and have a look around. If Dessalines is there, as well he might be, we will return in force and with the cannons."

163

At a certain point they left the path and took to the leafy darkness of a small forest. They exchanged no words and crept toward the ancient ruins that were generally judged to be Arawak or Carib. Dessalines was not there, but the French officers were satisfied that he had been. They saw garbage and human excrement, and, on the far side of the powdery ghost of a rampart, there were two dead mulattoes not yet decomposed.

"Sir," one of the white officers asked, "what would you suppose was the crime of those men?"

"They were probably spies," Christophe replied.

The crime of the two men had been obvious to him. They had happened to be mulattoes at the unfortunate point when somebody's urge to create a realistic setting for a typical Dessalines encampment demanded the presence of corpses.

"We must search farther," he said. "He cannot be very far from here."

He saw that the white officers were impressed that he had led them directly to where Dessalines so recently had been.

"We will go to the crossroads now," Christophe said, "and take possession of our cannons. We will be in battle shortly."

He ordered the black officers to go prepare the troops for immediate conflict and to lead them forward in all readiness.

"The people around here must have known that Dessalines was encamped in the ruins. If I see any of those villagers who lied to us yesterday, it will go hard with them."

At the crossroads there were no horse-drawn cannons, no cannons at all. Christophe uttered an oath. "We need those cannons. From the evidence, there were a couple of thousand men with Dessalines."

There was one young French lieutenant waiting at the appointed place. He saluted and handed Christophe an envelope. Christophe read:

General Christophe,
I am pleased to notify you that the generals Toussaint and Dessalines have surrendered and that your orders have thereby been canceled. You are now instructed to

return with the men under your command to the garrison
at Le Cap.

C. V. E. Leclerc
Commanding General

The astonishment on Christophe's face was held long enough
to guarantee that all three French officers had noted it. Then he
passed them the message.

"A pity," he said. "No battle, and we are at such distance
that we must also miss the festivities at Le Cap."

The reception of Toussaint and Dessalines was only super-
ficially festive. The women were at the gates, smiling and tossing
flowers at the soldiers. There were salutes from the fleet and the
forts as Toussaint, in dress uniform, entered the city, accompanied by his staff and an escort of four hundred cavalrymen.

The white residents felt that Leclerc should have greeted
Toussaint and his men with a hail of grapeshot. The arrogance
of his bringing that beautifully drilled cavalcade to wheel and
prance and display themselves as though they were heroes!
Why, the whole thing had resembled a conqueror coming to
claim a vanquished city, rather than the arrival of an outlaw
who had been too generously forgiven.

Toussaint, because of ill health, was spared a social encounter
with General and Madame Leclerc. He conversed privately with
the General and retired from public view.

The white spectators in the city had been annoyed by Toussaint's cavalcade. They were sickened an hour later, when Dessalines was welcomed at the gates. Toussaint had held himself
aloof from the crowds, replying with neither a smile nor a nod
to the cheers and songs. But Dessalines was absolutely hostile.
He glared at the people and let his huge, repulsive body slump
as he rode along, as though no respect was owed to anyone. The
whites turned their backs at the ridiculous sight of blacks falling
to their knees as he passed and calling out words of praise and
even adoration.

"Why," the whites asked each other, "did they not put on that disgusting show for Toussaint? He was the one who caused all the trouble about getting them their freedom."

"Ah," others answered, "Toussaint is an educated man. He is not one of them. Don't you know that the vast majority of blacks can only admire another black if he is as stupid and as slovenly as themselves? Once they realize that their idol has soared above them, they would willingly tear him apart. Dessalines is a proper favorite for them."

"Yes, but what is Leclerc going to do with him?"

Leclerc made him commander of the district of Saint-Marc and gave strict orders to his staff that under no circumstances were arrangements ever to be made which would bring Dessalines into his presence.

Toussaint went, at the first possible moment, to his plantation house near Les Gonaïves. Christophe visited him there and was saddened by the appearance of his old commander. Toussaint was shrunken in face and form. He sat idly in a tamarind grove and picked without interest at the food brought to him by the woman who had been Bréda's cook.

"How does it all go?" he asked Christophe.

Christophe laughed. "For us French? Unsatisfactorily. We have taken, three times over, the whole of the South, all the plain of the North and most of the western coast, but it never really belongs to us. Somehow those awful blacks get back in and burn everything we've fought for. They keep opposing us, so it's not easy being French. We don't get a peaceful day. The black soldiers are so ignorant they can't count. They don't know they're badly outnumbered."

Toussaint looked with affection at Christophe. "Very kind of you to translate tragedy into comedy. Our best men die while other blacks tend their farms and will not fight for Haiti. Well, I will speak more of that in a moment. Let me show you a letter that awaited me upon my arrival here." He searched through a pile of papers that lay in a basket beside him. "Ah, this is it."

Leclerc had written: "I had hoped to have your brilliant mind as a fount to which I could turn at any hour, any day, but you desire repose and you deserve it. After a man has sustained for several years the burden of the government of Saint-Domingue, I apprehend he needs repose! I leave you to enjoy your estates as you please. I rely so much on the attachment you bear to the colony of Saint-Domingue as to believe you will employ the moments of leisure you may have in your retreat in communicating to me your sentiments respecting the means proper to be taken to cause commerce and agriculture to flourish once more."

Christophe said, "General, I hope you won't bother to think of 'means proper to be taken.' You look so tired."

"Tired? Yes, I am tired, but I am also very ill. I have great pain, no appetite and each day it is more difficult to make the journey from my bed to the pleasant place where I now sit. Christophe, do not try to find words for an answer. I have not spoken of my illness in order to receive sympathy or advice. I but wanted you to know that everything in the world has a use. My illness has a use. Were I young and strong, I would be less inclined to die inconspicuously for Haiti. Perhaps I would not have the courage to go to my death without the excitement of a battlefield or the joy of taking many Frenchmen with me."

Christophe waited.

"If I were in fine health and still had years before me, I would not let myself be kidnapped."

"Kidnapped!"

"Long years ago, a commissioner named Sonthonax invited me aboard a French ship for dinner. It was on the day I first met Rochambeau, and we three were to dine aboard. I refused. Though Sonthonax was a good man, I was not sure what orders he had been given. I took great care of myself, for the years ahead were promising. Now I am ready to go aboard a French ship. There are only months left to me, and they will be filled with pain. Christophe, the French are not smart enough to leave me here in retirement, not shrewd enough to let the blacks entirely forget me. They have not the cunning to permit me to die unnoticed. Because the French demand trophies, they will insist upon making a martyr of me. Leclerc is under orders to send me to France."

"I remember that shameful note he wrote asking that I betray you."

"Bonaparte will censure him severely if I am not delivered up to French justice. He accepted my surrender because there would have been further delay before he could seize me as an outlaw. Leclerc's gracious gestures and his kind letter are intended to lull my suspicions. It will all be easier for him if I obligingly walk into the trap he will set."

Christophe jumped to his feet and began to pace. "What can I do?"

"Please do nothing. You will rob me of my one last attempt to strike a blow for Haiti." He looked at Christophe, and for a second there was the old glitter in his eyes, the old communicable excitement. "You must take the news of my disappearance with no show of rage or sorrow. Then you must be sure that every black who has failed to rally to the Haitian Army knows the truth. Spread the news in every way that will not reflect back on you. The woman who was Bréda's cook will be of boundless help. Tell the blacks something they will understand. Tell them that slavery could not be restored as long as I lived and breathed among them. Tell them that is why the French took me, and that farms must be forgotten while blacks go fight again for freedom. If they do not fight, then slavery is the next step. Tell them."

Toussaint brought himself tremblingly to a standing position. "General Christophe, these are your orders. Do not interfere with my deportation, but, when I am gone, inspire the blacks to fight for Haiti. Tell the drums to beat until there is no black man in any valley or on any mountain peak who does not know that slavery is on its way back. Tell them! Tell the drums! Go tell the blacks to fight!"

Christophe saluted and, without looking again at Toussaint, marched away. He sat straight and disciplined until he had ridden a mile beyond the plantation. Then he took his horse off the road and, under the black sablier trees, he hid himself to weep.

Toussaint, left alone, wondered how long he would sit await-

ing the next French move. It seemed he had spent a hundred
years watching the French, outthinking the French, hating the
French.

This time he had only a week to wait. A soldier brought a
letter from General Brunet, Commander of the French troops at
Les Gonaïves:

> We have some matters to discuss, my dear General,
> which it is not possible to deal with by letter but which
> an hour's conference would settle. I am overwhelmed
> with work and petty problems and so, if you have re-
> covered from your indisposition, will you come here?
> And let it be tomorrow, since one should never be laggard
> in good works. You may not find in my simple quarters
> all the refinements that I would wish to provide for your
> reception, but you will find the candor of a man of honor
> who desires nothing but the prosperity of the colony and
> your personal happiness.

Toussaint had a manservant help him into the uniform he had
worn for state occasions as governor-general of Haiti. It no
longer fit his emaciated body, but it suited well his state of mind.
He was ceremoniously escorted to General Brunet's headquarters
by French postilions, and ushered immediately into the inner
office.

General Brunet greeted Toussaint warmly and invited him
to sit in the most comfortable chair. "I will tell the boy to bring
some refreshments," the General said, and darted away.

Now there was only a moment to wait. Toussaint turned to the
window, to fix forever in his mind a last, loving view of Haiti.

A major with a squad of grenadiers came crowding noisily
into the room. They advanced on the small, sick man, who regarded them disdainfully.

"What? You enormous fellows are going to tie my hands?
Really? Why, even the Corsican would laugh at you."

Toussaint was carried out of the house and bundled into the
back of a farm wagon. As though there were a chance of escape

or rescue, the grenadiers held him down and stuffed his mouth with a handkerchief.

At the harbor of Les Gonaïves he was placed aboard the frigate *Créole* and lay, sick and injured, his hands still tied, the handkerchief gagging him. As the *Créole* moved away from Haiti, Toussaint fainted, and when he recovered consciousness he was aware that his hands had been untied. He felt no gratitude. Someone of the French crew had had to untie his hands in order to steal his splendid uniform.

Ah, yes, you must have your trophies, he thought. But now, Frenchmen, it is June. We held on all winter, and you did not beat us down. It will grow harder, Frenchmen. It is June.

In the marshes and all along the bay and even in Le Cap and Port-au-Prince, where swamps had been clumsily filled in with bits of wood or pebbles, mosquitoes were breeding. They were breeding fast. And it was June.

. . . .

Never before had the President invited the entire Cabinet to dinner without inviting the wives.

"Explain to your dear Dolly that this will not be an entertaining evening. Please ask her to be so kind as to let the other Cabinet wives know that she understands and is not offended."

"I will suggest that she invite the ladies to dine with her," the Secretary of State said.

"I would appreciate that. Perhaps I overestimate the importance of having the good will of the ladies, but I cannot separate myself from the notion that in every Cabinet member there is a mystical reflection of his wife's attitude toward me."

"Dolly is very fond of you."

The President nodded in pleased agreement. "And from which of my advisers do I get the most assistance? Truthfully, James, I need not have had this dinner. We could have met in the morning in my office, but that would have excited the interest of too many people. Besides, I have discovered that primitive forces influence the most civilized gentlemen. Good food and the intimacy of a comfortable room with a roaring fire en-able us to talk more easily. Somehow the atmosphere produces the feeling that our ideas are received by a band of friendly listeners."

Madison thought about that. "Yes, perhaps you are right, but do not be disappointed if the Postmaster General has no ideas at all to contribute."

"God knows there is no point in his being present, but courtesy forbade me omitting only him. He has been alarmed by my invitation. I think he expects me to announce that the end of the world is upon us. He cannot imagine that anything less would bring him into discussion with you and the Secretary of War."

Madison's eyes were suddenly veiled, and the President did not fail to notice.

"What is Granger alarmed about, James? Possibly you can shed some light on the meaning of a remark he made to me. He mumbled something conventional about placing himself at my service—" Jefferson hesitated. "I think he then said that he would take the opportunity to express his admiration for the silent dignity of my stand. He was quite pale and uncomfortable. Since he doesn't know what I have to tell him and the others, what was he talking about?"

Madison had not yet adjusted himself to Jefferson's phenomenal talent for completely putting from his mind all matters with which he did not intend to deal. There was a certain majesty in the ability to forget totally those things that would move lesser men to rage or explanation or denial. It was a remarkable, almost godlike quality, but it sometimes made difficulties for the Secretary of State.

"What's troubling Granger?"

"The newspapers."

The President was amused. "They're attacking so harmless an institution as the Post Office?"

Madison remembered an editorial of comedic spirit that had appeared in a friendly magazine, suggesting that Mr. Jefferson, the great diplomat, and his Secretary of State must conduct some extremely recondite conversations, even when weather was the topic. "Remember," the editorialist wrote, "that a diplomat feels

himself obligated to make no statement that is not open to a
dozen interpretations and which does not lend itself to immediate retraction. How on earth does one suppose Mr. Madison
speaks to President Jefferson?"

Very bluntly when there is no choice, Madison thought. Aloud
he said, "No, Mr. President, the newspapers are, at the moment,
too busy to attack the Post Office. They are attacking you.
Granger, who has an almost excessive regard for propriety,
winces at the idea that our meeting tonight will deal with their
detestable charges."

A look of sorrow appeared on the President's face. "Oh,
James, forgive me. I hadn't meant to embarrass you. I really
dragged that from you, didn't I? And I should have realized
Granger's position. Being a Northerner, he must have to defend
me against his friends every day. Do the newspapers keep that
shopworn story ready to print—with only a change of name—
every time a Southerner becomes prominent?"

"Mr. President, surely you have recognized that this filth was
not printed simply for the profit that lies in catering to infantile
minds. Certain newspapers are manipulated by your political
adversaries. For verisimilitude the name of a particular slave
woman has been in various items."

Jefferson rubbed his forehead just above the right eyebrow,
where the pain always struck. "My poor daughters. My poor
little girls. What hell I have put them through by my talent for
making enemies."

"Is there a woman at Monticello named Sally?" Madison
asked.

"Of course. That was a simple thing for the mudslingers to
find out. As a child, this good young woman was rather a pet of
my wife's. I send her to help my daughters when there is a new
baby on the way or an illness in the family. Both Martha and
Maria love her. I suppose the special privileges extended to
Sally lend credence to the allegations."

Madison said, "Most of the opposing press mentions her name.
Your name, too, is clearly stated, though one newspaper coyly

refers to you as 'the man whom it delighteth the public to honor.' "

"I think I recognize that too clever journalistic gentleman." Jefferson raised his aching head, and sudden pride shone in his eyes. "My God, Madison, what a country we have! Is there any other that would invite scoundrels to see if it can be torn apart? Do me a favor. Tell Granger that tonight we are going to speak of something which the President regards as important. And to pay him back for his concern, give him a small hint of what the subject will be."

Madison walked away wondering if there was anything small about the subject to which the President referred. Even a hint could assume enormous proportions in the time it took to travel from his mouth to Gideon Granger's ear. The subject was not a healthy matter for speculation.

I could quiet Granger's nerves by saying this is an international question, Madison thought. But what is gained by having him carry his curiosity to Levi Lincoln or Robert Smith? No, I will say nothing to anyone.

On second thought, it occurred to him that the President's lightly spoken request that Granger be given some idea of the upcoming disclosures might have substance and should not be ignored. Perhaps it was of consequence that his very words be repeated to Granger. Madison, somewhat surprised at his own momentary obtuseness, revised his thinking. Of course. How better could Jefferson indicate his lack of concern at the slander directed against him than by sending the message "Tonight we are going to speak of something which the President regards as important"?

Madison thought of a phrase Dolly employed when impressed by subtle use of color in a room or a particular presentation of a play. "It has style," she would declare solemnly. Yes, he said to himself, Tom Jefferson has style, and the person who is asked to carry his words to another ought remember that.

He found Granger behind the frosted-glass door of his office, consulting with two assistants on the feasibility of a plan for postriders to deliver mail to places as remote as Natchez.

173

"It could be done," Granger was saying as Madison entered. "In a matter of fifteen days a letter could reach an anxious relative in Natchez. It would be another contribution of a compassionate government to the comfort of its people. Fifteen days! Think of it!"

Madison thought of something quite different in connection with the Post Office. He thought it would be splendid of Granger to devise a means by which citizens could be assured of privacy in their correspondence. Tampering with letters had reached the stage where people having news of a confidential nature to disclose went to the public coach station and selected an honest-appearing passenger to whom the letter could be entrusted.

Granger dismissed his assistants and peered apprehensively at Madison. "Does the President still intend to have the dinner this evening?"

"Yes, indeed."

The Postmaster General shook his head worriedly. "I just don't know what Connecticut is saying about all this. Much as I enjoy my work and continue to take pride in the President's having called me to Washington, I wish I were back home now. After all, I was one of the few strong voices in Connecticut for Mr. Jefferson. If I were there now, I could control opinion somewhat. I could say the whole thing is a pack of lies. I could—"

Madison said, "Please don't excite yourself, Mr. Granger. If Connecticut chooses to believe that Virginia gentlemen are swine, I don't know who can convince them otherwise."

"Well, there is something that can be done. Connecticut and the whole country can be stopped from reading such dirt in the public press. The minute we are asked for our opinions tonight I'm going to give mine. I'm going to say that I think the newspapers should be suppressed."

"That's going to be your statement?"

"It certainly is. I believe all newspapers that have printed things about our President's having black concubines should be closed down."

Madison laughed. "Mr. Granger, you are really going to say that the minute you're asked for your opinion?"

"You can wager on it."

"Even if we're not talking about black concubines? Suppose the President has called us together for the purpose of discussing the trading posts of the Chickasaw Indians. When he asks your opinion, are you going to say you want the newspapers suppressed?"

Granger's jaw dropped and he stared at the Secretary of State. Was it possible that with his personal reputation at stake Mr. Jefferson was going to discourse on matters quite apart from that?

"Mr. Granger, tonight we are going to speak of something which the President regards as important."

"You mean he doesn't regard as impor—" Granger stopped right there. A dark-red flush spread over his face, and he was silent for a long moment. "I guess I didn't realize how big a man he is, Mr. Madison. I've admired him for not making an issue of all this foul talk, but I thought he must be troubled by it."

"Would you like to know what troubles him? Any suggestion that newspapers be suppressed. Some people have low taste and undeveloped minds and will read trash, but they are still citizens and have rights. This is a free country. For that the blood was spilled, Mr. Granger."

"I know. But I hate to see those vindictive scribblers— I mean to say, the President is so defenseless. An ordinary man could sue, but with the high honor of the presidency it is very unlikely that—"

"Very unlikely." Madison turned toward the frosted-glass door. "He's not going to talk about Chickasaw Indians, either. An international matter will be under consideration."

Granger seemed uninterested in international matters. "I feel such a fool. I made some silly remark to the President about—"

"Console yourself. He never listens to us unless we're saying sensible things."

The dinner was as perfect as one had come to expect at the table of the President. The emphasis was on hardier fare, more full-bodied wines. It was a masculine dinner. Madison offered a

175

silent tribute to superlative teamwork. The orders Jefferson had given Meriwether Lewis had been passed to the steward and on to the chef and butler without misunderstanding or blunder. Women could do as well, of course, but they wearied themselves and others with a plethora of directions and dark premonitions of failure. Men simply stated what they wanted and were astounded if anything went contrary to their expectations.

At table, conversation was cheerful and animated. No one showed signs of concern or indicated that something of significance had brought them together. Madison noted that the President's headache had left him slightly wan. What were those peculiar attacks that caused severe pain above one eyebrow and momentarily distorted vision? What a pity the President had experienced this suffering today, when there were so many pressures on him. However, he was laughing heartily at Gallatin's imitation of himself speaking Pennsylvania Dutch to his farm workers—with an Italian accent.

And after a time the President led his Cabinet into a small sitting room, where the fire was warm and welcoming. He asked them to seat themselves, but he remained standing. As they looked up at him he seemed awesome, with his grave face, his height of six feet three inches and his straight, square shoulders. His black velvet jacket was worn and out of fashion, but it had a certain classic correctness, and it could be guessed that it had been tailored in Paris. Perhaps for Mr. Jefferson's presentation to the unfortunate King.

"Gentlemen, we are here to speak of a weighty problem. I will appreciate your questions and comments or what may be called mere conversation. As you know, several months ago Bonaparte sent an enormous fleet to the Caribbean. The stated purpose was to bring back into the French family the delinquent island of San Domingo or Saint-Domingue. I did not believe then, nor do I believe now, that Bonaparte has in mind only the recapture of that colony. I am convinced that his aim is to establish French domination on this continent. At the time that the Spanish Intendant in New Orleans canceled our right of deposit in his city, Mr. Madison and I were aware that we were facing a somber situation. The most immediate manifestation was the threat of a great commercial loss to our citizens who depend on the use of the river to transport their agriculture. I say it was the most immediate, which is true, but it was certainly not the most worrisome."

The President paused while the butler arranged a decanter of port, glasses, tobacco and sweets on the low table within reach of all. Secretary of War Dearborn began to nibble nervously on a peppermint from the candy dish.

"The Marquis de Casa Yrujo was summoned and he assured us that his king could not have ordered or approved the Intendant's action. Shortly thereafter we had a letter from the Spanish Governor explaining that the right of deposit had been restored to us, and there were expressions of gratitude and apology. To the superficial view, there was no further need for concern. I doubt many people were disturbed that the French fleet, in all its might, was and is still in the Caribbean."

The Secretary of the Navy fidgeted in his chair.

"A question so soon, Mr. Smith?"

"Yes, if you don't mind, sir." Smith's handsome face was puckered in puzzlement. "The word is that Bonaparte has sent his best generals and the greatest soldiers France ever had. Now, sir, they're just fighting a tatterdemalion mob of ex-slaves. So what's delaying the French in taking back their San Domingo colony?"

"That's a reasonable question, Mr. Smith. For the moment, I shall answer it this way: Blacks have limited intelligence and no organizational ability. They are not a match for French generals and French troops. Please accept a somewhat cryptic reply— The French are purposely delaying their victory. There is a time element which they must observe. I will clarify that later."

Gallatin poured port for himself, and served Lincoln. No one else desired wine just then.

Jefferson continued. "Naturally, Mr. Madison and I were pleased that the right of deposit had been returned to our people but we felt no complacency. A warning had been sounded. To be utterly truthful with you, I would not have been surprised had

Bonaparte's forces landed at New Orleans within a month or two of going ashore at Saint-Domingue. I assume that it is clear to you that the French need the island for a supply base and permanent garrison. They will not make a move toward New Orleans until they have secured Saint-Domingue."

"Well, bless the blacks for delaying them," Dearborn said.

A vein in Jefferson's temple throbbed, but he spoke gently to Dearborn. "As I stated, I do not believe the blacks are delaying them. If I should be wrong, Mr. Dearborn, and blacks are indeed capable of souring the cream of Bonaparte's army, then we have another problem, which has no place in this discussion." He was briefly silent. Then, "Yes, I will say a word on that tangential subject. My own state has just suffered a small slave rebellion. It has been successfully quelled, and I have asked Governor Monroe to order as few executions as possible."

The three native Northerners in the room fastened their eyes upon the roaring fire. Smith, of Maryland, munched a chocolate. Albert Gallatin, of Switzerland and Pennsylvania, considered slavery quite unrelated to the Treasury Department. He made it a point not to think about slavery.

"I am constrained to mention, gentlemen, that a free nation of ex-slaves functioning in triumph would create a dangerous climate for the people of the South. Perhaps even for all Americans. Who is to say that the little country would not choose to earn its living in the manner of Tripoli and Algiers? They might become pirates and smugglers."

"As I recall, sir, we do business with those potential pirates and smugglers. We buy their wares and they buy ours. Mr. President, don't we even sell them a full range of weaponry?"

Jefferson nodded. "Yes, we do, Mr. Smith, and that's lamentable. They are rebels and barbarians, but other countries will trade with them even if we do not. Our people would like the government to be uncomplicated and easily understood, though nothing else of importance in life meets those specifications. Governments will forever keep disappointing the governed. Why? Because a government is nothing without high ideals. It is also nothing unless its economy is sound. On one level, a nation is a noble and beautiful goddess to whom we build monuments and sing joyful praises. On another level, a nation is an unfortunate wretch who has to sell whatever he can so that his people will prosper. Pray for the day, Mr. Smith, when there will be citizens so clear-eyed that they will see that the monuments and songs come in one package and the nation's prosperity in another. Pray, too, that they see how necessary it is that we have both packages." The President dropped into a chair. "Enough of that. Where was I?"

"You were saying that you would not have been surprised had Bonaparte's forces landed at New Orleans within a month or two of going ashore at Saint-Domingue," Madison said.

The President, with his elbow resting on the arm of his chair, turned back toward the others. "I spoke to Mr. Madison at that time about the possibility of buying New Orleans."

Dearborn and Smith gasped. Granger gave his head a short, sharp shake, as though he suspected there was water in his ears. Lincoln put on his legal expression. And Gallatin asked, "What figure had you in mind to offer Spain?"

"I did not give a thought to cost, Mr. Gallatin. My intention was to confer with Mr. Dearborn and Mr. Smith and to hear their opinions before talking to you about money. You see, I wanted New Orleans in order that we could place fighting men there to keep Bonaparte off this continent."

There was a hush in the room so deep that Granger could hear the pounding of his heart. He looked at the other Cabinet members. Lincoln, like Gallatin, saw everything in the cool, steady light of his department's applicability to the problem at hand. Madison had known the situation for some time. Dearborn and Smith were leaning forward avidly, waiting for the President's next words.

"I still want New Orleans," Jefferson said quietly. "We need the river and cannot tolerate having its free use obstructed capriciously."

Lincoln spoke the logical question. "Why did you think Spain would let Bonaparte use New Orleans as a steppingstone?"

"There was the matter of the right of deposit having been

interrupted. Would it not seem strange to you that Spain could have let that happen even accidentally? We were forced to invoke the services of their minister here and our minister there before we had satisfaction."

"But obviously the whole thing was a mistake and—" The Attorney General let his words trail limply into silence. It had occurred to him that this dinner, this meeting, had not been planned merely to review the past. Hastily, on short notice, the President had called them all together. Certainly, his purpose was not to announce that months earlier the Intendant at New Orleans had been guilty of an error. Lincoln was remembering that Mr. Jefferson had begun his remarks by stating that they were gathered to speak of a weighty problem. He saw that the others in the room were remembering, too.

Dearborn said, "I don't believe Spain would let Bonaparte land at New Orleans."

Smith shook his head. "No, Spain wouldn't. But if, for some reason, such permission were granted, we could put up a fight impressive enough to make—"

The President raised a quieting hand. "Mr. Smith, there is now no question of fighting. The situation is far too serious for war."

Dearborn was startled. "Too serious for war, Mr. President?"

"Yes. Perhaps with tremendous effort we could have repulsed the French landing at New Orleans. If their action was contrary to the wish of Spain, we might even have had some small help from King Charles." The President pressed his hand to his eyebrow and said, "That is the way we saw it. But that is not the way it is. In possessing himself of New Orleans, Bonaparte will be proceeding with law and reason on his side. The fact is, gentlemen, Spain has effected a Gargantuan alteration on our world. In exchange for Tuscany she has given Louisiana to Bonaparte."

It was a measure of the stunned incredulity of the Cabinet members that when Smith asked, "You mean, Bonaparte now owns New Orleans?," every eye but Madison's clung to the President, every ear but Madison's moved closer to him, waiting to be assured that what he had called a fact was not a fact at all.

Jefferson did not speak at once, and Madison knew that he was irked by the empty question. The President would hold his answer until he could reply without sharpness in his tone.

"Mr. Smith," Jefferson said, finally, "Bonaparte owns Louisiana, which indeed includes New Orleans. Louisiana itself is a gigantic land mass which extends from the Gulf of Mexico to Canada. New Orleans is important to us and we must try to annex it. That is our duty, but never lose sight of the danger the United States faces from now on. With Bonaparte in control of a portion of the continent that is larger than our country, there will be little hope of harmony. I do not believe he will let us live."

Lincoln watched the firelight play on the rich color of his wine. "I suppose every last loose end has been tied up between France and Spain on this business."

"Virtually," the President said. "My information is that they're at a stage comparable to one man's having made an offer on a house and the other man's having agreed to sell. After the handclasp there are always a few arguable details—a demand here, a refusal there, but no one expects the transaction to be nullified. The eager buyer feels quite safe in hiring an architect to do some remodeling." Jefferson went on after accepting a glass of wine from Madison, who was pouring. "My personal suspicion is that the particular eager buyer we have in mind overstepped himself somewhat. I think he was responsible for the revoking of our right of deposit in New Orleans. I don't suppose we will ever have positive evidence, but I believe he persuaded someone to bend to his will. He took the gamble that King Charles of Spain does not inconvenience himself to listen to every complaint. Bonaparte must have been disappointed when reminded that, though he may have his architectural plans drawn, he cannot build a fence until the deed to the property is in his name."

Granger took a pinch of snuff and asked, "Why would Bonaparte bother about trying to revoke the right of deposit? He can do it easily enough when he's in full power in New Orleans."

"It was a way of finding out what we would do and how King

Charles would react, and perhaps even a probing investigation into which man or men in New Orleans could be subverted. Mind you, Mr. Granger, this is a very private meeting convoked for the purpose of expressing ideas that could not properly be said in any other company. For all I actually know, the Intendant at New Orleans made an honest mistake or carried through some old ruling without consulting his government."

Again, Smith had a question. "Why would Spain trade Louisiana for Tuscany, Mr. President?"

"If you meet a highwayman who offers you a penny for your boots, accept his offer quickly. He might decide to keep the penny, give you a bloody head and run off with your boots whether you will or no. Spain can't defend Louisiana, Mr. Smith. She grows weak with age. A great pity."

"England would help Spain if there was a question of Bonaparte's trying to take Louisiana by force. England doesn't want France in the New World. She doesn't want France close to Canada, or in the Caribbean, either." Dearborn's gaze wandered from the President to Madison. "Is there a channel through which you could inquire if England would support Spain against Bonaparte's robbing her of Louisiana? If England, in the difficult language of diplomats, would say something that you could interpret as an affirmative, could we not then imply to England that we would join her in beating off Bonaparte? Could we not then tell Spain that she need not trade Louisiana for Tuscany?" It was clear that Dearborn was delighted with himself. Never before had he had an opportunity to point out to the Secretary of State just how things ought to be done. "And in payment for our efforts in keeping that huge land mass safe for Spain, all we'd ask is that she give us New Orleans."

James Madison did not enjoy squelching a well-meaning man, so he looked away from Dearborn as he answered. "Do you think Spain would still have New Orleans to give away after England had decided what her payment should be? Besides, once we have invited England in, who is going to invite her out?

182

If she decided she'd like to have New Orleans herself, I don't see how our position would be vastly improved."

Dearborn was busily working out a reply when the President spoke. "Yes, well, all that is in the realm of fancy. Spain has been a good, comfortable neighbor to us, but we have not earned equal praise from her. She will be glad to exchange Louisiana for Tuscany. She is not only afraid of France, gentlemen; she is also afraid of us."

Granger found that almost impossible to believe. "Afraid of us, Mr. President?"

"Yes. Spain today is largely financed by the mineral wealth of Central and South America. We were colonies that freed ourselves. Spain lives in horror that her colonies might learn how we did it. Also, she sees us as a rowdy young man with no respect and a great deal of avarice."

"That's unfair of her."

Jefferson smiled ruefully. "I wish you could read Spanish, Mr. Smith." He took a moment to reflect, then sighed almost inaudibly. "I can tell you with all honesty that as a nation we have not planned to plunder Spain's empire. Not as yet, we haven't, though a future administration may find the temptation too great to resist. We will grow stronger and Spain weaker, and the map makers will mark man's greed by new boundaries. For now, I repeat, as a nation we do not menace Spain's colonies, but as individuals—Mr. Smith, Spanish officials could tell you that the violations by United States citizens are numbered in the thousands. The frontiersmen boldly cross borders and, by sheer bullying and disregard of property rights, live where they choose and take what they want."

"Why not deprive them of citizenship for acting in a manner that shames us?" Lincoln suggested.

The President, a dark silhouette against the fire, spoke sadly. "They have no ties and no loyalties. They can be neither frightened nor punished. They are freebooters. Spain frets that they will grow in numbers and that their rapacity will constantly increase."

"Mr. Madison, can't you delicately intimate that we will look the other way while Spain hangs a few of them?"

Madison eyed Smith with disfavor. "Would you really like it if Spain felt free to hang any American who happened to get himself disliked while in Spanish territory?" When there was no answer, Madison added, "That could easily happen to you, Mr. Smith."

Jefferson said, "Spain has both the feebleness and the wisdom of age. She understands that we will damn the conduct of our citizens and weep for their depredations against her. But let one American citizen be roughly treated in a foreign country and we will tremble with rage and call the evildoer our most gallant son. It is the way we are and Spain knows it. She wants no trouble. Though she recognizes that we are not a strong country militarily, she is, on this continent, weaker than we. Moreover, she does not dare place guns in the hands of her colonies. They might turn them against her and keep the wealth of Central and South America for themselves. Spain is tired of being polite to us. She is tired of being afraid of us. She is transported with delight at accepting Tuscany and letting Bonaparte block our frontiersmen from striding across Louisiana into her great southwestern territory. Have done with trying to devise means by which Spain can keep Louisiana. She is happier than she has been for years. Not only has Bonaparte promised her lovely Tuscany, but he has also relieved her of bothersome neighbors, neighbors of whom she has had her fill."

"Tuscany is not lovely," Gallatin said. "At one time, long ago, it had cultural and commercial importance. It is now a worn-out, war-ravaged piece of earth."

"You have seen it, Mr. Gallatin?" Jefferson asked.

"I have seen it, sir."

The twist of the President's mouth was too grim to be called a smile. "Then you alone in this room can realize how anxious Spain is to leave our side. I am informed that when Bonaparte proposed the trade of Louisiana for Tuscany, King Charles was moved to tears of joy and spoke of the Tuscans as 'people mild, civilized and full of humanity.' You see, he does not care in what condition his new possession is. We have taught him to appreciate gentle people."

A question came to Gallatin's mind, but he did not ask it immediately. He sensed that Mr. Jefferson would welcome a small respite. To insure it, he walked about the room offering wine to the others, passing the candy dish, engaging in brief, meaningless remarks. The President sat very still, his eyes closed. Gallatin felt a glow of satisfaction that he had provided this moment of rest. By opening the second bottle of port on the tray, he gained another minute or so for the weary President. Then he went back to his chair and asked his question.

"Mr. President, won't the French be tempted by Spain's southwest territory? Has Spain no need to doubt France's desirability as a neighbor?"

Jefferson's eyelids rose, and he answered without hesitation. "No. The French Revolution did not result in setting men free to be as good or as bad as they wished. It resulted in Bonaparte, who controls his people. He will settle Louisiana with farm families and governable workingmen. There will be no marauders or rogues who wish to prey on their neighbors. I would like our citizens all to be as decent as the peasants Bonaparte will select to tame the wilderness. It is undeniable that we number among us many villains. It is the chance a nation takes in choosing freedom." The President let a silence fall before he spoke again. "Bonaparte will ask for volunteer emigrants; then he will have them painstakingly examined as to their qualifications for developing a valuable territory. As for French national ambitions, Spain knows she has no worries. Bonaparte's path is east from Louisiana, not west. We are in danger, not the Spanish colonies."

Dearborn gave Jefferson a long, hard look. "Mr. President, would you really not consider war?"

Jefferson got to his feet and began to walk up and down before the fireplace. Madison thought of the threadbare carpet in the President's office. It might have belonged to Adams, but Madison knew now that a threadbare carpet was as much a part of the presidency as the seal of office. Only constant replacement of carpets would preserve the comforting illusion that a man who headed a nation always sat calmly in his chair.

"Mr. Dearborn, I would consider war after I had considered every other thing in the world that is not dishonorable."

The Secretary of the Navy could not conceal his surprise. "Sir, may I ask why war did not seem so obnoxious to you when you first realized that Bonaparte's fleet was on this side of the ocean? You told us that it had been your wish to buy New Orleans for the purpose of mounting an action against Bonaparte there."

The President ceased pacing and faced Smith. "Yes, it was my wish to mount an action against Bonaparte. But remember, Mr. Smith, it was my intention that we be in legal possession of New Orleans when we stood and fought him. The simplicity has been removed from my plan. The situation is changed. Now when Bonaparte sends his fleet to New Orleans, he will have every right to do so. The city and its harbor will belong to him." Jefferson began to pace again. "The opinion of civilized nations would not be on our side if we fought to keep France off her own property, and it would ill become us to accuse Bonaparte of scheming to destroy us. We have no evidence that that is his purpose. Common sense is not evidence. He is but postponing his conquest of that small Caribbean island until all courtesies with Spain have been exchanged and all signatures properly witnessed."

"Mr. President, you believe that on the day he has the deed to Louisiana in his hand he'll order all rebels on San Domingo executed, that then he will set sail for Louisiana, arriving as the respectable new owner of a million square miles of this continent. Is that it?"

Before answering Dearborn, Jefferson again seated himself close to the fire. "I believe something like that."

The Secretary of War looked from one Cabinet member to the other. When his eyes reached Madison they waited.

Madison said, "New Orleans is the problem. The territory of Louisiana will have to be established, populated and made a viable entity before it is a danger to the United States. Another generation will have the woe of a strong Louisiana to contend with. There is no way we can protect the future. New Orleans and the present is our worry. The longer Bonaparte holds his fleet in San Domingo, the more time we have to develop our ideas on obtaining New Orleans." He looked at Jefferson. "Mr. President?"

It seemed that Jefferson's mind had wandered elsewhere. It would be slightly insulting, Smith thought, if the President were not closely following the remarks of Cabinet members. Perhaps he had not listened even to Madison.

Jefferson had listened. "I wish there was a way to safeguard the next generation but that is beyond our power. We can only hope to procure unhindered use of the New Orleans harbor for the agriculturists of today. War is unthinkable except as a desperation move, and we are not yet desperate. It seems to me that never before has there been so fine a parade ground on which diplomacy can display its worth."

"But why would France sell New Orleans?" Smith asked. "It's the only city in the whole territory, and it has a first-rate harbor. Why would Bonaparte even consider selling?"

Jefferson sat back in his chair and brought his gaze to meet Smith's. "Diplomats exist to prove that the obvious conclusion need not always be accepted. I will admit that on the surface there is no reason for Bonaparte to sell us New Orleans. We must furnish him with a reason."

Gallatin moved away from the fire and touched his handkerchief to his forehead. "Are you speaking of a large amount of money, Mr. President?"

"No. I am speaking of a large amount of diplomacy. We are not a rich country or a well-armed country, but, Mr. Gallatin, it is my belief that we have among us men who can think as deeply as any others, and can handle a delicate situation with grace and imagination."

"Well, yes, of course." Gallatin looked sharply at Madison. "Would you go in person to speak to Bonaparte?"

Madison made a quick reply. "No." He turned his eyes toward the President, again giving him the stage.

"Robert Livingston, our Minister to France, is a distinguished member of world society," Jefferson said. "His family is highly regarded and he is one of the great legal minds of the day. And no one has forgotten that Livingston was given the honor of administering the oath of office to President George Washington."

Strangely, it was Gideon Granger, the provincial Postmaster General, and Albert Gallatin, the suave former European, who caviled at the mention of Robert Livingston.

"Livingston's deaf," Granger objected.

"People are very courteous to Livingston. They pitch their voices to accommodate his infirmity."

Gallatin's protest was stated with diffidence. "Mr. President, I must remind you that Robert Livingston's French is not very good."

"Not very good? A mild criticism, Mr. Gallatin. Livingston cannot manage a complete sentence in French, but he is an eminent man and very wise. The First Consul's advisers cannot fail to respect the reasonableness of whatever he suggests."

"But how will they know, sir, what he is suggesting? Surely the conversations will be too confidential to permit of an interpreter."

"Livingston will probably not see Bonaparte or any of those ubiquitous brothers to whom he sometimes listens. Charles Talleyrand is foreign minister, and his English is as good as Livingston's French is bad. So there is no stumbling block in that quarter."

"Livingston's deaf," Granger said again.

This time the President chose to ignore Granger. "It is my conviction that intelligent, patient men, talking sensibly together, achieve the truly great victories. Peace is demonstrably man's solemn testimony to his superiority, since animals, lacking the gift of speech, are forced to settle differences by bloodshed and death. In the short time that is left to us before the French fleet sails into the harbor at New Orleans, let us hope that Robert Livingston and Charles Talleyrand may face each other and talk."

And now a protracted silence fell. No glances were exchanged.

No words were whispered. The President did not rest himself. He sat forward on his chair, his eyes narrowed, his mind no longer reaching out to touch other minds in that fire-lit room. Madison felt he knew the President's thoughts. Of what other thing could Thomas Jefferson think than the excitement of being Robert Livingston and testing his skill against Talleyrand of France? Madison even sensed the moment in which the President turned from his futile regrets. He saw Jefferson becoming aware once more of the Cabinet members, and he saw, too, that Jefferson had had enough of them for the evening.

"I wanted to acquaint you with the problem," Jefferson said, at last. "Perhaps what I really mean is that I wanted to be the first to acquaint you with the problem. There will soon be rumors and even newspaper articles. A matter of international concern is not long hidden from the press. Once the news is out in the open, we will discover that I am unprincipled, unpatriotic and, of course, unworthy to lead the nation. There are senators and congressmen who will not consider the merits of buying New Orleans but will study instead how well the idea lends itself to disparagement of me. There are leading citizens who will give not a thought to the well-being of the United States but only to the opportunity of returning their party to power. Their philosophy is 'Let us get the votes; then we will worry about the country.' " Jefferson rose from his chair and offered the parting smile of an amiable host. "And now I cannot think of any unselfish reason for detaining you further. Thank you for coming." He shook hands with each of the Cabinet members as they filed out of the room.

When he was alone, Thomas Jefferson went upstairs, and although he permitted his valet to put away the black velvet jacket and help him into his dressing gown, he did not think of retiring. He walked the floor and pictured France already in physical possession of Louisiana.

What turmoil could the French create without a shot being fired, without provable breach of international law? Jefferson did not have to waste much time on the question. He saw what France would see, or perhaps what France already saw. It would not be difficult for a handful of French *provocateurs,* armed with the innocent claim of love for mankind, to stir the Indians into a frenzy. The French need only preach "the earth is the Lord's, and the fulness thereof" to remind the Indians that they had less earth today than in the past. The French, casting pious eyes toward heaven and murmuring that no child of God is less deserving than another, would drive the Indians to burning and looting a settlement.

Nor would the French, with Saint-Domingue so fresh in their minds, forget the slaves in the Southern states. The French knew better than any other nation what horror blacks could wreak once they turned on their masters. Bonaparte would realize that France's reputation as a slaveholder might be well known to the blacks of the United States, so for inciting rebellion he would employ some free blacks and a great many venal Anglo-Saxons.

Those were a few of the things one could envision with little effort. He thought of Moreau de St. Méry and his bookshop and the continual stream of French arrivals to Philadelphia. Bonaparte had had time to prepare a long list of possible ways of generating chaos in the United States.

Jefferson walked to his desk and made a note to have Indians removed from all land bordering on Louisiana Territory. There was no point in making it easy for the French to establish a warm friendship with the tribes. Very little could be done to protect the South from aroused blacks. Though the French might have to pay conscienceless troublemakers to insure organized insurrection, Jefferson knew that there were many decent, sincere whites who regarded slavery as a wicked practice. Never would they encourage blacks to murder or to destroy property, but it all came to the same thing in the end. Since blacks could not understand the difference between freedom and license, the mildest word spoken against slavery was explosive. Of course, someday the blacks would all be free. Anyone who thought otherwise had no knowledge of the nature of change. Something would occur that would make it necessary or practical for Southern economy to advance without slaves. And what would the poor things do then? Who would take care of them when they were ill? But that would not be his concern. Perhaps his grand-children's. Not his.

Sometime after midnight he went to bed. He thought of Livingston, who was indeed deaf and whose French was extremely poor. All very well to say that Talleyrand's courtesy and fine English would erase both difficulties. All very well to say it. Only a fool would believe that a talent for foreign languages and sharp ears with which to pick up gossip were not among a diplomat's most valuable tools. But Livingston was brilliant and intuitive. Moreover, one must content oneself with Livingston. He was the United States Minister to France.

By the time the Seventh Congress convened, the world would know that Bonaparte owned Louisiana. Hamilton's friends, in and out of Congress, would recognize the dangerous situation as their last chance to discredit the present administration. If they did not sink Jefferson and his party now, they were lost. They were obliged to force a war, if possible, to make a mockery of Jefferson's peaceful negotiations. When the Treasury was drained by the terrible cost of conflict, and a humiliating peace had been pressed upon the United States, Hamilton would have had his way. He would have proved that in Thomas Jefferson the nation had made a sorry choice.

Jefferson tossed in his bed and tortured himself, guessing at the tone the antiadministration newspapers would take. As the sky grew pale and his head throbbed more violently, he knew he must somehow calm himself. Where was the wisdom in drinking the hemlock before it had been set before him? He was not without self-control and not without power or accomplishments. Even on this desk in his bedroom there must be at least a dozen letters and documents to prove that diplomacy was no feeble weapon. There was, for instance, a communication that had been sent by Lord Hawkesbury, British Foreign Secretary, to Rufus King, United States Minister to England. In his second paragraph, Hawkesbury had written one potent line—

Jefferson got out of bed, lighted a candle and went to the desk. He would hunt for that letter, and the reading of it would soothe him. But before he found it, he found another letter. It was from

France, and it had no connection whatsoever with Bonaparte or Talleyrand, nor did it bear any relationship at all to the dark, menacing cloud that hung above Louisiana. The manner in which Thomas Jefferson had been addressed revealed that the sender had his own views on ranking a man's achievements. And though Jefferson smiled, as when he had first seen the envelope, it placed matters in proper perspective for him. He sat in the light of the trembling candle flame and read again:

> To His Excellency Thomas Jefferson
> President of the American Philosophical Society
> Member of the Institut National de France
> President of the United States

He told himself that he was worthy of none of those honors if he was going to sit here looking for Hawkesbury's letter, or lie in his bed dreading the opening session of Congress. He extinguished the candle, went back to his pillow and, remembering with amusement the envelope from France, fell asleep.

But he woke up thinking of Congress, and neither the morning, now bright blue and sunny, nor another look at the envelope from the Institut National de France cheered him. He would spend the day writing his second annual message to Congress.

The message was numbingly commonplace and dull. Alexander Hamilton's newspaper called it a lullaby. Jefferson thought that a fair critique. He had aimed at boring Congress. There was, he felt, a reassuring ring to a presidential message that provided the wish to yawn. He had spoken of the happy continuation of prosperity, freedom and peace. Since it was now known to all, he acknowledged that Louisiana had been returned to French ownership and that this could change the aspect of foreign relations in some unspecified decade. He took note of the fact that the country was still slightly bothered by warlike actions from Tripoli. Morocco had grown belligerent during the year but seemed to have withdrawn now from any alliance with Tripoli.

Nobody was interested in Tripoli or Morocco. Congress

wanted to hear about New Orleans. Jefferson did not speak of New Orleans. He left it to his enemies to open the subject. Let them spark the flame.

They began almost at once by labeling him a coward and a betrayer of American rights and dignity. Senator William Plumer, of New Hampshire, was quoted as saying that the President was weak and timid, and that the United States should take immediate possession of that city which Jefferson was too scared even to mention.

In the House of Representatives the President's friends brought a quick finale to what could have been a season of lengthy wrangling. Roger Griswold, of Connecticut, offered a resolution calling upon Jefferson to lay before Congress all papers and information respecting the retrocession of Louisiana. James Varnum, of Massachusetts, took the floor and began to speak. Jefferson's enemies could not have been said to listen to Varnum. Instead, they listened for the moment in which to cry out their displeasure.

"Adhering to that humane and wise policy which ought to characterize a free people and relying with perfect confidence on the vigilance and wisdom of the Executive—"

Griswold's clique shouted him down. Vigilance! Wisdom! In such men as Jefferson and Madison! Varnum's expression of confidence must be expunged from the record!

John Randolph, of Virginia, with the strange quality that was known as his cold passion, confounded the President's detractors. Before the intemperate name-callers and chronic hairsplitters could get themselves properly organized, the assembly had defeated Griswold's resolution.

There was no John Randolph in the Senate. Everybody in Washington knew that a spectacular drama would be played there. Party hatreds had become torrid. There had been insults at dinner tables, slurring remarks and rumors of duels. Ladies canceled their tea parties and card games to be present when Senator James Ross, of Pennsylvania, rose to destroy Jefferson.

"I know negotiations are in progress concerning New Orleans," he said, "and I would not think of speaking a single sentence to thwart or embarrass the President. But I do believe it is necessary for us to give profound thought to something that happened not so long ago concerning this very same New Orleans." Ross paused then, to be sure he had full attention from the people who had crowded into the hall. Kentuckians, Tennesseeans and Ohioans who regarded Jefferson as their champion must not miss a word. "Westerners who have no resources other than the products of their farms were unable to send these products to market. The harbor at New Orleans was closed to them. Though western farmers were still obligated to pay debts and taxes, their crops were rotting for want of a waterway. Now this is what I want to ask: What language, what methods would have been used had such indignity been offered to the Atlantic coast? Why this callous indifference to the vital interests of Kentucky, Tennessee and Ohio? Do you suppose there would have been only sweet, patient speeches from the Administration if the commerce of eastern cities had been in peril?"

Ross paused again for the pleasure of listening to his applause. He gauged the moment well and continued his speech on the very beat at which the clapping hands began to tire.

"And this I also desire to ask: Can it not all happen again to the good, industrious people of the west? Can not this humiliation and dishonor be visited again upon the United States? Spain or France, what difference? Do we expect them to give our people more tender consideration than does our faint-hearted President? Why not seize what is so essential to us as a nation? Why submit to tardy, uncertain negotiations? Shall we, fellow Americans, wait till the French are settled in and prepared to fight? And what is this empty talk of France selling New Orleans?" Ross raised his head and went through the mummery of searching for a gullible citizen who could believe such nonsense. "Only when we are in possession of New Orleans will we negotiate with advantage. The French might sell—and very quickly—if they find us armed and resolved to stay in New Orleans. I am presenting what I hope you will recognize as a sensible and honorable proposal. I want the Army and Navy to take forceful possession of New Orleans. I want the militia to the number of fifty thousand called out. I want the sum of five million dollars to be appropriated for the use of buying our nation's self-respect in the only way that this blessed commodity can ever be bought—by fighting men and self-sacrificing patriots."

The New York *Evening Post* naturally reflected its owner's opinion, though the editorial did not carry the name Alexander Hamilton. "The spirited and well-timed resolution which Mr. Ross has brought forward in the Senate can not fail to excite the applause of every true American." The newspaper also published Ross's speech in full. A few days later it had the speech of Senator Samuel White, of Delaware, with which to inflame the people. One question of White's was repeated in every gathering place of the United States. It was repeated with glee by his supporters and with abhorrence by those who respected Jefferson's serene efforts to prevail without injury to the nation.

"Why negotiate when war would serve?" Senator White had demanded.

Thomas Jefferson, sitting on George Washington's sofa, sipping a glass of wine, looked toward his Secretary of State. "How is it that there are Americans who do not retch at that question of White's?"

Madison shook his head in weary disappointment. "Thank God the matter cannot be submitted to popular vote."

"No, they cannot vote us into war, and I don't think they would. Actually, James, it is rare that public sentiment decides immorally or unwisely." Jefferson's expression suddenly became that of a man who for the first time looks with a critical eye upon his own work. "Why, I have spoken those words before. I said them to Gouverneur Morris. They are the very words which led him to charging that I believe in the wisdom of mobs. I do not, you know, but if I am going to go around quoting and requoting myself, I must clarify that thought, giving it purer definition."

"I wish you had not mentioned Gouverneur Morris," Madison

said. "You have reminded me that when he takes the floor he may be more damaging to us than Senator White."

"He is an insidious fellow. And yet—"

Madison hoped the President would continue. One could scarcely urge him to do so. Perhaps an eager, inquiring glance would not be judged ill mannered.

"And yet, Madison, when I was Secretary of State, and he had my former position as Minister to France, I had reason to respect him and be grateful for his good sense. He was in Paris when the Revolution became the Terror. He saw people butchered in the streets and he was suspected of royalist sentiments, but he never asked me to relieve him of his post. He was the only representative of any country who remained in France throughout the Terror."

"No one has ever accused him of lacking courage."

"You are quite right. In my position, however, the thing I appreciated most was his refraining from ever asking what policies to adopt toward the French. What policies could we adopt? Morris was smart enough to see that I could offer no guidance. France was insane. Her citizens ran the gamut from worshipers of the King to murderers of servant girls who had once scrubbed the royal kitchens."

Madison nodded. "It's strange how few people realize that madness really had gripped the country. They don't know anything about those servant girls. I suppose it's easier just to believe that all decent, hard-working French rightfully took up arms to rid themselves of oppressors. People like simple pictures."

"Yes, they do, Madison. They find facts very confusing. Between thirty-five and forty thousand French citizens were cruelly deprived of life, but the average person is comfortable thinking that a cold-hearted queen, a vicious king and their sycophants received the punishment they deserved."

"It makes a romantic story."

"For numskulls. To execute royalty is merely a grand-scale version of the principle of whipping a spoiled child. Kings and brats are the victims of those who, after encouraging selfishness and undisciplined behavior, suddenly lose their tempers. Those poor, shallow Capets should have been exiled to a beautiful country estate with fifty servants and a score of good friends. Consideration was owed to them. They had been raised, with the full complicity of church and populace, to think of themselves as gods. How could they know they weren't?"

Madison smiled. "You're not a royalist, are you, Mr. President?"

"I would have been judged so in Paris for those remarks. Many who said less went to the guillotine."

Madison's smile widened. "Many who said more went to high government posts right here in our own democratic society. If you had been at the Constitutional Convention, you would have heard Alexander Hamilton suggest that the Senate be limited to the landed gentry, and serve for life. I wish you'd seen the expression on Ben Franklin's face when Hamilton added that the poor should never be permitted to vote for a president."

Jefferson stretched his long legs and sighed. "I am glad I was not there. I enjoy remembering a time in which I never had to think of Hamilton."

Madison saw that the interlude had ended. "Breckenridge and Clinton are going to take the floor tomorrow," he said.

Jefferson stared moodily into his wine glass. "I am pleased to have their friendship, but it seems that fervent orators are always in the opposition camp. On Thursday the Senate's most inspired speaker will do his best to equate peace with cowardice."

"Oh, yes, Gouverneur Morris again. The spellbinder."

Morris was that and more. With his sublime speaking voice, he began on that Thursday by reviewing the facts concerning Louisiana. Then: "So Louisiana has been ceded to France. Had Spain a right to make this cession without our consent? I say that no nation has a right to give to another a dangerous neighbor without consent. Yet although we have ministers in Paris and Madrid, our Government was not consulted. We were scorned."

Somebody coughed, and Morris glanced with patronizing

good humor toward a man who had been weak enough to catch cold.

"In Bonaparte's splendid career he must proceed. When he ceases to act, he will cease to control France. He is condemned to magnificence. Impelled by circumstance he rules in Europe and he will rule here also unless, by vigorous exertions, you set a bound to his power. Is Bonaparte a child whom you may bemuse with soothing sounds? What in the name of heaven are the means by which you would render a negotiation successful? Have you any magic spells? We have no hope of peacefully annexing New Orleans. We must take immediate possession."

Morris's jubilant admirers cheered lustily and doubled their cries of approval an hour later, when he finished his speech and sat down.

Senator Stevens Mason, of Virginia, was a dying man, and there was no one in the Senate unaware of his fatal illness. With difficulty, he rose to his feet and made a motion for adjournment. It was eight o'clock in the evening, he said, and though he wished to reply to Senator Morris he found himself unable to do so without resting. There was a great clamor against the motion, and a vote was taken. Aaron Burr, presiding, announced a tie and voted against adjournment.

To everyone's astonishment, Senator Plumer, who was a venomous enemy of the administration, demanded to know the exact manner in which the voting had gone. Burr slyly pretended to have been caught in error, and Plumer asked that the Senate be polled. This time, Plumer was revealed to be a man more merciful than political; he voted for adjournment.

Gouverneur Morris lost his courtliness and chivalry. "Senator Plumer, when a man is resolved to act only according to the convictions of his own mind, the party to which he belongs can never depend upon his support."

"And that will make for an excellent country," Plumer replied.

So Mason had twelve hours of rest before he need speak. His condition was pitiful when he took the floor. He apologized for his quavering voice and inability to stand upright. But there was no weakness in his words.

"What is this talk I have heard here? Ross tells us there need not be war. Need not be war? If he had his way and sent fifty thousand militia and the whole naval and military force? Why, it would amaze any thinking man if such a force did not find itself bombarding the city and desolating the farms. Now Morris is different from Ross. Morris did not equivocate. He told us that war is his favorite mode of negotiating, that war gives dignity to the species, that it draws forth the most noble energies of humanity. And at length, after more than two hours of praising glorious havoc, we are told by Morris that this young country must restrain the overgrown power of France. Well, let us try to do so. Let us astound the world with the force of intelligent speech. I am weary of the story of David and Goliath because I am weary of blood and the high-flown phraseology that seeks to mask the horror of war. If it is our national destiny to be David, let us, in God's name, overcome Goliath with the strength of reason, the weapon of intellect. If young men must die, let them die trying to establish an admirable precept. If they must live, let them live with the knowledge that a mindless creature originated combat but that it takes a genius to avoid it."

Someone brought a glass of water for Mason. He drank hastily and looked around him with deep sadness.

"I have much to say but I lack the endurance to say it. I leave you with this thought, this picture: Robert Livingston is in France working and praying that no blood be shed. He is representing us in all good faith. He trusts us to conduct ourselves in a manner that does not make peace impossible. In the name of civilization, do not invade the city that Livingston, with dignity and honor, is trying to obtain for you."

When Mason sat down there were shouts of acclaim. The vote was taken, and it was not close enough for Aaron Burr to influence in any way. The United States had declined to march on New Orleans.

"But, by God, Livingston had better find a way to buy us that city." Jefferson's color was high with the excitement of the message that had been rushed to him from the Senate chamber. Madison said, "Mr. President, I have had a letter from Livingston. I withheld it until the messenger's arrival. I felt that we might be unable fully to digest its content while we were unaware of how the vote would go."

Jefferson glanced at the Secretary of State, trying to assess the tone of Livingston's letter, but Madison could be a sphinx when he chose. The President swiftly read what Livingston had written to Madison.

> Sir:
>
> I have made several propositions to Talleyrand on the subject of New Orleans. He told me that conversation was premature, that the French Government has determined to take possession, that there is nothing at all to discuss now and that there may never be.
>
> Nevertheless we meet, Talleyrand and I, for conversations on diverse topics. It is to be hoped that my opportunities to see him will continue. . . .

Jefferson tossed the letter to his desk. Madison picked it up at once and neatly tucked it into his leather case. "Mr. President, I regret that there is not better news from Livingston. If Talleyrand is speaking truthfully, or believes he is correctly expressing the thoughts of the First Consul, then today's vote of the Senate becomes less valuable. I fear we are on probation, and that, although some senators are willing to give us time for negotiation, they will listen more sympathetically to war talk when there is nothing to negotiate."

"Yes, if the French government has determined to take actual possession of New Orleans, then the situation is even more difficult than we supposed. I have had a letter myself. Do you know Pierre Du Pont de Nemours?"

"Not well, but I know his son, Irénée, the one who has a gunpowder plant in Delaware."

"It is the father who is my good friend. He sometimes gives

me the benefit of his thinking." Jefferson lifted a paperweight and scanned the letter on top of the pile. "He writes this from New York and, in part, he says, 'Offer France enough money so that she will agree to the sale before she takes possession of New Orleans. Once France is in there, you will not move her. The men Bonaparte appoints to high positions in New Orleans, and the commercial companies that will immediately ensconce themselves in the city will convince the First Consul that French interests demand his standing firm.' You see, Madison, France will not talk until she's in New Orleans. And once she is in New Orleans she will not get out. Have you any ideas?"

"Yes."

Jefferson's keen gaze turned attentively to Madison. "Tell me."

"I am not underrating Livingston, Mr. President. I am not suggesting that he disappoints me. However, I think someone else should be sent, not to replace Livingston, but to emphasize the importance of the business we wish to transact."

Jefferson nodded thoughtfully.

"I do not believe, Mr. President, that Talleyrand would fail to mention to Bonaparte that the Americans had sent reinforcements, so to speak. I can imagine Bonaparte saying something like 'Those fellows are really serious. Maybe they would pay a lot of money. Go ahead, Talleyrand. For curiosity's sake, find out what figure they have in mind.' "

"That's a plausible premise, Madison. Have you a reinforcement you would like to send?"

Madison busied himself with the straps on his leather case. "I thought of James Monroe, Mr. President."

Jefferson made a small sound of dismay. "Why is it that the names of Virginians come so readily to us?"

"Livingston's a New Yorker, sir."

"Yes, and that does not make it easier. Livingston is not human if he feels no twinge of resentment at being—reinforced. He might suppose that Virginians are closing in on him."

Madison shrugged. "That can't be helped. I would have wanted Monroe regardless of his native state. There will be ugly words from here and there, perhaps, but I am not going to take a lesser man than Monroe just to prove I have no regional partiality."

"James, there are those who will tell you there is no lesser man than Monroe. I'm sure you remember that George Washington came to have little respect for him."

"Since those days, Monroe has been a successful governor of Virginia."

The President grinned. "I am afraid that is as dazzling a recommendation as saying that he was always highly regarded by his mother."

Madison did not return the grin. "It is not a small thing to have been Governor of Virginia."

"I enjoyed it, in a strange way," Jefferson said.

"Besides," Madison continued, "Monroe has a fine mind and a persevering spirit."

"And now, James, we are beginning to overlook the basic purpose of your appealing notion. We wished only to catch Bonaparte's interest by doubling the ministerial mission. If Bonaparte is not piqued by the arrival of a second minister, then Monroe's qualifications are of no consequence. If Bonaparte will permit a discussion of New Orleans, then it is Livingston I would choose for that discussion."

"Mr. President, before Monroe is exposed to either a snub or a welcome from France, we must have him approved by the United States Senate. It was of that I was thinking."

"And quite rightly, James, quite rightly. For a moment, I had forgotten the United States Senate."

The Senate had not forgotten James Monroe. George Washington had recalled him from France, and Monroe now read in the newspapers that his election to the governorship of Virginia had so shocked the great man, in his retirement at Mount Vernon, that death had come a day after his hearing the announcement.

At any rate, the Senate confirmed Monroe's appointment by fifteen to twelve, and Gouverneur Morris busied himself writing to his old friend and fellow New Yorker Robert Livingston, commiserating with him on having been superseded in authority and dishonorably treated by the administration. Morris's communications may well have succeeded in distressing Livingston but they were hardly needed. Assiduous servant to his country though he was, Livingston could sulk with noble dignity.

Secretary of State James Madison
Dear Sir:

I have received your letter notifying me of Mr. Monroe's appointment. I shall do everything in my power to pave the way for him, and I sincerely wish his mission may be attended with the desired effect. It will, however, cut off one resource on which I have relied. I had established a confidence which it will take Mr. Monroe some time to inspire. Enclosed is a letter to the First Consul himself, and sent him by hand before I heard of Mr. Monroe's appointment. Of my own knowledge I can state that the letter has been delivered and I have been told there will be an answer. What that answer will be I know not, but I have been indefatigable in my application, and if Mr. Monroe can suggest any improvement in my course I will be surprised though attentive.

Things every day look more toward a new rupture between France and England. Politicians think otherwise. I believe a war not very distant, and I am endeavoring to show Talleyrand in what way the money and friendship of the United States, gained by the sale of New Orleans to us, would be a great service to Bonaparte. I am pointing out to Talleyrand that England might seize New Orleans.

In short, I am saying and doing and have said and have done everything that could occur to the mind of mortal man.

R. R. Livingston

When James Monroe received word that the Senate had confirmed his appointment, he hastened to Jefferson. For days, the President, Madison and Monroe sat in the office with the books, the charts and the impudent mockingbird. They talked and listened, thought and questioned. Their minds sought every possible proposal that might be made; then they challenged the proposals and found new answers, new probing questions. They were aware that in the taverns and drawing rooms, and on the highroads and muddy pathways of the United States, they were being jeered by their countrymen for their niggling word games. Why did the President not realize that the sword was the only manly solution?

Jefferson fixed his blazing eyes upon Madison and Monroe, and said to them, "On the event of this mission depends the future destiny of the Republic."

Monroe found it difficult to relate Jefferson's solemn statement to the meager salary he would receive. Nine thousand dollars a year, scaled downward, of course, if a full year of his time were not required. Monroe controlled his laughter, remembering that Madison had added, "And you will have a right to bill the government for your postage expenses."

Surely he would never rebuild his financial strength after this voyage to France. He must learn to accept his appointment as an honor and to regard his empty wallet as evidence of his patriotism. It had, however, been a shock to learn that he was not permitted to travel on a frigate.

"In compliance with economic reforms of this administration," Jefferson had explained, "I fear our gentlemen on European missions are now treated less tenderly than in the days of Washington or Adams. Pinckney was denied a frigate for Spain, and Rufus King has been refused one for his return from England. Mr. Madison's friendship and mine for you being so well known, the public will have an eagle eye to watch if we grant you any indulgence out of the general rule. Of course, we will pay for a small private cabin for you on a commercial ship."

A small private cabin. Monroe had promised himself that he would not be parted from his wife and children. That meant the government would be contributing only a tiny portion of the traveling expenses. The living costs in Paris would be enormous, for he and his family had accustomed themselves to low-priced accommodations no more than had Jefferson. He thought of the stylish home he had owned in Paris. It had been sold with the understanding that he would be allowed to rent it furnished if at any time he returned to France on a diplomatic mission. He had notified the owners that he expected to take possession— good God, what rental would they ask? There had been no discussion of that.

The *Columbian Centinel* was thinking of money, too, but in quite a different way. "Monroe is directed to buy New Orleans even should it cost forty millions of dollars. What will Bonaparte think of us? He will consider us blockheads who deserve to be gulled, and he will shrug his shoulders at Mr. Monroe and say that he did not expect our millions, but that since Monroe has brought them, he will gladly receive them as a pledge of the attachment between our two countries."

Jefferson and Gallatin had set a figure far below that which had enraged the readers of the *Columbian Centinel*. Jefferson, with the advice of Du Pont de Nemours still greatly influencing his thinking, implored Gallatin to put no coldly frugal hand upon the negotiations.

Gallatin said, "I think five million dollars is a fair price."

Jefferson closed his eyes and bit into his lower lip.

"I see you are distressed, Mr. President. I should not have wasted your time with a businessman's appraisal of the property. We can manage to pay ten million for New Orleans. Remember, sir, we can manage. I beg of you, tell Monroe, and have him tell Livingston, that this figure must not be instantly announced if Talleyrand ever asks what payment the United States would make."

"I respect your judgment, Mr. Gallatin. I will encourage Monroe and Livingston to begin at five million. I will impress upon them the fact that if there is haggling they must try to close at eight million."

And so Monroe was instructed. "Never mention ten million dollars. Never. If there is the chance to bargain, and the French demand that price, state clearly that it is impossible. Yield only when it becomes apparent that France will accept no less. Tell Livingston that the United States Treasury names ten million for New Orleans as the absolute maximum."

"Yes, Mr. President."

Jefferson was silent for a moment. This was not an easy interview. Monroe had been his good friend, his generous campaign adviser and his volunteer bulwark against all enemies. Now, as a reward for his loyalty, he was being sent as mere window dressing for Livingston's presentations to Talleyrand. Impossible to tell him so. Monroe saw the appointment as an honor. Impossible to soothe Livingston by confiding in him that Monroe's presence would be no more than a theatrical trick to draw the attention of Bonaparte.

"There is something else to tell Livingston. Tell him that you bring the latest news on the climate of American thinking more vividly than it could be written in a letter."

Monroe's gaze was as unwavering as the President's. "There is no way, sir, to lessen Livingston's scalding pain at having to accept me. He sees himself, and quite rightly, as the one who has done all the work. He sees me as an opportunist who will take the credit for success, if success there is. But he and I are both sensible men, devoted to our country, and so I expect that we will give the best of our abilities, though neither liking the other very much."

Jefferson sat rigidly, his hand closed tightly on the arm of his chair. "Please don't speak of disliking Livingston. It is an open secret that he has dreams of becoming president when my task is finished. He has counted on concluding the New Orleans mission in so brilliant a manner that his name and accomplishment will be known to every citizen. Have sympathy, for he believes that now his fame will be, at best, halved."

"I don't know what to say, Mr. President. I have no ambitions beyond keeping busy in the service of my country or my state. But I know how gnawing ambition can be. Livingston has my pity."

Jefferson stared down at the articles on his desk and seemed dissatisfied that the letter opener had been placed to the left of the inkwell. Carefully, he moved it to the right, then found a new location for the paperweight. "There is one thing more. I cannot let you go without warning you about it. If the mission to buy New Orleans is a failure, you might live the rest of your life with Livingston and his friends blaming you."

Monroe summoned a pale smile. "I have been blamed before, Mr. President."

Jefferson did not comment on that. He changed his position in his chair and began to speak somewhat in the manner of a schoolmaster. Or, at least, that was the thought which passed through Monroe's mind.

"Now, listen carefully. Livingston has this order among his private papers, and you have it in the batch Madison gave you. I am going to go over it once more right now. It is so important that it cannot be out of anyone's thoughts for a moment. You must, by making every possible effort, convince the French that it is sensible to sell us New Orleans. If a positive and final no is given, your work is not done. You then have to apply yourself, perhaps more diligently than before, to urging them to sell us a portion of ground contiguous with the river that we may use as a deposit for our products. If even this appeal is beaten back, you must persist. Ask then that the French sell us jurisdiction over a space on the Mississippi River where we can establish a small town dedicated only to the shipping of our wares. If this is denied, we are almost, but not quite, defeated. You are ordered somehow to wheedle us a piece of commercial real estate on which we can set our bales and barrels before loading them on boats. Do you understand?"

"Yes, Mr. President."

Jefferson stood up and held out his hand. He had become so accustomed to looking downward at his five-foot six-inch Secretary of State that it rather startled him to find a pair of eyes on a level with his own.

"Good-bye and good luck."

"Thank you, Mr. President."

When Monroe had gone, Jefferson opened the door of the gilded cage and permitted the mockingbird to strut across his desk. They had reached a pleasant relationship of trust and affection. Each was certain that the office was his private holding, and would have been deeply disappointed had the other infringed upon duly recognized rights.

Jefferson bent low over a drawer of his table, and, pushing aside the garden implements, a few rough drawings of a refracting telescope suited for both terrestrial and celestial objects, a Hindi dictionary, diagrams for a polygraph machine and a carefully designed plan of a steamboat, he came at last to the stack of papers he sought. He ran through them rapidly, searching for one small item. Was it on Monroe's list? Had it been sent to Livingston? Infinitesimal as it was, it still might be of value. Jefferson had learned that there was no way of accurately measuring the importance with which a comment would be received. One could drop, as an afterthought, some idle word, only to discover that to the listener it had emerged as the most significant remark of the entire conversation.

Jefferson hurried his eyes over the section in which he and Madison had suggested what could be said in colloquy with Talleyrand. "Remember to mention," Meriwether Lewis had written, "that even the mild people in the New World are not always easy to govern. For instance, tell Talleyrand that the Ursuline nuns are abandoning New Orleans and moving to Havana. Explain that Spain provided the perfect atmosphere for intense religious worship, and the church has no wish to remain in New Orleans under French domination. Remark that what France called a revolution concerned itself far too much with exercises in losing for man his soul and his God. Tell him that the people of New Orleans will resent a nation once Catholic, and now indifferent to religion, more than they would resent good Christians who happen to be Protestants."

That was it. There it was—the small bit of information about the Ursuline nuns moving out of New Orleans. Talleyrand might laugh or might not even notice the remark pertaining to this pathetic exodus. But, if mentioned to Bonaparte with a thought of amusing him, it might be more disturbing to the little man than any other thing that could be said. The First Consul was an interestingly complicated creature. He was, so ran the story, shaken by nothing except the disapproval of his mother. Jefferson chuckled, wondering if Pierre Du Pont de Nemours would know a way of getting the news about the Ursulines to Napoleon's mama.

Well, that was that. Nothing could be done now but wait for word from Paris. Any further attention given to the situation would belong in the fruitless category of anxiety and obsession.

Jefferson drew a sheet of stationery from under the feet of the mockingbird and began to write:

Dear Dr. Priestley:

Thank you very much for your pamphlet entitled "Socrates and Jesus Compared." I do believe you should enlarge your treatment so as to fully explore the moral doctrines of the chief philosophers of Greece and Rome, and the doctrines of Jews and of Jesus. I had once thought of doing this very thing myself, and if I no longer regret that my time must be devoted to the contemporary world it is because in your writings I have discovered someone who will use the material far more expertly than I.

Thomas Jefferson

As he reached for a second sheet of note paper, he was fascinated by another proof of the mockingbird's undeniable learning ability. This time the bird stepped back and off the stationery as the human hand approached.

"Good boy," Jefferson murmured.

Dear Maria:

I am so sorry that Martha's children and yours have been exposed to measles but such things will happen. My disappointment at having the visit once again postponed is very great. However if you and Martha and your families stay well I will be happy.

I beg of you never again to cancel our plans for being together just because no horses can be spared from your plantation operations. You did this last time that I expected you and Martha here. It was very unnecessary and naughty of you to deprive me of the joy your visit would have brought. I can always send horses and any number of servants to make the traveling easy for you. It would be no trouble to me, though I know you fear that it would. I have heard of an excellent inn where you can rest over night on your journey, and also I hear that the roads have been improved. . . .

FOUR

Generals and Diplomats

. . . .

$\mathcal{S}$OMETIMES ROCHAMBEAU LAUGHED DERISIVELY at how cheaply Christophe and Dessalines had been bought. The price had been no more than two new uniforms and two commissions in the French Army. It was hilarious that those boys thought they were French generals.

"As I told you, blacks are inferior humans, if one can call them human at all. They have no loyalties. For instance, what black man has shed a tear over Toussaint's disappearance?"

Leclerc said, "I don't know whether tears have been shed or not, but when you use the word 'disappearance' you give an aura of mystery to the proceedings. I told Christophe quite frankly that Toussaint had been arrested and deported."

"And what did he say?"

"Very little."

"That was wise. He wouldn't want his beautiful French uniform taken away from him, would he? Odd that it doesn't seem to occur to him that he and Dessalines could follow their old leader over the ocean." Rochambeau looked questioningly at Leclerc, inviting a confidential word on the subject. "They're no less dangerous than Toussaint was."

From the gallery of his hilltop home, Leclerc stared out at the shimmering blue water and moved his chair beyond reach of a hot, piercing ray of sunlight. He mopped his face and thought of the cool, grassy villages of France. "You knew Sonthonax, didn't you?"

"Who? Oh, Sonthonax. Yes, I knew him."

"What possessed him to give those guns as personal gifts to

Toussaint's soldiers? When I first heard the story I thought it was a local legend. Was he crazy?"

"In my opinion he was. How could a sensible white Frenchman trust a black as he trusted Toussaint? And he married a mulatto woman, you know. Of course he was crazy. As to the guns, he was so grateful that he could report peace to the Directory that he would have given Toussaint's army anything."

Leclerc smiled weakly. He was wondering what he would give today to an army that brought peace for him to take home to Bonaparte. What would be good enough to offer? What would—

"I have heard from a dozen sources," Rochambeau was saying, "that he told the soldiers some sort of rubbish about never parting with the guns, that the men who took them would reinstate slavery."

"It was not rubbish, Rochambeau. He spoke solemnly and the men believed him. That's why only Christophe and Dessalines can get them to surrender the guns."

"What do you suppose they say that is so effective?"

"Christophe tells the gun owners the truth. He tells them that anyone on the island possessing a personal weapon will be hanged. Then he asks for the gun, explaining—quite emotionally, I imagine—that the last thing he wants to see is a soldier of the great old army put to death. Even though Christophe is now a French general, the peasants don't think he'd send them back to slavery."

"Dessalines probably demands the guns and kills anyone who refuses right then and there."

"Yes, that happens. But in the end, he gets the gun."

Rochambeau's conviction that he was a better general than Leclerc triumphed over his discretion. "When you asked me about Sonthonax I thought you were trying to avoid speaking of the deportation of traitors. I see now that you were making the point that they can be useful. I hope, General, that you are having a close watch kept on what Christophe and Dessalines are doing with the guns they collect from the peasants."

Leclerc shook his head. "No, Rochambeau, you cannot have

it both ways. Either you are right that we bought the black generals cheap or you are right that we have not bought them at all. Which is it?"

Rochambeau scrambled for an answer. "It is that I have such an overwhelming desire to see this damned island safe in our hands that sometimes—"

Leclerc said, "I know. I know, Rochambeau. It is all very wearying. Please excuse me now. I am not feeling well and I wish to lie down."

Rochambeau murmured politely and departed. There was no doubt that Leclerc had been annoyed with him but no doubt either that Leclerc did not look well. The heat was abominable and the frustrations of fighting barbarians on their own ground was enough to sour the temper of any commanding officer. Still, at this season of the year in Saint-Domingue, and when a man's skin had that pasty look— How many men were dead of the fever so far? Rochambeau tried to recall. Was it fifty or a hundred? That was not so many. Maybe the fever season would take a light toll in contrast to battle losses. No part of the island stayed captured and secured. If old Toussaint were still sitting under the tamarind trees at Gonaïves, Rochambeau thought, one might suspect that he was whipping up a new fury. But the old man was lying in a French dungeon and his influence was at an end.

Yet, there was no peace. Every single black was, within himself, a seething, hot mass of lava that erupted at sight of a French soldier. Leaders rose overnight to take the places of those who had been killed or corrupted. Hercule Drouet was one of the shiny new heroes, pledged, the spies said, to murder Christophe for forsaking the rebel cause. What fanatics they were, the blacks. Rochambeau still thought that to hang every one of them and repopulate with slaves from the Guinea coast was the only answer. God, how blistering the sun was, how uncomfortable the miserable little island. Perhaps he would ask to be returned to France. But if Leclerc had the fever— Rochambeau pictured the First Consul saying, "It is a pity about my sister's husband,

but under your command, Rochambeau, we won back Saint-
Domingue, so it was fate."

Leclerc, lying on his bed in the hilltop house, was in possession of more facts than was Rochambeau. Leclerc knew that so
far in this month of June three hundred and twelve men were
dead of the fever. He knew, too, that he himself was a sick man.
The flagship doctor had told him that he was overburdened with
work and worry, and that the climate did not agree with him.

"A man who falls victim to this island fever does not feel
sick one day, better the next and so-so on another, General
Leclerc. Men die swiftly, some within hours. But I will tell you
this, sir: any condition that tears down normal vitality and
resistance invites the disease. You must write to the First Consul
and state that you are ill. You must ask for a successor here."

"I don't think I could do that."

"May I do it for you, General?"

"No, no. I thank you, but please do not. Perhaps I will bring
myself to write when I have thought it over."

Leclerc had written, not to the First Consul, but to the Minister
of Marine, because he had not felt well enough to choose words
carefully or to write a pretty description of how Pauline and the
little boy amused themselves on the island. This was a minor
showing of cowardice, for, of course, he expected the letter to be
laid before Bonaparte.

"If the First Consul wishes to have an army in Saint-Domingue
in the month of Vendémiaire," he wrote, "he must have it sent
from France, for the sickness here will very likely spread vastly.
Even now, at only the beginning of the intense heat, not a day
passes without my being told of the death of someone whom
I have cause to regret bitterly. Man cannot work here without
risking his life. Since my arrival, I have often been in very poor
health. The government must seriously think of sending me a
successor. It is out of the question that I remain more than six
months. I expect by that time to hand over the colony, free from
a state of war, to the one who will be designated to replace me."

He read the letter over after elaborating somewhat on the

possibility of peace within the year. Had he placed enough emphasis on the need for more troops? Scores of vicious skirmishes were a steady drain on the common soldiers, and even some officers had been lost. The island was under martial law, but the blacks were not intimidated by French edicts. Leclerc recognized that he was up against one of those unscientific facts that had baffled all French since the first slave uprising. "They do not think as we do." A bit of nonsense, a cliché, a demonstrable untruth, and yet Leclerc had noticed what other French had not: for blacks, there were no realities unless all people involved in a situation were black. Black was real. Death was real. Therefore, death could be envisioned and feared only if it were threatened by another black. Death could be dealt by Dessalines, or even by Christophe on occasion. Death from Leclerc was an unimaginable fantasy made up of crackling paper with printed words upon it and no actuality to frighten anyone. He had seen blacks die by noose and by fire, and he had seen them laugh as though they had obligingly joined in the antics of badly behaved children. Here in Saint-Domingue he had learned why the slave had stolen an egg even though he might pay for it with his life. He had learned why black soldiers, raked by grapeshot, would sing as they marched on a redoubt in tight columns that never wavered, never stepped back. Within their minds there was no apparatus that enabled them to picture the white man as an agent of anything so real as death.

Leclerc became aware that the pillow beneath his head was unbearably warm and moist. Had he been asleep? Or had he been thinking? Of what? Oh, yes, martial law. He reached over and took Pauline's pillow from its blue satin sham. Ah, how cool it was, how fragrant. He lay back and tried to think of something pleasant. The white residents of the island approved of martial law and they had congratulated him on the arrest and deportation of Toussaint. That was pleasant. The French planters knew that he was doing everything possible to bring peace.

A strange question came to him as he lay there discovering that Pauline's pillow was, after all, just as warm and moist as his had been. Why was it that all French planters said the same thing? "We always hated Toussaint, you know," and "We are people who want to live in peace." Well, Toussaint had made peace, and they had lived in it with him and they had prospered. Now the First Consul had sent them another bloody war, but they blessed his name and made obeisance to Pauline as they would to Marie Antoinette if she rose from her grave. "They have no loyalty," Rochambeau had said of the blacks. Leclerc asked God a question now. From whom would the blacks have learned loyalty?

Who was worth all the blood that had dripped and streamed for Saint-Domingue? And after a time, he took a spoonful of the medicine the doctor had given him and he felt stronger. It was then the idea came to him of establishing upon the island a form of government modeled loosely on the Directory that had ruled France before Bonaparte had dispossessed it. If twenty-four men were selected, eight of each popular shade, and they sat as a deliberative body, how could anyone be displeased? He would be relieved of so many ponderous duties, and there was no gainsaying the dignity of parliamentary procedures.

The more he thought of the idea, the better he liked it. He began to make a list at once of the men who would be suited to such high station. Unfortunately, it was finished with only twenty-two names. He had selected a pair of splendid officers from the fleet, but, even as he wrote, word came that, along with eight soldiers, five officers had died of fever during the afternoon. His two choices had been among the dead, and he could think of no other names with which to replace them.

Christophe had been first on his list, and when asked to join what Leclerc called the Provisional Assembly, Christophe accepted without much discussion. Leclerc was relieved on two counts. He had no wish for a debate, but, more important, he had need of a black with brains, manners and a good reputation. Those answering all specifications were not to be found in great numbers.

Leclerc issued a proclamation to acquaint Saint-Domingue with its new form of government. He declared that he had chosen men of lofty principles, and the whole island should rejoice at his unwillingness to subject it to the rule of any man who was not personally known and approved by himself.

As it turned out, the Provisional Assembly was a less than successful experiment. The word flew swiftly that the majority of the hand-picked twenty-two, including mulattoes, was for restoration of slavery. Opinions on this matter had not been unknown to Leclerc. He had counted on fourteen of these influential islanders, with their friends, families and personal prestige, to be of assistance to him when the blacks were returned to what Bonaparte called "the only worthwhile contribution they are capable of rendering to us."

What did stun Leclerc was the stupidity of these Assembly members in revealing their sentiments so far in advance of the propitious time. One member had actually proposed that blacks who had not been free prior to 1794 had no claim to freedom now. They had never been legally manumitted, he stated, but had escaped slavery by means of rebellion and murder. For weeks the Assembly wrangled over that proposal, while fighting intensified on the island. The burning of plantation houses again became common practice, and in the town of Céret all white residents were brutally slain.

"I hope," Leclerc said to Christophe, "that you are strongly opposing that awful proposal."

"I am strongly opposing it," Christophe said.

"Some very good black troops who came over to our side with you and Dessalines are now deserting us. Do take time to assure those who are still with us that the opinion of one elderly man is not the opinion of the French command or of the First Consul."

Christophe's voice was only a polite purr, but Leclerc thought he detected a sullen burn in the black eyes. "General, may I respectfully suggest that the First Consul is as responsible for the trouble here as the elderly man of whom you speak? It is my guess that Bonaparte takes for granted that no black can read. Otherwise he would have instituted a law that French newspapers may not leave your country. They come to this island from the United States and from Spain and from all over. Not

only do some blacks read, but they read aloud to their uneducated brothers."

Leclerc nodded sympathetically. "I know of what you speak.
I, too, saw in some journals that black and mulatto French
nationals are no longer allowed to enter France without special
permission. That isn't the truth, you know, Christophe."

Christophe shrugged. "It is the thing that least distresses me,
General Leclerc. I am speaking of something much less trivial
than who may or may not visit France. I am speaking of the
French Caribbean islands which England captured from your
country and has now returned under the Treaty of Amiens."

"Yes?"

"I am saying that the French, with all their liberty, equality
and fraternity, have immediately reinstated slavery on those
islands."

Leclerc said, "Your charge against us proves how irresponsible newspaper editors can be. Why don't they tell the whole
story?"

"Which is?"

"Which is that slavery has not been reinstated. The First Consul has quite rightly demanded that plantation owners who grew
wealthy from the labor of blacks now feed and house them until
the French can teach them to bargain for wages and put their
skills to the best use. Besides, this has nothing to do with Saint-
Domingue. Saint-Domingue was never captured by the English."

Christophe's sudden smile was surprising. "No," he said.
"Saint-Domingue was never captured by the English. We had
Toussaint to thank for that, didn't we, General?"

When Christophe left him, Leclerc suffered one of his frequent attacks of nausea. Nervous disturbance, the doctor had
said, and no doubt he was right. Had ever a commander more
reason to be nervous? Leclerc had boiled at seeing the French
newspapers. He had not then dared write to Bonaparte. There
had been the danger of expressing his anger too forcefully. And
he had boiled at Christophe's casual manner of saying what he
thought. Who did that black bastard think he was? And again
he, Leclerc, had been prevented by circumstances from making

known his rage. Christophe, if he so decided, could renew his enmity against France, and then the island would indeed explode.

If I could vent my anger by speaking my mind to Bonaparte, if I could shout my fury at Christophe, my stomach would not be sick. My worry and cares are a poison inside me. I would be a healthy man were I not a general.

And because he was a general, he dragged himself to his desk and wrote to his brother-in-law:

> . . . as those of my reports which you permit to be published finally arrive here along with other impolitic news items. I implore you to appoint a bureau of intelligent men who have the wit to read the papers from the standpoint of a Saint-Domingue native. Also, please, I beg you to forbid the printing of any more of those supposedly humorous remarks at the expense of blacks. They do not appreciate them. People are sensitive about their origins. I think you can understand that. Pauline has told me that, at one time, it was not fashionable to be Corsican.
>
> For the love of God, send me the twelve thousand reinforcements for whom I have asked. Over the last weekend one hundred and six additional men died of fever, and more than seven hundred have been killed or severely wounded in combat. The blacks attack like whirlwinds and slaughter everything in sight, then disappear into the mountains. Of course, dear sir, they are pursued. Military honor demands pursuit, though there is not a military man here who can give a sensible reason for ascending those awful cliffs to meet death in a dozen different savage shapes. It is absolutely necessary to see the country to form an adequate idea of the difficulties which it presents at every step. I have never seen in the Alps any obstacles equal to those which my soldiers face every day.
>
> Pauline and the child are on the island of Tortuga in a house which was built in a few weeks. There is no need

for sturdy materials and excellent workmanship on islands that never know a cold day. One needs only a good roof against the winter rains, which are unbelievably torrential. In any case, Pauline is delighting in cool breezes and the fragrance of fruit blossoms. She has a native group collecting a gift for the Menagerie in the Paris Jardin des Plantes. There will be dozens of small tropical animals sent there along with indigenous trees and bushes. Pauline has a cage of parrots and monkeys for her own amusement on the gallery of the Tortuga house.

I know you will be pleased that she is enjoying herself. . . .

Leclerc hoped the gossip hadn't reached Bonaparte. Pauline naturally had taken her ladies and some of the young lieutenants to Tortuga. She could not have been expected to go unaccompanied by friends and protectors. Of course, flirtations and love affairs flourished. He had steeled himself against the first terrible anguish that had come with the realization that Pauline never would be faithful. It was, however, quite another thing to know that Napoleon enjoyed the situation unless news of it threatened to reach the ears of all twenty-six million French citizens. Josephine had slept with everyone of any importance in Paris. First to save herself from the guillotine, and later to maintain an elegant little house for herself and her children. To reasonable people, her behavior, considering the terrible circumstances of her life, did not seem unforgivable. But somewhere along the way Josephine evidently had begun to rather like the payments that had been required of her. Now no longer a petitioner for her life, no longer fearful that her children would be reared in poverty, Josephine, First Lady of France, still wandered charmingly from one bed to another. Napoleon had yet to steel himself against the suffering, but it comforted him to hear that other men were also cuckolded. Leclerc had a suspicion that it particularly pleased Napoleon that Pauline was as generous as Josephine. Did the knowledge that his own sister regularly committed adultery argue that Josephine's morals were really quite in accordance with the times and nothing to cause distress? Or did Napoleon harbor some hidden dislike for Pauline's husband? Or was it all much more complicated than that?

Leclerc, recalling the anonymous notes that had reached him, concluded that few who wished to report to Napoleon on Pauline's island activities would be likely to talk of the young lieutenants. That was just the old story with a change of geographical background. What would seem more fascinating, more novel, was that Pauline had cleared a section of the Tortuga acreage so that eighteen or twenty young black men and women could use it for dancing at night. She had ordered torches to burn and rum to be conveniently placed. She had been particularly insistent that no one was to disturb or restrain the poor things in their pleasure. It was said that, from a couch in a small garden house concealed by vines, Pauline watched the wild dancing and the orgiastic culmination that never failed to occur.

Leclerc wondered what Napoleon would think of that. He wondered what he thought of it himself and, after deliberation on the matter, was surprised to find that he felt no more than the same disgust that he had always felt for voyeurism. It startled him that he was inclined neither to excuse Pauline nor to disbelieve the unsigned letters that had been delivered to his house and to headquarters. So much for the efforts of enemies who hoped they were making a contribution toward shattering the composure of the French commander. On the contrary, in being forced to examine his feelings, he had discovered that, as far as Pauline was concerned, the suffering was at an end. The thought came to him that prolonged pain over infidelities of a mate might not really exist. One took for granted that the pain persisted until there had been earnest promises, forgiveness and a new beginning. No such thing. One should remember to explore one's state of mind at proper intervals.

On the first of July reinforcements arrived. Leclerc had originally requested them in May, so there had not been too great a delay. But in May his men had been dying in the traditional way of soldiers. Now there was the fever. He had planned a celebration for Bastille Day, believing that such things reminded the troops of patriotism and caused them to feel important and more willing to accept the beastly burdens of soldiering. There had been no celebration. By July 12 almost four hundred of the new arrivals were dead, and an equal amount would not live through the night. Seven of the dead and dying were officers, but Leclerc issued an order that all military funerals were to be discontinued.

"I am sorry to hear that, General," Rochambeau said, flicking a furry spider off his sleeve. "It is an honor we always accord our brother officers."

Leclerc took a swallow of his medicine. Rochambeau was very trying. "It is an honor that draws attention to our mortality rate. We cannot afford to hearten the blacks. God knows they are bold enough. During the past week, in spite of martial law, large groups of them gathered on the plain and even right here in Le Cap. They claim they wanted to discuss new agricultural methods that were printed in some newspapers that came from the United States. I am told they were actually hatching a plot to massacre all whites on the island."

"Did Christophe tell you that?"

"I would rather not say."

The cold light of Rochambeau's eyes did not match the warmth of his words. "General, personal fondness for you forces me into saying something I would prefer not to say. Living as we do with a plague and a brutal enemy, none of us dare stay aloof from others. You, who are still young and resilient, will certainly outlive me by many years. However, there may be a few days or even a week when you are unable to function at your best. Wouldn't you feel more comfortable knowing that I am completely aware of the measure of Christophe's trustworthiness, and what chain of contacts you've established to bring you news and what sort of—"

"General Rochambeau, you astound me. We are soldiers. We are not old ladies sitting under a shade tree planning our obsequies and deciding to which of our nieces we will bequeath the silver fruit bowl."

Leclerc was not certain whether he had lost the knack of masking his dislike for Rochambeau or if the direct questions concerning Christophe had infuriated him. Nobody, absolutely nobody must know that he now suspected Christophe of treason. An odd way of putting it perhaps, since Christophe had been a traitor to France through all the years of Toussaint's governing the island; and, then, if one found tenable excuses for his devotion to the land he called Haiti, he had betrayed Haiti to become a French general.

But I am only human, Leclerc thought. I count his treachery from the day it involved me, and I know now that he never did betray his Haiti. He never did become a French general. I call him traitor because I was fool enough to trust him. And now I cannot even rely on him to treat me with a feigned respect that will preserve my standing among my own kind. What must I do? If I deport him now—if I could deport him now—the reprisals would be so monstrous that not a white would survive. The same disaster would result from Christophe's meeting with an "accident." Must I pretend that I suspect him not at all, and that he and I well understand each other's bitter moods? And, dear God, what has he done with the guns he took from the peasants? I dare not ask him. By asking I could be setting off the signal for Armageddon.

It soon seemed clear to Leclerc what Christophe and Dessalines had done with the guns, those cursed gifts from Sonthonax. They had distributed them widely in sections of the island that had been unarmed. There was a massacre at La Fondrière and another at Le Rouet, and suddenly one on the island of Tortuga. Leclerc sent a thousand soldiers to bring Pauline, the child and the elegant little imitation of a royal court back to the relative safety of Le Cap.

Citizen Consul:
Half the soldiers that I sent to La Fondrière and to the island of Tortuga died, only a few of wounds. Most

dropped dead en route. The fever mounts and spreads, and I must have reinforcements. You cannot picture this island. It smells of disease and death, and the air hangs dark with the smoke of battle and arson, and all the time there is the beat of the drums, the drums, the drums. I am fatigued and perhaps seriously ill, but you have never responded to my request for a successor. At any rate, I intend to send Pauline and my little boy home to you, depending, of course, upon conditions. . . .

But Pauline would not go. "What am I in Paris? Napoleon Bonaparte's sister, to be sure, but he has two other sisters and a mother and a bevy of sisters-in-law. Here I am as important as Josephine. In this particular place I am first lady."

"And God help you if anything happens to me."

She laughed. "Never worry about your Pauline. Every white on the island would die gladly to protect me."

"Unless a powerful black were in command. Then they'd be so damned busy bowing to him that they'd never notice you were being beaten to death in the public square."

"Oh, that reminds me—do you remember me telling you about seeing Louis Fréron in the Place d'Armes the first day I came ashore at Le Cap?"

"Who's Louis Fréron?"

"The old fellow who'd been a commissioner to Marseille, and had voted in the National Convention for Capet's death. He was only a civilian clerk with the Army here, but, anyway, he died of the fever. He fell right down dead in the street and everybody ran from him and he just lay there till some priests dragged him away and buried him. I thought you'd be interested, but if you didn't know him—" She pressed a heavily perfumed handkerchief to her nose. "Why do you suppose we don't get this awful sickness?"

"Because we're related to Napoleon," he said.

She was delighted. "I will tell him you said that."

There had been a time when he would have asked her not to repeat the remark, but he no longer cared. Napoleon's displeasure was not even on the long list of items that made Leclerc's life almost unendurable, although, as a military man, he often found himself speculating on how Bonaparte would handle the terrible island were he commander. And the thought came back to him again and again that one learned all one could of the art of commanding and then, with a reasonable degree of bravery, set forth on one's career. After that, it was a matter of luck. One was given the opportunity to shoot down citizens on the streets of Paris and thus become admired by the Directory. Or, on one's way to oblivion, one was set the task of conquering an island that was unconquerable. Unconquerable? Probably. Leclerc had heard his soldiers singing the *"Marseillaise"* as they marched against black men on this Godforsaken island, and he had heard the black men sing the *"Marseillaise"* right back at them. And something deep within him had been touched, for the white soldiers sang their anthem with the pride of men who had vanquished their oppressors, and the blacks sang it with defiance, as once upon a time the whites had sung it. Only, now the men who had toppled a dynasty were the oppressors, and it was the sad way of the world that this should be the truth. And Leclerc sometimes tossed restlessly in his bed thinking that Napoleon would have found a way to subdue the blacks.

He is a better general than I, and that may be only because he is a man who would not notice that both sides sing the *"Marseillaise."*

The Provisional Assembly was still locked in dispute. The island had forgotten its existence. No word came forth that gave the people anything to discuss. The Assembly had never advanced beyond the slavery question. Meetings were useless confrontations in which insults instead of opinions were exchanged.

Leclerc still held stubbornly to the notion that the Assembly could, if it operated properly, create an illusion of stability. He decided to give a banquet. In the atmosphere of a wholly social evening, he could suggest that the slavery discussion be laid aside and that less explosive issues be brought under consideration. He could have walked into the council room and given such an order, but he was reluctant to make so clear the utter powerlessness of the Assembly. It would be far more tactful to dine and drink with the members and to place himself in the position of a helpful friend who had a few ideas that might be acceptable.

He had set the date and had arranged for the banquet to take place at Government House. He had been told that the dining room was downright dirty, with unswept floors and unwashed windows. Former civil servants were occupied with insurrection. If no one else could be found to give the place a cursory cleaning, then he would send soldiers to do it. Pauline had argued, reasonably enough, that her home was not a place for political meetings.

Two days before the date set for the banquet, the frigate *Cocade* arrived in the harbor of Le Cap. No one paid any particular attention to it. The *Cocade* had been first to Guadeloupe, which was one of the islands recently restored by England to French ownership. The frigate, no doubt, had messages for the fleet or perhaps needed repairs. Nobody in Le Cap would have given the *Cocade* a second thought except that from her deck several desperate blacks hurled themselves overboard. Those who survived the sharks came ashore at Saint-Domingue. The *Cocade,* they said, was filled with blacks picked up at Guadeloupe to be used as forced labor in France. It was difficult to disbelieve the statements of the distraught arrivals. No one offers himself to sharks on the gamble that he will live to tell a malicious lie.

"They are selling blacks in Guadeloupe as in the old days," the half-drowned men gasped. "And they are beginning to sell mulattoes."

The *Cocade* had left the harbor with an abruptness that could only add credibility to the story. In the mountains the drums were thundering. The island seemed to vibrate with the ceaseless beat of their anger.

Leclerc sent soldiers to bring the Guadeloupe refugees to headquarters. They were questioned separately first and then in a group. Neither stern doubts nor smiling suggestions that they had mistaken French intentions changed any story in the slightest.

"Take them to the hospital for examination," Leclerc ordered. From his office window he saw that hundreds of blacks had gathered outside. They were watching intently that no harm befell the unfortunate men from the *Cocade*. They even followed to the hospital, still watching.

"What will you do about our guests when the doctors find them fit?"

Leclerc turned slowly and gazed at Rochambeau with cold eyes. "I am going to befriend them. They are not being sent back to Guadeloupe."

"They're dangerous. Tomorrow they'll join the rebels."

"What do you recommend? That we kill them tonight so that tomorrow every defenseless white will be murdered in retaliation?"

"Why do you suppose they did not jump into the sea the first day they were in harbor?"

"I suppose it to be a bitter coincidence. Nobody swam out there to tell them there's a political meeting tonight at Government House."

"Oh, I had not meant to imply anything like that. I was just curious." Rochambeau signaled a change of topic by walking away from the window. "Is Government House quite safe?"

"From what standpoint?"

"It's been set on fire so often, it must be structurally weakened."

"No. Its exterior walls are sooty and hideous but the building is firm. And now, if you can think of no other disturbing thing to mention, I shall go home and sleep for a time."

He did not sleep but lay thinking of how he had planned to use the banquet. Wisely or foolishly—and no doubt foolishly—it was to have been an occasion on which the members would be encouraged to set aside all deadlocked issues and urged to consider matters that might lend themselves to solution. Now, as he lay in the debilitating heat of midafternoon, he decided that the banquet should have quite a different purpose. It would be a farewell dinner to the Provisional Assembly. A word of thanks for having served, a word of regret that agreements had been impossible to reach, and several words explaining that sole responsibility for the island now once more rested with him.

What nonsense the whole idea had been. In a country where three-quarters of the population were ex-slaves how could an assembly rule? There was only one way to govern such people. That was by the order of a leader having absolute authority.

And I must take absolute authority, Leclerc thought. I will be lenient when I can, and I will not hesitate to be harsh when the situation demands.

For a time he felt almost comfortable thinking of his new government, under which he would be respected for his decisions, which would always be just. Evil people would fear him. Law-abiding citizens would admire him. Perhaps he would remain forever on this island, bringing it the benefit of his wisdom, sharing with it the richness of his experience and—

He knew he had not been asleep, so he was somewhat troubled by the foolish daydream in which reality had completely slipped from him. He had actually forgotten that he was here, not to rule a country, but to extinguish an insurrection. What could he rule except his army and the small segment of population that was not against him? To whom was he going to show leniency? To warring blacks whom he had already fought against in every conceivable way? To whom was he going to be harsh? To plantation owners who were his supporters? What a strange picture of existing conditions his imagination had presented to him.

The water in the pitcher beside him was warm, and his stomach was queasy again. On the gallery Pauline was laughing, and in the mountains the drums were throbbing. He grasped his pillow in both hands and pressed it against his ears.

Later, the breeze rose from the sea and breathed benevolently upon him. He took a double dose of medicine and dressed for the banquet at Government House. He felt curiously drained and ineffective. He knew he was not thinking well enough to make a speech dissolving the Assembly. He thought now of smiling at everybody, of making it clear that this was an evening for chatting pleasantly of unimportant things.

He arrived late at Government House. Somehow, he had lost

contact with time. He was astonished to see that the building was surrounded by heavily armed black soldiers who must have been of his command, for they wore French uniforms of recent issue. However, from his personal guard he heard a mutter of surprise and dissatisfaction. He lowered his eyes swiftly to avoid an incident. He had not been saluted. Damn those people who had thrown themselves off the *Cocade* and had come to make trouble for him. A pity that any of them had reached shore. What were sharks for? What were these black soldiers for? Who had ordered them to Government House tonight? Who had— Of course. Why had he not realized that Christophe would fear the banquet to be a trap, set and ready to hustle him off to the dungeon at Fort de Joux, where Toussaint lay dying?

In the dining room, which had been given the most perfunctory dusting and sweeping, the grimy windows stood open to invite a breeze, but the room smelled of neglect and mold. The guests were already at table, and wine had been served to them. Four white men, one mulatto and one black stood as Leclerc entered. His eyes went at once to Christophe, who remained seated and did not look in his direction.

Leclerc saw that to attempt handshaking all around would be as provocative of a small crisis as would have been a demand that he be saluted. He merely took his place at the table, apologized for being late and told his adjutant to send word that dinner be served. The man at his right spoke of the weather, and Leclerc amiably responded, although he was taking note of other things. The tablecloth that once must have been magnificent enough for a palace, now grayish, poorly pressed and scorched upon its lace panels. The unpolished silverware. The carelessly washed glasses, finger-marked and chipped. And Christophe, hot-eyed and very still.

Leclerc wondered why Christophe had come. If this was the end, why had he not simply vanished with his loyal men? Ah, yes, he wanted first to make a speech. Despite what Rochambeau kept saying, they were human. Like all men filled with rage and hatred, Christophe wanted to loose a stream of burning words.

The slow-moving waiters, in their soiled livery, began serving the first course. The man beside Leclerc spoke of the summer of 1780, when it had been noticed that those who recovered from the fever were safe from it for five years. Leclerc heard himself replying that that was interesting. He watched and waited. What would give Christophe his opportunity to announce that he was finished with the French?

Or am I too trusting?

The thought had come suddenly that perhaps those black soldiers outside were not there to protect Christophe but to slaughter his enemies.

Are they awaiting a signal? Is it I who have walked into a trap?

Leclerc beckoned his adjutant and whispered an order. The adjutant nodded and walked away as though he had been asked to query the steward regarding the paucity of candles or the total absence of proper forks for the crab meat. He had been told to ride nonchalantly toward the garrison and gallop back with two hundred white soldiers.

Though no one had addressed a word to the obviously angry Christophe, the silence toward him was now broken. The man who in the Assembly session had proposed a return to slavery felt that he had caught the spirit of the evening. Calm, pleasant conversation was its purpose, and, as in all things, he was willing to do his stupid part.

"General Christophe," he said chattily, "I have often wished to ask you about your accent. You are not of this island, are you?"

Christophe brought his gaze from the far distance and leveled it stonily upon the man on the other side of the table.

"I don't mean that your French is not perfect, but there is that small, interesting trace of another language, another place. Are you perhaps English? Are you perhaps—"

Christophe made a quick movement, as though he intended to fling himself across the table. Then he settled back and said loudly, "I am a Haitian. Not a Saint-Dominguan, not an English-man and certainly not a Frenchman. I am a Haitian."

There was no way now of pretending that nothing was amiss.

He has caught the attention of all, Leclerc thought. He is ready to speak. God, let him speak quickly and go. I am so sick.

Christophe was standing. His height gave additional theatricality to the power of his voice and the flash of his scornful eyes. Leclerc forced himself to look and listen with courteous detachment. He was the commanding general of the island and, sick, frightened or dead, he could not shrink timidly back in his chair as the others did.

"The men who jumped from the *Cocade* had thought themselves Frenchmen," Christophe shouted. "They believed in your Revolution. They prayed for England to give up Guadeloupe so they could share in your beautiful liberty, equality and fraternity. And what did you French do to them? Tell me, if you dare, what you French did to them."

I should walk out, Leclerc thought. It is the prescribed behavior for high command when the country is insulted, but of what use is prescribed behavior in this hellhole? I would please him if I placed that much importance upon his ranting. He is planning a spectacular exit, no doubt, and let it be soon, for I did not give the order that is most crucial of all. I neglected to say that no one may fire a shot at him. Let the soldiers be delayed, for, now that he has bellowed the *Cocade* story to everyone within earshot, the waiters will spread the word that I had him killed for telling the truth.

Within the room the dusty draperies fluttered. Christophe raised his head and looked through the window into the dark Haitian night. Leclerc knew that he felt at one with darkness, with danger and with courage. An exultant glow was upon him because he had marked the white man's Revolution for the gigantic hoax that it was.

But, Christophe, there is no other kind of revolution. If it is black or white, it is a delusion of the masses, for, in the end, leaders are needed. And when that fact is acknowledged, then once again, no matter what terminology is used, there are only the rulers and the ruled.

"Do you believe in slavery, you French? Some of you say you do. But you do not enslave white people. Why not? Because it is not really slavery in which you believe. It is only degradation and oppression of blacks. Ah, how you lie about your treatment of us. There are even pretty stories told about how much you have done for us. Frenchmen, I have my own list of what you've done. But you are not ashamed, are you? We are not people. We are only senseless, unfeeling clods. We are better off enslaved. Very well, those are your convictions. Mean, base convictions, but they are yours. Go fight for them! I will fight back. As long as I live, you will have to deal with Christophe!" He paused and let his eyes rest questioningly on the other two black men at the table. Unexpectedly, he bent toward them, and, lowering his voice, he said almost entreatingly, "Follow me." Then he turned, walked out to the gallery, leaped over the railing and issued a ringing command to his waiting soldiers.

The men he had left behind at the table sat motionless, listening to the hammering hoofs and the singing and laughter that swept past the windows of Government House.

Leclerc raised himself from his chair. "Gentlemen, if you will excuse me—"

No one said a word.

He walked outside. His personal guard was waiting. One of the men helped him mount his horse. "I'm very sick," Leclerc murmured. "Two of you remain here. Tell Captain Guilbert, when he arrives, that the soldiers are not needed. I want to go home."

In the drawing room there was quiet music and the hushed wave of genteel voices engaged in badinage. Leclerc made his way to the bedroom and fell fully clothed upon the bed. What had happened? What had really happened? Anything of great moment? Did matters stand at a different angle than they had last week, last month? Was Christophe a more dangerous enemy than he had ever been?

Yes. Now that the masquerade was over, Christophe could operate openly. Surely, while acting out his deception he had been unable to take the whole black population into his confidence. Now relieved of any reason for trickery, he would encourage companies of soldiers to desert. Every black would be reminded each morning of Toussaint's fate and of the men who had jumped from the *Cocade*.

But my mask is off, too, Leclerc thought. I will hang every black man, woman and child who speaks an ill word of the French, who carries a message for the rebels or who walks outside his house without a reason. I will defeat these people if it means killing every one of them. Again I will declare Christophe an outlaw. This time I will offer money for his capture, and then we will see how much the blacks love him.

And into his mind for the first time that evening came the thought of Dessalines. He, too, was a danger. Now, while he was still unaware of Christophe's defection, was the time to arrest that disgusting animal. Leclerc pulled the bell cord and, impatiently, after only a moment, he pulled it again. When a servant responded, he sent him to fetch a soldier from the gatehouse or the back garden or any soldier at all who was closest at hand.

While he waited, he swallowed a spoonful of medicine and put a wet cloth to his temples. The soldier who entered his room was of the sort Leclerc liked. Alert, attentive, an intelligent light in his eyes.

"There are two hundred men on the road between the garrison and Government House. Or perhaps they have already returned to the garrison. They must be found and sent immediately to Saint-Marc. Another thousand are to be made ready to follow them. This is the order: Arrest Dessalines. If they have to kill him, so be it. Tell them it is my order that if he is dead they must bring his body to Le Cap. If he is alive, guard him heavily. I am going to have him hanged. Do you understand everything I said?"

"Yes, General. I understand."

"Then go. Take a horse from my stable and hurry."

The soldier was already gone.

Leclerc began to undress. Had he felt better, he thought regretfully, he would have led the troops to Saint-Marc himself. He pulled the bell cord again. "Bring me fresh, cool water, please."

He stretched out once more upon the bed. In imagination he followed the young soldier. How much time should it take?

Would any officer doubt the authenticity of the order simply because there was no signed slip of paper? He should have written a proper command, but he had been so anxious to get the action begun. If two hundred soldiers had started off, completely armed and prepared for anything—

Leclerc sat bolt upright on the bed. Of course they were not prepared for anything. What was the matter with him? They had not been followed by wagonloads of food and water on the march to Government House. All this would have to be provided for them now. There would be a delay, a terrible delay.

He sank back upon the pillows and wondered why it was that nothing, nothing at all, ever went well for him here on this island. He closed his eyes and permitted all the frustrations and disappointments to parade in sequence through his mind. He was hardly surprised that, just as he came to the moment when Christophe leaped over the gallery railing, the drums began again. A mad clatter of excitement in the nest of beaters perched nearest Le Cap. Attention. Attention. Attention. That signal he had learned. And, though he could not decode the message, he knew very well what it was. Christophe had quit the French. He was on his way back into the mountains. The message would be relayed throughout the island before the wagonmen had even decided whether to load the water or the food first. And nobody was going to take Dessalines by surprise. Nobody. The drums, the drums, the Goddamned drums.

There was no point in trying to sleep. He left the bed and went to the window. He looked into the night and thought of Christophe. Where was he now? On a narrow mountain path riding toward some secret meeting place? Or had he reached it and was he, with his men gathered about him, celebrating his most recent betrayal of the French? Leclerc pictured the scene, felt the throbbing excitement and heard the laughter of the black soldiers. Why was it that rebels always seemed to be enjoying a war while legally constituted forces suffered and fretted and had no time for laughter? Was it because the natural qualities that produced a rebel crippled the capacity for imagining failure?

As he stared down into the city of Le Cap, he saw a great flame jump toward the sky. Rebels had so many ways of celebrating.

He thought that soon Pauline would come into this room and prattle to him as she prepared for bed. He thought of the long night in which he would not be able to sleep. He dressed again and went stealthily out of the house and rode down to headquarters.

The wagons were being prepared for the expedition to Saint-Marc. He did not countermand the order. Saint-Marc must be provided with some sort of French authority. The fire brigades had gone out to save a row of small buildings, including two brothels and a tavern that catered exclusively to white soldiers and sailors.

Leclerc went to his office and sank down on the cot he had recently ordered installed there. He asked a lieutenant to bring the latest reports.

"Yes, General." The young man started for the door but did not open it. Instead, he leaned oddly against the jamb and then slid to the floor, where he lay still.

Leclerc, trembling with shock, called for the guards. The door was blocked by the body of the young lieutenant, and there was something so unbearable about watching it being forcibly pushed aside that Leclerc shouted angrily for the men to enter through the windows.

After they had carried the corpse away, Leclerc sat at his desk with the room reeling about him, the perspiration soaking through his uniform.

I can stand no more, he told himself. I can stand no more.

But at his desk, respectfully awaiting his attention, was another lieutenant. "The latest reports, General."

Leclerc looked up at him, and, because the boyish face was expressionless, calm, a tremendous surge of pride in his army gave the General new strength, new determination.

"Thank you, Lieutenant."

The reports were dark and bloody. Another massacre in a town near Jérémie. Ten men killed in Le Cap within the hour by rebels who had set the fire. Rebels thought to be hiding somewhere in ruins behind the cathedral. Search in progress. Colonel Thermes taken to hospital with little hope of recovery. Ninety-three soldiers, eleven sailors dead of fever since noon. Blacks from frigate *Cocade* examined, fed and released. Hospitals too crowded to give them beds for the night. Colonel Foix—

Leclerc looked up from the report. "Where did they go, Lieutenant? The men from the *Cocade*, where did they go?"

"They stood outside the hospital somewhat bewildered, General, not knowing what to do with themselves. Then, just about an hour ago, a wagon came and rounded them all up and—"

"What wagon? Who came?"

The Lieutenant said, "I don't know the names of the men in the wagon, but it's there in the report, General. Colonel Foix signed the men out to two members of the Provisional Assembly who were considered perfectly correct custodians. They are the two members who make up the black contingent of the Assembly along with General Christophe."

Leclerc sat in heavy silence. Rochambeau had been right. Tomorrow the men from the *Cocade* would join the rebels and fight against the French. And Christophe had been more effective than one could have guessed when he had bent toward the two black men at the table and asked them to follow him.

Why is everybody right except me? Why is everybody effective except me? Why can I not do one single thing on this terrible island that turns out to be right or effective?

"Lieutenant, I have something to add to the report and I want it circulated widely and swiftly. Christophe is no longer part of the French Army. His commission has been taken from him and he is to be regarded as an enemy of Saint-Domingue. I shall issue a proclamation with further directives on this matter in the morning. The commission of Dessalines has also been revoked. Both men are rebels and traitors and are to be viewed as such by Army, Navy and civilians."

"Yes, General."

"One more thing. The Provisional Assembly has been dissolved. Add that to the report, though it is of little significance to anyone."

Leclerc sat at his desk through the night, composing the proclamation, which had to be printed and distributed no later than
the following day. In it, he once more declared that Christophe
and Dessalines were outlaws. This time he offered "a considerable sum" for the capture of either or both. "Since these men
were given trust and respect and have chosen to become enemies
of duly authorized government, it must be clear to all that it is
impossible to distinguish between mendacious citizens and those
who are faithful. Therefore, with sorrow, and owing completely
to the deceit of Christophe and Dessalines, all must suffer. The
laws will be more stringent and more sternly enforced than ever
before. Crime will now include any assistance of any kind given
to any rebel by any person in any station of life of any age and
of either sex. The penalty for such action is death by hanging,
and the sentence will be carried out at the time and place of the
discovery of the crime."

He wrote more, much more, and was still writing when the
blazing sun rose and beat upon him, parching his throat and
blurring his vision. He drank a glass of water and lay for a time
upon the cot, thinking what else must be stated in the proclamation, what else must be threatened so these people would understand they were dealing with the power of France.

The doctor from the flagship dropped by the office, and
Leclerc guessed that some well-intentioned officer had sent for
him.

"I'm feeling very well. For the first time, I am optimistic. I
believe I can tame this circus of wild animals." He told the
doctor about the proclamation and why he could not rest. "I
must finish it. It must be distributed today."

The doctor nodded. "I see the need for that. But you yourself
are delaying the distribution. The more time you spend writing,
the longer you hold your decrees from the printing press. You
can always issue others on another day."

Leclerc's proclamation went to the printing press, and he consented to drink an ounce of liquid that tasted vile. He slept
throughout the day on the cot in his office. When evening came,
he went home and slept again. The following morning he ate a

breakfast that seemed delicious to him, and he sat up in bed and listened while Pauline spoke of her concern for him. He found himself believing her. He found himself enchanted with her.

When the doctor arrived, there were pleasant, reassuring words. "You were overtired, General. You've been overtired for weeks. Don't let yourself get in that state again."

"I shan't. I've had terrible things to face, and they still must be faced, but I feel able to do it now."

Good God, the doctor thought, how can a man of thirty become an aging forty within the span of months? "Take another day in bed," he said, and went away feeling depressed.

It was a splendid day. Pauline gave him her full attention and brought the little boy to visit for a time.

This is the world of men who did not choose to be soldiers, Leclerc thought as he played with his child and fell in love again with his wife.

At six in the evening General Rochambeau was announced. Leclerc could not refuse to see him. "Tell him the doctor said I am allowed only fifteen minutes of conversation."

Pauline was pleased at the opportunity of delivering a curt command to Rochambeau. She had heard that it was he who had first said, "The old law that orders the deportation of French women who have had black lovers has to be suspended. Its enforcement would embarrass Bonaparte."

Rochambeau came into the bedroom smiling genially at Leclerc. "So you are feeling better, General? I am overjoyed to see that you are obeying the doctor."

"Yes, I am resting, and though I admit that I should have done it sooner, I still feel a sense of guilt at my laziness. There is so much to be done."

Rochambeau said, "You may rest with no sense of guilt. Your words are at work. The proclamation has been distributed throughout the city and slightly beyond. Within the week it will be known to the whole island. Already we have hanged twelve people today."

Leclerc looked away from the bright excitement he saw in Rochambeau's eyes.

"Three women and a boy of fourteen. All bearers of messages. The other eight were part-time fighters for the rebels, informants and that sort of thing. Everybody seems quite impressed by the new laws. A white planter said to me, 'General, it's a new reign of terror.' "

"By God, I make a poor Robespierre," Leclerc said. "I am already wondering if the twelve people were truly guilty."

Rochambeau's hands moved in a gesture of indifference. "If they were not, then their neighbors are. The sight of dangling bodies may teach them something."

It was what I intended, Leclerc thought. I meant to be merciless. It is the only way to subdue the insurrection. And yet, it is not what I call soldiering. It is not a thing that a man can view with pride.

"Why would a white planter call it a reign of terror?" he asked Rochambeau.

"You have one little phrase in your proclamation that startled them, General. They've never seen or heard it before. Through generations they've been pampered by our government. Now they realize they cannot depend on special treatment from you. By saying 'of any station' in your proclamation, you have suddenly stripped them of the protection their positions had guaranteed them."

"That's ridiculous. When is a white planter going to carry messages, or fight or do any favors for black rebels?"

"General," Rochambeau said, and, though he used the proper form of address, there was somehow the implication that he would have preferred to say "young fellow." "General, rich planters are not always white. They are sometimes mulatto, and though never on equal footing with aristocrats, money bought them a lot of respect."

"They're not apt to favor the blacks, either, Rochambeau. They hate each other."

"When you're up and around, you won't be so sure of that. The news those black bastards brought from Guadeloupe about mulattoes being put up for sale is causing them to reappraise their situation. Two mulatto majors and a captain have deserted

241

us. You also have to remember that white plantation owners
often have mulatto mistresses. Even in Capet's day the black
parts of the girls' families were always shown consideration if
the plantation happened to be one of the big ones. The man I
spoke to was probably thinking that he'd lost the influence to
save his mistress's uncle from being hanged."

"And he has," Leclerc said. "Rochambeau, I don't know
whether you came here to tell me I've acted wisely or to tell me
that I've acted like a bloody fool. In either case, the proclamation stands as written and I expect my officers and men to uphold
it and give it unquestioning support."

"All I was trying to say, General—"

Pauline appeared on the threshold. "I heard your voice all
the way down the hall, dear. I don't think you should let anyone
annoy or anger you. General Rochambeau, you will have to
excuse us now."

Leclerc watched Rochambeau walk out of the room. What
had the man come to say? Or had he come to confuse? If so, he
had been successful. His first words had seemed vaguely con-
gratulatory, but then had followed hints that mistakes had been
made, situations not thoroughly understood. Leclerc tried to
recall the particular remark of Rochambeau's that had caused
him to raise his voice. All he could think of now was the
reference to a reign of terror. And it occurred to him that this
was what Rochambeau had come to say. He had manufactured
the white plantation owner so that he could pass his own opinion
off as a quotation from a prominent citizen.

I did not mean to institute a reign of terror.

A frightening question came to him: Had Robespierre meant
to institute a reign of terror?

When he returned to headquarters the next day, the reports
handed to him were all disheartening. The town of Jérémie was
in complete revolt. Troops had been dispatched there. The two
hundred men sent to Saint-Marc had been surprised midway by
encountering a portion of the army of Dessalines that was
withdrawing from the area. The French, small in number, had
attempted to fall back, in hope of being joined by the thousand

men following on the same road. The blacks had pursued, and there had been a sharp, brutal battle. More than sixty per cent dead. No sign of Dessalines. Several hundred black troops had deserted the garrison during the night. Deaths from fever for a twenty-four-hour period had reached the highest figure so far recorded. Many new cases today. Suggestion made by hospital staff that Government House be furnished with cots.

Leclerc asked a major of the administration department if any files had been kept on black soldiers. "Do we know their names and their villages? Were any of the deserters men from Le Cap?"

"Such information was never kept. A majority of the blacks came to us with the surrender of Christophe and Dessalines. In the first few weeks of our arrival here we got black enlistments because they were then convinced that their generals, by opposing us, would bring disaster upon small farms that were black-owned."

"Don't give me long answers. We don't know anything about the black deserters. Is that right?"

"That is right, General."

"Then send a squad into Le Cap with orders to hang a dozen men of military age."

The major tried not to look astonished.

"Don't stare at me. Ask your damned question, whatever it is."

"What if these men—the ones who are hanged—are not deserters?"

"What difference does that make? Our object is to teach these people, once and for all, that the French are in power. And if you're thinking that the blacks who stay with us will make damned poor fighters after the hangings, cease worrying. We will have no more blacks in the field. They will take over all menial work at the garrison, the harbor and the hospitals. We're so short of decent French soldiers that I won't have white men performing tasks that should rightfully be done by blacks."

The new orders generated a riot at the garrison. Eleven whites shot. Fourteen blacks hanged. Two hundred and seven blacks unaccounted for; presumably, they had fled into the mountains.

Leclerc sent riders around the island to order all commanders who had suffered desertions to hang a few blacks in the public square nearest the local army post.

"Deserters represent new fighters against us," Leclerc said. "We may have to hang a lot of women to make their men stop and think. By God, we're going to beat these people yet."

The doctor looked out at the city, where smoke billowed like thunderclouds against the rust-colored sky, and blazing lumber in the street gave melancholy evidence of Leclerc's intention to rebuild once again. "What is there to win, General?"

"The richest island of the Caribbean. The First Consul wants it, and I was sent to get it for him."

A sorry errand. He has not rested since his collapse, and he is hounded by a desire to succeed. God help a man who must please a famous brother-in-law. "General," the doctor said, "if the First Consul saw this island, I doubt that he would bid you to fight on."

Leclerc did not reply to that, although more than once he had longed for a sensible, trustworthy person to whom he might speak of Saint-Domingue's place in the First Consul's pulse-quickening designs. He looked away lest his eyes reveal that Saint-Domingue's geographical location was of a value beyond mahogany or sugar.

"Have you been able to meet with any black doctors?" he asked. "Were they able to tell you anything of the fever?"

"Their people are not susceptible to it, General, so they have made no study of the fever." He seemed slightly embarrassed. Then, "I talked to a black man who is—well, I suppose it's only honest to say that he's a witch doctor. I don't know the native terms for these fellows. He made a chart of how the sickness would go with us. It has no scientific importance but you might be interested."

"Yes, I would like to see it. How were the reports from the hospitals today?"

"Depressing. Each day now is worse than the day before."

Indeed worse. Men died of fever and of fighting. The blacks swooped down out of the mountains and attacked military posts, murdered civilians and threw flaming torches at homes, shops and churches. They vanished, leaving few of their own dead behind, since the advantage of surprise was always theirs. No enemy could hope to launch a sudden attack upon Haitians in their own mountains. When blacks were encountered about the plain or in a village, it always seemed clear that this was purely accidental. Surely it was not upon a traditional battlefield that blacks expected to triumph. There was never a sign of organizational technique in their fighting. It stunned the well-trained French over and over again that there was obviously no pre-arranged system of performance. Each black took as great a toll as he could while retreating. Each fought his individual war, animated only by a fierce compulsion to disappear in the mountains.

The French asked each other what had become of Christophe and Dessalines. Among the blacks, there seemed to be no officers, no authority, only the passionate desire to survive while doing as much damage as possible in a limited time. The French pursued, not always any more, but sometimes. It was never a good idea. Often a man who had been with Leclerc in the valley or with Rochambeau at Crête à Pierrot died wondering why white officers still believed they could interpret the actions, the expressions and the thoughts of a black army.

Every evening in Pauline's drawing room there was music. The military band played because the time had gone when the gentle plucking of harp strings or an old, sweet song could hold attention. Loud music was wanted, and Pauline encouraged dancing, mad games and contests. Everyone drank too much and laughed hysterically, and couples collapsed on the floor, screaming helplessly because a joke had been too funny or a witty remark simply devastating.

A member of the band fell dead in Pauline's drawing room. A young plantation owner whose father had died the week before dropped out of the dancing and expired before reaching a chair. The house on the next hilltop burned, and Pauline's guests stood on the galleries and pretended they were watching fireworks in

Paris. They cheered and applauded and sang bawdy songs from early Revolutionary days.

Most nights, Leclerc stayed at headquarters. He did not wish to be identified with the happenings in his home, nor did he like the coterie with which Pauline surrounded herself. It troubled him that he understood these people, understood why lust and drunkenness had come out of hiding. To those who crowded into Pauline's drawing room, the island represented the world, and therefore the world was going to pieces. The future was unmentionable, the present unendurable. Fever stalked the island. Who would die next? Houses flamed and smoldered, and even the most witless knew that the unseen hand that had set the fire would set another. Where? The stench of the island, the corpses lying unburied or left to swing and decay in the heat of the diabolical summer, the triumphs of the blacks, their hatred— who could not understand why the brittle shell of elegance had splintered?

Leclerc sometimes spent the entire night writing letters.

Citizen Consul:

Months ago I entreated you to do nothing which might make the blacks anxious about their liberty until I was ready. Suddenly, and to my astonishment, the slave trade was authorized in Guadeloupe. I was robbed of all possible hope that anything could be accomplished by persuasion. I can depend only on force and I have no troops.

Citizen Consul, if you wish to preserve Saint-Domingue, send a new army. If you abandon us to ourselves as you have hitherto done, the island is lost and, once lost, you will never again regain it. Death has wrought such frightful havoc among my troops that I confess to sitting here dazed and unbelieving. What general could calculate on a mortality of four-fifths of his army? I respond to all my difficulties with severe penalties. Terror is the sole resource left me. I employ it. I had sixty blacks hanged today. Bear in mind that you must send me a successor. I have no one here who can replace me in the critical situation in which the colony will be for some time.

Send me reinforcements. . . .

Leclerc was never sure that his brother-in-law read his letters. The Minister of Marine was certainly obligated to do so.

Citizen Minister:

If the French government wishes to preserve Saint-Domingue it must, on receipt of my letter, give orders for ten thousand men to sail at once.

The mountain chain from Vailliéres up to and including Marmelade is in insurrection. Not a village or an individual is a friend of France. I will be able to protect the plain only supposing that the fever stops in the first ten days of Vendémiaire. The flagship doctor has spoken to a learned man who says it might well do that but since 8 Fructidor the fever has assumed a new force. I lose a hundred to a hundred twenty men each day. To hold these mountains when I shall have taken them I shall have to wage a war of extermination and it will cost many lives. Please send ten thousand men in addition to the reinforcements already promised.

I have to fight a war besides counting off my losses in the hospitals. Men die of fever as they prepare for battle. They die sometimes before they have even been instructed on how to fight these people.

I was hoping you would name my successor to me or send him here without any more talk on the subject. I wish you better health and more pleasant thoughts than mine. Do something for us. Do not leave us abandoned. . . .

Where was the harm, Leclerc thought, in writing again to Bonaparte?

Dear Brother-in-law (or Respected Citizen Consul if I am no longer cherished as a member of your family):

I was told that in Vendémiaire the sickness should taper off but it did not do so. The month of Fructidor cost me more than four thousand men. Today I am told the sickness may not abate until the end of Brumaire. If that is true and it continues at the same intensity, the colony is lost.

No general commanding an army has ever found himself in a more trying situation. The troops that arrived a month ago no longer exist. They have all succumbed to this terrible plague. Rebels carry out attacks on the plain every day. They burn whatever still stands and the sounds of battle can be heard at Le Cap. It is impossible for me to take the offensive but we who are your soldiers fight as well as we can while we still breathe.

The black troops are deserting me by companies. Some mulattoes remain but many have disappeared. Today I have only nine hundred and twenty troops fit for duty and seven hundred and fifty-nine convalescents. In the outposts the situation is as bad or worse. For God's sake, send me twelve thousand men. . . .

Leclerc was not the only one who knew that the hospitals housed more soldiers than the garrison, and that the strangely idle ships of the fleet cradled only dead and dying sailors.

On an October night a French artilleryman burst into headquarters with the news that five to six thousand blacks were massing for an attack on Le Cap. He had been serving with the mulatto general Clervaux when Pétion, second-in-command, had deserted and, with all black troops following him, had joined the rebels.

Leclerc listened to the story with a great deal of suspicion. "How is it that you live? Where are other Frenchmen? Where is General Clervaux?"

"General Clervaux was permitted to ride away safely. He is a friend of Christophe's, as is Pétion. Clervaux will join the rebels when he has thought the matter over. He and Pétion embraced and wept in parting. Clervaux begged that white soldiers not be mistreated, so we were only disarmed and released. We all started from Le Haut-du-Cap together, but I outdistanced the others."

"How can I believe you?" Leclerc demanded.

The artilleryman gazed boldly at the General. "Sir, has the time come when this army is as rotten as theirs? If not, why do you mistrust one of your own good soldiers?"

Leclerc sent for Rochambeau and ordered him to be responsible for the safety of Pauline and the child.

"Put my family and household on any ship that has a healthy captain and crew. Tell Admiral Villaret de Joyeuse to give the sailing order. I can leave you a few hundred men, but no more. Use them well to protect the civilian population."

"What is your order concerning blacks who did not desert us?"

"Herd them onto one of those ships where everybody is dead, and hang them."

Leclerc, with three hundred and eighty French soldiers and a thousand National Guardsmen, took the road to Le Haut-du-Cap. Rochambeau had urged him to stand and defend the city. Leclerc did not waste time in argument. The risk could not be taken that thousands of blacks, ready to launch a violent assault, might stampede the defenders and run loose among helpless residents. Leclerc would have to stop the rebels as far away from the city as he could. And if he could not stop them at all, then God must help Le Cap.

Rochambeau dispatched a grenadier and four sergeants to bring Pauline, her child and her ladies to the docks. He sent word to Admiral Villaret de Joyeuse that Leclerc's household must sail as quickly as could be arranged. He then called out all able-bodied white residents between the ages of fifteen and sixty to act as guards and defenders of Le Cap. The city was in turmoil. Women ran screaming through the streets toward the harbor, imploring that they be placed immediately on ships bound for France. Pauline, who was commanded to do the very thing for which these women begged, refused to obey.

In negligee, she sat in her drawing room with the dried bones of some small animal arranged in a cryptic design before her. An old black woman hobbled away as the grenadier entered.

Pauline shouted at him. "Get out! I even dismissed my friends because I was having a very private reading about my future, and you dare to charge in here as though my home were public property. Get out! Don't you hear me? Get out!"

"I have been ordered to take you to the harbor, Madame. You must leave the island."

"I will not go," she said, and settled herself comfortably in an armchair, with a glass of wine in one hand and her mirror in the other.

"It is an order, Madame," the grenadier told her.

She reached back into her Marseille girlhood and selected a few orders of her own that caused the grenadier to blanch.

A sergeant came into the room, bringing the child, who was in night clothes. The governess and nursery help walking behind him were pale with terror. Pauline looked at them contemptuously.

"You are not afraid, Dermide, are you?" she asked. Then she turned to the grenadier. "This boy is the nephew of Napoleon Bonaparte and it was Bonaparte himself who named him. Dermide. He chose that from a favorite book of poems. Don't ever forget the boy's name and who named him." She bent her head back to catch the last drops of wine in her glass, then smiled sweetly at the child who had been clever enough to have Napoleon for an uncle.

The other sergeants had finished gathering together all occupants of the house. Pauline's ladies and servants, rubbing their eyes and buttoning their clothes, straggled into the drawing room.

"All accounted for?" the grenadier asked. He swung Dermide to his shoulders and said to Pauline, "We go, Madame."

"You think you can order me around, do you?"

The grenadier signaled the sergeants, and they picked up the chair in which Pauline sat.

She found an entirely new shower of words from the Marseille waterfront, but she was carried out of her house with the members of her domestic establishment trailing behind her. "We look like a Mardi Gras parade," she said. "I am the first lady of this island, and you are making a spectacle of me."

At the harbor her chair was set down to await the launch that was on its way to her. Two of the sergeants stood beside her, fending off the people of Le Cap who beseeched her to take them with her to France.

"I'm not going to France. I am staying right here. You are afraid to die. But I am Bonaparte's sister and I am afraid of nothing."

When elderly men whom she had known as dignified and respected residents of the island began to approach her with requests for space on her ship, she eyed them chillingly.

"If you're afraid of death, start learning bravery," she taunted them. "Blacks or no blacks, your time is nearly gone, you dried-up old sacks of bones."

Her ladies, standing behind her, whimpered and trembled in fear of the people Pauline insulted. She scalded her little court, her mouth so twisted in disdain that for a moment she strikingly resembled her brother.

"So you're the daughters of the old aristocracy, are you? No wonder that in order to be strong France had to murder your kind of scum. Stop sniveling. You're going back to Paris. I'll wait right here for my husband, who will end the night by hanging every black on the island."

Leclerc was less optimistic. The blacks came against him a little after midnight. They came with savage cries, their hard bodies glistening beneath the moon, their eyes wild and pitiless. Leclerc saw the depth of their imposing columns and he prayed. He prayed and he fought, and in a corner of his mind he counted the dead of both sides and realized that the French could not afford even a victory. Little by little he gave ground, his men dying around him, struggling to fire once more, struggling to hold the road to Le Cap.

But it was lost. The road was open. Leclerc had been beaten back.

He sent a messenger galloping to Rochambeau to say that Pauline and the child must sail at once, if even on a small boat, if only to another island. With fewer than fifty men, he stationed himself in the darkness of a palm grove just below the fort, which bulked weirdly on the rise of the hill. It had been a symbol of French predominance. It had become a charnel house. If a man still lived behind its walls, no one had seen or heard of him in more than a week. The fort was quiet and sinister. The moon skimmed low and turned the observation towers and embrasures ghastly white.

"Fire at those black bastards as they pass," Leclerc ordered his men. "Get as many as you can. Then disperse and hope they won't stop to search for us. Was the National Guard wiped out? Where is it?"

"They lost a few hundred, sir," someone said. "After that they withdrew."

Leclerc waited for the triumphant dark columns to appear on their laughing, singing march to Le Cap. There was not a sound on the road. No thunder of rolling cannon, no beat of footsteps. Even the black voices raised in the jeering staccato style in which they constantly communicated were silent. An hour passed in complete stillness. Then suddenly the sky reddened a few miles to the east of where the fighting had taken place. Almost simultaneously flames sprang up a mile away from the first fire.

"What are they doing?" one soldier asked another.

Leclerc did not explain, but he understood what was happening. Somehow, the black army was out of hand. The commander of that great fighting force had lost the ability to control his unpredictable men. No doubt the voice of authority had shouted, "On to Le Cap," but the blacks, dazzled by seeing the French General run, had stood where they were, slapping each other on the back and shouting with joy. Their objectives were limited. The ambition span of the average black reached no farther than one accomplishment. They had routed the French, hadn't they?

That was enough work for one night. Some other time they'd march on Le Cap. Right now, they were going to celebrate. My, my, didn't those French just get out quick? Let's go burn a few plantation houses.

So they had scattered in all directions, slaughtering anyone they saw, throwing torches at buildings, looting, raping, sometimes pausing just to laugh and tell each other all over again how the French had run. And there lay Le Cap, almost undefended, certain to fall with no more than a scream of anguish into the hands of any army that would simply keep marching. Leclerc shook his head in wonderment. He thought of Toussaint, for whom men like these had thrown three European nations off the island. He thought of Christophe, who had the cold talent of command. He thought of Dessalines, who terrified the ignorant common soldier. Where were Christophe and Dessalines tonight? He knew they had not been killed or captured as outlaws. No demand had been made on the government for the reward. The artilleryman who had reported Pétion's abandoning the French had not seen either of the two highest-ranking black officers. Who, then, was the man who had been powerless to drive his troops to complete victory? Was it Pétion, the gentle revolutionary, the sometime poet, the quadroon with white skin and black sympathies?

The moon was obscured now by smoke. The familiar acrid odor of burning buildings filled the air. Rebel soldiers, stimulated and uncontrolled, wandered the island. What would they do next for excitement? His question was answered swiftly. He heard voices, black voices, chattering, arguing, advising, refusing, agreeing. They were approaching the fort. He could hear the cannons being dragged into place. Stupid bastards. With the city of Le Cap lying helpless, they had decided it would be fun to shoot at the fort. Their so-called commander, whoever he was, must be going mad with frustration and rage.

Leclerc and his men waited, listening. The cannons roared, and bits of the old fort's masonry flew high and fell to earth, making solid, thudding noises. There were howls of glee, and the cannons fired again. It came to Leclerc that this was not

253

simply the joy of vandalism. They were actually trying to shoot their way into the fort. Ah, yes, of course. What pride, what pleasure it would give these idiots to possess a French fort.

The cannons roared once more, and this time a mighty cheer rose, and, with cries of exultation, the blacks could be heard lunging through the breaks they had made in the fortifications. And suddenly there was a sound so astonishing that Leclerc's heart leaped. There was firing from the fort. From the fort!

The fusillade was spaced, thoughtful, accurate. But now the blacks had help. The sound of cannon had drawn wanderers who couldn't think how next to squander their dangerous energy. Leclerc heard the short, sharp exchanges between the rebels and the fort. Then the boom of the cannon again. No swift answer from the fort. A black voice shrieked "Advance" and followed the command with a whoop of boisterous laughter. Leclerc pictured a lowly soldier, ebullient, wild with delight at having shouted the most inspiring word in a soldier's vocabulary.

Now, after a prudent delay, the cannons from the fort fired again. The blacks were no longer talking or laughing. They could be heard moving through the trees, addressing themselves differently to the attack. Leclerc sensed the change of mood. It was there in the slap of hands against musket butts, the heavy tread of large men who were once again soldiers, the eerie quiet of the night. When those voices that could be shrill or mellow dropped to a whisper, there was always something to fear. Massing now. That was what they were doing. Massing to storm the fort. But from behind earthen ramparts came a sting-ing volley of death, and Leclerc heard a long, mournful wail. It came from a single throat and was heard but seldom from these men who ignored their dying and never picked up their dead. The advance wave against the fort had been thrown back with heavy losses, and one man had cried out. One man.

By God, Leclerc thought, when they put their minds to it, they are really soldiers.

The wail had scarcely died in the night when a rallying shout shook the stillness. They were ready to try again. To try what? To take the fort they did not need and had not had as an objective. Now it became the center of all satisfaction, a goal worthy of any sacrifice. A fort. Why, telling about the taking of a fort would give more pleasure than describing how the French General had run away.

Where are their leaders? Leclerc's military mind suffered for the misdirected efforts, the waste of lives, the failure to march upon and occupy a city that controlled not only the harbor but also, perhaps, the future.

There was a silence again, a delay. The fort waited, too. Why? And then Leclerc knew what the observation towers had seen. He heard the yells and the running feet. More blacks had given up their plundering and burning to unite with their comrades, who had found something really wonderful to do.

Frenchmen would have debated strategy, mapped out orders for a score of officers, even fed the men while proper organization was under discussion. The blacks only raised another terrifying shout and threw themselves against the fort.

God damn them, Leclerc thought. If they succeed, they may then remember Le Cap, and they will be so intoxicated with having a French fort in their hands that not even a white kitten will survive.

But the cannons of the French fort blazed again, and the leaderless blacks were dying or falling back. And Leclerc caught his breath, for on the Le Cap road, flying toward him, was the sound of horses' hoofs. He stepped from the grove and, squinting, saw the outline of uniformed men. It was the National Guard coming back to fight again. Five hundred, Leclerc judged, peering down the long road into the darkness. This time, about a hundred were mounted, swinging sabers and looking fierce and determined.

"General Leclerc here," he called as the riders drew near.

"The city is in convulsions, General. The black residents are so sure they're winning that they've gone wild and are attacking the whites. We have to cut them off here." The Guard Major gestured toward the cannon fire. "How did the fort get involved?"

Leclerc said, "The blacks fired on it. Let them try once more, then we'll go after them."

Somebody gave him a horse. He held the impatient Guard and waited as a blood-curdling yell split the darkness, and the fort responded with deadly fire.

Once again Leclerc heard the mournful wail, and he said to the Major, "Let us try it now."

The mounted men sped up the road, whipping their horses and ascending the hill to the fort with the momentum of fury. The cannons of the fort had wrought carnage, but the blacks, in blind hatred of the French, ignored what had already happened to them. They rushed forward in screaming frenzy. Sabers made sibilant, whistling sounds, and heads dropped to the bloody ground. Leclerc whirled on a black who carried a French sword. He shot and the man fell, but not before imbedding the sword deep into the stomach of Leclerc's horse.

The foot soldiers reached the hill, and, because of what was happening in Le Cap, they fought as though they were the angry victims raised from the dead for an hour of vengeance. And the remnant of an army that could have, on that night, repeated the triumph of Toussaint L'Ouverture streaked toward the mountains. The brilliant, laughing army that could have sent the feeble French forces racing for their ships either lay dead or crouched, demoralized, in the caves above the city.

The pale light of morning revealed a sight of unbearable horror. Leclerc turned from it, faced the fort and called out to the silent concrete bastions. "It is Leclerc. Admit me." After a moment, he called again. "You saved the island. Let me salute you."

A man appeared on the parapet. "General, don't come in. We are sick."

Leclerc backed away, gazing upward to get a better look at the man. "By all that is holy, soldier, you did not act sick when we needed you."

"There were fourteen of us left, General. Two died while firing. There is no one here who has not died within the week and none who will live until tomorrow."

Leclerc felt the cold tingling of his scalp. "God, man, is there nothing I can do?"

The soldier crossed himself and began to weep. "Have a mass said, sir. Not here on this cursed island, but if you ever get to Bordeaux—" He swayed and fell backward.

Leclerc shouted but no one answered. And, though he stood there shouting again and again for several minutes, no one ever answered. He turned away thinking of the courage of those who had defended the fort, the handful of dying men who had known they had nothing to gain or lose and had still fired the cannons.

Suddenly, he was tired of courage and killing and victory and defeat. He became aware of the blood on his uniform, the splattered blood of blacks and whites. He looked again at the sprawled bodies, the crushed heads, the severed limbs that had been trampled upon. From the rise of the hill he looked out at the sea as it lay, soft and green, in the new morning. He saw the French fleet and was surprised that it could seem so gallant and good and innocent.

Brother-in-law, there would have been no harm in their keeping the island. Why didn't you welcome them as a valiant little nation that had won its right to live? I was trained to defend the glory of France. Is this glory? Is this even a thing that can be asked of a man? Brother-in-law, I tell you in all sincerity that I hope you roast in hell.

He walked over to the surviving officers of the National Guard, who awaited him. "I'm afraid someone will have to give me another horse."

They rode back to Le Cap. Leclerc remembered as he rode that he would have to give the order for a hundred blacks to be hanged. Murder of white residents could not go unpunished. But, then, did anything go unpunished?

He did not give the order. He went directly to his house. Pauline met him on the gallery, but she recoiled when she saw his bloody uniform.

"Go have a bath and then we'll talk. Dear husband, I have so much to tell you."

"I'm going to bed. I'm tired and sick and—"

"You can't go to bed. You're a hero. Everyone is saying that only one more battle and then the island is Napoleon's forever."

He walked past her without replying. He went to the bedroom and rang for the servant whose duty it was to carry the tub water. He took off his uniform and told the man to throw it away.

"General, I can clean it for you."

"Throw it away," Leclerc repeated.

He lay in his bath for a half hour; then he crawled into bed.

Pauline came to the door and smiled at him. "I was so brave," she said. "Even when the real trouble started I was—"

"I'm sick, Pauline. Very sick. Go away."

"You'll feel better when you get up."

Only, Leclerc never got up again. He died thirty-eight hours after the battle of Le Haut-du-Cap. He died saying that Napoleon Bonaparte was the most vicious, most destructive man alive.

"He couldn't have meant that," Pauline said. "He was delirious, wasn't he, Doctor?"

The doctor thought her question over. Then he said, "Yes, he was delirious."

"Well, of course he was. He couldn't have said such a thing if he'd been in his right mind. Doesn't everybody get delirious with the fever? He did die of the fever, didn't he?"

Again the doctor did not give a quick reply. Finally, he said, "Yes, he died of the fever—I think."

. . . .

She hated them all, but when they gathered on Mont Vautour, the woman who had been Bréda's cook greeted them and gave them coffee. Christophe had asked her permission to hold a meeting on what she considered her private estate, and she had agreed. Toussaint would not have liked her to refuse Christophe a safe place to talk.

"The Colonel will be here," he had said apologetically.

"It is a matter of indifference to me. I have nothing to steal. But why, when he has always been ignored by good fighting men, do you have to acknowledge his existence?"

Christophe had looked troubled. "He has many soldiers and, for some reason or other, he claims he wants to be part of a legitimate effort to defeat the French."

"I would say that is not to be believed. I have heard that, though he calls himself 'Colonel,' he was never more than a man without rank in the Martinique National Guard. People say he has amassed a fortune in jewels that he has taken from the rich houses. You had better be careful of the Colonel. He is a ruthless man."

Christophe had averted his eyes. "We are all ruthless men. All of us."

Now, with some curiosity, she studied the Colonel. He was tall and bony, with a narrow nose and thin lips. He had declined the coffee and sat drinking rum, which he had carried with him. The friend he had brought accepted coffee and had even smiled, but she had not bothered to smile back. The man was so obviously a toady.

She rested her eyes on the trim Christophe; on Clervaux, the mulatto; on Pétion, the quadroon. How very much like gentlemen they were. To be sure, Bréda never would have permitted Christophe or Clervaux at his table, for one was *café noir* and the other *café au lait*. Pétion was as white as Bréda and far more elegant of speech. It amused her to think that if Pétion had been introduced to Bréda, say, in Paris, Bréda would have supposed him to be a French nobleman and would have been proud to claim acquaintance with him.

She wondered if the newcomers to the circle noticed how brilliantly Pétion maneuvered so that he need never look at Dessalines or become involved in any talk of which he was a part. The old hatreds festered long in mixed-bloods. Blacks were different. They either killed you immediately or forgot what it was you had done to them.

Her gaze went to Hercule Drouet. She knew him well. She had carried the messages and had been a faithful intermediary when Christophe had lived as a French general and Hercule had made himself famous as the rebel leader sworn to murder him for his betrayal of Haiti. At Christophe's order, Hercule had sent his men throughout the island to spread the news of what the French had done to Toussaint. She, riding on her mule, had traveled from village to village, talking only to women, telling them that unless their men fought against the French their children would be sold into slavery. She had convinced the women that Hercule Drouet must have soldiers. She had done all there was left to do for Toussaint. So had Christophe and Hercule and Dessalines. How could she hate them? It was easy to do. She hated all men who were alive on Mont Vautour tonight while Toussaint died in the dripping damp of a French prison.

There had been some inconsequential conversation. Now Clervaux held up his hand, and said, "Let us talk of serious matters."

The woman who had been Bréda's cook had expected Christophe to take charge of the meeting. True, Clervaux was also a general, but he had never possessed the authoritative bearing of Christophe. She saw the Colonel's eyes wandering away from Clervaux, drifting scornfully over Christophe and Dessalines, and returning to Clervaux. She listened as the Colonel spoke.

"I told you I would come, and I'm here. I'm here to say that you can't serve the French and defeat them at the same time. Two of your friends who are present are spies of the French, lackeys of the French, tools of the French."

Clervaux said, "Not so."

"Don't tell me it's not so. I don't trust you very much, either. For a kind word from a white man, you mulattoes would crawl on your bellies."

Clervaux did not flinch. "You have been aching to say that for a long while, haven't you? Well, now it is said. May I proceed with the plan for opening constructive discussion?"

"I can't think of anything more constructive than getting rid of French officers. Unless Pétion would like to tell us what happened at Le Haut-du-Cap, where he lost an army."

Pétion said, "That night I was a poor field commander. Does that satisfy as an explanation?"

"It might if you fellows weren't so friendly with them." He

pointed toward Christophe and Dessalines. "What the hell is this meeting all about?"

Clervaux said, "If you will be silent for a short time, Colonel, I will—"

"Don't call me Colonel. I was a colonel when I thought I was a Frenchman. I haven't been in their rotten army since the day I found out that to them I wasn't a Frenchman. I was just a nigger. That's what we all are to them. Yes, even you, Pétion, with your milky-white skin."

Dessalines got up slowly from the rock on which he had been sitting. There was the feeling that he had risen to remind the Colonel how huge he was, and that he had moved slowly to emphasize that nothing so insignificant as this man could drive him to swift action.

"Listen," Dessalines said. "I want you to Goddamned stop talk about what color is somebody's skin. How it beat the French if I got a behind white like cloud or black like iron stove? Much better you talk war pretty soon or I go home."

The Colonel said, "I intend to talk war. I have eight thousand troops, and I didn't let Pétion throw any of them away trying to take a fort. Who's got more than eight thousand live, strong men?" He looked challengingly around the circle of faces.

Dessalines was quietly laughing at him. "You got eight thousand live, strong men, Colonel, because they do not die trying to take a fort. They do not die trying to do nothing. You save them up like, when little boy, I save a piece of cake some lady throw away. They never fight nothing but children and women. You not fighters, none of you. You looters. While we fight and make everything noisy and scary, you walk in houses and grab pretty things and run. It take eight thousand of you to rob jewel things from two old ladies."

The Colonel contented himself with a sneering glance at Dessalines, and another swallow of rum.

Clervaux said, "I don't see how this meeting will benefit us unless we concentrate on the only thing that has any meaning. Can we, as commanders, agree to pool our strength and—"

The Colonel's companion spoke up. He was copper colored

and, like Christophe, had in his speech the accent of another island. "I have three thousand men. Unlike some people, I'm willing to admit that's small compared to the Colonel's army. Therefore I'm not going to call him 'Colonel.' I say he's general. General of the whole, the entire North Province of Haiti. You bring your little bunches of two or three thousand each, join them to the General's army, and then we have something worthwhile. Later we'll talk sense to the South and West provinces, but for now we'll just show them how to win in the North."

Nobody replied. The Colonel, who had appeared to close his eyes in complete indifference to reactions of the others, stole a quick look around. He was thunderstruck to see Christophe nod as though saying to himself, A good idea. Now, that would be a piece of luck. Christophe was a fine leader. To have Christophe on his side really would guarantee success. Expecting nothing but hostility, counting Christophe as lost from the outset, the Colonel had decided to be first with the insults. He had learned that it always sounded well to doubt another man's patriotism. It was not a tactic that inspired affection, yet there was no denying that a certain respect attached itself to the accuser. Hell, if he had known that Christophe was going to listen with interest and perhaps even approval, he would have taken a different tack. What did it matter whether or not Christophe had been loyal to Haiti? That kind of thing was for stupid people. Besides, Haiti was going to be a different sort of place when he was in power. The United States had kept the rulers of Tripoli and Algiers in luxury by bribing them not to plunder their merchant vessels. Well, the United States could pay Haiti's ruler, too. He knew almost to the dollar what it would cost for the ships he would need, and he had every dollar ready and waiting. He thought of the pearl necklaces, the gold and the diamonds in his possession, hidden away to be exchanged for a private fleet that would be the terror of the Caribbean. Negotiations would start on the day that the French were beaten off the island. Everything was at a standstill until then. He needed competent leaders, and here was the place to find them.

He shot another quick glance at Christophe. Deep in thought.

Yes, he had impressed Christophe with the mention of the eight thousand men. It would be helpful to have Dessalines as well. The man had a great reputation among soldiers. How did one go about placating a wild animal?

Pétion said, "From the silence, I gather that everyone has been thinking over the last remarks we heard. I hope that all of you will be as frank as I am going to be. I very much want eight thousand men who have not been really fighting the French to come fight them now. I will not make a lengthy explanation about what happened at Le Haut-du-Cap. It is sufficient for me to say that I am in no position to stand in the way of another's assuming leadership."

There was a long, shuddering sigh from Hercule Drouet before he spoke. "Yes, I've been thinking over the remarks we've heard, and I'm going to be as frank as man can be." He carefully set his coffee mug on a tree stump and addressed Clervaux firmly but without fire. "I am not going to fight under the leadership of the Colonel. I am only a major, as rank goes, but I have men who will obey only me. I am not going to say how many men I have, but there are enough of them. The fact that I was invited here proves that. My men are very experienced. I'm not going to risk them by putting them into battle with those who have been taught nothing but how to loot houses."

"All soldiers loot," Pétion said.

Drouet flashed his fine white teeth in an honest smile. "Agreed, General. All soldiers loot. But I object to looters who have never soldiered. When did these men ever help us? When did the Colonel come galloping against the French? He has a mob which he calls an army."

"Watch yourself, boy," the Colonel cautioned. "Who in hell are you anyhow?"

Dessalines roared with laughter. "See, Drouet, he don't know you. That prove he not never go to war. If he would go, he would see you and know who you are."

Clervaux tried not to be amused. "Please, Dessalines," he said, "be serious. Hercule, you have something to add?"

"Yes, I have. Since General Pétion has not wished to explain the disaster at Le Haut-du-Cap, I would like to do so." Drouet looked away from Clervaux and addressed the others. "General Christophe was to lead the attack on the city. He was ready and God knows he was able, but when the word spread that it would not be General Pétion in command the men threatened to desert. Do you know why?" He looked at the Colonel. "Because the same garbage I've heard here tonight was scattered through the ranks. Christophe was a traitor to Haiti. He had served with the French and was their man. So General Pétion was at the head of an army that had already dictated the terms on which it would fight. It was so all powerful it could choose a commander and do as it damned well pleased. When it saw Leclerc run, there was no holding it. It had refused one general and had defeated another, so in its pride it got itself torn to pieces. I'm not going to fight under any Goddamned idiot who says the same things about Christophe and Dessalines that a bunch of sons of bitches said before they got themselves slaughtered."

Dessalines shook his head disapprovingly. "Such words, Drouet, when the woman who was Bréda's cook, she sit right where she hear such dirty things." He cast a glance at the small, gilt chair near the dying fire. "No. She go. You right, Drouet. Only sons of bitches and Goddamned idiots think me and Christophe ever trait against Haiti."

The Colonel ran his hand almost bashfully across his face. "All right, Dessalines, I guess I was—"

"*General* Dessalines," the big man said.

"You're right again. You deserve your honors. What I wanted to say, General Dessalines, is that I guess I was a little rough. It's been said that I've used the war as a cover for looting, but I don't hold that against anybody. We've all done a little something that we don't want out in the open."

"Not quite the truth," Clervaux said freezingly.

"What do you mean by that?"

"I mean, you must speak for yourself, Colonel."

Pétion smiled good-humoredly at Clervaux. "I'm surprised at your implication that some of us are angels."

So, the Colonel thought, the fine three-quarters white man is also impressed. Maybe I could use him. Nobody away from the islands could tell that he's just another nigger. Maybe he'd be helpful in putting my propositions to United States naval officers and people like that.

Clervaux said, "Let us not waste time. Who agrees that victory in the North Province depends on unity?"

Dessalines had questions. Propped up against a tree, he was idly whittling a small whistle with a very large knife. " 'Unity' means all together? We all fight to beat hell out of French?"

"That's right," Clervaux answered.

Dessalines cocked his massive head to one side. "Who command?"

"We'll open that to discussion."

The Colonel said, "I'm sorry, General Clervaux, but I don't see any need for discussion. If I am not immediately named general of the North Province I'll have to prove my supremacy by using my eight thousand men in a way I had not planned on."

Clervaux blinked his eyes nervously and turned to Pétion. "Suppose we chose the Colonel as our leader. Would you take orders from him? Would you carry out those orders faithfully?"

Pétion seemed startled. "We have reached the heart of the matter very early, haven't we? I would think it necessary to reflect well on all that has been said before declaring any man our leader. I feel it only fair, however, to state that I am inclined to favor a united army, and if that means accepting the Colonel I do not believe I would be much opposed."

Clervaux looked at Dessalines with the disinterested expression proper to a capable referee. "General Dessalines?"

Dessalines frowned at the small piece of wood and the large knife. "I command my army till day I die. You know that, Clervaux."

The Colonel smiled quite charmingly. "General Dessalines, earlier I said harsher words than I really meant. I apologize. Please don't vote while you are angry at me. Take time to think."

Dessalines made no reply and did not even glance at the Colonel.

Clervaux's gaze passed to Hercule Drouet. "Yes or no?"

"No."

"Christophe?"

There was no immediate answer. Dessalines and Drouet looked at him anxiously. His eyes were fixed on some far-distant point. He moistened his lips, but still he did not speak. Perhaps he had not heard.

"Christophe?" Clervaux said again.

"I want to whip the French," Christophe said after another few seconds of thought. "I believe we might be able to do it if we pool our forces. So I am certainly for that. As to the Colonel being placed in full command, I have reservations. I am not acquainted with his leadership. He may be an impulsive man who marches his men into traps. He may be an overcautious man who fails to grasp opportunities. As I sit here, I simply don't know enough about him."

The Colonel extended his hand to Christophe. "I want to say I like your attitude. I like an open mind."

Christophe clasped the offered hand, and said, "Thank you."

Dessalines gaped at him. "What in hell happen here?" He turned to Drouet. "You understand what happen?"

Without replying to Dessalines, Drouet asked, "General Clervaux, how do you vote?"

The mulatto made it simple. "No."

Dessalines said, "I hear three very big, strong *no* words, and I hear two very weak, little *maybe* words. The Colonel, I think he vote *yes*, so we don't need ask. What good only one *yes* word against three *no* words and two *maybes?*"

The Colonel again smiled charmingly. "General Dessalines, we aren't quite finished. My friend has not yet had the chance to vote."

The small, bloodshot eyes of Dessalines narrowed in contempt. "I trust you with secret, Colonel. Three thousand men don't get him nothing up here except a cup of coffee."

"And I say anybody with three thousand men deserves a vote."

"That what you say, Colonel? All right. Drouet, you call the woman who was Bréda's cook. She going to vote. I just give her four thousand soldiers."

Clervaux bent toward Dessalines and in a playful manner slapped his shoulder. "You're not behaving. You can't give away soldiers just to get someone else a vote."

"Why can't I do that, Clervaux? That's what the Colonel do."

The Colonel leaped to his feet. "I'm going to tell you men something. You better listen to Pétion and Christophe, who, I think, are being fair. You'd better listen to them because I've got my army in a howling mood to fight."

Dessalines went back to his whittling. The candlelight flashed on the blade of his knife, and he cast one quick upward glance, as though measuring exactly where the Colonel stood.

"I'm a stranger, an outsider, but I want the French off this island as much as you do. Maybe more. You're never going to run them out unless I'm on your side." No one tried to silence the Colonel. He had a great deal to say, and his voice grew strident as he continued. "I'm an educated man. Maybe I'm not a scholar like Pétion, but I know things that you'll need when the fighting is over. Who the hell here understands administration and the banking business? I do. Put me in command of the North Province Army and I'll soon control the whole island. I'll make every one of you so rich that you will live like kings. I want power because I deserve power. No one's going to stand in my way. I tell you——"

They let him talk. They listened. They watched him. After twenty minutes of his boasting, wheedling and threatening, Dessalines, the illiterate, the uncouth, dealt so refined an insult that Clervaux was filled with admiration. Dessalines had simply looked up, studied the Colonel for a moment, then quietly put his knife away.

"I wasn't always in the Goddamned French Army. I once occupied a position that would make you blink with surprise and maybe even bow with respect. I'd like to work with you. You're splendid fellows and we belong together. I'm going to accomplish mighty large things. Nothing is going to hold me back. I have to destroy whatever interferes with my advance in life. I don't like to do that, but when a man knows——"

Dessalines stood up, yawned, stretched and, without a word

to anyone, lumbered toward the twisted, rock-hidden path that led down the mountainside. Hercule Drouet hesitated only a second, then followed.

Clervaux said, "I'm afraid we have not had a successful meeting."

"Well, I'm not the one who is going to regret it." The Colonel looked from Christophe to Pétion. "You two gentlemen have been very open-minded. I tell you what I'd like to do. I'd like to give you a chance to know me better. Maybe after we have talked and played sort of a question-and-answer game, you'd call another meeting. At that time you might give me a whole-hearted endorsement."

"It's not beyond possibility," Pétion said amiably.

Clervaux stood up and brushed fastidiously at the seat of his breeches. "Let's not meet here again," he said. "Pétion, you must know a place that would be clean and comfortable as well as safe."

The Colonel laughed sourly. "How do you know you'd be welcome at the next meeting, General Clervaux?"

"I trust my friends, Colonel. For now, I will leave you with them so that they may get to know you better." He bade a cordial good night to Christophe and Pétion, and departed.

Because Clervaux had presided over whatever order there had been, the rock upon which he had sat became the position of importance. The Colonel immediately took it as his own and looked good-naturedly at the remaining two generals. "My whole life story or just the last few years? Or would you rather I began with my thoughts on the future? Of course, you can interrupt with questions when you choose."

Christophe considered the options. "Personally, I'd like the whole life story. I'm sure it would be extremely fascinating, as well as helpful, in giving us a base on which to build our judgments. Besides, you speak so well that it would be enjoyable to listen."

The Colonel grinned his pleasure and glanced at his copper-colored friend, who grinned back at him.

"However," Christophe went on, "I have to agree with Clervaux that this is not the most comfortable place to be."

"Where else could we go?" Pétion asked.

Christophe's disappointment was evident. "I thought sure you'd know some place. Even Clervaux seemed to think you would."

"Well, Clervaux was mistaken. I don't have a home, and the young lady who permits me to visit her at times—" He paused. "Oh, I see what Clervaux had in mind. Yes, I have a few white friends, but they are not going to invite me to conduct rebel meetings in their drawing rooms."

Christophe chuckled. "You just gave me an idea, Pétion. I know where we can go."

"Where?"

Christophe smiled slyly. "Not so fast. I have to be careful. I'm not only a rebel, I'm an outlaw, remember. The place I'm speaking about isn't this isolated. We can't approach it as though we were on parade."

The Colonel said, "Hell, I parade everywhere I go. I've got three hundred troops waiting for me down below. You mean I can't take them?"

"Oh, I'd say you and your friend could each take one man as a guard. Pétion and I will do the same."

"Let's stay here." The voice of the Colonel was oddly high pitched.

Christophe shrugged. "As you say." He and Pétion exchanged glances.

The Colonel saw their eyes, not unfriendly, but suddenly uninterested. What was that Christophe had said? He would have to know something about the character of a leader, and he would reject an overcautious man as quickly as one who was impetuous. These were tough campaigners who would not have survived had they not made harsh judgments swiftly. And they were making harsh judgments as they looked at him now. How would they vote if asked at this moment to accept him as their general? Of course, the whole thing was a test, his first test, and he was not coming off very well.

Pétion glanced up at the sky. "Actually, it's getting rather late. If you don't mind, I think I will be on my way."

Christophe walked a few steps along the ledge and called out, "Thank you for the coffee. We're leaving." He came back and picked up the candle. He offered it to the Colonel. "I would guess that an unfamilar path disquiets you. Do take this so you may feel quite safe."

The Colonel laughed raucously. "This is a new experience for me, gentlemen. Nobody has ever before mistaken me for a coward."

"Who said that of you, Colonel?" Christophe asked.

"Listen. Let me explain myself. I didn't think we were so bloody uncomfortable sitting around here. I'm used to a rough way of living. I'm not like Clervaux, who evidently needs a brocaded chair and cushion. I didn't see any sense in going to the trouble of moving from one place to another. But if you're anxious to do it, I'll be glad to oblige."

Pétion said, "I'm not at all anxious. Are you, Christophe?"

Christophe shook his head, and again he offered the candle. "Colonel, I advise you to take this. I don't want you to hurt yourself."

The copper-colored man spoke unexpectedly. "The Colonel has explained, and he's willing to go wherever it is you want to go."

Pétion looked unutterably bored. "Oh, very well. What's another hour?"

Christophe blew the candle out, tossed it aside and started down the path, with the others following. The walk was long and no word was spoken. At the bottom, Pétion asked, "Where are we going? What do I tell my men?"

"You don't tell them anything. Do you think I want the whole island to know where I am? Pick out a man to ride with you, and order the others to meet you later somewhere. You must have a favorite rallying point."

It was unnecessary for the Colonel to ask any questions. He had heard the directions given to Pétion. He mounted a horse, disappeared briefly into the darkness and came back with another rider. His companion did the same. The horses of Christophe and Pétion were brought forward by properly uniformed soldiers, who then hurried away to summon the particular man each general had requested.

"We go very quietly," Christophe said, "drawing no attention and engaging in no conversation. When our destination is revealed, please make no exclamation of surprise."

They rode through the night, each man with his guard beside him, alert, wary. The shadowy darkness closed in on them, and they rode without haste, keeping the horses at a pace that would suggest no urgency, arouse no suspicion. After a time, they left the road and followed Christophe over trails untraveled by any Frenchman. They skirted a blighted forest that still smelled faintly of fire. Small, gentle hills. Up. Down. Finally, though there was not even a murmur, it was clear that they were directed toward the city of Le Cap. Christophe led onward to a hilltop, and his hand, raised high against the veiled sky, could be seen in a commanding gesture. The horses stood motionless. The men looked at a deserted house, its blind windows and wide galleries looming ghostly in the night.

"It was Leclerc's," Christophe whispered. "Everything is gone except some furnishings which Madame did not take back to France with her. I have felt a compulsion to examine the premises and I have been here more than once." He beckoned forward with a wide sweep of his arm.

He and Pétion, with the two guards, walked their horses past the abandoned gatehouse. The four men behind them followed slowly, quietly. Suddenly, there was a low, sharp order. The Colonel found himself separated from Christophe and Pétion. He and his companion and their guards were alone and surrounded by a dozen men with quick, silent bayonets. The thud of hoofs pounding across the lawns toward the far slope of the hilltop was the last sound the Colonel ever heard.

Christophe and Pétion galloped on until they were down the hill, over a picturesque bridge that spanned a ravine, and into a clearing circled by tall trees.

"I built that bridge when I lived on the hilltop," Christophe said as they dismounted.

Pétion caught his breath. "My God! Is that all you can think to say?"

"No. But I supposed you would prefer it to the obvious 'I told you so.' At what point did you realize that I was right, and that we could not afford the Colonel as either friend or enemy?"

"I knew it as soon as he spoke. Didn't my performance indicate that I recognized him as a liability?"

Christophe peered into the shadows and saw the two guards, also dismounted, waiting at a respectful distance. "It hurt me," he said, "to disappoint Drouet so deeply. He has not the type of mind that sees through a plot. He is courageous and obedient, but he does not understand the deceitful things one must often do."

Pétion said, "I understand the deceitful things well and I do not like them or myself any better. Do you think we will now be able to attract the men who are without a leader?"

"As I told you yesterday, if we fail to enlist them they will be a nuisance. But with the Colonel commanding them they were an outright danger. He would have ripped our troops, out of sheer vengeance, whenever he could. He left us no choice. He had to die."

"Yes, he had to die." Pétion's voice was weary. "I never get used to it."

"You are more sensitive than I."

"Was Clervaux informed in advance?"

"One of us had to roundly oppose the Colonel. I was fearful that Drouet would be taken in by his rough, direct way of speaking and vote yes. I was certain Clervaux would vote no without any coaching, but I needed him to introduce the idea of moving off the mountaintop. Coming from you or me, the suggestion might have been viewed with suspicion." Christophe reached into his pocket and brought out a knife, which he tried to hand to Pétion. "Give me a deep gash on my arm. The left arm."

There was a rustling of low bushes as Pétion stepped swiftly backward. "I can't, Christophe. So help me God, I can't."

"What? Pétion, you have to. We can't be without wounds. I want the Colonel's men to believe that, although Leclerc's house has not been patrolled since his widow left it, tonight the French were there. Pétion, didn't you guess that we'd both have to show signs of an encounter with Rochambeau's men?"

"Yes, there must be wounds," Pétion said. He moved closer and guided the knife in Christophe's hand toward his own thigh. "Go ahead. Plunge deeply." He made no sound as Christophe's knife was driven into his flesh.

"Are you all right, Pétion?"

"Of course. It is not pain that distresses me. It is the inflicting of it."

Christophe grunted. "You were not that squeamish when you and Rigaud fought against Toussaint and me at Jacmel."

"Even then, Christophe, when we of mixed blood were at war against blacks, I could not have stabbed you. In those days I would have been delighted to kill you, but with cannon or musket. Never could I have used so personal a weapon as a knife."

With a low whistle Christophe called his guard to him. "Right here," he said. "Make a sharp, hard cut. Pull the blade a few inches so it is no mere scratch."

Pétion placed himself on the ground against a tree. There was a flash of his white handkerchief in the darkness as he applied it to his wound. "I am ashamed of myself, Christophe."

"We all shrink from something, Pétion. I had not the courage to do my own work. I had to have the guard do it."

"What about our guards, Christophe? Why were they not attacked by the French?"

"Because we left them outside Leclerc's gatehouse to give warning in case such was needed. Remember, we did not expect the French to be inside, although that, regrettably, is where we found them. I wanted all four guards to watch the approaches to the house, but the Colonel insisted that his men stay with him."

"I see," Pétion said. "Who will believe us, Christophe?"

"At the moment, I don't care. My arm hurts."

"Is it bleeding badly?"

"I hope so. I need a very convincing, very bloody sleeve. How is your leg?"

"It throbs. We cannot stay here and bleed to death."

"I do not think there is that danger. However, you go to the young lady who permits you to visit her at times."

"And you?"

"I will manage, friend."

They separated, each riding into the night with his guard. Christophe knew that he must present himself to the Colonel's men wherever he could find few or many of them. They must not be casually informed that the Colonel had been found bayoneted to death. No profit could come from that. He himself, still bleeding and breathless, must be the one to carry the news. There was a chance, just a chance, that the Colonel had ordered his men to wait where he had left them.

"We must ride back to Mont Vautour," Christophe said to the guard.

"It is a longer ride than is good for you, sir."

"The only thing that is good for me is to find some of the Colonel's soldiers."

"If we find them, sir, we are alone and at their mercy. You ordered our men back to the encampment."

"I can think of no better proof of innocence than fearlessly to bring the story of the night's happenings."

The guard, emboldened either by affection for his general or by full knowledge that he must be accepted as a partner in the adventure, spoke bluntly. "What is to prevent the brigands from seizing you as an outlaw and delivering you to Rochambeau for the reward?"

"There is nothing to prevent them except an ingrained hatred of legal authority. It would keep them from turning to the French even if they were starving. You will see. They might kill me themselves, but they will not do anything that improves France's reputation as a tireless pursuer of evil."

It was dark and still at the foot of Mont Vautour. Christophe leaned forward upon his horse and rested. He could feel the pain now from wrist to shoulder, and the bleeding had not ceased.

I had not counted on weakness. The loss of blood will leave me unable to ride farther. Yet I cannot allow these men to find me on a day when I am without a wound.

"Call out," he said. "See if there is not someone."

The guard dismounted and walked across the narrow, stony span to the black trees that stood motionless in the night. "General Christophe is here," he said to the trees. "He is badly wounded, but he has come to speak to you."

Silence.

"General Christophe has come to bring you news concerning the Colonel."

Silence.

"If you can hear me, then answer, for there is something you must know."

Christophe felt a presence in the lonely night. For a moment he thought it part of the curious fancy that may come to one before fainting or dying. With great effort, he turned his head and saw beside him a man as large as Dessalines. A man who spoke to him in English with a voice as gentle as a woman's and an accent that did not belong to any island.

"What must we know? What has happened to the Colonel?"

"He is dead."

"But you are alive? Is General Pétion also alive?"

"I don't know what happened to Pétion."

With hands and arms operating as giant tongs, Christophe was plucked from his horse and laid upon the ground. Out of nowhere came a crowd of hard-eyed men and a young boy bearing a candle. Christophe's guard wheeled in astonishment at the voices and the flicker of light.

The large man said, "General Christophe, you had better pray that you are not slightly wounded." He spoke in French to the others, "Take off his coat."

"Carefully, I beg of you," Christophe gasped.

His clothes were torn from him. He was pulled from side to side, the wound examined, the flow of blood thoughtfully noted.

The man who spoke English seated himself on the ground beside Christophe.

"Tell me what happened."

Christophe took a deep breath. "I had a house which I burned when the French came. Leclerc built his on the same site. Always I have returned with longing to that place." He paused to gather strength. "Since his death and his family's departure I have noticed that no one has gone there. I thought it was safe so— May my guard tell more while I rest?"

The wide bottom rolled forward, the enormous head nodded at Christophe's guard. When the story was finished there was a thick hush, during which everyone stared at Christophe.

At last, the gentle voice asked, "Do you want to add anything to your guard's account, General?"

"Yes. I'm sorry the Colonel was killed."

"Thank you. We will miss him. He was a fine man."

The faces that bent above Christophe were blurred and indistinct in the candlelight. He could hear the thump of his heart as it pounded in bewilderment, trying to discover why every beat was worsening the situation. All that had happened, all that was happening would be for nothing, Christophe thought, if by a consenting silence he marked himself as one who did not value truth. He took another deep breath and tried to live.

"It was not my impression that he was a fine man. I found him to be a braggart and somewhat ill-natured. But I needed him and I think he needed me."

The gentle voice again. "General Christophe, is it altogether unreasonable for us to suppose that you set an ambush for the Colonel?"

"Altogether unreasonable. If I had killed him I would not be here. I'd be in hiding with a guard of a thousand men around me."

There was another silence. Then Christophe heard the gentle voice say, "Pour water slowly into his mouth. Give only a little at a time. Make sure he's swallowing. That's very important."

After that, Christophe thought he slept. Later, he heard the voice again. "Now give him rum in the same way. Slowly, slowly."

He knew that it was all a dream because the sun was shining and the woman who had been Bréda's cook was sitting on her little gilt chair, talking earnestly to the huge man, who spoke both French and English with a strange accent.

"I regret that you did not know Toussaint L'Ouverture. He was a remarkable man. It is for him that I have done what I could for General Christophe. Christophe was as a son to him."

"But Christophe betrayed Toussaint, Madame. Christophe went over to the French and with false promises talked Toussaint into surrendering."

The woman who had been Bréda's cook said, "As you see, I am a poor old woman on a lonely mountaintop. I can know nothing of Haiti or of Toussaint or of Christophe unless a man who is an escaped slave from New Orleans bothers to come here to inform me."

Christophe heard the soft laughter of the big man. "Forgive me, Madame. I am not only a carrier of hearsay but a simpleton. Let us see if our patient is still sleeping."

"I am awake," Christophe said to them, and he knew that none of it had been a dream. He was lying on a blanket outside the cave where, in another time, Toussaint had often slept.

"How do you feel?"

"My arm aches and I am weak."

"You will regain your strength. The bleeding has stopped. The ache will lessen."

"Are you a doctor?"

"That is a title which has not been bestowed upon me. Would you take food if it were offered to you?"

"I would do as you say."

The large stranger sat beside him as Christophe ate the beaten eggs that had been brought to him.

"I visited the grounds of the Leclerc house," the gentle voice said. "I examined the bodies of the Colonel and the others." There was a small wait, and then the voice went on, now with a note of mild reproach. "You were not wounded with the same sort of weapon that was used upon the dead. They were slashed with bayonets. You were stabbed with a knife."

Christophe said, "I believe I can explain why—"

"It would bore us both for you to try. Let us pretend the explanations have been concluded. From that point we would speak of how matters stand now. So let us do that. General Christophe, matters stand this way: the Colonel's men were never informed where the wealth he had accumulated was hidden. Since they had done the work and taken the risks, it was always accepted that they would be generously rewarded when the jewels and other valuables were eventually sold. The Colonel was a man acquainted with worldly negotiations not even vaguely understood by his followers. They knew only that he was smarter than they, and believed that one day a ship full of money would, by his arrangement, sail into the harbor. They were satisfied to wait until that day came. They thought that the Colonel would exchange the jewels for the money and then make distributions in proper shares and everyone would be very happy." A sardonic gleam appeared in the man's eyes. "They are now killing each other as they scatter into small bands, each claiming certain sections in which to search. They are digging in valleys and caves, at the bottom of dry wells and at the top of high mountains. Meanwhile, they are murdering everybody who seems to have selected a more likely place than they, and are torturing anybody they suspect may be able to give them a clue."

"Do you suppose the Colonel ever trusted anyone with the location of his hiding place?"

"Oh, I think his friend knew, but you have made it impossible for him to be questioned."

"Was there really an army of eight thousand men plus the friend's three?"

"More like five thousand in all. Only a small percentage of them were actually involved in looting. The rest functioned as a standing army in case the French or one of you generals decided to run the Colonel out of business."

Christophe winced suddenly and grasped his arm, which was

wrapped in what seemed to be an old petticoat. "May I see this painful thing?"

"Some other time. It will frighten you. I did not have the materials with which to accomplish a very pretty piece of work. You are going to have a bad scar."

"Your master was a doctor, I take it."

"Yes. I assisted him when, as a favor to his friends, he set the bones or sewed up cuts of valuable house servants. In time, he permitted me to go alone to the plantations to render these services. I once saved the life of a butler who had cost two thousand dollars."

"My friend," Christophe said, "you have come down in the world."

"Not so. I have come up considerably—provided that the French do not win their war here. It was to help defeat them and thus find a place for myself in life that I went through hell to reach Haiti. How I became part of a brigand army is another story, one that would too blatantly expose my naïveté."

Christophe regarded him thoughtfully. "As I remember it, you had a great deal of influence with the men who gathered around me last night."

"That was not last night, General." And, allowing no time for questions, the man continued. "When you met me I was in a position of leadership. A few hundred men had been instructed to obey me in any emergency that concerned my specialty. The Colonel had an idea that in the event your meeting turned unfriendly he could be wounded. That's why I was present. Evidently he learned to trust you." The sardonic gleam again. "Now he and I stand quite evenly if anyone wishes to measure the level of our naïveté."

Christophe asked, "When will I be well enough to pursue my fight against the French?"

"It is a matter of strength. You are out of danger, but, as you said yourself, you are weak."

"The fight is not all on battlefields," Christophe said, and closed his eyes. When he opened them the candle was lighted, and Dessalines was drinking coffee and patiently waiting for him to awaken.

"How you feel, General Christophe? I hear you and General Pétion both terrible sick. Too bad. Of course, I don't visit him, but I hear he not sick like you sick. He sick in big bed. Black man bring him fancy things to eat. Girl with blue eyes sit on chair beside him and make sorry noises like he dying. I tell you, white people know how to get sick very stylish."

Christophe said nothing. The pain of being black, the envying hatred felt toward white-skinned mixed-bloods never ended. It showed itself in foolish jokes and in unspeakable barbarities.

"Christophe, I tell you something. Any time Pétion want to leave Haiti he can go to other place and be white. Me, I cannot do that. I think if I go to middle of Africa, people point and say, 'Look at the black man.' You laugh? Good. I cheer you up? Then, that's enough cheer up. Now I very serious. When you ride a horse?"

"Soon."

"Better be very soon. New meeting coming up. Not like last one. Big generals from all over island. No little thing like just us and that piece of guano who say he colonel. We all ride far, to Geffrard's post in South, and talk about making unity and picking one general who tell us all what to do to beat French." He winked at Christophe. "I don't make unity with nobody. First time somebody tell me where to place my men and how to use them I kill him dead. Get well enough to ride horse, Christophe. This going to be big thing."

Christophe was well enough in another week. The drums beat out the news that he was riding south. It was well known now that Rochambeau had no one to interpret news for him as it came thundering from the mountainsides. Christophe listened, noting that no reference was made to his recovery or to the bandaged arm. Some nicety was intended here. He wasn't quite certain to whom it was directed. He rode with the man he called Doctor on one side and Hercule Drouet on the other. Behind them followed a guard of one thousand men. They were needed.

At every crossroad there was a skirmish and a death or two. The brigands had chosen to harass Haitians instead of French.

As the generals gathered, Christophe thought again of the brigands and was shamed by the antics of his mind. It was no mean cause for which the generals had fought. Their goals had been sufficiently noble. They had thirsted for a land of their own and freedom. But an outsider would find it difficult to perceive why the brigands did not fit quite comfortably into the bloody pattern of Haitian behavior. Almost every man on the island had fought a variety of adversaries, had changed sides, had learned to kill an old ally or embrace yesterday's enemy.

It was undeniable that Pétion had deserted Toussaint to join Rigaud. The mulattoes had been defeated, and Pétion had gone to the French. After that, he had deposed Clervaux and marched the troops over to the black rebels. He had been a colonel then. When had he become a general? By whose authority had Pétion become a general? Had he rewarded himself for his miserable showing at Le Haut-du-Cap? Why, a sergeant with a firm voice could have routed the French that night. The outsider, perhaps laughing now at Haitian vagaries, might ask, "And is Pétion one of the candidates for unifying the armies and becoming commanding general?"

Clervaux, unlike many others, had not fought for every possible army. He had been a loyal French officer. It had taken Pétion to bring him to the rebels. Without Pétion's example, Clervaux probably would be at this very moment Rochambeau's second-in-command. No, that was not true, but only because Rochambeau detested mulattoes and would not have offered the honor to Clervaux.

Christophe walked about, greeting officers he had not seen for some time. He talked with them, remembering their military records, searching their faces, asking himself if this was the oak from which a commanding general might be carved.

Food was served by the soldiers of the host General, the majestic mulatto Nicolas Geffrard, who was not accustomed to seeing so many blacks. They rather frightened him. He had to keep reminding himself that his friend Christophe was black and a very decent fellow just the same. Everyone enjoyed the conch stew and the sweet-potato pudding. Much laughter and a feeling of excitement took over the gathering as rumor and recollection ran from group to group. There was a moment of reflection on the terrible fate of Maurepas, the black General whose allegiance to the French had remained steadfast. Rochambeau had had him tortured in the presence of the Maurepas family. Later, the black General, his wife and children had been bayoneted and thrown into the sea.

"Rochambeau grows frightened," Colonel Paul Romain said.

Geffrard was surprised. "I have heard that Bonaparte has sent more men, the fever is subsiding and those who recovered have no chance of suffering it again for five years. Why is Rochambeau frightened?"

"Because there is no one upon whom to blame his failures," Clervaux said. "He thought Leclerc inept and often implied, even to lieutenants, that, were he in command, he would do much better. Now Bonaparte extends himself for Rochambeau as he never did for Leclerc. He gives him full freedom of policy, without criticism or rebuke, and sends fresh troops regularly."

"Why is that?" Geffrard asked. "Leclerc was his brother-in-law."

No one had an answer, so Gérin, the dignified adjutant, suggested that it was time for more important discussion.

A church had been requisitioned by Geffrard to serve as a meeting hall. The officers entered with a respectful mien that was totally unrelated to the small building's intended function. Most of those present had concluded long ago that gentle Jesus and heaven and hell were only crafty inventions with which whites had hoped to keep their slaves harmless and submissive. A meeting hall in which decisions could be reached inspired a realistic faith and hope.

In the same incongruous manner that the rebels had continued to sing the *"Marseillaise"* and to wear the uniforms Sonthonax had ordered for Toussaint's tattered warriors, they still regarded the French flag as somehow belonging to them and their island. The pulpit had been converted into a speakers' rostrum, and in routine fashion the flag of France was displayed behind the lectern.

General Geffrard opened the first session with a welcoming word and then consulted his notes. Many officers were anxious to address the meeting, and an alphabetical arrangement had been placed in effect.

The first speaker, a gaunt, nut-colored man who was a survivor of Buckman's rebellion, rasped his way through a long speech filled with hyperbole and inappropriate references to the past. His listeners finally discovered that he was in favor of unity. The second, third and fourth speakers were also for unity. The fifth was for limited unity. He wanted every leader who could command five thousand men to retain full authority of his army but to support earnestly any other leader who needed his assistance.

The sixth speaker said he had come only to warn that unity would be a disastrous mistake: "Unity presupposes one army and one commanding general. Who is going to relinquish his laurels to become only a liaison between his men and this powerful figure who will rule everybody? More puzzling, dear friends, is this question: Who is the man we could trust with the formidable army you would give to him? Where is the man among us who has proved himself to be so honorable, so incorruptible, that none has ever questioned his motives?"

The speaker may have had more to say, but he was silenced by a rustle of dissatisfaction that grew to an argumentative roar. Christophe found it depressing that the original proposition had been momentarily forgotten. No one was enraged or even disappointed that there had not been a unanimous cry for combining forces. Instead, it appeared that no one in the little church was willing to have himself judged as anything less than the strong man of integrity that speaker number six had demanded. Christophe watched and listened as officers leaned toward each other, angrily remarking on the insult suffered by everyone present. Others stated that they had never wanted or expected to be commanding general, but surely their characters were known to be without flaw. Pétion was standing on a chair, demanding an apology. Clervaux had the appearance of a man who has been dazed by a hard slap.

Geffrard was at the lectern, suggesting that everyone must be tired by the lengthy session and that it would be a fine idea to meet again at noon the next day.

Dessalines came up the aisle, moving slowly, yawning. His eyes seemed even smaller than usual, more sullen.

"What did you think of all that?" Christophe asked him.

"Like I think before. I don't give my army to nobody."

"Then you were pleased with the last speaker."

Dessalines yawned again. "He talk. I sleep. Someone holler in my ear, so I guess meeting finish."

When it resumed the next day, the atmosphere was charged with cold rage. One speaker said that, with fever season behind him and new troops arriving weekly, Rochambeau would be able to destroy separate armies one by one. The man who followed him to the rostrum agreed and added that if Bonaparte came to Haiti offering to change sides and fight against Rochambeau, personal ambition would cause some idiots to reject him. The idea was advanced that unity should be accepted but with six commanding generals of equal rank acting as an administrative board. Derisive laughter drowned that speaker out. His supporters became infuriated at the laughter, and there were a few loosened teeth and some bloody noses dripping on elegant dress uniforms. The meeting was adjourned.

The evening session was no more productive until toward the close, when Geffrard gave the floor to a less prestigious officer, a man of whom he had never heard.

"Major Hercule Drouet."

Hercule jumped to his feet and into the secularized pulpit. He flashed his bright, boyish smile and thanked the assemblage for permitting him to speak.

"Most of you don't know me and that isn't surprising. I'm only a peasant who turned to soldiering because Haiti needed all the soldiers she could get. A friend of mine told me that Thomas Jefferson, President of the United States, has said that blacks can be led and can sometimes lead but are incapable of co-operating. Since Mr. Jefferson is president of a country that allows slavery, and is himself a slaveholder, let's make a liar out of him. Let us co-operate."

Thin but friendly applause was heard.

"I am going to ask you to picture a situation in which there is no question of a commanding general, no thought of losing one's own army and one's own personal power. How would you feel about unity then? Isn't unity the only way to fight France? Isn't it true that, say, a hundred thousand men working together in one determined force is better than ten separate forces that won't even tell each other what they're doing? Now, because it is all an imaginary game, it is not binding, but just let us see where we stand. Forgetting a commanding general, forgetting the sacrifice that all but one of us would make, let us take a vote. Let us find out if, with other objections removed, unity seems desirable."

There were murmurs of approval and a few shouted insults. Drouet went back to his seat. Geffrard said that, in his opinion, the young man had presented the first creative idea.

It was difficult to take a secret vote, because fully one-third of the impressively garbed officers could neither read nor write. In the end, the priest was awakened, and he came to sit unhappily in the confessional recording an individual voice vote. The affirmative view was favored by all but six voters. Geffrard then closed the session with a comment that Major Drouet's game had been diverting and that some might enjoy thinking about it during the night.

Christophe let an hour pass; then he sought out the strongest leaders. Some had brought tents. Others lay like common soldiers, sleeping beneath the trees. Geffrard was to be found at the post, lying wakefully upon a cot.

"Someone has to lead, Nicolas, or we are ruined. The results of the voting indicate that most of us know there must be one single army and one single leader. Toussaint proved that was the only road to success."

"But we have no Toussaint today."

"Does that mean there is nothing to do until the French are ready to clasp the chains upon us?"

Geffrard's patrician face expressed some embarrassment. "Christophe, I have a great deal of personal admiration and affection for you. You are an intelligent commander of unquestioned courage. I am sorry to tell you that your fellow officers will not have you. It was your man and your ideas that forced the voting tonight. Everybody knows it. The incident caused them to speak their minds. Some said quite plainly that they will not have you."

Christophe nodded. "Many have hated me since the days when I owned a hilltop home and gold place plates. Others believe my surrender to the French was genuine and therefore a betrayal of Haiti."

Geffrard's eyes wandered to Christophe's bandaged arm. "There is dissatisfaction with you based on a more recent occurrence. You and Pétion—and no one believes Pétion would have thought of such a thing—are suspected of killing a brigand leader. There is no grief for the brigand, and I do not suppose that anyone of our acquaintance is shocked by murder. However, opinion is that your act has created more enemies for us. The brigands who know the island as the French never will are now vengeful and will give Rochambeau information and—"

"Foxes are not likely to do favors for hounds, Nicolas. But all this is beside the point. I know I cannot be commanding general. Whether or not I would like to be is immaterial. The important consideration is defeating the French. We need unity and we need a capable leader. We have no officer who enjoys the favorable regard of all, no officer who is free of the taint of treachery, and no officer of note who, on one day or another, has not led French soldiers against his own blood brothers. Let us admit that the life we have lived has deprived us of everything but the determination to survive. Let us cease to dream of a leader with fine personal qualities. Let us ask only that he be the most resolute, the most terrifying commander on the island. Now, who is the man answering that description, Nicolas? Who is he?"

Geffrard sat back in his chair and half closed his eyes. "We have many excellent fighting men. Some I do not regard highly as companions or—"

"I would like you to forget everything except ability on the battlefield. Who is the best, Nicolas?"

Geffrard shrugged. "I would have to say Dessalines."

"Yes, indeed, my friend, you would have to say Dessalines."

"But he is a beast."

Christophe said, "Saint George is not available. If you want a fighting general who can lead an army to victory, you'd better stop thinking that he will look and speak like Clervaux and Pétion, and have your grace and good manners."

"But Dessalines is ignorant and dirty, and he is so cruel that even the most insensitive among us are nauseated by his misdeeds. He is a horrible creature who—"

"Who happens to be the best commander we have."

There was pain in Geffrard's eyes. "Christophe, I couldn't choose Dessalines."

"Then you choose French rule and slavery. Is that it, Nicolas?" Christophe paused and let a cold moment fall between himself and his friend before continuing. "Listen to me. Dessalines is the most cunning, most forceful fighter we have, and you will lose him. He will never give his army over to any other man and he has twenty thousand tough, hard troopers who would not be unified with ours." Christophe bent closer to Geffrard and said, "Nobody knows Dessalines as well as I. Yes, he is dirty of body and evil of soul, but I swear to you that if he is given the opportunity to express his thoughts, you will be surprised at the quality of his mind. As a slave, his treatment was brutal beyond anything you could imagine, Nicolas. Warped he is, but not stupid. He is— But it does not matter what he is. If Dessalines is no more than an ape with a gift for war, we need him. For God's sake, Nicolas, think of that. We need him."

Geffrard looked across the candles into Christophe's blazing eyes, and a sudden excitement possessed him. In this room, at this dreary outpost, the fate of Haiti could be decided. And there was something more. If the vile Dessalines had been born for a purpose, if he existed to be used for one startling moment in history, then life was not the meaningless, haphazard thing it had seemed.

"Have you spoken to others of this?" Geffrard asked.

"Yes, and I will speak to many more before the night is out. I have had no enthusiastic responses. The most encouraging are those who have promised to consider the matter. You are a man of influence. You are the one who drew us here. Even those who despise the idea of unity came from far away because of you. These are the names of men to whom I spoke. Go tell them that without Dessalines there is no hope. Then go to your closest friends and ask them to do this momentous thing. Ask them to trust Dessalines."

"I will. Does Dessalines know of all this?"

"No, and he will undoubtedly insult us as he accepts the honor."

Christophe and Geffrard spent the rest of the night speaking to those who had large troop followings or had earned reputations for wisdom. Some who had listened with disgust to Christophe's campaigning for Dessalines changed their minds and attitudes when it was the mulatto Geffrard who begged them to judge Dessalines by battlefield accomplishments. And there was no doubt that black men who thought Geffrard singularly innocent concerning the character of Dessalines were impressed when it was Christophe who was willing to gamble all there was on the fearsome General.

Though Christophe had left Pétion to be convinced by Geffrard, Pétion came limping to Christophe.

"So your leg is still bothering you, my friend?"

"Do not speak of my leg, Christophe, and I shall not speak of your arm. I have come to tell you that you have debased Geffrard in making him party to your wicked plan. He thinks he knows the worst of Dessalines. He does not. When Toussaint sent that fiend against Rigaud and me at Jacmel, we saw horrors that we can never forget. I will not call that savage my commander."

Christophe raised his eyebrows. "Are you perhaps getting ready to desert the Haitian Army again, Pétion?"

"Call it what you will. I cannot accept Dessalines as a leader. He burned prisoners alive. He beheaded babies. His soldiers were instructed to slit open the bellies of women they had raped. He—"

Christophe said, "We are agreed that he is a monster. The only question now is which monster you prefer. Dessalines or Rochambeau? Because you are almost a white man, I presume you will opt for Rochambeau."

"God damn you, Christophe."

"God damned all Haitian patriots a long time ago, my friend. You can scamper away to Rochambeau, who despises mixed-bloods, or you can do what Dessalines orders you to do. There is one more choice. You can kill yourself."

"Do you want to be commanded by Dessalines?"

"I want to win a war. What in hell is it you want, Pétion?"

General Geffrard opened the fifth session with a plea, almost a prayer, for selfless devotion to Haiti. There was no one who did not notice that the General's hand trembled as he reached for his notes, and that, although he looked haggard, he evidenced no lack of spirit.

"Friends, last night you clearly indicated that most of you favored unity. Now, let us suppose that that was a binding vote and that today we are committed to finding a commanding general for the huge Haitian Army we have created. You must ask yourself, 'What do I want that man to achieve?' and your reply to that question can be only, 'Freedom.' "

Geffrard went on, using all the persuasive arguments Christophe had used, and giving all the answers to all the questions that had arisen during the night. He did not mention the name Dessalines, but he edged toward it delicately, hinting that the best soldiers were not always one's favorite people and that the hope of Haiti did not necessarily rest with a man whose uniforms were designed by French tailors in Philadelphia.

The officers listened, sensing that something dramatic was

about to occur. And as Geffrard spoke the words "For this magnificent task, for this uncommonly difficult assignment I would choose—"

Two things happened: the priest appeared from nowhere and slipped into the confessional; and there sounded the measured tread of Geffrard's troops, assembling outside the church.

"Dessalines!" Geffrard finished his sentence with a triumphant shout.

"Dessalines!" echoed the voices of officers upon whom Geffrard and Christophe had counted.

Some men sat stunned and silent, unable to believe what they had heard. Others, who had digested the proposal more swiftly, were already on their feet, screaming objections or pummeling a neighbor.

Christophe glanced at Dessalines. The sullen-eyed giant sat undisturbed and, to all appearances, disinterested. It was a remarkable fact that to the men around him he was so unlikely a member of the human race that no one approached him to say a cordial word and no one choked back a derogatory judgment. It was, Christophe thought, as though a horse had been put up for sale and one had no reason to suppose that the horse understood any of the discussion that whirled around him. Christophe wondered if Dessalines just happened to be the only man in the church who remembered what it had been like to be the horse. Was Dessalines the only man who had never recovered from the ignominy of that experience?

Owing to the noise and the fighting, Geffrard ordered fifty soldiers to stand in the aisles and insure serenity. Now that the name of Dessalines had been mentioned, he was able to describe with clarity and a degree of candor Haiti's desperate need for Dessalines.

"Who else has the power? Who else has the talent? Who else will stand with me and say he wants Dessalines?"

Fifteen men rose and cried out their approval. Another five did the same a moment later, Clervaux and Pétion among them.

The man who had survived Buckman's rebellion stood up to

ask a question. "Is this just for the hell of it, like the vote last night?"

The church shook with the knowing laughter of black men. "Be still, old man," someone called. "We are picking out a commanding general for the United Army of Haiti."

Geffrard nodded solemnly. "Is there another name anyone wishes to mention?" He turned his back to the lectern then, signifying that he would give them time to think, to consult among themselves. There were whispers, grave glances, nervous movement, but no one addressed Geffrard. He let the matter lie. No one must say that he had brought about a hasty and unwise conclusion.

The soldiers stood motionless in the aisles. The whispering died away. There was silence. Five minutes of utter silence. And suddenly Dessalines, black and huge, got to his feet and walked toward Geffrard.

"I talk now, General?"

"You talk now, Dessalines."

Dessalines stared up at Geffrard on the rostrum. "I don't talk good, but I want to stand where you stand."

Geffrard moved aside, and Dessalines took his place at the lectern. He looked out at the eyes fixed upon him. With the quick leap of an enormous cat, he turned and clawed the French flag from its stand behind him.

"That I want to do all the days I sit here. I do it now. Why you fools never do it before? With that dirty rag, they make you slaves, they beat you, they kill you, they throw you to pigs for swill; but where we go you hang their flag and they laugh like hell at you. I fix that. I fix that now."

With his tremendous hands he ripped the tricolor down one side and up the other. The white stripe he spat upon, then tossed it from him. He pressed the blue against the red and said, "New flag. Flag of Haiti. Blue and red. What we want with white?" For a moment he held the blue and red stripes where the French flag had hung. Someone raised a cheer. Dessalines scowled. "Never mind cheers. You going to have hard time under that flag. At finish if you alive, you cheer." He took the two stripes and stuffed them into his pocket. "I tell you other thing I think all the days I sit here and all the years I fight. This island black. I never see no white people grow sugar or cut mahogany. I never see no white people do nothing but own the land and be rich. I tell you, when we get French soldiers to go home, we going to send French civilians with them. We are strong army then, and we make man who is king or president or something of Haiti sign a law. We make him sign that no white own nothing on island, at no time, at no place. And no white have no kind of vote in Haiti, at no time, at no place, too. And no white never sit down at no big desk and do no lawmaking for us. This is our country."

Now Dessalines' scowl could not silence the cheers. He stood, impatient and annoyed, waiting to speak again. At last, he thundered at his listeners, "Hey, you, stop it. If you tell the priest you want me to show you way to beat French, then you better find out fast two things. You look at my face. If it don't look like I like what you do, you better stop what you do. Right now I don't like that big yell you make when I say something you like. You know why? I tell you. If you cheer when I say something you like, then you have to cheer all the time I speak, because when no cheer happens it gets to mean you don't like what I say, and you have no right to tell me you don't like what I say. If you vote for me, I am commanding general; and I don't know no army where commanding general gets told he say something nobody like. So you keep quiet all the time and I will not know what you think and that will be one damn good thing for all of us."

Dessalines paused, and there was not a sound. Nobody turned to look at a neighbor. Nobody moved.

"Now, other thing. If you say to priest I am commanding general, don't never come to me and say you should have promotion or I told you a lie or did this or did that to you. I am here in Haiti one long time now, and nobody never think I am nice fellow. If you vote for me, you know you are voting for son of a bitch, and don't never expect me to be nothing else. If you hate me bad enough, then you kill me if you can, but don't run to me with your eyes crying because you don't like this little thing or that little thing I do. You just do what I tell you, and if I want to hear you speak with me, I will let you know I want to hear you speak with me. We are going to win a war. Pretty soon we make Haiti all for us, but before that happen you learn lesson. You learn that Rochambeau is also son of a bitch and, if you think you see hard war before, what you see now will scare you bad."

Dessalines' glance prowled the church. Each man had the feeling that he had been noted, his expression studied, his thoughts read.

"You think that if you say I commanding general that right away I ride out on horse with a hundred thousand men behind me all howling and screaming together? You want to think that quick we kill French like they hill of ants? Pretty picture, sure, but it don't happen. Listen, I talk to the stupids here. Other kinds of people better listen, too. We never going to beat French with big battlefield winning. Toussaint know it. I know it. He pray for fever to come wipe out French Army. Fever big Goddamn help. When Bonaparte count how many men he lose in Haiti, he don't say this many men killed in battle and that many men die of fever. No. He look at numbers and say, 'Good Christ! Fifty thousand of my soldiers pissed away on that rotten island.' We got to see that he don't get one single day with good news in it. One single day with good news in it make him think things better, and so he send more troops, more cannon. But if no good news never come to him, he say at last to Rochambeau, 'What you do there, you big jackass? Get the hell off that island while I still got some French soldiers.' You see what I am meaning? We fight like crazy men and make sure Rochambeau never have good news for his boss. Every battle got to come out even. If it cost a thousand men to keep the French from taking one dirty little pile of garbage, we pay one thousand men. We don't retreat. We don't do no fancy withdrawals. That's for the French. We got to fight and die to keep Rochambeau from writing to say, 'Hey, Bonaparte, we win glorious victory. We take big important hill.' You see what I am meaning?

"Sometimes we win a battle, but if you in charge of men, don't never come tell me you lose while you got soldiers alive. Any time you do worse than come out even, next time I go myself to lead your troops and you don't get them back no more." Dessalines took a deep breath, and his eyes were hot and angry. "Anybody with sense know from way back that Haitians will beat French only because Haitians don't mind to die for Haiti. What the hell we got if we don't got Haiti? The French got clean, pretty place to go home to. We only got Haiti, and if we start counting how many men die, then we don't got Haiti. We hang on. We keep fighting, only more hard than before. We kill all the French he send, and, one day, if we kill enough of them, Bonaparte say, 'Let them keep that pile of dung. What I want with it? What I want with wild animals that nobody can whip hard enough to make them good slave?' "

Dessalines was suddenly quiet. He gazed out at his listeners. Their eyes were lowered, their faces sober.

"If I commanding general, I don't want nobody to sit on ass thinking fancy words and just defending. I tell every general what to attack, with how many men, and how to do it, at what time. I watch lots of years and I listen. I see generals read books about war. I hear them talk. I am Goddamn sick of books and talk. Maybe all right for soldiers who, if they lose war, still have a country and don't get to be slaves. Haitians different. We got to die and kill all the time. Everybody got to fight like hell and never give up. We going to hang on to rope with teeth and bite at the same time. Not possible to hang on to rope with teeth and bite at same time? Haitians show French lots of things nobody think possible. We fight for day when Bonaparte say, 'Rochambeau, you bastard, I think you lose war.' "

The thought of that beautiful day, which now did not seem so far away, caused a young officer to raise a lonely, but lusty, cheer. Everyone around him turned and stared, as though this manifestation of enthusiasm had never before been heard anywhere.

Dessalines ignored the incident. He said, "One more thing. Very important. We not all always true to Haiti. We fix that now. We make swearing to each other and to Haiti. We swear nobody never again fight for France, nobody never again live under French rule. We kill ourself if we are last Haitian alive on island. We kill a friend if he do bad to Haiti. Everybody who swear to that now stand up, so then all of us know forever we got a unity that is more big even than putting all armies together. What you swear now is real, even if you tell priest I am not commanding general."

Every man in the church rose to his feet. Because Dessalines was already standing, he pulled the remaining blue and red stripes of the tricolor from his pocket.

"This Haitian flag," he said, and kissed it. There was a moment of silence; then Dessalines abruptly stepped from behind the lectern and walked up the aisle. The soldiers moved aside for him, and, when they were slow about it or undecided, he pushed them out of his way. He walked straight to the door of the church and disappeared from view.

Geffrard returned to the rostrum. His face had a curious ashen tint, and his hands trembled more than ever. He asked, *"Now* is there another name someone would care to mention?"

As before, there was a long silence, which he did not interrupt. Then Pétion stood up but made no move toward the rostrum. He spoke three brief sentences.

"Dessalines is a terrible man. We need a terrible man. Is it necessary to vote?"

Christophe brought the news. Dessalines had given the order to break camp, but he had no intention of waiting until his men had completed the task. He and his guard were already mounted and ready to ride.

Dessalines nodded in satisfaction at Christophe's message. His small eyes narrowed until they were no more than glinting slits.

"You tell Drouet he promoted to colonel. Tell Pétion he now real brigadier-general and he in charge of West Province. Tell Clervaux he follow me right now. He major-general, too, like Geffrard. Tell Geffrard he stay here because he do good in South

Province. I take Clervaux with me. He sit at big table with other officers when we have war talk. I go everywhere and tell everybody what to do, only maybe I make Clervaux say it for me in words I don't understand. Christophe, you lieutenant-general. You get whole of North Province to command. You live maybe in Toussaint's house at Gonaïves. I call everybody together for meeting soon. That's all."

"Don't be in such a hurry. Wait one minute, Dessalines."

The glinting slits widened to gaze with black iciness upon Christophe's detaining hand. "Who in hell you think you talk to, eh, Christophe?"

Christophe used his outstretched hand for the purpose of giving a smart salute. He turned and walked away.

The drums were giving the message. It was Dessalines! From the South Province the news would be relayed across the island until there was no one beyond the sound of the booming, clattering, thundering drums. It was Dessalines! Dessalines, the black brute, riding into Haitian history. Toussaint L'Ouverture was a small, pitiable figure on a distant shore, quietly, courteously slipping from one's memory.

It was Dessalines who had torn the white stripe out of the tricolor. It was Dessalines who had declared that never again would there be white property owners or white laws. It was Dessalines who had forced an oath of loyalty that no man could ever deny having taken. It was Dessalines who had been shrewd enough to throw a noble bone to the quadroons and mulattoes and, while honoring them, had placed Pétion and Clervaux where they could be watched.

It was Dessalines! Boom boom boom boom boom! It was. Dessalines! It was Dessalines! It was Dessalines!

. . . .

If one had a choice of only three categories in which to place all male humans of the civilized world, it would be necessary to list Robert Livingston as a gentleman. Certainly Livingston was not a peasant or a member of the *bourgeoisie*. He was a gentleman, but Talleyrand, French Foreign Minister and aristocrat, would have preferred a fourth category. Livingston ought to be designated an American gentleman. The adjective would operate as sort of a minus symbol, warning Europeans not to waste subtleties or profound truths upon him. An American gentleman's manners could be relied on at a large dinner party, no matter how formal and exquisite the table setting; but at a dinner for two or four, the banality of his conversation would destroy the most piquant flavor and reduce the evening to tedium. An American gentleman was, at best, a bore, Talleyrand thought as he laboriously dragged his deformed foot across the room. He would sit beside Livingston on the sofa. The unfortunate man was deaf, and probably sensitive about it. It wouldn't do to keep shouting at him.

Livingston courteously averted his eyes as Talleyrand made his way toward the sofa. Let him believe that others were fooled by the pathetic pretense that his advance was slowed only by affection for certain pieces of furniture. He clutched a chair back and pointed out the perfection of its needleworked cushions; a table top and gave a brief history of its marquetry design. Good God, why didn't the poor devil use crutches or stay at his desk and frankly admit that he was lame?

One could pity Talleyrand, but it was impossible to like him. There was an unwholesomeness about a man who had been bishop of Autun and had all too swiftly learned another profession when his country had gone into religious bankruptcy. How could one trust him, when it was he who had proposed the sale of ecclesiastical property and joked about his excommunication? Had he ever believed in his church? Had he ever believed in his country? He had abandoned both and then returned from England and America to swear allegiance to Napoleon Bonaparte. And there was more that Livingston found obnoxious. The flaunting of love affairs, the pride Talleyrand took in bedding down someone else's wife or mistress. There was a streak of childishness in the French. They seemed to think they had invented mating. One could be amused, but Talleyrand's background tended to kill the laughter. Though not a Catholic, Livingston was filled with disgust at the casual references to illegitimate children Talleyrand had fathered while still a churchman. One could not dismiss the offensive remarks as a cripple's pitiful attempt to establish a reputation as the welcome guest in innumerable boudoirs. The reputation had already been established for him, and by high-ranking ladies. There was no doubt that Talleyrand was attractive and fascinating. He was speaking now in that deep, dramatic voice, so resonant that no strain was placed even upon an American gentleman who was losing his hearing.

"When the First Consul summoned me yesterday and you generously permitted me to terminate our conversation, I believe we were talking of George Washington."

Livingston sighed. Why did Talleyrand constantly arrange appointments as though they were of the utmost importance and then make every effort to limit them to unprofitable, chatty exchanges?

"No. As I recall, we were talking of New Orleans."

"So we were, but there is a question it would give me pleasure to have you answer. I believe myself entitled to any information which may be in your possession concerning James Monroe. I am sure you will understand my curiosity when you consider that it will be my duty to meet with him as I meet with you."

Livingston stiffened. Was Talleyrand implying that he planned on private conversations with Monroe? Would he then decide which American he preferred and drop the other from his calendar?

"Why did Washington recall James Monroe? Why wasn't Monroe a satisfactory minister to France? There must be an explanation. It is a blemish upon Monroe's career."

Livingston was not inclined to please Talleyrand at the expense of a fellow American. "I do not regard Monroe's career as having been blemished. You know as well as anyone that diplomacy is an art. Let us say that President Washington ordered a painting, and, though it was excellent, it was not what he had had in mind. He then did what is usually done under such circumstances. He commissioned another artist."

Talleyrand nodded. "I see. I had been in doubt. It is comforting to have the matter so thoroughly clarified. There is just one question remaining. Why did Washington recall Monroe?"

Livingston decided that the truth might be more embarrassing to Talleyrand than to Monroe, and, since the man insisted— "I am not sure you know this, but President Washington did not feel there were any similarities between your revolution and ours. He was proud that our people, no matter how deeply they desired freedom, did not slaughter neighbors who preferred to honor the King of England. George Washington liked to say that we produced a disciplined army rather than a bloodthirsty rabble. He often said that our people would have scorned to have the word 'freedom' associated with the brutal murders of a weak-minded man and a frivolous woman to whom you had once sworn a solemn oath of fidelity and whom you had called your king and queen. James Monroe displeased President Washington by giving the impression that France and the United States were revolutionists together. Washington, who had not an uncivilized bone in his body, was sickened."

Talleyrand examined his beautifully groomed hands, and said, "I am not certain that neighborhood atrocities were as lurid as Washington was told. They well may have been. After all, we are Latins. People keep forgetting that by nature we are quite violent." He used his lace handkerchief to buff a fingernail he thought less highly polished than the others. "Latins are not sticklers for fair play, as a rule, but the royal couple was treated in sportsmanlike manner. There was an assembly vote, and the Capets lost by only fifty-three points. Of course, I was not here during the Terror, so I can't say, by my own knowledge, how bloody that was. Incidentally, I arrived in your country with a letter to George Washington, but he declined to see me."

"A pity."

Talleyrand made a careless gesture. "His refusal was couched in terms of the greatest civility. I was satisfied, and I met many delightful Americans who, perhaps, were more in tune with my temperament. On the matter of Monroe—I believe it was his duty to show a spirit of affability toward the members of the Directory. In all truth, he had not been sent here to insult them."

"It is not my intention to suggest that Monroe was wrong and Washington right, or the other way around. Unfortunately for Monroe, Washington was president and had the last word."

"Really? Isn't Jefferson adding another? By sending Monroe here now, isn't he criticizing Washington's action just a little?"

"I don't think so. Other times, other purposes. Monroe, on this occasion, will not feel it needful to comment on our revolution or yours. He will be concerned only with New Orleans. It may come as a shock to him that you shun the mere mention of that city."

"Now, do not exaggerate. We have spoken often of New Orleans and we will continue to do so. I will keep you informed of any changes in the First Consul's thinking on the subject, and I will carry to him, as always, your rather dismal accounts of this land that Spain has so cunningly foisted upon us. For the moment, you and I are rather marking time, are we not? How are we to speak seriously of New Orleans while Monroe is hurrying to us to add his opinions? It would be terribly rude to chatter like magpies and finish the conversation before Monroe arrives."

Livingston was silent, thinking about what had just been said. Finish the conversation? Was Talleyrand in a position to do that? Had Bonaparte already decided about New Orleans? If there was no way for the United States to acquire the city, why did Talleyrand spin away time and unfailingly conclude each meeting with an appointment for the next? And if Talleyrand knew there was a firm basis upon which discussion of terms could begin, was it not maddening that he thought it necessary to wait for Monroe?

"Monroe may be delayed," he said. "He became ill in New York, I understand, and took a later sailing."

"That distresses me. I trust he will not come to us coughing and wheezing. I am terribly sympathetic toward people suffering pain, but minor illness I find intolerable." Talleyrand stared absently at the flower-decked nymphs on the arras that covered the opposite wall. "There was something I wanted to ask you about President Jefferson. Now, what was it?"

"Did it concern New Orleans?" Livingston asked, a bit testily.

"Oh, I know what it was. Is it true that he never suppresses a newspaper?"

"Quite true."

"Has he never felt that he would like to?"

"I have heard that he has been angered occasionally, but never by his detractors. It is the newspapers which favor the President that sometimes exasperate him. In their zeal to denigrate the opposition, they are often more despicable than the enemy press."

"What do you mean by that?"

"Well, for instance, Alexander Hamilton was born in the West Indies. That makes it easy to hint that he may be part black. It is President Jefferson's custom to send a sharp rebuke to any editor who prints that sort of thing."

Talleyrand made a steeple of his long, thin fingers and seemed lost in admiration of it. "President Jefferson is a gentleman of lofty Christian principles and high ideals. But wait—he is, after all, a politician. Could it be that he fears the populace will suspect he directed his editor friends to print such innuendoes?"

Livingston said, "You speak without knowing the character of President Jefferson. He does not think small, nor does he care for the opinions of those who do."

"I will wear him in my heart's core. And how thoughtful he is of Alexander Hamilton. Do tell him he has my gratitude. Hamilton is one of my dearest friends."

"I know that."

"We are realists, Hamilton and I. We are without sentiment and, I suppose, without patriotism. Patriotism is but excessive sentiment, is it not? The thought of a terrorist sobbing over humanity, or a slaveowner shouting for freedom amuses Hamilton, as it amuses me. Incidentally, suppose Hamilton were part black? What would it matter?"

Livingston turned and looked squarely into Talleyrand's brilliant gray eyes. "You are testing my patience, sir. I am a New Yorker, and New Yorkers do not own slaves. For the

Americans who do, I will say that no Frenchman is in a position to speak as though he accepts a black man as an equal. You are now engaged in the business of murdering an entire nation of blacks. When you cease that heartless slaughter, and form a friendship with a black man as deep as the one you enjoy with Hamilton, then you may ask me again why it would matter if Hamilton were part black."

Talleyrand said, "Oh, that tiresome Saint-Domingue thing. It works its way into every conversation. Did you know that General Leclerc, the First Consul's brother-in-law, died in Saint-Domingue?"

Livingston overcame the annoyance of the moment past and presented a face as bland, a manner as unruffled as Talleyrand's. "Yes, I heard that he did. I was grieved by the news."

"Madame Leclerc brought his body home to us. She had cut off all her hair and placed it lovingly in the coffin with her dear husband's remains."

"I sorrow for her sorrow. How is she now?"

"Bathed in tears."

"Time will dry them."

Talleyrand said, "Time is causing the tears. She wants to marry Prince Borghese. The First Consul has threatened to send her into exile if she doesn't wait until she has been a widow for at least a year. My heart breaks for her. You know, it isn't every day that one has the opportunity to become a princess."

It was a habit of Talleyrand's to treat the cheap and foolish aspects of human nature as though they warranted particular understanding.

"How do things go now in Saint-Domingue?"

"Things will go splendidly very soon. We are sending another thirty-five thousand men. The subject of Saint-Domingue bores me."

"Then, perhaps we can speak of New Orleans?"

Surprisingly, Talleyrand shrugged and said, "If you like."

"Yesterday, when the page came with the message that your company was desired by the First Consul, I had just mentioned that the Ursuline nuns would not live under French domination and were moving to Havana."

"Yes, yes. Some nonsense about the Revolution's depriving men of their souls. The Ursulines are given to theatrical displays. Actually, they are well aware that piety isn't a matter of geography."

"It may be history that disturbs them," Livingston said.

Talleyrand smiled. "You do hate us, don't you?"

"No. In my own country I have a reputation for being very partial to the French."

"Give me a small demonstration of how that rumor got about."

"It is more than a rumor. The fact is that most Americans are fond of the French."

"What you mean is that most Americans are fond of Lafayette. They don't know anything at all about the French. And if they knew anything about Lafayette, they would give up naming towns and streets after him. My God, he's a bloody nuisance. What did you people want with him?"

"I'm amazed that you haven't guessed. We needed a foreign hero, and we couldn't spell the Polish names."

Talleyrand threw a sharp glance at Livingston. "You wanted to talk about New Orleans."

"Yes, with this slight digression: I want to assure you that Americans have a deep affection for France. We can think of nothing on an international level that would give us more pleasure than the knowledge that peace between our two countries will last forever. Now that I have stated that truth, I am led quite naturally to ask a significant question. Has it occurred to you that our need of the New Orleans harbor makes any nation who owns it our potential enemy? We cannot wholeheartedly love a government that is placed where it can choke off our access to some very rich markets."

Talleyrand raised his head haughtily and stared at Livingston. "I do not remember that my government has solicited your love. And if we, as owners of New Orleans, spark your enmity, I believe we can somehow weather that frightful storm."

The cold sarcasm was calculated to remind Livingston that he was the emissary of an upstart country. The point could not be successfully argued, so Livingston used it as advantageously as he could. "It is my custom," he said, "to regard myself as a laborer for the well-being of the United States. To me, that means not only in my lifetime, not only for the period in which I represent my country, but forever. That is because I am authorized to make agreements which will eternally bind my countrymen. Assuming that you feel an equal responsibility toward the people of France, I will say this: the United States is young, not wealthy and without a powerful army or navy, but the passage of time is no more certain than is the fact that the United States will prosper and strengthen. Someday it will become absurd for her to accept dictates from any other nation, and she will look with angry eyes at the harbor of New Orleans. Then France and the United States will engage in a conflict that you and I could have prevented."

Talleyrand's tone was disbelieving. "You're threatening France?"

"With what, sir? You knew before I told you that we have not the means to make war. I am indulging in prophecy. In my life span, we will be helpless to take New Orleans from you by force—unless, of course, we acquired a mighty ally." Livingston let a small silence fall. Then, "That would be bad for both of us, I think."

Talleyrand bent down and stroked his crippled leg. When he straightened himself once more against the sofa cushion, he was frowning. "What is all this sudden anguish your country suffers concerning New Orleans harbor? She has lived her entire life with the bothersome thing in the hands of Spain."

"Let me quote Montesquieu's famous remark. You must remember that he said, 'It is happy for trading powers that God has permitted Spaniards to be in the world, since of all nations they are the most proper to possess a great empire with insignificance.' Unfortunately, you French don't know how to do anything insignificantly."

"Thank you."

"Oh, you've earned the compliment, if that's what it is. In

truth, we did have a scare, even from Spain, when the port was closed to us for a brief time. Error though it was, it alarmed us enough to begin examining our situation. Now I am back at the beginning again, asking: Can we embark on discussions relative to the possible sale of New Orleans to the United States?"

Talleyrand looked as astonished as though he had never heard the question before. Livingston waited while the Foreign Minister arranged his reply and shifted his expression to one of reproach.

"My dear Mr. Livingston, I have told you that that question is premature. The First Consul will not even consider a discussion of whether or not we would sell New Orleans until we have taken possession of the Louisiana Territory. What more can I say?"

"Speaking of questions that have been too often repeated, that last one of yours has a familiar ring. I remember my first visits here, when you were still unwilling to agree that France had bartered Tuscany for Louisiana. You insisted that you knew nothing about it."

"And what harm did that small untruth do? You didn't believe me."

"No, I did not."

"Then I have failed. It is well known that a diplomat needs the faculty of appearing open, yet remaining impenetrable, of being reserved, yet with all the manifestations of candor."

Livingston could not resist a quiet chuckle. "Are we to meet again?"

"Naturally. I have promised to keep you informed of the First Consul's thinking. Besides, we cannot be rude to Mr. Monroe. Think of the long, hard voyage he will have had for nothing if we close shop before he arrives."

The bitterness returned to Livingston. It was obvious that Talleyrand had no wish to terminate the talks. Probably, Bonaparte had said the equivalent of "Hang on to him. We might do business with him one of these days." What a miserable piece of luck it was that Jefferson or Madison had thought it necessary to send Monroe. If New Orleans was to be brought to a grateful nation, the people might long remember who had brought it.

One man might be covered with lasting glory for such an achievement. Two men would drag each other down into oblivion.

Livingston rose. "I will take leave of you now."

Talleyrand asked, "Will you stop by tomorrow morning?"

"I would prefer the afternoon."

Talleyrand's lips tightened as he looked at Livingston with displeasure. "I must keep tomorrow afternoon flexible."

"Then I shall not trouble you. Perhaps one day next week would suit us both."

"Is your morning really completely taken?"

"It is."

"Then come in the afternoon. I am accustomed to inconveniencing myself for others."

When Livingston was ushered into Talleyrand's presence on the following day, he found the Foreign Minister already seated upon the sofa. Talleyrand evidently had decided to take that painful walk across the room while still alone.

"Do sit down, Mr. Livingston. You look very tired. I trust your morning was not burdensome."

"Not at all. I had a very pleasant drive."

"Drive?"

"Yes. Hadn't I mentioned that I was going to Passy to see Ben Franklin's old neighborhood?"

Talleyrand shook his head. "Americans baffle me. You come to France to look at places where Americans once lived. Meanwhile, with great difficulty, I reshuffled all my appointments to accommodate what I supposed to be pressing business of yours."

"I told you that next week would be as satisfactory as today."

Talleyrand said sadly, "You are trying to play a game, Mr. Livingston, and it is not becoming to you. The true secret of diplomacy is not petty ruse and ingenious trickery, but, instead, it is the simple virtue of good faith."

Livingston laughed, and, when Talleyrand gazed at him questioningly, he did not explain his laughter.

"I am also baffled by what causes Americans to be amused, but no matter. Mr. Livingston, the First Consul receives with interest your descriptions of Louisiana, which I carry to him. In a most cordial manner, he has requested that you speak more on the subject."

"But I have given no descriptions of Louisiana. It has been seen by almost no one except Indians, fur traders and priests. From its source in the Northwest to its mouth, there are long miles of Mississippi River banks that are pathless wilderness. I hope you have not represented me as an authority on Louisiana. No one is. The territory is too vast and wild to be easily traveled. Of course, New Orleans, as you know, is another matter."

"The First Consul is well informed about New Orleans. He would like to have your impressions on Louisiana."

"I suffer deep chagrin at being empty of impressions. I will recount, though, what I have heard of the territory. There will be difficulties for you to face. Among the Kentuckians and Tennesseeans, there are those who think of Louisiana as the highroad to the conquest of Mexico. Twenty or thirty thousand of these Westerners dream of coming down the river on flatboats, sweeping everything before them."

"But they are your citizens. You must control them."

"They are an army unto themselves. We are not equipped to control them. Besides, they are no menace to us. They never approach cities, and do not bother us, except that we lament their behavior toward our neighbors. They are an undisciplined horde who do not need the supplies and provisioning of regular soldiers. They are a contrast, indeed, to your fine French legions, though in marksmanship they equal the skill of anyone. Their habits of living in the woods and of conquering fatigue render them almost invulnerable to the sufferings of traditional soldiers. They stalk across Spanish lands as though God had given them the right to do so."

"You are not ashamed of an unorganized army that behaves as it will? You do not blush at claiming lawless creatures as citizens?"

Livingston smiled. "The United States looks ahead to the children and grandchildren these strong, fearless men will give us. A carbine and a little maize in a sack guarantee their health and survival. They slay deer with a cleverness that mystifies the savages. Your soldiers will not find the New World a place of boredom and routine. What I am telling you is only what I have heard. Why don't you ask some of your Spanish friends if I have been fooled by tall stories?"

Talleyrand's lips twisted contemptuously. "I will give you a piece of valuable information, Mr. Livingston. An organized army will, at any time, under any circumstances, tame any number of disorderly, plundering wretches."

"Probably, probably," Livingston agreed. "The unfortunate thing is that the wretches are not tamed immediately. In the interval between their first secret move into your territory and their last shot at your organized army, there will be dreadful unfriendliness. You will be killing our citizens and we will be killing your soldiers. That leads to all sorts of things. Truthfully, I don't believe we can live side by side without becoming enemies."

"You must grow accustomed to French borders abutting those of the United States. You must teach your scoundrels that France will not tolerate their using Louisiana as the route to the Spanish Southwest."

"We can teach them nothing. You will have to keep constant guard if, by any chance, you have promised Spain that it is your soldiers who will die to protect her riches."

Talleyrand said, "Your sympathy for French soldiers is touching."

"Yes, well, they are an unfortunate generation of fighting men. Reared in the innocent belief that France would use them on European soil, in contests against soldiers much like themselves, they have been shipped to Egypt, to Saint-Domingue, and now on their itinerary is the wilderness of Louisiana. It is a bitter cup the First Consul has brewed for them."

Talleyrand's eyes slid sidewise so that he might watch Livingston's face while appearing to look straight ahead at the nymphs upon the arras. "Americans are known to be a direct people, Mr. Livingston, unencumbered by evasive tactics. Yet I am worried by the possibility that you are attempting to cultivate the nasty skill of devious approach. I ask an honest question which I hope will be answered honestly. Are you trying to say that if we would sell you New Orleans you would, by super-human effort, manage to keep your dangerous citizens out of the rest of Louisiana?"

"Good heavens, no. We can't restrain those fellows. They'll run all over you, and there's nothing we can do but regret it. We'd like to buy New Orleans, so I sincerely wish there was something above money I could offer. There is not."

Talleyrand considered the last statement. "In the sort of thing we have before us, money is of great consequence. It can be used in many ways. Of course, sometimes one's ideas are so limited in scope that it cannot be used at all. Shall we let our minds wander and see what paths they take?"

"If my mind wanders, it will not go far from New Orleans. It might glance casually at the Treaty of Amiens, which is little more than an excuse for parades and fireworks. You are going to have another war with England. When that happens, there will be such trouble in the Caribbean and in the Mexican Gulf that discussions about New Orleans will become purely academic."

"I do not foresee war."

"Of course you do."

"How ridiculous to argue with me over what I do or do not see. In any case, our fleet that is now in Saint-Domingue would hurry to the harbor at New Orleans to preserve its safety."

Livingston looked at Talleyrand with interest. "You have a date, then, for the surrender of Saint-Domingue?"

"Virtually. Rochambeau is a magnificent soldier."

"Leclerc was not?"

"I will not be drawn into unkind criticism of Leclerc. Let me say only that he did not understand the enemy he met in Saint-Domingue."

"And Rochambeau does?"

"With no further elaboration, I will simply say that, yes, Rochambeau understands the enemy."

"And when Rochambeau vanquishes this enemy he understands, then you will take possession of the Louisiana Territory, including New Orleans?"

"Yes."

"And you will be at war with England, who does not want you on the North American continent."

"We have as much right there as the English have."

"If you choose to debate that question with England, using, instead of words, such expensive articles as ships and weapons and troops, then your treasury will be glad of a windfall. Sell us New Orleans, and you will have additional funds to throw away on other projects that seem worthy to you."

Talleyrand yawned behind his lace handkerchief. "Let us speak of something less tedious than that bloody part of the world which you inhabit and which seems notable for a variety of savages and a total absence of good will. Are you interested, Mr. Livingston, in the customs of antiquity? Take, for instance, the formality of excommunication. Everyone is aware that that is the process by which Mother Church unfastens some poor sinner and sets him adrift, but there are certain punishments added to his disgrace and to his loss of all sacraments."

"Really?" Livingston drew out his own handkerchief, which was severely unadorned. He, too, yawned, but with little attempt at concealment.

"When I was excommunicated I discovered that all good Catholics were obliged to refuse me water and fire. Isn't that an interesting relic of ancient thinking? I wrote a note to a young lady of my acquaintance, and I said to her, 'Console me. Let me come to supper. Remember, you must not give me the comfort of fire or water, so let us have cold pheasant and iced wine.'"

"Very witty," Livingston said, without a trace of a smile.

"Oh, do you think so? I am very pleased. I meant only to entertain you, but I believe you now know more than the Pope does on the matter of excommunication. I would wager that he is ignorant of the true rigors he is imposing on the poor sinner. He thinks only of souls, as I did myself in the days when I dreamed boyishly that someday I might be pope."

"I would like to know how one dreams boyishly of being pope."

"I couldn't dream girlishly of it, could I? At any rate, Mother Church and I have decided to forget the past. We have again embraced. I am in excellent ecclesiastical standing. The First Consul thinks his own and his official family should set a high moral tone for the nation. Livingston, did I ever tell you about meeting Benedict Arnold?"

"Yes, you did. You met him in an inn at Falmouth. You asked him for letters of introduction to Americans, and he said that he was the only American who could not give you letters to his own country. Isn't that the way your story goes?"

"With all color and flavor removed from the encounter, yes. Shall we meet again tomorrow?"

"I cannot come tomorrow."

"Then I shall save the questions for Mr. Monroe."

It cost Robert Livingston a frightening pain in his chest, but he said, "Yes, do that."

"You could not come even in the late afternoon?"

"I am sorry."

"Very well. I shall send a page in a day or two to inquire as to your convenience. Mr. Livingston, you puzzle me. What on earth could be more important to you than these discussions of ours?"

Livingston said, "A satisfactory sign that these discussions of ours are important to you."

Talleyrand looked distressed. "One gets such blunt replies from Americans."

"I suppose one does. But you try for them, don't you? You are a highborn gentleman with an extraordinary education. In America, the same is said of me. America is crude in many ways, rustic and even uncivilized. Yet, had you come to me with a matter of infinite importance to our two countries, I would not have thought it courteous to speak, as you have, of the days when you shared a mistress with Gouverneur Morris, and of your excommunication, and of—"

"I believe I have horrified you, Mr. Livingston."

"At times. There is a certain reticence among Americans. We have many preposterous characteristics. One of them is that when tasks have been assigned to us we do not rest until we have performed them as well as we can." Livingston stopped speaking and looked searchingly into Talleyrand's eyes. "Can you believe that I am so engrossed in the subject of New Orleans that when anything else is mentioned I regard it as a tiresome waste of time?"

"That is very selfish of you. Other people are terribly weary of New Orleans. Do you speak of it all through dinner?"

"Very often, I'm afraid."

"Oh, your unfortunate table companions. Who are the victims this evening?"

"I have been invited to the home of Barbé-Marbois."

"Was it discreet to say so?"

Livingston smiled. "If you really wanted to know where I was dining, I would have been only the first you would have asked. Barbé-Marbois was a friend of mine long before he was the First Consul's Minister of Finance. He liked my country so much that, while there, he took an American lady as his wife."

"Yes, I know. So you have discussed New Orleans with them?"

"Why not? What you and I are talking about is not a secret to any newspaper reader in the entire world."

"How does our Minister of Finance feel about your quest to acquire our North American city?"

Livingston said, "Since that is about the only thing that is a secret to newspaper readers, I don't feel free to repeat his remarks. Certainly, you have a right to ask him."

After dinner at the home of Barbé-Marbois, Livingston thought Talleyrand had determined to do that very thing. Coffee and liqueurs were being served when the butler whispered to the Minister of Finance.

Barbé-Marbois turned to his wife. "I may have to leave our guests for a time. Talleyrand has arrived. Possibly there is something he will wish to discuss."

Madame Barbé-Marbois frowned. "Doesn't he know you have an office, and that you can be found there during the day?"

Ladies who had heard the small exchange looked away, seemingly overcome by their hostess's straightforward expression of her distaste at the intrusion. Livingston observed the small, forgiving smiles that the ladies finally managed. They were remembering that poor Madame Barbé-Marbois was, after all, an American.

The Minister of Finance went to the archway to receive his unexpected guest. There was quite a clever performance as Talleyrand embraced him and leaned upon him until they had advanced as far as a tapestry which Talleyrand could admire while supporting himself against a heavy table. The rest of the walk to Madame Barbé-Marbois's chair had to be negotiated without assistance. Talleyrand, looking quite handsome and elegant, retained his dignity as he limped forward.

"So kind of you to make room for the uninvited." His appealing, well-practiced smile was offered generously to all. Livingston thought that Talleyrand's charm would persuade an outsider that this was his drawing room and that he was graciously dealing with the awkward surprise of having all these people descend upon him unannounced.

Talleyrand selected a seat next to Livingston. "Is everyone talking about New Orleans?"

"No, but if you'd like to do that I'll ask Barbé-Marbois to lend us his private sitting room."

Talleyrand laughed. "I believe you would."

"You can be quite certain of it. You have placed me in a predicament. My government will consider me a very indolent negotiator."

"I will give you a certificate attesting to the fact that you are the most importunate I have ever met." Talleyrand turned then to listen politely as an elderly gentleman explained why he had refused the excellent brandy. One would have supposed that nothing had ever interested the Foreign Minister more. When the temperance lecture had ended, he gave his attention back to

313

Livingston. "As a matter of fact, I have news for you. That's why I invaded this dear little house."

Livingston was torn between curiosity and resentment. It was detestable of Talleyrand to refer to Barbé-Marbois's home in such a patronizing manner. It was a beautiful home, even luxurious by the standards of those who had never used their positions for dishonest gain.

"Offer Talleyrand two hundred thousand dollars if he is aloof and difficult," Gallatin had said. "He will not be insulted unless he considers the bribe too small. Never talk about it to Jefferson. He knows the world is full of venal men, but he hates to hear about it."

Livingston decided not to defend Barbé-Marbois's house against the sneers of Talleyrand. His curiosity, he discovered, was stronger than his resentment. "You have news for me? What sort of news?"

"James Monroe arrived today at Le Havre."

Livingston's heart began to pound. He felt a deep shame for the bitterness that welled within him at the thought of Monroe. To share, with a man who had failed as Minister to France, the mission that might have catapulted the name Robert Livingston to— Not even to himself would he acknowledge the dream that he had lived with for more than a year. He looked at Talleyrand, and saw that Talleyrand had been looking at him.

This wicked ex-bishop knows how the minds of men work. He has been following my thoughts as easily as if he were reading a letter in which I had written to him of my hopes and ambitions. But how in hell does he know that Monroe arrived today at Le Havre?

"Is not the heliograph used in America, Mr. Livingston? The names of all arrivals of any importance are flashed across the country from major harbors. It is a clever signaling apparatus that is worked with mirrors and sunlight from one town to the next until it reaches Paris."

"I know," Livingston said dispiritedly. "I just wasn't thinking. When will Monroe be here?"

"I would suppose in two or three days." Talleyrand sipped

his brandy and looked up to smile at a yellow-haired girl who had been aching for his attention. "Who is she, Mr. Livingston?"

"I have no idea. Two or three days?"

"You mean, you did not catch her name?"

"He is traveling with his whole family. If anyone is ill, he might be delayed in Le Havre for a while. Yes, I caught her name. I've forgotten it."

"How could you?"

"But assuming that they are all well— She is a goddaughter of Madame Barbé-Marbois, from America."

"Oh. Well, in that case, why don't you have dinner with me tomorrow evening?"

"Thank you. I have been invited elsewhere."

"I shall master my disappointment. However, it amazes me that you would accept an invitation to dinner for tomorrow evening. Madame Bonaparte's reception—"

"That is at five o'clock, and surely foreigners such as myself will be in and out within twenty minutes."

"Perhaps." Talleyrand lapsed into thought. After a time, he said, "It is customary to make no social commitments that directly follow a Bonaparte reception. An outsider will never forgive your last-minute apologetic note."

"How can you be sure I am dining with an outsider?"

"An insider would have known better than to invite you."

"You're an insider."

"Yes, but if it becomes necessary for you to cancel dinner, I shall be so busy myself that I won't notice."

"Why should I cancel anything simply because Madame Bonaparte is going to smile politely and make certain that I have partaken of the refreshments and have received a nod from the First Consul?"

"Sometimes I think you are an impostor. Did you toss the body of the real Robert Livingston into mid-Atlantic after robbing him of his credentials? Or have you really moved in diplomatic circles before? My God, Mr. Livingston, at these pseudosocial gatherings, so artfully named for the lady of the house, astounding things have been known to occur. You meet someone from an embassy and you don't want to leave him because he has drunk just enough to make him talkative. He invites you to dinner, but there you are, already pinned down to a dreary evening with some old friend who knew Benjamin Franklin. Worse than that, you may want to spend hours writing a detailed letter to your Secretary of State on what you have deduced from a quick word or a sudden, surprised look that was not intended for you to catch."

Livingston shook his head. "We live in different worlds, I fear. For me, these receptions are quite rightly named for the lady of the house. I have heard nothing but gossip. I have seen nothing but bulging eyes, fixed on the First Consul, and I have deduced nothing that Mr. Madison would care to hear about."

Talleyrand said, "I find you absolutely amazing, Mr. Livingston."

Livingston remembered that portion of the conversation on the following evening as he penned a note of regret to the very kind people who had invited him to dinner. The mail would be going out to America within a few hours. He must get his letter in the diplomatic pouch, and yet it must be written without haste. To lend import to his account of Madame Bonaparte's reception, he decided to write directly to President Jefferson. If Madison were displeased at this snub, so be it. It was undoubtedly Madison who had thought Monroe was needed in Paris.

Livingston sat for quite a time, recalling the startling scene at the reception. Then he began to write:

> Today I attended a reception at the Tuileries given by Madame Bonaparte. A circumstance happened there of sufficient consequence to merit your attention. After the First Consul had gone the circuit of one room, he turned to me, and made some of the common inquiries used on those occasions. He afterwards returned, and entered into a further conversation. When he quitted me, he passed most of the other ministers merely with a bow,

316

went up to the British Ambassador, and, after the first civilities said, "I find, Lord Whitworth, your nation wants war again." Lord Whitworth responded, "No, sir, we are very desirous of peace." The First Consul seemed not to have heard the answer for he remarked, "You have just finished a war of fifteen years." Lord Whitworth remained calm. He said, "It is true, sir, and that was fifteen years too long." The First Consul apparently had made up his mind what he would say to the British Ambassador in public, and was not to be put off regardless of what Whitworth said to him. Quite contemptuously, the First Consul said, "But you want another war of fifteen years." Lord Whitworth was certainly uncomfortable though clear-spoken. He said, "Pardon me, sir, we are very desirous of peace." In reply to that the First Consul said, coldly, "I must either have Malta or war." Lord Whitworth, as embarrassed as any ambassador would be at having such words directed to him while the entire room listened, retained his courtesy. He said, "I am not prepared, sir, to speak on that subject, and I can only assure you, Citizen First Consul, that we wish for peace."

The prefect of the palace, at this time, came up to Bonaparte and informed him that the ladies were in the next room, and asked him to please go in and greet them. Bonaparte said nothing. He bowed to us and retired, omitting altogether any presentation of himself to the ladies. Obviously, the entire reception was arranged so that all embassies might see with what disdain he treated the English, and might hear with what fearlessness he demanded Malta from them.

I have long been of the opinion that those two countries would soon be at war. It seems I am the only one who saw the writing on the wall. Today everyone can see it, but I do not expect that most people will remember who saw it first. . . .

Livingston rewrote his letter in the cipher that Jefferson insisted be used even when nothing of a secretive nature was imparted. Thomas Jefferson was unquestionably a great and learned man, but Livingston could not help thinking that the President was a little too proud of the complexity of his cipher.

I ought to be flattered that I was given the key to it. After all, I am not a Virginian. Damn you, Livingston, you become more malicious by the hour. You were not always so. People would not like you if they knew how difficult it will be for you to speak civilly to Monroe. Why can he not be delayed by a broken leg or a bilious attack? If only—if only there were some word I could get from Talleyrand that would prove I had made progress while Monroe was still sitting around Le Havre. If only I could write to Thomas Jefferson saying, "Mr. Monroe has not yet arrived in Paris. However, today I made great strides toward our goal. Without Mr. Monroe's valuable assistance, I extracted a promise from Talleyrand that—"

Livingston scarcely knew how to finish the imaginary sentence. What promise could be extracted from Talleyrand? The situation might well be more hopeless than ever. The Corsican's mind was busy with England. Yes, but couldn't that be a favorable turn of events? Talleyrand had once said that the First Consul would send Rochambeau thirty-five thousand fresh troops. Livingston didn't quite see how thirty-five thousand could be spared. The talk was that more than fifty thousand had already been squandered on that peculiar thing happening in Saint-Domingue. Could Bonaparte fight England and still keep replenishing Rochambeau's army? If he could, then he was indeed a genius. If he could not, he would have to abandon hope of conquering Saint-Domingue. In that case, common sense would indicate the impossibility of taking possession of New Orleans. The French islands of Martinique and Guadeloupe were too far away to serve Bonaparte as a North American foothold.

No use asking Talleyrand whether or not Bonaparte, after his fiery demand for Malta, could still send thirty-five thousand men to Saint-Domingue. Talleyrand would say only that there was no reason to suppose he could not. Rufus King, the American Minister in England, had described French attitudes perfectly when he had said, "The policy of the French is to keep crying 'Victory!' until they are obliged to retreat." But there had not been anyone like Bonaparte within the memory of man. Perhaps he could accomplish feats beyond imagination. One who said he could not was, perhaps, only demonstrating the narrowness of his own vision.

Talleyrand had the grace not to gloat over Livingston's canceled dinner or his own prescience. When the two men sat together the next day on the sofa, the Foreign Minister asked if the works of Voltaire were popular in the United States. Livingston said they were not, then sat back and listened to a discourse on comparative literary tastes throughout the world. Talleyrand could be interesting and informative, and Livingston was grateful that no personal reminiscences, at least, were— With an agonizing shock, it came to him that Talleyrand had chosen literature as a subject because, today, anything relating to New Orleans must be avoided. Talleyrand was waiting for Monroe. No further word of importance would be uttered until Monroe, too, sat in this room. No, no, that could not be tolerated, Livingston thought. He deserved some small scrap of hope or information that had been gathered before Monroe's appearance. From the tormenting Talleyrand he must elicit a private bit of knowledge spoken to him alone. He must get the conversation on a many-forked crossroad.

"Did you ever notice the great significance islands play in the life of the First Consul?" he asked.

An irrelevance—and an interruption, at that—was not calculated to please Talleyrand, but time was flying. Monroe was, no doubt, in a coach at this very minute, on his way to Paris.

"Islands?" The gray-green eyes were cold.

"Yes. He was born on one and so was his wife. There may have been others which I am overlooking. But there were Corsica and Martinique in the past, and Saint-Domingue and Malta in the present. Some records and writings even refer to New Orleans as the 'Ile d'Orléans.' "

"Mr. Livingston, I was speaking of Goethe."

Livingston smiled ingratiatingly. "I have warned you that I cannot keep my mind away from New Orleans."

"It is interesting," Talleyrand said thoughtfully. "I mean your reference to the First Consul and islands. Yes, quite interesting. Still, he will probably never bother to look at Corsica again. He has never seen Martinique, Saint-Domingue is practically in his pocket, and the English will hand over Malta. So perhaps there will be no more islands in his life to stir your imagination."

"You did not mention New Orleans."

"A map maker's error, one supposes. It is not really an island."

Livingston said, "But it is New Orleans, and you know it is of that I wish to speak. Will you consider selling it?"

The lace handkerchief. The yawn. "Why would anyone sell New Orleans?"

"I thought I had given you many reasons. I will gladly give them again."

"Please do not."

"Let me give you one, just one. The English could take New Orleans from you if the war extended to the Caribbean and the Mexican Gulf. If that happened, you could not defend Louisiana."

Talleyrand bent forward and turned his head so that he was gazing straight into Livingston's face. "Mr. Livingston, my poor American friend, how can you be so dense? What good is Louisiana without New Orleans?"

"What good is Louisiana! God Almighty, it is a million square miles of territory which, when developed, will be as fertile as any land in the world. Sell us New Orleans, and Louisiana will be safe. England is our friend today. She will not touch New Orleans if it is ours."

"Is Louisiana really so fertile as you say? Is it so desirable?"

"It is a wilderness, as I have told you. The potential, however—"

"What would you give for all of Louisiana?" Talleyrand asked.

It was the first time he had ever spoken without Livingston's being absolutely certain of what he had said.

"I beg your pardon. Would you repeat that? And, please, a little louder."

Talleyrand yawned again. "I only asked what the United States would pay for all of Louisiana."

Livingston felt a sudden trembling in his limbs. He knew that his forehead was wet and that it would take him a moment to find the words to fit the situation. Then he remembered what Lord Whitworth had said to Bonaparte. "I am not prepared to speak on that subject."

Talleyrand shrugged. "Neither am I. The thought just came to me as we were talking. You seemed so terribly enthusiastic about Louisiana's potential."

The trembling continued, and, though Livingston's mind was whirling with thoughts and questions, he dared speak none of them for fear of floundering. He stood up. "I must go," he said.

Talleyrand raised his eyebrows in surprise. "Really? There is nothing for you to think over or to write to Madison about, you know. I just happened to give voice to an idle thought."

"Still, I am afraid I must leave."

Livingston went home and seated himself in a quiet upstairs room. His nerves were jangled, and he could not seem to view with clarity the various lines and curves that presented themselves to his puzzled mind. After a time, a degree of calm returned. He even smiled, remembering that he had hoped Talleyrand would say something worthwhile before Monroe's arrival. Well, Talleyrand had said something worthwhile. It was a lie, of course, that he had voiced only an idle thought. Foreign Ministers voiced no idle thoughts on matters of international interest. It had been after discussion with the First Consul, and possibly with Decrès, Minister of Marine, and Barbé-Marbois, Minister of Finance, and perhaps those excitable Bonaparte brothers, that the decision had been made to place the idea on the table and see what Livingston did with it.

And what had Livingston done with it? For a long, dark hour, the distinguished New Yorker who had administered the oath of office to George Washington sat deep in thought. He knew the French well enough. They would insist that the ocean was too wide, time too valuable. Impossible for him to write and receive letters from Jefferson and Madison. The chance to buy Louisiana must be accepted or rejected without delay. No, New Orleans was not for sale by itself. The Americans would have to buy all of Louisiana or none of it. What will you pay, Mr. Livingston? Will you sign or not?

These were the questions, these were the misgivings that had sent him home to sit in a quiet room. How he would welcome the sight of Monroe standing before him, explaining that he had just arrived but would be willing to get to business immediately. He wanted to shake hands with Monroe and feel the strength of another American, a man whose duty it was to listen and advise.

During the long, dark hour, Livingston went over everything in his mind. Quietly, he retraced his steps to the moment in which he had first learned that Monroe was joining him in the mission. The resentment, the anger, the jealousy. The effort to prove that Monroe had never been needed. The passionate perseverance to draw from Talleyrand some proposition that would need a cool appraisal, an incisive intelligence and a flashing display of courage. Now here was the opportunity that would give wings to ambition. And all he could think of was his need to talk to Monroe. Ridiculous. Still, he could not boldly state that he would buy Louisiana, when he had been sent to fetch only New Orleans. Did the United States even want Louisiana? And did refusing Louisiana definitely mean that New Orleans was lost? Yes, that is what it meant. Why would anybody sell New Orleans? Livingston, my poor American friend, how can you be so dense?

And now what? Now what? Where was James Monroe? Why was he dawdling on his way to Paris? Good God, suppose he had broken his leg or been taken ill?

If the news comes within the next day or so that something

like that has happened to him, I shall go to Le Havre. I must
see him.

Monroe was not ill, and on his first day in Paris he spent nine
and a half hours with Livingston. They read each other's instructions, checking carefully to see if anywhere there was a phrase,
a word or hint that could be interpreted to cover the situation.
Was there a hidden order to discuss nothing beyond New Orleans? Was there a subtle invitation to probe the possibility
that the First Consul really did not want all of the wilderness?

Monroe looked up from his reading, and said, "Tom Jefferson
sends a ton of closely written pages when he wants someone to
buy only a horse for him. Wouldn't you think that he'd have
been more explicit in his directions to us?"

"Madison wrote our instructions. If Jefferson had done so,
there would have been a beautifully phrased paragraph warning us precisely what not to buy."

"Oh, don't think Tom didn't tell Madison what he wanted
included here."

Livingston looked thoughtful. "Yes, you're quite right. You've
called my attention to the most significant fact of all. The President didn't waste time cautioning us not to buy Mongolia or
Timbuctu. In the omission is our order. We're not to buy anything but New Orleans. I remember now that the alternative
to the purchase of that city is not on an upward scale but downward. If we are denied New Orleans, then we are to try for a
portion of ground contiguous with the river, and if that is
refused, then we are to ask for jurisdiction over a—"

Monroe burst into laughter. "Isn't it incredible? We were
told to settle, if necessary, for a piece of real estate just big
enough to stand our barrels and crates upon. Now we're worried
sick because they want to give us a million square miles."

"They don't want to *give* us anything, Monroe. The price that
will be demanded is the serious problem. We cannot consult
with Jefferson and Madison, so we have a choice between exceed-
ing the amount we've been directed to spend or—"

"I know. Or letting New Orleans slip out of our grasp."

Monroe was no longer laughing, and his eyes seemed to have suddenly hardened. "Livingston, I will not be a party to breaking the Treasury of the United States, but neither am I going to let Gallatin lose us New Orleans. Our country needs that harbor. If it is going to cost a few million dollars more than we're authorized to spend, I'm going to be in favor of spending it."

"Even though we have no directive even to discuss anything more costly than New Orleans?"

Monroe was silent.

Livingston said, "It strikes me as quite unlikely that Jefferson never thought of possessing all of Louisiana. The fact that he did not mention it to us may be a sterner warning than had he written on every sheet of paper that we were not to consider the whole territory."

Monroe sat back in his chair and gave courteous consideration to Livingston's remarks. Then, "Think about Louisiana for a moment. Imagine the extent of that territory. It would increase the size of the United States by one hundred and forty per cent. It will give us exclusive navigation of the entire river, and the calm of having no neighbors to dispute us. We could live forever with no war to dread."

"Inviting. No question about it—very inviting. But I still believe the President thought of all that and put it from him. He is in possession of information that, quite properly, is not shared with those of us in whose department it does not belong. Would you concede that there might be military reasons, secret agreements or whatever that have put the President under obligation to abstain from dreaming of Louisiana?"

Monroe said, "You have a knack for complicating the complicated. I love Tom Jefferson as though he were my brother, and I believe his brain is the finest in our country. But he is human, Livingston. He behaves as others do. Did you ever think there would be a chance to buy Louisiana? Of course not. Neither did he. And if he had thought of it, he'd have dismissed it from his mind immediately, fearing that the price would be too high."

"And perhaps it will be."

"Perhaps. However, there are two things to remember. One: Talleyrand asked if you'd buy it. You didn't ask if he'd sell it. That's a point for us. Two: the situation as it faces us is something Jefferson could never have imagined. The French won't talk to us about New Orleans. We shall have to buy the entire territory or nothing. They want to get out, Livingston. Bonaparte's decided that Louisiana is on his unlucky side of the world."

Livingston began to remember why he had seldom liked Virginians. Monroe was talking as though it were he who had sat through the meetings with Talleyrand. All that Monroe knew about any recent remark or happening had been told to him this very day by the man to whom he would now explain the situation. There was a way to deflate his unbearable self-confidence.

"When you are presented to the First Consul, Monroe, I would advise you to be as cordial as he will permit, but do not grow effusive and compare our two countries."

Monroe reddened and opened his mouth to speak what could be only an angry word. Surprisingly, he did not speak it. Instead, he reached across the table and laid his hand on Livingston's arm in friendly fashion. "That's right, I haven't met him yet, and I'm already as nervous as a cat. I certainly admire the way you've stood up during this long, hard pull, Livingston. You must be a man of iron."

That was another thing about Virginians. One could never guess what on earth had changed their moods.

"I hope you have planned to dine with me, Monroe. There are still a few things—"

"I'd be delighted. I need all the pointers you can give me."

Well now, that is better. Monroe might still prove to be the useful sounding board I wanted after that astonishing last meeting with Talleyrand. He isn't needed here, God knows, but, since he has come, I shall try to be amiable.

Dessert had just been served when Livingston, glancing through the lace draperies of the dining-room window, saw a man strolling in his garden. Since the butler was ill, and only the elderly cook and a scatterbrained waitress were on duty, Livingston thought he had better question the intruder himself. He made an excuse to Monroe and, by way of the corridor and library, went out to the garden.

"Don't be alarmed, Robert. It is I." The man who approached was Barbé-Marbois, the French Minister of Finance.

"Why, good evening, François. What are you doing in the garden?"

"I peeked through your window to see if you are alone. I am disappointed to see that you are not. Could you, by any chance, come to my house tonight after your guest has departed?"

Certainly Barbé-Marbois must know that the guest was James Monroe. Then it was to Livingston alone that the First Consul would have his messages delivered. Livingston felt an upsurge of pride and a small twinge of pity for Monroe, who was not really a very fortunate fellow.

"That probably wouldn't be until eleven o'clock or so."

"I'll be watching for you."

The rest of the evening was difficult. Livingston asked himself if he only imagined Monroe was scowling at him. Could Monroe know that the man in the garden was Barbé-Marbois? Nonsense. Monroe didn't know there had been a man in the garden. Another annoying thing—Monroe was mumbling his words. Livingston found himself requesting again and again that Monroe repeat what he had said. It occurred to him that the fault could be his own. Perhaps he was not concentrating as he usually did. It was impossible to keep his mind from straying, from guessing, from anticipating. Suppose that when he entered Barbé-Marbois's house he would encounter the First Consul. If an answer were demanded right then and there, should he say that he was obligated to consult Monroe? Or should he resign himself to the sorry fact that Monroe was a less distinguished American?

"I'm afraid you are very tired," Monroe said. "We can talk again tomorrow. I will bid you good night."

"What's that? What did you say?"

It was only nine thirty. Was it too early to go to Barbé-Mar-

bois's? No doubt the First Consul would not yet have arrived—
Livingston, you are going crazy. Nothing was said of the First
Consul. He is not going to be at Barbé-Marbois's house.

And, of course, he was not.
"Tell me exactly what you said in answer to Talleyrand's
question," Barbé-Marbois demanded, in some excitement.
"There was nothing of importance I could say."
"You mean that Talleyrand surprised you?"
"Oh, I am not easily surprised."
"But we have not heard from you."
"I have been busy with Monroe. There is much to think and
talk about. For instance, what is the actual size of the Louisiana
Territory?"
"Nobody knows that, Robert. You must take it as Spain
handed it to us: unmeasured, but huge and very valuable."
"Well, I can't just take it. I'm obliged to consult with Monroe."
"Yes, yes, of course, but forget Monroe for the moment. Let
us talk as friends. I will tell you candidly that the First Consul
has had a terrible shock. How could he have supposed that
Saint-Domingue would still be holding out against him? Think
of the quality of our soldiers. Think of our resources and
strength. If all had gone as expected, we would be successfully
established in New Orleans today, and we would be examining
the uses to which our vast territory might be put. My God, that
damned black island has been an expensive disappointment."
"So Bonaparte will fight Englishmen instead of blacks. He
will take Malta instead of Saint-Domingue."
"We have not yet abandoned Saint-Domingue, Robert. It
belongs to us. As to Louisiana, I am glad you did not have any
definite statement for Talleyrand. He is opposed to selling." ·
"Is he really?"
"Indeed. So are the Bonaparte brothers and Decrès."
"What are their objections?"
"I do not know about the brothers, but Decrès is a profound
thinker. He is as concerned about the future as if Bonaparte

and he were immortal, and in a hundred years or so he would be blamed in public for the sale of Louisiana. He is saying that France needs colonies for her support. He is in favor of developing the territory, which he thinks may be very lush land for agriculture and cattle raising. Also, he is saying that one day, somewhere south of Mexico, we may want to build a canal uniting the Atlantic and Pacific oceans, and that, when that occurs, New Orleans and all of Louisiana will be enriched by it."

"Why is Talleyrand opposed?"

"Do not answer me yes or no, but I believe you have not bribed him."

"So it is you and Bonaparte only who are willing to sell?"

"Bonaparte vacillates. If he did not, it would be unimportant what Decrès or the brothers say. He would simply order everyone, including Talleyrand, to be quiet. It is that there are days on which he doubts he can hold the territory when war with England is declared. On those days, he is very determined to make certain that England will not have both Canada and Louisiana. There are other days when he believes he can defend Louisiana against the devil himself. You know the temper of a youthful conqueror. Everything he does is rapid as lightning. One of these mornings he'll make up his mind, all within five seconds, that you are or you are not to have Louisiana."

"On his dark days, does he ever think of telling the Spanish King to take it back?"

Barbé-Marbois smiled. "No. Bonaparte does not want Tuscany returned to him, as King Charles would courteously insist upon doing. Also, Bonaparte needs money in the Treasury. You know you're getting that information from the main source, my friend, when you're getting it from me. That's why I am for selling Louisiana. That's why I asked you here for this little talk. Robert, give me a figure I can mention to Bonaparte when he's in a selling mood."

"François, I cannot do that. I cannot disregard Monroe."

Barbé-Marbois stared at him reproachfully. "I have told you things that, if revealed, would ruin my career. I trusted you.

328

Are you now saying to me that in the quiet of my home, coming here at this hour, as only a friend could come, you will refuse to utter any word that would not be spoken in a formal meeting with the First Consul and his ministers?"

Livingston saw the justice of Barbé-Marbois's hurt. "It isn't that, François. Of course I will confide in you as you have in me. Whenever there is time, I will tell you much that I would not tell Monroe. The trouble is that I am almost ashamed to mention the paltry sum of money that is at my disposal. Has Bonaparte, when contemplating a sale to us, ever stated the amount he would expect?"

"Yes. One hundred and twenty-five million dollars."

Livingston was stunned. "Good God! That is a madman's price."

"I told him it was exorbitant. He said you would have to borrow it. I explained how that would beggar so young a country, and he turned the conversation to another matter. Please mention some figure that I can give to him when he is again receptive."

Livingston made no reply.

"Could I say that you might pay sixty million?"

"No. That is beyond our means. Far beyond. Remember, I came here to buy only New Orleans."

Barbé-Marbois looked at him with compassion. "There was never a chance of that. I believe that Talleyrand finally asked you what good Louisiana was without New Orleans."

"Yes. Evidently he grew bored waiting for me to see for myself why the meetings went on and on without progress."

"As I told you, he is against the sale, but on a day when the First Consul was in favor of it, Talleyrand was ordered to keep talking to you. We'd have had a better position if it had been you who had brought up the question of the entire territory. How is it that the brilliant Jefferson failed to see that no one would sell New Orleans alone? It's the only city, the only harbor, the only—"

"The only thing President Jefferson wants, François. The United States needs it, and will have it. I must recommend now that we fight for it. Bonaparte, in his madness, has given us a sure ally."

"England? Why, if you were fortunate enough to capture New Orleans, England would take it away from you."

"That would be a bitter blow to us, and one that would in no way profit France. I guarantee you that if we join forces with England, Bonaparte will suffer the shame of losing his North American territory instead of selling it. He will have made an enemy where he could have made a friend."

"Yes, you are right. Name a figure, any sensible figure that I can bring to him."

Livingston suddenly became conscious of a scraping irritation that had caused him, over the last few minutes, to speak sharply to Barbé-Marbois. What was it? He was startled to discover that it was mistrust. Of course, mistrust. This man, his old friend, had known that New Orleans was not for sale. Months ago he could have dropped a hint, and there would have been time for correspondence with Jefferson and Madison. And perhaps there would never have been a thought of sending Monroe.

"I cannot name a figure for a head of state who deals in fantasies. I repeat, I will recommend that we fight for New Orleans." Livingston started toward the door. "Thank you for all you have done, and for all you could have done. Thank you very much."

The Minister of Finance rose slowly, hardly believing that his guest intended to leave. "When Monroe got home tonight, there was a message awaiting which informed him that he will be presented to the First Consul tomorrow. If you give me a word to carry to Bonaparte tonight, I will press for an audience immediately following the presentation. You will have to put some sort of proposition to the First Consul. He is going to Brussels the day after. Every moment is precious."

"Yes," Livingston said acidly. "Every moment is precious because France says so. The United States sat here for months, but now, all of a sudden, Bonaparte is in a hurry. You asked for a word to carry to him. This is it: tell Bonaparte that if I go back to America without a peaceable agreement by which we own New Orleans and its harbor, then Jefferson will be discredited. He will be defeated at the next election, and power will be thrown into the hands of men who are most hostile toward France, men who are shouting now for war. Ask Bonaparte if he wants that."

"Of course he does not want that, Robert, but—"

"The buts are finished. I have heard many from Talleyrand, and am unwilling to hear more. I must confer with Monroe before I mention money to anyone. Try to impress upon the First Consul that he has an opportunity to make the United States a loyal friend forever. If that sounds like small satisfaction, tell him what I told Talleyrand. Nothing is going to hinder the development of the United States. France may live to rejoice in our friendship."

"France deeply desires the friendship of the United States."

Livingston looked long and hard at Barbé-Marbois. "Really, François? All I can say is that you people have a hellish way of showing it."

He went out then and got into his carriage, giving the coachman Monroe's address.

It took several minutes before a servant was awakened to open the door, several minutes more before Monroe, in dressing gown, came down the stairs. It was astonishing to Livingston that Monroe looked very wide-awake and self-possessed.

"What has happened, Livingston?"

The question was unsettling. Livingston had been thinking of Louisiana, not of etiquette. For the first time, he realized that an explanation and an apology would have to be spoken. He had committed a grave diplomatic discourtesy. Monroe had every right to boil with rage at having been neatly maneuvered out of what could prove to be the pivotal moment of the mission.

Livingston described briefly how he had spent the last hour. It troubled him that he said twice, and almost pleadingly, "You see, François Barbé-Marbois and I are very old friends."

Monroe nodded curtly. "He is Bonaparte's Minister of Finance. Nothing else about him is of interest to me."

Livingston sighed with relief. Monroe would not dwell upon his injury.

"Did you get the message that you are to be presented to the First Consul tomorrow?"

"Yes."

"Directly after the presentation, I expect Barbé-Marbois to gain an audience for us. Bonaparte has named a hundred and twenty-five million as his price for Louisiana. Barbé-Marbois thought sixty million more realistic. Monroe, what on earth can we say? What can we do?"

"To begin with, let us sit down."

It struck Livingston that he had never noticed before what tremendous dignity James Monroe possessed. He did not appear either odd or amusing casually seated in his dressing gown amid such priceless objects as Chinese porcelains, Egyptian cats, Roman medallions and silver candle lamps. What a splendid place he had rented. Livingston would have liked to ship the room intact to his house on the Hudson.

"We have been instructed to offer five million for New Orleans and, if necessary, to allow ourselves to be pushed as high as eight million," Monroe said tonelessly. "There is, as well, the possibility that ten million would neither shatter our economy nor drive Gallatin to suicide. Therefore, I suggest that we simply announce that our figure for Louisiana is ten million, and no more."

"Monroe, we can't begin with the top dollar."

"We can't begin with the bottom one, either. Bonaparte will. get up and walk out of the room. Five million is so small an amount that he will feel justified in indulging his passion for dramatic exits."

Livingston thought about that. "You believe ten million will hold him in his chair?"

"It will quicken his interest."

"I should hope so. That's absolutely as high as we can go."

Monroe said coolly, "Don't delude yourself. He will not accept ten million. That is only the amount with which we can catch his attention. It is a respectable amount. It does not shame us to offer it. It does not shame him to consider it."

Livingston felt a degree of alarm. "Suppose Bonaparte calmly invites us to double it."

"I would not dream of doubling it. If we sense that he is definitely going to decline our offer, I would think it proper to go to fifteen million. If he attempts to draw us to still higher ground, then it is you and I who must walk out of the room."

"Fifteen million was never mentioned in Washington, Monroe."

"Louisiana was never mentioned in Washington, Livingston."

The silence that followed lasted many minutes, while each man thought his thoughts. Livingston hoped he was as expressionless as Monroe. From what source had the Virginian drawn his tranquillity and poise?

Monroe finally spoke. "I am assuming that you have already sent to Bonaparte by way of Talleyrand and Barbé-Marbois every one of the dire warnings a diplomat keeps ready for delivery."

"I don't think I have missed any."

"Have you also conveyed to the First Consul all the advantages that would result from harmony between the United States and France?"

"That, too, I believe."

"Did you make it a point to say that by adding to our power and prestige Bonaparte will be creating a nation that will forever keep England's stature somewhat modest in North America?"

"Of course I said that."

"Good, Livingston, good. Go home and sleep now. Within a few hours we will have bought the Louisiana Territory for fifteen million dollars."

"How can you be so sure?"

"Bonaparte must sell it or have it ripped from him."

"If we all know that, then he knows it, too, and will not stalk angrily from the room. So why do we not offer him eight million, or even five?"

Monroe smiled, but not exactly at Livingston. The smile was distant and introspective. "It is always bad business, Livingston," he said, "to give a man a reason to feel that he has been insulted."

FIVE

The French, the Haitians and the Yankee Flag

．．．．．．．．．．．．．．．．．．．．．．．

$\mathcal{D}$ECRÈS HAS SENT HIS REGRETS," Barbé-Marbois said to Talleyrand. "He wrote a brief note that was not very friendly. His opinion is that there is nothing to celebrate."

Talleyrand nodded. "If you would like to offer me a glass of good wine, I would not refuse it, but I, too, see nothing to celebrate."

Barbé-Marbois smiled. "You do not have charge of the Treasury."

"I know what your situation was. The American money will be a help. You and I are on a seesaw, François. The times when you are without worries are often the very occasions on which I have to perform most arduously."

"Yes, you will have to be charming to Spain. You hinted that there was something—" Barbé-Marbois frowned in an effort to remember exactly what Talleyrand's problem was. "Precisely what have we done that will anger King Charles?"

"Oh, only a little thing," Talleyrand said. "We have sold what we did not own."

The Minister of Finance was startled. "We gave them Tuscany, and received Louisiana in an honest trade, did we not?"

"Nothing is ever that simple, and you know it." Talleyrand paused, then questioned plaintively, "François, you *are* going to offer wine, aren't you?"

"It is on its way."

"Delightful. I trust the delay will not be unbearable." He paused again and sighed. "There is a slight wrinkle to iron out with Spain. Deplorably, she has our solemn promise that the

Duc de Palma will be king of Tuscany and acknowledged as such by all European powers. Do you know who the Duc de Palma is?"

"No. Who is he?"

"He is either the son-in-law of the King of Spain or his brother-in-law. I really didn't listen closely. Sentimental family attachments bore me. However, our ownership of Louisiana rested on this gentleman's receiving the royal position we promised. Well, he didn't receive it. England and Russia asked a question very like yours: Who is the Duc de Palma? François, I can say only that if he is not king of Tuscany we did not own Louisiana."

"My God, Talleyrand, how could you make a treaty that depended on the acquiescence of foreign rulers?"

"I don't know, except that it's the sort of thing one is always saying in treaties. One gets carried away, you know. Ah, here comes the wine. And such attractive things to eat." He smiled warmly at the butler and his assistant. "Do fix me a small plate of pâté and lobster and sturgeon."

Barbé-Marbois sat in silence while Talleyrand beamed at the servants and encouraged their comments on wine and food. So like him to treat his own household with princely disdain, and to create the notion in the minds of other men's servants that he was the only one who thought them human.

When they were alone again, Barbé-Marbois asked, "Do you think Spain will cause difficulties?"

"It is hard to say. I shall have to guide their ire so that it falls on England and Russia. I will swear that we did not sign the treaty until we had the promise of every royal house that the Duc de Palma would be acknowledged as king of Tuscany. Of course, I shall have to say the promises were only verbal, and admit that we were too trusting. It might be a nice touch to add that we had believed the word of all rulers to be as sacred as that of the King of Spain." Talleyrand nibbled delicately and drank. His eyes, Barbé-Marbois observed, had taken on a new, contemplative expression. "Yes, yes, I think I can deal quite successfully with Spain on *that* matter."

"On *that* matter? Is there another?"

Talleyrand bit into a chocolate-covered cherry. "I'm afraid there is. We had to include in the treaty an agreement never to sell or cede Louisiana to any other nation without informing Spain and receiving her permission."

Barbé-Marbois felt a chill pass over him. "Good God! You will wreck France with your dishonest dealings."

Talleyrand looked hurt. "Was it I who wanted to sell Louisiana?"

"You could have reminded the First Consul that it was not for sale without Spain's permission."

"Oh, Spain would never have given permission. She is frightened to death of the United States. When the whole Louisiana Territory lay between the Yankee Doodles and the Southwest, Spain feared that she would be robbed of her lands. Now she's really in jeopardy. There will be nothing but screams from Spain for another thirty or forty years, and then the United States will grow tired of the noise and will strangle her."

"But we can't allow that."

Talleyrand raised his eyebrows. "Why, François, it is not our business. Didn't that good man George Washington say something about avoiding foreign entanglements?"

Barbé-Marbois was not amused. "You are the worst foreign entanglement we have. We are now obliged to inform the United States that their fifteen million dollars cannot be accepted and that the negotiation is canceled. I suppose we can explain that we've just reread the treaty with Spain."

Now Talleyrand became serious. "I beg of you not to express such a thought to the First Consul. Today he would do just that. He is in a regretful mood. He is viewing Louisiana as paradise lost. He is berating even those who opposed the sale, saying that we should have firmly protected him against his own foolishness, and kept our valuable portion of North America."

"Probably Spain will settle the argument by throwing Tuscany back in our laps."

"Forgetting the Spanish complications for a moment—I do not believe Bonaparte could have retained Louisiana, but I did

339

want him to try. There's something so seedy about selling one's property. It would have been glorious to make the attempt to save the territory, though without Saint-Domingue our navy has no shelter and no supply base. The First Consul, I think, consented to the sale because now there is no way to prove that he couldn't have held Louisiana. I'm sure you know that he's not going to hold even Saint-Domingue."

Barbé-Marbois said, "I really don't understand war. I will tell you that I have searched my mind ever since Leclerc's failure to gain immediate supremacy. I can find no logic in a magnificently trained, well-organized, self-respecting army getting beaten by a mass of aborigines."

"Oh, their leaders are not that low on the scale. Most of the commanders had French training, you know. Then we suffered the calamity of fever season— But I am talking to you as I talk to outsiders who are occasionally my dinner guests. They ask questions about Saint-Domingue and I respond patriotically. The truth is that the slaveowner in Saint-Domingue was allowed to abuse his human property without ever a word of rebuke from France. Blacks who owned blacks were brutal beyond words. So were mulattoes. So were whites. We never sent anyone of integrity to enforce laws that gave protection to the poor devils. For that reason hatred was directed against the whites. There was no black too ignorant to know that it was France's business to run the island by the laws of God and man. We never did it. We just imported mahogany and sugar, and got rich on the suffering of others. By purest accident, the Directory once sent a commissioner who gave them their freedom and sailed away. Toussaint L'Ouverture took over and governed the island better than it had been governed at any time in the past, and probably better than it will be governed at any time in the future. The First Consul destroyed Toussaint and the island. It would be very difficult to understand why the blacks would not fight well against us."

Barbé-Marbois refilled the glasses. "You are telling me that the strongest force is hatred. I have always known that. Why do fools keep saying it is love?"

"Because fools can't gauge the depth of either one. Actually, most people go through life without experiencing anything that inspires the majestic emotions. Yet the words are sprinkled about as though everyone was acquainted with their meaning."

"Curiously, they both demand self-sacrifice and enormous energy."

"Yes, few of us have the capacity to love or hate. We are too practical and too lazy." Talleyrand's eyes turned toward the tapestry he had admired on another occasion. "François, on this Spanish imbroglio—"

"I don't want to speak about Spain. That troubles me, and I may not keep my temper if we discuss it further. I don't want to speak about Saint-Domingue, either. I suffer for Toussaint, although I am a sensible man and have to recognize that the island belonged to France. He had no right to it."

"You have opened the door to a philosophical debate, François."

"You are mistaken. I have closed the door to anything that does not amuse me."

"Shall we talk about America?"

"What is amusing about America?"

"What isn't? Livingston wearing his honorable position like a Sunday hat? Monroe just waiting to tell his fellow Virginians that Livingston, figuratively speaking, tried to stab him? Jefferson worrying that he can't walk on water? Madison fretting that Jefferson will learn how to do it? But the most wonderful absurdity about the Americans is the boast that their country was founded upon the consent of the governed. Now they are going to rule over a people whose land has been annexed without anyone consulting the preferences of the new citizens."

"The new citizens will consent, Talleyrand. Man is a commercial creature. It is not Spain or France that fills the New Orleans harbor with shipping. It is three hundred thousand American farmers who have cultivated the plains and sent their produce to market. New Orleans knows that. She won't quarrel over being adopted by a rich family."

Talleyrand reached for another chocolate-covered cherry. "I

wonder if the elegant scholar who wrote the Declaration of Independence, with some small assistance from Benjamin Franklin and John Adams, ever read the American Constitution. I took a quick look at it the other day. It appears to me that it's quite illegal to purchase foreign territory and incorporate it into the United States. Acts of the national government are valid only when specifically authorized by the Constitution."

Barbé-Marbois's exasperation was very evident. "Really, Talleyrand, you're not in such a state of legal grace that you can cast aspersions on Jefferson. If he has done something wrong, he will right it. He never plans to be dishonest."

"Oh, I had forgotten that Madame Barbé-Marbois is American. Forgive me. But, just as a point of interest, did you know they look upon our revolution with contempt?"

"Much about our revolution deserves that view."

"You must stop listening to old royalists and start reading some of the documents which prove that, in our darkest, most bloodthirsty days, man was thinking of man. In Robespierre's time, generally known as the Terror, among the human rights declared by his party were public assistance to the aged, the infirm and those without work. Public education was proposed for everybody. When did the United States ever suggest legislation so noble and unselfish as that?"

"When did France ever do more than suggest it?"

"That's not the point. The point is that the United States simply doesn't recognize our virtues. She doesn't have a warm feeling toward us. She doesn't even seem grateful for all the financial help we gave during her revolution."

"*We* gave? Talleyrand, this firm was under different management in those days."

"But France is France."

"Yes, that's what we keep telling the children."

Talleyrand made an impatient gesture. "I thought it would be amusing to talk about America, but you're in a bad humor, François."

Barbé-Marbois shook his head. "On the contrary, I was very happy until I heard that I may not receive the fifteen million dollars from the United States. The Treasury needs that money. Talleyrand, you have done the most outrageous thing ever done by any man who has been trusted to represent his country with honor."

"That's exactly what will save us. Governments tend to accept the outrageous because it is too intricate to explain. They go to war only over things easily understood by the common people of their nations. What ordinary Spaniard is going to be furious because the Duc de Palma is not king of Tuscany? What American is going to shoulder his musket because France did not ask Spain for permission to sell Louisiana? You see, to make war, a country has to have a reason that the people take seriously." Talleyrand suddenly smiled. "You have a beautiful soul, François. While talking to you, my doubts have disappeared, a sense of serenity has settled upon me. I know there is nothing to worry about. Are there any more chocolate-covered cherries? And perhaps another bottle of wine?"

. . . .

On the island of Haiti, which once had been green and beautiful, French blood flowed in the hills and mountains and upon the plain. Haitians died, too, but they had expected to die. No Haitian soldier was ever heard to say "When the war is over . . ." They held in contempt all men who lived beyond the years of strength and fervor. They jeered at mention of the future and made songs about the shame of taking up room when one was no longer wanted by an army or a woman.

Rochambeau could not still their songs or their laughter, for the blacks themselves did not realize that, despite its flowers and shimmering sea, Haiti was an extraordinarily harsh land. They knew no basis for comparison. Death by cruelty was commonplace in all the world with which they were familiar. When Rochambeau crowded blacks into small, airless spaces and suffocated them by the burning of sulphur candles, it was the end of life for them. No more, no less. When they were handcuffed together in long lines, taken aboard a ship and dropped for the sharks, it was only the sort of thing one could expect. Who would not do a similar thing to a prisoner? And who wanted to live to be old? Fighting and dying was the business of the young. There were troops now that did not remember slavery. They were not sure what to fear when the word was whispered. They did not know of whom their elders spoke when sometimes the name Toussaint L'Ouverture was breathed in gratitude.

The young Haitians were afraid of nothing on earth except the anger of Dessalines. Some had never seen him, but they believed their officers, who shivered when they told of him. For the soldiers of Haiti, there were Dessalines and the French, sunlight and rain—and sometimes a girl. These were all the things there were in a life so short.

Rochambeau imported dogs from Cuba. Special dogs that were adept in hunting runaway slaves. In Haiti, they would seek out black soldiers who waited in ambush. Prisoners were being used in their training. Rochambeau invited guests to watch as the dogs, made eager by starving, were loosed upon naked black prisoners.

Dessalines had prisoners, too. He hanged five hundred Frenchmen one morning, each on a separate gallows. He chose a high hill near Le Cap so Rochambeau and his men could see. It was not a spectacular sight for Dessalines. During the previous month, his soldiers had captured and killed the brigands of the island, who had turned out to be very poor fighters. The captives were burned to death.

"Ammunition getting too low for polite killings, and hanging too good for brigands who steal people from villages and make slaves out of them to do their Goddamned digging. Haitian people never be slaves again. Brigands ought to know that. Stupid bastards."

"The fleet doctor has warned Rochambeau that there are too many dead bodies washing up on the shore," Clervaux said. "It is an unhealthy situation."

"What he think to do? The whole island smell of dead people for long time now. What anybody expect when is war between beasts like French and beasts like us?"

"I would suggest, General, that we make a forty-eight-hour

truce with Rochambeau and collect all dead from beaches, mountains and so forth. They could be transported on a French ship to one of the uninhabited islands for mass burial."

"You so dainty, you mulattoes. I tell you something, Clervaux: never going to come a day so long I live that French soldier walk on Haiti sure he not going to get killed."

The rainy season descended on the island. Day after day, the Haitians broke through opaque sheets of rain and attacked. The French gasped for breath and fought back, fearing the enemy less than the unbelievable downpour that could fill a man's lungs with water or hammer him into the smothering mud. Nobody gained an inch of territory, nobody unfurled a flag or claimed a victory.

The French soldiers thought they detected the reasonless action of primitive man in these mad onslaughts that took place under pouring skies. It was encouraging to think that the blacks had no plan or purpose. Some pagan ritual was probably celebrated at the beginning of the rains, and the warriors were overstimulated by frenzied dancing. But the French dead were as numerous as if a determined military leader had spurred the black men on.

In time, the rain ceased, and the island skies were as blue as the sea; but there was never a day on which Rochambeau could write to Bonaparte saying that he had scored an impressive victory.

The war was eternal, unalterable, a fixed certainty. Then, suddenly, there was a difference in tempo, meaning and intention. Everything changed, intensified, grew darker, grew brighter, exploded. Rochambeau took fifteen thousand men to Port-au-Prince. Dessalines could guess they were to be deployed in the annihilation of the West and South provinces.

"I let Geffrard handle business in South, but I go to West. Pétion too dreamy-face for what going to go on there. You send twenty thousand men after me. Get word to Christophe that something happen."

But nothing at all happened in the West Province. Or in the South Province. Rochambeau and his fifteen thousand men returned to Le Cap without eating a meal in Port-au-Prince or firing a shot.

Dessalines came back to his headquarters on the old Fayolle plantation. He was mystified and crestfallen.

"I attack Rochambeau, but that be thing only big fool do. When I not know what happen, I wait till I know what happen. Fast French ship in harbor at Port-au-Prince. May bring him some message. I do not know what it do there, if no message. You find that French clerk fellow and tell him come here after dark. Maybe he know if strange thing happen someplace."

The white civilian clerk hated Rochambeau so much that he had permitted himself to be bought by Clervaux. He came after dark. He was sweating and pressing his stomach as though that was where the misery lay.

"General, may I stay here after I have told you all I know? Rochambeau will suspect. He will torture me."

Dessalines glowered at the clerk. "You talk quick and true, or maybe you got me to be more scared of."

The man steadied himself by clinging to the wall. "May I sit down?"

"No. You talk."

"A message from Bonaparte went to every harbor where Rochambeau could possibly have been. General, the Treaty of Amiens is no more."

"Big thing, eh? Who Amiens? What in hell he got to do with anything?"

Clervaux had leaped excitedly toward the clerk. "The Treaty has broken down?"

"Yes, sir."

Dessalines roared, his eyes red with rage. "What in Goddamn hell you two talk about?"

Clervaux said, "France and England are at war, General."

The clerk nodded and was waved from the room by Clervaux.

"They at war, for true? Good God Jesus, Clervaux, we got something better than fever season. France and England fight?" Dessalines pounded his fist exultantly on the table. "They fight?

God damn, Clervaux. God damn. You see something now. Write a letter. Write a letter quick."

Clervaux was puzzled. "To whom, General?"

The cords in Dessalines' thick neck bulged. "I got to know his name? That's your business. Who you write to when ammunition running little? To your mother? No, you fool, you write to man in big job on Jamaica. Jamaica English. English fight French. Tell English in fine, big words like I don't understand that we their dearest friends in Caribbean. Tell them if they our dearest friends in Caribbean to send ammunition, and together we beat French here in one hell of a hurry. After that, Haiti at peace and then need to buy everything for rebuild cities. Tell them we buy everything from England, and be friends together for all time."

Clervaux delayed a moment to stare at the black commander with the massive hands that had never held a pen or a book. He had not known the meaning of the Treaty of Amiens, but already he was familiar with ways to use its collapse.

"I never thought of Jamaica," Clervaux said. It was an admission of admiration.

"Better you not think of Jamaica before I do, Clervaux. We get along good so long you don't think faster than me."

Governor Nugent of Jamaica was also a fast thinker. He sent his emissary to Les Gonaïves to confer with Dessalines, who was at the residence of General Christophe. Governor Nugent would be glad to give General Dessalines military supplies and unlimited support in crushing the French.

"In return," the very English Captain Walker said, "the Governor requests two ports to be used as British trading posts when peace is restored. But, of course, there are requirements in the present. Two fortified bases, the one at Tiburon, the other at Môle-Saint-Nicolas. Governor Nugent suggests that the English, in occupying these two bases, could bring a conclusion to hostilities in the Caribbean more speedily than the Haitians could."

Dessalines looked at the Englishman across a desk, which had nothing at all upon it but a framed piece of embroidery that represented the blue-and-red flag of Haiti, and a prayer book that had belonged to Toussaint.

"What else your Governor Nugent want?"

"Oh," Captain Walker said lightly, "I suppose one would mention the ordinary decencies of war: protection of white civilians, and return of their property when peace has been made."

Dessalines sat in silence for a time, his eyes still riveted on the Englishman's pink, plump face. "I answer you backwards," he decided. "Last things you say I answer first. White civilians don't got property for us to return to them. You don't read Haitian new laws, I guess. White people not allowed to own anything here. I protect white civilians like Governor Nugent ask, unless they make us fight them. French shoot at us, we kill them, even if they little old ladies sitting in pretty garden. That what happen in war." Dessalines' unblinking gaze remained fixed. "I tell you, Captain Walker, I awful Goddamn sick in my stomach at way you talk. French is enemy of England, but you like your enemies more better than you like your friends. You worry that French people be safe and comfortable. You don't worry about Haitian people. What the Goddamn hell you think we be? Bat guano, that you and French kick out of your way?"

Captain Walker said, "I meant no insult, General. The conventions of war are—"

"You got something to tell me about war, Captain? I don't think so. I tell you. I tell you that nobody treat Haiti like it slave quarters of France—or England. You get no Goddamn ports for trading posts when war over. Law against white people owning land in Haiti go for English just like it go for French. Nobody cut no slices off this country like it is pig you grab and gobble down. And you tell Governor Nugent that bases at Tiburon and Môle-Saint-Nicolas don't get no English troops— not now, not never. And we don't talk about that no more because so far I am talking very soft and nice, but pretty soon I think more about what Nugent send you to say and I start hollering."

The cool English voice, brisk, businesslike, responded as though nothing extraordinary had been said by the Haitian commanding general. "Let me get this straight, sir. What is it, exactly, you propose to offer England in exchange for her aid in ridding you of your long-time enemy? If we are to be cobelligerents, certainly it is reasonable to suppose that each makes a concession of sorts to the other."

Dessalines' laughter was deep in his throat, mirthless, mocking. "Oh, you so educated, Captain, I don't know what it is you say. I answer what I think you say. I tell you again what I tell you in first letter, only now I make it more plain. You give me things to make war with. I give you help of best Goddamn army you ever see. You bring your boats where you block French reinforcements and supplies from come in harbor. I push French off island right onto decks of your navy. War over in Caribbean. Nugent get medal. Maybe you, too. We got Bonaparte in middle if you decide black people almost human. If you decide no, you guess what happen? I tell you. French let Haitian Army rest. French not stupid. They know we can't chase them across Jamaica Channel. We got no navy. They let us sit while they take biggest fleet this side of world ever see and they go get Jamaica. King of England say, 'You idiot bastards, Nugent and Walker, you lose Jamaica. You had chance to make chicken bones of French if you know how to handle Haiti and that black son of a bitch they got for leader.' "

Captain Walker's smile was stiff and somewhat forced as Dessalines continued, "Now, Captain in English Navy, I am very kind and honest with you. I tell you truth about everything, and I don't get mad and holler even once. Now your turn to be very kind and honest. You sit here all day and you tell me what Nugent tell you to try to get from me. It is time you tell me what he is willing to settle for."

That autumn, Le Cap fell to Christophe, and Port-au-Prince to Dessalines. The torrential rains began again, and for three weeks the blockaded French, starving, miserable and drenched to the skin, could not see, through the downpour, the enemy that harried them day and night. As the French ate their horses, their mules, and finally the man-hunting dogs from Cuba, it occurred to them that perhaps they had not been fighting primitive men at all.

In November, Rochambeau sent a message to Dessalines. Clervaux read it aloud: "Commanding General of the United Army of Haiti, I request you to withhold any further attacks upon my army as with this message I unconditionally surrender to you. I am at this hour opening negotiations with Captain Loring of the British Navy on the subject of terms for capitulation. Rochambeau."

Dessalines took the sheet of paper from Clervaux and looked at the writing upon it, writing that he could not read. Then he placed it flat between the palms of his big hands, as though this were another way that the words of Rochambeau could be committed to memory.

"We hang on, eh, Clervaux? We hold the rope in our teeth and we keep biting at the same time, and at last something very great happen. It was good thing we hang on till Bonaparte do something stupid. I tell you true, Clervaux, France never bother us no more. They learn that we hang on. They learn with more than fifty thousand of their dead, and Christ knows how many of ours."

Clervaux said nothing. This time he was thinking faster than Dessalines. He was thinking that Rochambeau was a lucky man. The English would never hand him over to the Haitians. Loring and Walker would agree that of course the French were enemies, Rochambeau was despicable, but, after all, my good fellow, one doesn't toss a white man to the cannibals, does one? For the first time in his life, Clervaux did not feel like a mulatto. He felt like an angry black.

"Clervaux, order wagons for me and order my men up. No little boys. Men. Men who be with me in most terrible times. I ride with them to harbor. We see what go on there."

In the harbor lay all that was left of the French fleet. Two frigates and fifteen small ships. The English Navy had done for the rest, and the English Navy was now in charge of what had been the stupendous armada that had brought General Leclerc and Bonaparte's finest soldiers to Saint-Domingue. There were seven thousand Frenchmen aboard, survivors of a campaign that might never be required reading in the school system of Napoleonic France.

"Where Rochambeau?" Dessalines demanded.

"Admiral Walker said to tell you that Rochambeau is a British prisoner."

Dessalines glared at the navy captain who had been sent to answer his questions. "I make that Goddamn Walker an admiral. Without me, he lose Jamaica. Tell him I want to see Rochambeau."

Very respectfully, though with a trace of a smile, the captain said, "I don't think it's possible, General. The wind, at last, has shifted. Rochambeau is on his way to England."

"Who say he can go there? Rochambeau surrendered to me."

"Admiral Walker felt you might be disturbed, General. He instructed me to say that, since you did not grant trading posts or fortified bases, England was entitled to bring the King some small souvenir from Haiti."

"That suppose to be joke, eh? I don't laugh. I tell you two things. I tell you that Walker son of a bitch. Other thing I tell you is I big fool if I don't know from start that England get something from Haiti. Thank Christ, it only Rochambeau you get."

Dessalines stood watching the French sail away. He squinted until the ships, small and harmless, finally passed beyond his range of vision.

He turned then to his veterans, and shouted, "I bring you here to see what you do. You tear to pieces Goddamn fine army, that what you do. For years you fight. If not, you be slaves right now, and no Goddamn English come help slaves. They only come make friends with army so strong that England needs them bad. Now, if you got home, you go find it. You free men in free country. Go get your women. Go get drunk, if that what please you. Do what you like. This part of great Haitian Army is dismissed forever. Get to hell out of here. Why you grin and look proud? What in hell you black bastards think you are? Heroes?"

. . . .

For the second time, the ladies had not been invited with their husbands to dine at the President's table. The President had apologized, declaring that he had deprived himself of their company only to protect them from boredom. Dolly Madison again entertained at what one Cabinet wife called a she-party. Very kind of Dolly, but Northern ladies found Mr. Jefferson's apology flowery and patronizing. They wished he would credit them with the sense to know that they were not Cabinet members and therefore not entitled to hear national secrets. Sometimes, he was just too Virginian.

To the room with the roaring fire, the butler had again, after dinner, brought tobacco, sweets and the decanter of port. President Jefferson, wearing his old black velvet jacket, sat meditatively in his chair. Candlelight and deep-blue areas of shade suggested that an artist had just arranged his pose and the soft gleam from the candelabra.

Madison was reading aloud a letter that had come to him from Spanish Minister Yrujo. Everyone listened attentively.

Sir:

It was with extraordinary surprise that the King, my master, heard of the sale of Louisiana made to the United States in contravention of the most solemn assurances given in writing to His Majesty by the French Foreign Minister with the consent and approbation of the First Consul. The King, my master, charges me to remind the American Government that the said French Minister gave his word and the word of France that the Province of Louisiana would never be sold without Spanish concurrence. The sale of this province to the United States is founded in the violation of a promise so absolute that it ought to be respected; a promise without which the King, my master, would, in no manner, have dispossessed himself of Louisiana. His Catholic Majesty entertains too good an opinion of the character of probity and good faith which the Government of the United States has known how to obtain so justly for itself, not to hope that it will suspend the ratification and effect of a treaty which rests on such a basis. There are other reasons no less powerful which come to the support of the decorum and respect which nations mutually owe each other. France acquired from the King, my master, the retrocession of Louisiana under obligations, whose entire fulfillment was absolutely necessary to give her the complete right over the said province; such was that of causing the King of Tuscany to be acknowledged by the Powers of Europe; but, until now, the French Government has not procured this acknowledgment promised and stipulated, either from the Court of London or from that of St. Petersburg. Under such circumstances it is evident that the treaty of sale entered into between France and the United States does not give to the latter any right to acquire and claim Louisiana, and that the principles of justice as well as sound policy ought to recommend it to their Government not to meddle with engagements as contrary in reality to her true interests as they would be to good faith.

Such are the sentiments which the King, my master, has ordered me to communicate to the President of the United States; and having done it through you, I conclude, assuring you of my respect and consideration towards your person, and of my wishes that our Lord may preserve your life. . . .

Attorney General Levi Lincoln said, "Of course, Yrujo only wants his objections preserved for history. He does not expect any more than that to come of the letter."

"I imagine the French got a sizzling tongue-lashing from the Spanish Minister in Paris," Dearborn said.

Granger nodded. "The Spanish have every right to be angry. If our need were not so great, I would be inclined to urge Mr. Madison to tell Talleyrand what we think of him and the First Consul."

President Jefferson smiled sadly at the Postmaster General. " 'If our need were not so great.' Those are the words man has always used when proceeding on a course of which he is slightly ashamed. Yes, our need is very great. We will have New Orleans harbor and the territory of Louisiana, but let no man tell me that only Talleyrand and the First Consul are behaving in a questionable manner."

Madison said, "Mr. President, I hope you will not suffer too deeply for Spain. When she was powerful, she was not famous for her sympathy toward others."

"I find that as empty of comfort as Mr. Granger's phrase. There was a time when we dreamed of doing better than merely measuring ourselves against the evils of old nations. We were arrogant in our youth. We believed no other group of men had ever thought of founding a government of high-minded citizens. God help us, as we live, we learn. A head of state is morally obligated to do the best he can for his own people. Those who look to us for leadership need the harbor of New Orleans. Where lies the greater sin? In being so pure-minded that they do not get the harbor? Or in becoming part of the First Consul's dishonorable dealings with Spain?"

After an interval of silence, Lincoln undertook to answer. "Mr. President, for myself I will say that one feeds one's own children first. Perhaps they are not better children, but they are the family for whom one is responsible. And I will betray myself as a small-minded man, no doubt, but I am not sorry for Spain. She made clandestine arrangements with France regarding Louisiana. Those who meet the First Consul secretly have to expect to be—er—despoiled."

Jefferson sighed. "There are a thousand justifications, and there are none. Let us leave the matter of conscience where it is always left, in the tool shed, along with the hinges and bolts and brads and chains and pieces of wire that we never use but cannot bear to throw away." It was clear that he would have liked to say more on the subject of conscience, but, purposefully, he pressed on to less abstract matters. "It is my wish to send William Claiborne, of the Mississippi Territory, to administer Louisiana, at least for the present. He will be there to address the citizens on the occasion of the raising of our flag in New Orleans."

"He speaks neither French nor Spanish," Gallatin objected.

Jefferson was unperturbed. "It is not a French or a Spanish city to which we are sending him. New Orleans is American."

"A century will have to pass before that's noticeable," Granger remarked. "For a long time to come, the people down there will hate what they are sure to call 'the Yankee flag.' "

"They will not exactly hate it, Mr. Granger. They will enjoy the prosperity which will come to them almost immediately, but, in common with other peoples of the world, they will observe that we are not particularly well-mannered or understanding of other cultures. They will spend American money happily, and, just as happily, they will thank God that they were born French or Spanish."

Dearborn said, "Yes, well, you gentlemen are talking of a time when we're settled in. I'd like to talk of the day when that Yankee flag, of which Granger spoke, is hoisted over New Orleans."

"I have a draft of a proclamation which will be distributed in three languages well in advance of that day. In it I am explaining that all white inhabitants shall be citizens, and stand as to their rights and obligations on the same footing with other citizens of the United States. The tone is conciliatory. We approach them as brothers, as beloved fellow citizens," said Jefferson.

"Sir, I know that is the way we will approach them," Lincoln said. "I know the people of Louisiana and New Orleans will be regarded as fellow citizens. However, they will be thinking that every conquering power has approached every subject people with just such words. It will take time to convince them that we intend to deal fairly. I do think there should be some American soldiers around for Claiborne's speech and the flag raising."

"Will that prove we regard them as brothers?"

"No, Mr. President. It will take years to prove that. What it will prove is our determination not to have Claiborne pelted with rocks or our flag torn down and ripped to pieces. There are bound to be some French or Spanish aggregations that don't want to be American. I can't think of anything worse than starting out by letting them make us look silly."

Jefferson lowered his eyes. "I have so much faith in people that I am inclined to overestimate their intelligence and good will. Mr. Dearborn, do see that there are enough soldiers to keep order in New Orleans. Not too many soldiers, please. There is more than one way of looking silly."

Granger said, "I know we were called here for something more than just talking, but, since that's what we're doing right now, I'd like to know how to answer people in Connecticut on this Louisiana thing. Before you know it, we'll be having elections again, and I'll be hearing a lot of questions. Was Louisiana a good buy?"

Everyone looked at Albert Gallatin.

He said, "Do you really want to talk finance?"

"No. The people of Connecticut who will ask the questions of me don't know any more about finance than a newborn babe. They'll just be wondering whether or not they should vote for President Jefferson again, and they'll ask about Louisiana."

"Mr. Granger, tell them it was the most spectacular buy in history, and that of course they must vote for President Jefferson."

Secretary of the Navy Robert Smith, who had been serving the wine, placed the decanter down suddenly, and his eyes met Gallatin's. "Can you explain what you meant when you asked Mr. Granger if he really wanted to talk finance? Is there anything we don't know about the sale?"

Gallatin glanced at the President.

Jefferson said, "If we can't trust each other, then I do not know why we are here."

"A contest of sorts developed between Livingston and Monroe," Gallatin explained. "The price for that huge piece of land cannot be judged excessive. I believe it comes to less than five cents an acre. The criticism might be that Mr. Livingston was too precipitate. More advantageous terms might have been obtained in the handling of the actual business. Mr. Monroe's rather good suggestions were not noticed in Mr. Livingston's pell-mell dash to get the papers signed. It appears that Cazenove, who is Talleyrand's privy counsel and financier, was in command. Needless to say, he would not regard the United States as the client to whom he owed his best advice." Gallatin divined the President's dislike of the topic, and finished quickly. "Louisiana might forever be known as the finest purchase ever made. Boast of it with complete assurance. It is only in the handling of terms and payments that we rather botched it, and that's a close Cabinet secret."

Madison said, "It must be just that, gentlemen, at least as long as Mr. Livingston is on earth." He turned toward the President. "Sir?"

Jefferson moved in such a way that the shadows fled from him, and the candlelight revealed the anxiety in his eyes. "I will get to the point immediately, and it is this: the Constitution of the United States has made no provision for our holding foreign territory, still less for incorporating it into our union. The Executive, in seizing the fugitive occurrence which so much advances the good of the country, has done an act beyond the Constitution."

Dearborn, Smith and Granger stared in shocked surprise. Then they all spoke at once.

"You mean we're not going to get Louisiana, sir?"

"Mr. President, then it would have been illegal even to own New Orleans."

"Sir, has that been a recent interpretation by which you learned only now that—"

Jefferson raised his hand to request silence. "We are going to get Louisiana if our House and Senate will agree that the Constitution was created by human beings who are capable of

357

error and omission. Surely the Constitution did not intend to limit our boundaries eternally. That, as I have said, will be for the people's representatives to decide. New Orleans, had we been able to buy it as a large block of real estate, would have had a different identity. I had thought it might exist as a separate city having the advantages of our protection in peace and war, a steady increase in wealth as our own fortunes advanced and a right to all privileges of freedom, except that of voting. Of course, no such simplistic system will work with a gigantic land that one day may be more thickly populated than our eastern country. No, there has not been a recent interpretation of the Constitution. I have long known its content, gentlemen. So well did I know that I never mentioned to Livingston or Monroe that they should price the whole. I thought of it because it seemed to me that, if the French refused, they would at least be willing to discuss a friendly partnership in New Orleans. I did not dare place the thought of Louisiana in the minds of our emissaries. I could not, for, if the French agreed to sell it to us, then the Executive would have performed an act which is unconstitutional. Now, by a whim of destiny, that has occurred."

Everybody accepted another glass of wine.

Smith said, "I believe in the destiny of people and of nations. Everything has worked toward our having Louisiana. Why, Bonaparte would be doing business there right now if the Haitian Army had not astounded everybody by its great stand. Those black soldiers didn't know they were fighting for us, but they were. Without them, the French would have been installed on this continent some time ago, and our days would have been numbered. Who would have guessed that that pack of ex-slaves had such military talent and persistence? Mr. Madison, did you ever think they would defeat the French in the Caribbean?"

James Madison gave his sober attention to the question. "If Saint-Domingue—"

"Haiti," Smith corrected.

"If Haiti asks for our recognition as an independent government and meets the specifications for taking her place among the family of nations, we will recognize her. But, Mr. Smith, Haiti did not defeat the French in the Caribbean. England defeated the French in the Caribbean."

Smith said, "Was it England that kept Leclerc from bringing his fleet into New Orleans harbor? Haiti was fighting all alone, Mr. Madison, when we were wondering how soon we'd have the French on our doorstep."

"Yes, Haiti delayed the French timetable."

"A meager admission, sir. The Haitians just kept fighting, and that is how they changed world history. Had they given up, the French would be in command of our waterways, and soon it would have been Americans instead of Haitians struggling for survival. Livingston and Monroe would have had nothing to talk about with Talleyrand had Haiti ever thought of surrender. Yes, I believe in destiny. The Constitution is a magnificent work of man, but destiny defined our future."

The other Cabinet members gazed fixedly at the handsome Secretary of the Navy, whose position was without genuine importance. How outspoken he was, how negligent of protocol. He had broken the President's train of thought. Suddenly, everyone looked away from Smith. If he were to be reproved by a few delicately selected words, it would be unkind to embarrass him by staring.

They had underestimated the President's ability to concentrate. When Smith finished speaking, Jefferson went on with what he had intended to say. He had, the Cabinet members decided, not heard any part of the Marylander's strange footnote to American history.

"As long as the United States endures," Jefferson said, "it will not regret that our ministers agreed to buy Louisiana. The legislature, casting behind them metaphysical subtleties, and risking themselves like faithful servants, must ratify and pay for it, and throw themselves on the mercy of their country for doing, without authorization, what we know the people would have done for themselves had they been in a situation to do it."

"Yes," Madison said gravely, "no one can doubt that the

people would have voted for the purchase had that course been open to them."

Jefferson moved in his chair, half turning from the others in the room. Light and shadow played upon him, and he became again a compelling figure once seen in a painting and remembered forever. When he spoke, no man thought he had been addressed. No man thought an answer was required.

"This is what I will tell the Senators: it is the case of a guardian's investing the money of his ward in the purchase of an important piece of adjacent property, and saying to him when of age, 'I did this for your good; I thought it my duty to risk myself for you.' "

. . . .

From Havana came the distinguished Marquis de Casa Calvo, who, in powdered wig, gold-laced coat and satin knee breeches, met at the Cabildo with Pierre Clément de Lausset, the prefect sent by Bonaparte to receive the colony. On the parade ground outside, the Louisiana Regiment of regulars, the Cavalry Squadron of Mexico and the New Orleans Militia were drawn up in battle array. After a long speech in Spanish by Casa Calvo, the territory of Louisiana was ceded to France, the people were freed of their oath of allegiance to His Majesty King Charles of Spain and the Spanish flag was hauled down. The flag of France was raised above the Cabildo.

Pierre Clément de Lausset knew that Louisiana would be French for less than three weeks, but he was a punctilious man. He proceeded as though three centuries had been named as the period in which French rule would be exercised. He replaced the hereditary Council with a municipal body of swiftly, but properly, elected supervisors, restored civil codes, appointed French officers to city and harbor posts and declared Spanish to be an inappropriate language for good citizens of France.

It was December 20 when William Claiborne, decked in a bright ceremonial sash, kept his rendezvous with Lausset at the Cabildo. Behind Claiborne marched lean, hard-faced soldiers armed with the long-barreled rifles that had made their marksmanship famous. The Mississippi Militia followed, and, since Claiborne spoke to the new citizens in a foreign language, these two detachments of military men gave the people all the understanding they had of the situation.

Claiborne, a very young man, a Virginian by birth, smiled attractively while speaking, and hoped that some warmth and friendliness reached his blank-eyed listeners. His performance was excellent, considering that, right up to the moment that Lausset absolved the people of their loyalty to France and presented the keys of the forts to Claiborne, Spanish intervention had been expected. Six thousand American militiamen were standing by in the event that Spain sent troops from Havana to seize New Orleans. All went peacefully. President Jefferson had once remarked, "Spain has both the feebleness and the wisdom of age." The quiet streets of New Orleans that day attested to his keen judgment.

The tricolor was slowly drawn from its place above the Cabildo, and a French officer bore it silently and reverently away. The American flag, in spite of efforts to raise it with a gallant flutter, remained, for quite a time, stubbornly fixed about midway up the pole. The spectators crowding the plaza and leaning from galleries and balconies held their breath and waited. It was not until the flag flew freely against the New Orleans sky that sudden, piercing cries of delight burst from one particular group. The isolated cheers intensified the gloom that emanated from the majority of those present. When the brief flurry of excitement died, it was possible to hear sighs and sobs from people born French or Spanish. Before leaving the plaza, everyone, whether friend or foe, threw a quick glance toward the Cabildo. Was the American flag still there?

It was.

FINAL WORD

In those first years of the nineteenth century, history unfolded before the wondering eyes of the world a surprisingly well-constructed morality play. It provided heroes and villains, rewards and punishments. The belligerent Corsican was thwarted in his desire to establish French power on the North American continent. The incredibly brave black soldiers of Haiti won their right to exist as free men in a free country. Thomas Jefferson, the philosopher, the man of peace, gained for his fellow citizens a million square miles of vast promise, a long, wide river and an outlet to the sea. It was such an inspiring play that it lifted men's hearts and gave proof that wickedness is without profit.

History should not have presented a fourth act.

First Consul Napoleon Bonaparte became Napoleon the First, Emperor of France. He was the man who could describe a bloody battlefield on which his wounded lay freezing beside their dead brothers as the most beautiful sight he'd ever seen.

The English found that fourth act quite unacceptable, so they wrote another and directed it themselves. They gave Bonaparte an island of which few had ever heard, an island whose importance he would create by his presence upon it. For the millions of words written about the world's most famous prisoner, the price came very high. It was his last island, and only in death could he escape from it. One wonders if, while on Saint Helena, as he complained about his doctor and his chef and the lack of stimulating conversation, he ever thought of Toussaint L'Ouverture, who had been thrown into a French dungeon and forgotten.

It was Talleyrand's statement that Haiti might never again be as well governed as it had been under Toussaint. Talleyrand was right. Dessalines, whose freakish gift for war had earned him respect, soon showed that he had no talent for peace. Worse, he had no interest in learning the fundamental principles of proper government. His countrymen whispered to each other that, after all, he was only an illiterate field hand who had been given too much power. Had Dessalines died in battle, he would have been deeply mourned. But he did not die in battle.

There was a cry for Christophe, but it came too late. The island had divided itself. The shining bond of brotherhood that had united all Haitians on the day Rochambeau surrendered lay tarnished in the dust. Pétion had his own army and his own ambitions. The same could be said of Christophe. All aspirations toward national success were stifled by the deadlock. Pétion and Christophe each ruled part of the island, ever watchful of enemies and mistrustful of friends. Haitians who had squandered their blood for freedom now feared men who had fought beside them. Both Pétion and Christophe were less than they might have been, and the fourth act as played in Haiti was a tragedy too terrible for tears, too chilling for hope.

In the United States, James Madison succeeded his friend Thomas Jefferson to the presidency, and was in turn succeeded by James Monroe. Robert Livingston had been dead for three years when Monroe took the oath of office. Thomas Jefferson was in uneasy retirement. His beautiful daughter Maria had died during his second term, and his sorrow darkened the remainder of his life. Also, his financial burdens were so immense that, although he still managed to cling to Monticello, he sold his acreage without even bothering to bargain shrewdly. He had never bargained shrewdly for himself. He trusted his friends and his relatives, and even some strangers. Who could refuse a man the chance to establish his own business? Who could foreclose on a plantation house? Where would the debtor and his family go? It was Jefferson's habit to lend money freely and to be very considerate of the unfortunate fellow who would certainly repay when in a position to do so. It was a pity to have to keep selling Monticello's acreage, but it was the only way one's own obligations could be met.

The magnificent book collection, which had been appraised at fifty thousand dollars, Jefferson offered to the government for half that figure, feeling that his books belonged in Washington. The government sliced two thousand off his named price. His debts mounted. His health failed. The state of New York sent a gift of eight thousand dollars to the man who had first envisioned New Orleans as an American city and had ended by persuading Congress that the Louisiana Purchase must be ratified. He had increased the size of the country by one hundred and forty per cent without shedding a drop of American blood. New York was grateful.

The fourth act in the United States was enlivened by gigantic patriotic pageants, memorable for bright banners, martial music and cheering crowds. Lafayette, of France, had come to visit! To this young nation, he was still a hero, still the dashing officer who had given to the American Revolution the romantic flavor in which it had been deficient. The visit was a great satisfaction to Lafayette. Americans were ever an appreciative people. They were delighted at the announcement that it had been resolved by the Senate and House of Representatives that, in compensation for important services, Major-General Lafayette had been voted two hundred thousand dollars and twenty-four thousand acres of land. . . .

A NOTE ON SOURCES

Whenever one is presented with a list of what the author has read in order to gather facts or surmises on a historical subject, it can be safely assumed that the list is far from complete. Many books written in the last century were ordered by proud families of famous men, and the material was therefore carefully selected to please the sponsor. It is necessary, then, to read almost everything available and to check one claim against another. The sources are endless, and to parade a hundred or more titles would be merely an accounting of what had been read. Instead, with gratitude and respect, I mention the books that I have used.

Jefferson in Power, Claude G. Bowers, 1936
Jefferson the President: First Term, 1801–1805, Dumas Malone, 1970
Jefferson's Decision, Richard Skolnik, 1969
The Lost World of Thomas Jefferson, Daniel J. Boorstin, 1948
Haiti: The Politics of Squalor, Robert I. Rotberg, with Christopher K. Clague, 1971
Black Majesty, John W. Vandercook, 1928
Christophe: King of Haiti, Hubert Cole, 1967
The West Indies, J. A. Thome and J. H. Kimball, 1837
Life in a Haitian Valley, Melville J. Herskovits, 1937
Haiti: The Black Republic, Selden Rodman, 1954
Pauline, W. N. C. Carlton, 1930
Pauline, Pierson Dixon, 1964
Napoleon, Emil Ludwig, 1953
Napoleon Bonaparte: An Intimate Biography, Vincent Cronin, 1972
The Life of Napoleon, Volume One, John Holland Rose, 1901
Thomas Paine, Liberator, Frank Smith, 1938
Tom Paine, W. E. Woodward, 1945
Louisiana Writers' Project, 1941
Creole City, Edward Larocque Tinker, 1953
New Orleans, B. M. Norman, 1845

Quasi-War: The Politics and Diplomacy of the Undeclared War with France, 1797–1801, Alexander de Conde, 1966

The Extraordinary Mr. Morris, Howard Swiggett, 1952

Talleyrand, Duff Cooper, 1932

Saints and Sinners, Gamaliel Bradford, 1932

Revolution and Imperial France, Ernest J. Knapton, 1972

The French Revolution, Georges Pernoud and Sabine Flaissier, 1960

James Monroe: Public Claimant, Lucius Wilmerding, Jr., 1960

James Madison, Secretary of State, Irving Brant, 1956

Moreau De St. Méry's American Journey, 1793–1798, translated and edited by Kenneth Roberts and Anna M. Roberts, 1947